pale shadows

an autobiographical novel

By

Angyl Nihthasu

Published by Angyl Nihthasu
Printed by Lulu.com

Excerpt from *Moon Magic* by Dion Fortune ©1956 Society of Inner Light used with the permission of Red Wheel/Weiser. 1-800-423-7087 www.redwheelweiser.com

"Everywhere That I'm Not" written by Steve Barton © 1982. Lyrics reproduced with blessings from Steve Barton and David Scheff

Cover art by the author.

ISBN: 978-0-615-25246-9

Printed in the United States of America

First Edition: October, 2010
Second Edition: July, 2022
Third Edition: January, 2025

Thanks to those whom have made this tome possible:

The Goddesses:

Alana my wife who has exhibited an artist's patience;

Olivia my late mother who gave me life, compassion,

and psychic abilities.

The Muses:

Andrea my oldest fan for the Brixton Contingent

and the Halloween castle readings;

Catherine for eagerly keeping me writing in a timely fashion;

"Amarantha" for returning to the darkness with me, providing

light and memories where needed.

The Smiths:

EOW writing group for their invaluable insights and wine;

Tony for repairing my high school Spanish;

Laura for proofing my work while under spiritual duress.

For "Marisa"

Who was in the midst of the chaos,

But never truly knew how deep,

And "Diana"

Who saved my life

After the storm had ended.

My eternal love.

aUTHOR'S EXORDIUM

This tale is based on the truth; thus, it contains many departures from the facts. The truth—in my eyes—is a subjective concept not constrained to the yellowing pages of a textbook or the fading inks of a newspaper. The truth lay in memories, and this is a retrospective rendering of events that occurred in the autumn of 1986.

I have often said that "Time and circumstance makes liars of us all," and so if any of the "pretty lies" in this *roman à clef* offend the people involved, know that they were not written out of malice. The names of individuals and places as well as some of the events within have, of course, been altered with absolutely no slight intended. It was done out of the need to protect the privacy and dignity of others, because of my biased recollections, and because of the desire to tell this tale in a digestible and entertaining manner. Life is not as neat as fiction.

This book is neither an endorsement for nor against occult practices, nor is it a primer to The Art. These are merely memories of Magick.

FRIDAY, SEPTEMBER 26TH, 1986

The pale-yellow field glanced Sol's spears, plunging them into my pinpoint eyes. I stumbled on unsteady stones and staggered with unsteady legs, yet I did not yield. Rocks shattered under my feet with the sound of an errant wind. No, not the wind at all, but a scream: a high, cursed wail.

Reluctantly, I took another step, rupturing another stone beneath my weight. Another scream drew my gaze earthward, and my heart became leaden.

A carpet of wind-pitted skulls stretched farther than the glare would allow me to see. Carrion-eating crows plucked dying grubs from hollowed sockets as they hopped from cranium to cranium. Death's stench stung my nostrils.

My belly convulsed and my throat tightened as I sprinted through the boneyard, crushing empty skulls and weathering the howls of dead souls. I ran until exhausted, then collected myself and finally stood my ground: 'twas no way for a servant of The Goddess to carry himself.

As the screams died, the distressed noise of rusty metal

1

grinding against rusty metal rose sharply in their stead. An ancient windmill appeared on the near horizon, its five blades turning against a nonexistent breeze. I approached the structure, and upon touch, its brown surface crumbled under my fingertips, and moist chips of corrosion fell on the sun-bleached skulls.

Then, carnal giggling invaded my ears. I turned toward the sound, and before me stood The Maiden, her naked form, golden hair, and dark eyes evoking visions of a sky-clad Venus within the shell of some monstrous oyster. She extended her lithe hand to me. I was moved and mimicked the gesture, but our fingers never touched. Her manic laughter mingled anxiously with the smell of patchouli and decay as she spun on her heels and flew over a ridge of bones.

Tugging my cloak tightly across my shoulders, I surged forward, intent on tracking down my apprentice; my friend. The pursuit proved to be painfully simple as a trail of blood marked her passage.

I scrambled up the ridge of precariously packed skulls and gasped in the carious air atop the crater's lip. I looked within the well, and I despaired once again.

The Maiden was bucking and laughing ecstatically beneath a nude beast of fierce beauty. Her neck was torn and bruised but bloodless. Her once radiant hair had dulled; her once supple body was spent. The Maiden was despoiled.

The creature between her legs silently invited me to join in, his angelic visage tarnished by the blood of my pupil.

I stepped back from the grisly vision, lost my footing on a loose skull, and fell to the bottom of the peak.

The crush of my body launched a hundred agonized screams skyward.

* * *

Laine Douglas's body spasmed as matter and spirit reunited in silent reintegration, his senses slowly bleeding back into the mundane world. As "reality" took hold, he opened his eyes to a room thick with golden smoke and sable shadows.

A disc of burning charcoal was fuming with a melangé of patchouli and dragon's blood resin in the brazier before him, and the flames of the four silver candles that encircled Laine sputtered and twisted in a breeze that stole its way in through a breach in the window. The room wore an unnatural silence.

Laine shrugged his stiff shoulders and stretched. Answering the riddle of his vision would take him a moment. Recovering from an astral journey had symptoms identical to waking from a lucid dream as, in fact, the mechanisms were the same. Even with his experience, Laine had to pause and clear his head.

"Preparations, preparations." Laine suddenly stood and rubbed his long thighs, restoring the circulation the floor had stolen from them and shocking his body into action. He tapped the pause button on the boombox sitting atop the blank TV, filling the room with a hiss followed by rimshots ticking, ticking, ticking like a stopwatch. Wire Train's "Slow Down": yes, something to ground and ready him.

A porcelain pirouette doll was leaning between the tape player and a small wicker basket decorated with a burgundy ribbon. Laine picked up the basket and opened its lid as the song's bassline slinked in. The aroma of dried rose petals anointed with Moon Goddess oil engulfed him as he breathed in the smell of the potpourri Amarantha Powell, his coveted pupil, had mixed for him early in their Magickal union. Laine smiled, then dipped his fingers deep into the bowels of the basket, feeling for its buried charm.

The phone rang jaggedly. "Laine," he announced into the receiver.

"Hi!" Marisa Chang's voice swept away Laine's mental cobwebs and spread warmth through his body.

"Hey, love, what's up?" he asked, resuming his search through the basket.

"Nothing much, I just got home. The Strand placed a

late print order." She paused, then sang, "Ooh, Wire Train, huh? Hah, I got you hooked!"

"Yeah, right, what you said," Laine grumbled jokingly, his fingers probing for the small metal hook still buried deep amongst the petals. "The song just fits my mood right now."

"Yeah, I've got them on too," she confessed with a subtle shift in her manner. "So, Laine, are we still going to Amarantha's party?" Her question contained equal parts brimstone and treacle.

Laine returned the attitude. "Of course. It's her birthday and only fitting that we welcome her home. She's been away over-long, and she and I have much ground to cover."

"Okay," Marisa said in a clipped fashion.

"You do know what's happening, right?" Laine pushed, his gaze locked with Trump the Pirouette's painted eyes.

"I only know what you tell me."

"All I can tell you right now is that we have witches' business to discuss. And anyway, Marisa, we won't be there all night. I'll just take care of business, we'll sing 'Happy Birthday', then we'll book. Okay?"

"Fine," Marisa said with a lingering hint of irritation. "I've already changed, so figure I'll pick you up in about twenty minutes?"

The ring of a tiny bell confirmed that Laine had retrieved his prize from the basket. Admiring the brass trinket in the candlelight, Laine said, "Perfect. I'll see you then. I love you, Marisa."

"I love you, too," she responded, the smile returning to her voice, then the connection died.

Laine replaced the receiver as he eyed the earring he held: a tiny bell suspended by minute, brass coils. The street merchant Laine had purchased it from two years earlier made only one pair, and he suspected Amarantha would wear its mate this eve, so it was a logical adornment. He prodded it against his earlobe as he walked from the dimness of his room and into the peach-green glow of the bathroom's fluorescent light.

4

Laine's reflection was a thesis of learned symbolism. Six-foot-three and slender, he'd often heard he had a royal bearing about him; an aura of ancient Egyptian aristocracy. He exploited those opinions happily by wearing the icons of the breed: silver *ankh* earrings; the eyes of Horus and Ra traced in kohl around his own; anointing oils bearing the names of those pre-Coptic deities. With his black tuxedo shirt and slacks, he would convey dignity and mystery, and with his moonstone pentacle—which he now hid beneath his shirt—he would express his true affiliation. Yes, Laine's costume was nearly complete, lacking only the earring which he now slipped into the puncture.

The Maiden was bucking and laughing ecstatically beneath a nude beast of fierce beauty.

Visions of Amarantha's deflowering rushed in tides of liquid smoke, their crests and eddies of grim remembrance smothering Laine's mind. The mental blow buckled his knees.

The creature between her legs silently invited me to join in, his angelic visage tarnished by the blood of my pupil.

His head erupted with a torrent of screams that dissolved into taunting laughter, then left behind a sharp ringing in his ears. Laine shook off his discomfort and stood once again to catch his image in the mirror. His eyes burned with a fiery quintessence; his heart was infused with newfound intent.

"So it appears my retirement has met with an unexpected challenge." The words boomed beyond the mundane limits of the room, touching the corners of astral reality. Breaking away from his reflected gaze, Laine strode determinedly back into the shadows.

He sifted through the contents of the nightstand drawer where his television rested: a replica pistol; a small library of occult references; old sketch pads bursting with adolescent doodles; an empty, black cardstock jewelry box. Shuffling those things aside, Laine pulled out a black Sharpie, a dove feather quill, and a small vial of wolves' blood ink. He shut the drawer, returned to the circle of silver candles before his altar, and rolled up his right sleeve.

"Only fools go into the unknown places sans compass or steel. I shall have both ready for my challenger." The candles' flames were flickering madly despite the current absence of wind. "That which goes hidden, let us embrace."

Laine's tongue tossed off sounds few modern ears would recognize in a rhythmic yet jarring chant. The candle fires ceased their dance and reached for the sky as thick and barbarous words tainted the heavy air.

The brief ceremony had begun.

*   *   *

Amarantha Powell tucked blonde tresses behind her left ear, then hooked the tiny bell earring into its piercing.

Her terracotta eyes smiled at her from the hand mirror as she checked the jewelry's security. Laine would surely appreciate the accessory. "I am ready, milord," she affirmed, "and I shall not fail you like your last."

After setting down the mirror, Amarantha lifted one of the six pink roses from its resting place, noticing it shared its hue with the surrounding candles on the vanity. One sniff brought Donovan Walsh to mind, and so vivid was the image of him that he must have given the flower "a touch". While Amarantha wasn't one for red Magick, love spells weren't so bad when the attraction was mutual. "I am ready, my sweet. Do not fail me like my last." Indiscreet knocking at Amarantha's door intruded the bedroom. "Come in."

The entrance swung open, and Heather Dominguez was thrown into the room by the doorknob. "Damn, Amy, when are you coming back? You've got a houseful of drunk people out here. Jimmy's sticking cream cheese labels on everything." The way Amarantha's best friend was swaying made it obvious Heather was a little worse for wine.

"So I see." Amarantha smiled and pointed at the day-glow orange decals on Heather's sweater.

"What the—that asshole!" A combination of

amusement and indignation colored Heather's smirk as she angrily tore stickers off her shoulders.

"Heather, calm down. Jimmy's probably just as drunk as you are." Amarantha laid the rose on her vanity altar. "And please watch your language."

"Sorry. So you gonna hide in here all night or what?" Heather balled up the labels with her palms and tossed them just short of a garbage pail.

"I've only been in here for ten minutes. Has Laine arrived yet?"

Amarantha could almost see Heather's brain stumbling through her mental fog. Finally, she said, "Oh yeah, that Black guy. Darth Vader. I ain't seen him."

"Heather!"

"Sorry, but that guy's creepy. He's always dressed in black, and he never talks, much less smiles."

"Hey, Laine only talks to strangers when he has something to say and only smiles when they amuse him. You just have to get to know him better, that's all."

"Whatever," Heather replied, unconvinced as she quickly checked her lipstick in a bureau mirror. "What about Luke Skywalker in back?"

"Donovan?"

"No doy."

"Just entertain him a little longer, please? I promise I'll be out shortly."

"Fine." Heather's grumble and side glance revealed her frustration.

"Thank you. I love you, Heather. And no more wine."

Heather softened a bit. "I love you too. And try to stop me." She exited as gracelessly as she entered, giggling all the way.

"You didn't shut my door!" Too late. Heather was already gone. Darth Vader, huh? Laine would just love that one.

Amarantha's domestic longhair scurried into the room and stroked its white body against her calf. Leaning over to rub an ear, Amarantha asked "What is it, Terra?"

The cat mewed a response.

"They're here?"

The doorbell rang over the synth intro of "Black Celebration". Amarantha rose from her vanity, made sure the altar settings were in place, and cinched up her dress to avoid trampling it as she ran out into the hall.

Two mythological creatures were lurking silently and still near the entrance: a tall, bipedal panther with a silver *ankh* emblazoned on its brow, and an avian woman with mint-green and ebony plumage. Amarantha gasped at the fetches, then grounded herself with a deep, cleansing breath before she walked to the door and slowly opened it.

Laine and Marisa didn't look all that different from their astral forms. Laine's black silhouette was broken by his dark gray overcoat and a purple string bean tie. His slightly-rounded flattop was trimmed into a Mephistophelian widow's peak and faded on the sides and back, bringing out the austerity of his face. Marisa was wearing a shimmering emerald dress beneath her black overcoat that was fitted just enough to suggest the contours of her body. It was far more modern than Amarantha's opulent gown but still appropriately formal. Marisa's hair was standing in punky spikes like an inky fountain frozen in time. In front was a lock of rich green hair—which Laine had referred to as her beak—that extended down to her chin, bisecting her round face. Amarantha knew there was also a "tail" just like it in the back.

"Laine! It's about time," Amarantha squealed as she gave him a rib-crushing hug.

"Sorry, we're a little late. Just being fashionable and all that." He returned the embrace, giving a small groan of pain for effect.

Something felt different about him. There was an underlying tension, and not just because Marisa was watching the embrace. Yes, Laine was distracted by his girlfriend but also by something else; something he was keeping well-concealed behind layers of Magick and a quietly focused mind. Amarantha released his torso. She would pick that lock later when they were alone.

Amarantha turned to the seemingly impassive Marisa and embraced her as well. Even though she harbored genuine respect for Amarantha deep inside, Marisa was also putting considerable effort into repressing her resentment towards her. This wasn't the first time a woman had felt threatened by her—silly as that was—and Amarantha simply noted Marisa's better instincts, letting them influence how she responded.

"And how have you been, Marisa?" Amarantha planted a kiss on each cheek.

"Great!" There was that smile: the one that had charmed a mage. "How was your vacation?"

"Tiring. It started out as a six-week visit and turned into a nearly three-month-long family obligation. Oh, I'm sorry, shall I take your things?" Amarantha nodded at Marisa's helmet.

"Yes, please."

"Follow me." Amarantha turned toward her room and called out, "Could you guys turn down the music, please?!"

"What are they playing?" Laine asked.

"Right now, Depeche Mode I think. Apparently, we have a new deejay, probably Jimmy." Upon entering her room, Amarantha assured, "Your things will be safe in the armoire."

Laine said, "Wow, your room is coming along great," after he secured their items. "I love the lavender walls."

"Thank you. I finished painting on Tuesday." Amarantha presented the two framed reproductions leaning against a wall. "I just found these Parrish prints on Haight yesterday, but I haven't figured out where I want to hang them yet."

Laine pointed at the larger one and said, "Oh, this one has to go next to the canopy bed."

"You think so?"

"Totally. It's got the right shape and size for the space, you got three women lounging by a pool—"

"Definitely," Marisa agreed. "The other one should go

on the wall next to your door."

"You know, that's a good idea. Oh, I almost forgot: happy first anniversary! I'm sorry I'm a month late. How did you guys celebrate?"

Marisa appeared pleasantly surprised that Amarantha remembered. "Thank you! Actually, I'd forgotten the date too," Marisa began, "But I came home from work one night, and there was this note sprayed with Grey Flannel and a red rose on my pillow."

Laine walked up behind Marisa and snaked his arms across her shoulders. The gesture emphasized their height difference.

"He'd made out the note to look like a coupon for a free dinner. I accepted, of course, and we went out to La Trattoria. The rest pretty much goes without saying." Marisa was rocking back and forth in Laine's arms. "Oh, and he bought me a lovebird the next day. I named her Misha."

"How romantic."

"Yeah, but now I have to top myself for her birthday in two days," Laine offered. "All you damned Libras," he added with mock disdain.

"Hey!" Amarantha and Marisa cried with Marisa elbowing Laine's ribs.

"Kidding, of course," he grunted.

Marisa slowly slid from his embrace. "Well, I guess you two need to catch up, so—."

"Well, there are plenty of drinks and snacks in back. At least there was twenty minutes ago," Amarantha said, placating Marisa. "Enjoy. I won't keep him long."

"Thanks." Marisa turned to Laine, kissed him tenderly on the lips, then left, avoiding eye contact with them both as she exited. The room fell quiet.

It was a pity that Marisa must be kept in the dark, but as Laine often said, this was witches' business, and what they needed to discuss wasn't for the ears of his first love, nor was where they were going for her eyes. Besides, Amarantha was confident that Marisa was privy to secrets

Laine would never reveal to her.

Amarantha and Laine gazed into each other for many moments, speaking without words and breathing as one. They shared a smile, then Amarantha walked to her dimmer switch and reduced the light.

"You know, my girlfriend doesn't trust you," Amarantha said about Heather.

"Really? What a coincidence: mine doesn't trust you," he joked, taking a seat at the vanity. The swaying altar light bestowed a solemnity to Laine's face. "By the way, is that one of your creations?" he asked, indicating her dress.

She smoothed its pink, silken folds. "Yes. One of my aunts gave me a sewing machine. I got a lot of sewing done while in Conway. Curtains will be next, and if you still want that cloak . . . ."

"Most certainly, Befana." Her Magick name now evoked, Laine's eyes drew Amarantha closer as he freed his pentacle from beneath his shirt with a bent finger. She crossed the room and knelt before him, their gazes never breaking and their breaths synchronizing again.

Laine reached out to touch her hair. "Nice earring." He smirked and tapped the jewelry hanging from her ear, filling the space between them with miniature chimes.

"Yours too, Lord Nihthasu."

They closed their eyes and interlaced their fingers, completing a cool-burning circuit. Amarantha swooned from the connection, surrendering her mundane mind and elevating her consciousness breath by breath.

* * *

I was awash with cobalt clouds punctuated by sparks of amber as I soared vertiginously through astral skies. Once my ascent halted, I slowly and reluctantly released the empowering touch of my mentor's fingers.

Laine was gone. Instead, Rorschachian shadows ebbed and flowed on a throne of hematite before me. Beyond this vortex, a vast, indigo sky sparkling with vagrant stars curved over the lapis landscape. I was seated on a scintillating bouquet that sprung from the soft, rolling earth, and each breeze carried floral notes and the chants of trees.

Something dark and hulking emerged from behind the throne and considered me with emerald eyes. After a cursory sniff, the black panther Neteru sidled up and nuzzled my face. I gave his neck a gentle rub.

Nihthasu's face resolved beneath a shifting pall. "Welcome back to Nihtheim, Befana Delafey." *His eyes were burning intensely beneath the shimmering* ankh *branded on his brow.*

"It's good to be home, Lord Nihthasu."

"Mother and Bride . . . ."

"Father and Consort . . . ."

"Sister and Chalice . . . ."

"Brother and Wand."

Nihthasu considered me with a smile. "It has been overlong, my kin."

"Indeed it has, my kin. I trust all is well with you?"

"All is well." *A disturbance in the jasmine-scented wind told me otherwise, but I held my tongue.* "We have much to discuss."

"Indeed." *I stroked Neteru nervously, composing my thoughts while the immense cat chewed Janus flowers.* "I have considered much in my absence," *I finally announced,* "and if it pleases milord, I wish to resume my teachings. I have missed your wisdom, your compassion, your trust. I have missed our friendship."

The cowl tried vainly to conceal Nihthasu's frown. "You will always have a place in my kingdom, and my knowledge is yours as ever. However, there really is little more of The Art that I can teach you, plus, as of late, my eyes and heart have turned towards retirement—and Marisa. Even if you weren't ready, I would have little time to instruct you." *Nihthasu smiled.* "But you are in fact more ready than you know, and I think that it's time to perform your Wiccaning . . . and free you from my charge."

I gasped and bowed. "Thank you, milord. I'm honored that you feel that I'm ready."

"Despite my previous misgivings, you have been ready for a while. Only now has it become convenient for me to tell you so. The true question is do you feel like you're ready?" *Nihthasu's chuckle was full of unexpected light.*

"Well, I guess I better be." *I added brusquely,* "And if not, I have of late kept company with a like-minded kinfolk. I had meant to introduce you once before, but you rushed off that night. If need be, he can walk the path with me when you can not. With your consent, of course."

Nihthasu flared, and I was certain of his impending rejection, but instead, he asked, "So you say? Can he be trusted? Is he driven by light?"

"You have all my assurances, Lord Nihthasu, that his heart is rightly placed and that his mind is clean and keen."

Neteru stirred and looked upon his liege with apprehension. Nihthasu's brow furrowed in reflection, but finally gave way to a reluctant placidity. "Then as you say, my kin. I trust your judgment, but I would meet this kindly mage for certainty's sake."

A weight lifted from the proceedings, giving calm to the very air around us, though Neteru was purring erratically.

"As is your will, so mote it be, Lord Nihthasu. You shall meet him this very eve." *I scribed an invoking star upon my bare breast with my fingertips and sighed, suddenly aware of the breathless minutes that had passed.*

Nihthasu's luminous eyes looked upon me with renewed concern. Catching me catching him, he broke contact and raised wards when I tried to skry deeper.

"Milord, what is it that you try to hide from me?"

"Hide?"

"Yes, hide. You have many thoughts locked up behind your eyes. Your student I may be, but not your fool." *My frustration caused Nihtheim's sky to burst in a scarlet flash.*

Nihthasu softened. "You are scarcely one and certainly not the other. You are my equal."

With a sigh and a sidelong glance, Nihthasu swept

away the wards. "So be it. I pray you vigilance. I've had a most distressing vision of a threat with its eye set upon you. You may even find this danger to be attractive and favorable, and I had hoped to identify and eliminate the threat quietly before you could be tempted. Because of this, I thought it unnecessary to divulge my suspicions to you."

"How certain are you of this omen?"

"Profoundly. I feel its stigma still. I . . . can not bring myself to describe it."

"Do you know whom or what it is that endangers me?"

"Not yet, but I will know it on sight."

"Thank you for sharing, milord, but if your vision proves true, I can't depend on you to be my shield, certainly not if you are retiring." *I set my jaw tight.*

Streaks of pitch rain were darkening Nihthasu's face, rendering it all but invisible beneath his cowl. "Oh, but you can. The business of war is a costly one. No victory— regardless of intention—leaves a soul unstained. These days, it seems there are far too many agents eager to exploit and taint the innocent." *Nihthasu unclasped his hands from mine and cradled my face, the soft gesture bringing me solace.* "I would be tainted in your stead. As your champion, that risk remains mine."

"As is your will, milord. Know this though: I, too, am versed in like matters, and though I am not blooded like you, I will go down fighting."

"I do not doubt you, but if the omen is true, you may not be willing to fight. Let me strike first and true. Just . . . remain vigilant, Amarantha."

* * *

The utterance of her common name brought Amarantha down into her room, back into her clothing and candlelight and clouds of incense. She rose and brushed the creases from her dress.

"I have already outlined most of your consecration ritual," Laine said, his eyes still shut. "We will get together sometime this week to go over the details, yes?"

"Yes. How about Monday?"

"That will suffice."

"So is class dismissed?" Amarantha asked, tongue-in-cheek.

Laine's eyes shot open at the joke. He smiled. "Class dismissed."

She kissed his brow. "Good. Then I can get you that bottle of '81 Cab I have stashed." Amarantha noted Laine's crooked smile and cocked her brow. "What?"

"You're just now turning eighteen, and you already choose your wines like an old pro."

Amarantha cursed the blush that came to her cheeks. "Must be all those rituals. One develops an expertise after a while. And it is a topic I'm learning about in school."

Laine viewed her with mock suspicion. "Yeah, right, what you said. Let's do it before Marisa has a conniption fit and—"

As if on cue, there was a knock at Amarantha's door. She moved to open it, increasing the light in the room as she did. Marisa stepped in.

"Hey. A couple of your guests are going on a beer run," Marisa informed. Her eyes scanned the room suspiciously before locking onto Amarantha. "Any requests?"

It was time to return to hosting duties. "Okay, I better get a move on before our wine vanishes."

"I can take care of it if you two are still busy—"

"No, no, we're finished," Amarantha reassured her, turning to Laine. "Right, 'teach'?"

"'Class dismissed,'" Laine joked through clenched teeth. Through the fading strands of their link, Amarantha could sense the tension pulling inside him, and it was all about Marisa. They needed time to talk alone. "Oh, Laine, can you put out my altar candles?"

"Yes. Absolutely."

Amarantha's, "Thank you," was tinged with *good luck*. Shutting the door behind her, a palpable increase in anxiety trickled from Amarantha's room as Marisa and Laine girded themselves for their inevitable conflict. Amarantha recognized her ineffectiveness when it came to the domestic disputes of others, particularly between brethren. The best thing for her to do was to just let them blow off some steam and settle their issues. She would await their return to the party when all was done, and once they did, Amarantha would be ready with wiles and wine.

And with Donovan.

* * *

Laine was looking upon Amarantha's altar with pursed lips. A love spell. A goddamned love spell. She of all people should know the dangers of red Magick. They were an affront to free will. What was his pupil playing at?

The lack of noise alerted Laine and turned him around to face Marisa. "You two must've had some important business," she said bitterly. "You were in here for quite a while."

Laine repressed a scowl as he turned back to the vanity altar. "What are you talking about? We were only in here for, what, ten minutes?"

"Try over twenty."

"Really? We must be rusty." Laine's watch proved Marisa right. Now he'd have to swallow shit. "As I said before, her absence was over-long." He took refuge in the cold, stone form of the Athena statuette on Amarantha's altar. "Much to go over."

"Like what?"

He could have just cited witches' business as a valid reason not to divulge what was shared, but seeing as it involved taking on Marisa fully as his next pupil, he might as well. Besides, revealing the heart of their congress could prove to be fruitful: it might result in some valuable insight from Marisa.

And if nothing else, it would at least get her off his ass.

Laine stood and faced her. "Well, she wants to resume training with me. In The Art."

16

Marisa waited expectantly. "And you said—"

"Yes. For now. However, I did tell her that our time together would be greatly limited. After all, I have other . . . pressing interests." Laine's impish smirk failed to charm Marisa. Her sharp stare remained.

"In any event, I'll be performing her Wiccaning soon, and she'll no longer be my student. Plus, it seems she has met another of our kin who will gladly assist in teaching her."

Marisa seemed pleased with this turn of events. "Really? Who?"

"I don't know. Haven't met him yet. Amarantha will introduce us tonight."

With a slow gait and her face nearly free of anxiety, Marisa stepped closer. "So it looks like everything has worked out after all."

"No. That's not all." Laine's attention returned to Athena's silent comfort. "Before you called, I'd just come back from a pathworking and experienced the most lucid and dire omen I've withstood in years." He clenched his teeth in remembrance of Amarantha's torn neck. "Amarantha is in danger."

Laine scarcely got his last words out before Marisa's protests began. "Oh what, so now you have to run out and rescue her?"

Laine proclaimed, "We protect our own,'" with a slow growl.

"We protect ourselves as well!" Marisa countered, "You're the one who keeps cramming down my throat how perfect and powerful she is. Maybe she can handle this herself. Maybe she doesn't want your help!"

Laine spun in outrage and burned an angry gaze into Marisa. "Stop! Did I just stutter?! She is in danger, and I am her mentor! I am honor and duty-bound to protect her!"

"Bullshit! This has nothing to do with 'honor'! It's all about you! You couldn't have her, and now you can't bear to let anyone else near her!"

Laine grinned despite himself. "This nonsense again?

I've told you time after time that what two witches share always looks more romantic to 'mundanes' than it is. They don't understand, and apparently, neither do you! She is my greatest student. I have invested much time and heart in her, and I'll be damned if anyone's going to undo that. Anyone!"

Marisa's stony expression showed she understood the full gravity of his affirmation. At this moment they were sharing the same thought: what about their relationship? Would he sacrifice that for Amarantha as well? It worried him that he didn't have an answer to the question that Marisa had been asking all along. It worried him a lot.

Damn the Rede of Chivalry. To be what Laine was demanded a code of conduct, for without that ethical context, unchained energies would consume the negligent in their hunger. Pain and madness were inevitable, and death—if one were fortunate—would follow. Laine had always effortlessly balanced his roles as liege and lover; his responsibilities to duty and passion. Now, with his oaths at odds, the scales were over-laden, and instead of possessing the strength of a fulcrum, Laine was feeling crushed by their combined weight.

"Marisa, I love you," he said at last, "but understand this is what it means to be what we are. Look, after this is all done—after her Wiccaning—I will retire as her teacher. She knows this. But until then, I won't stand down. I can't."

Now it was Marisa's turn to digest what had just been spoken. "I see," she said solemnly, staring at his pentacle. "Fine. Do what you want to; what you have to." Moist light was gathered in her eyes. "I won't mention it again."

Laine should have been satisfied with this rare victory. He wasn't. His stomach soured.

"Just be careful," she sharply pleaded.

"I will," Laine assured Marisa. He took her into his arms, content with the illusion of her civility. "One last crucible," he muttered, "and then it ends."

Laine's lips lingered on Marisa's. He fed on their warmth, their flavor, their shape, tasting them again and again. Reluctantly, he broke from their embrace and said, "Come. Let's join the others for a spell, then we'll be off."

They neatened their clothing in silence. Marisa was about to shut off the light when Laine said, "Hold on a sec. Before I forget . . . ," and turned a final time toward Amarantha's altar. He scribed a banishing star upon his chest and blew out the candles.

"*Now* let's join the party." Laine and Marisa shut the light and door behind them; shut their dispute behind them; shut Athena in the inky-black behind them.

They ventured down the high-ceilinged Victorian hallway, arms coiled around each other, admiring the intricate vine frieze snaking down the corridor; the floral bas-relief blistering the walls. Without warning, an inebriated young man staggered buoyantly up to them with a sheet of day-glow orange paper in his hand.

"Hey, what's up?" he bellowed and slurred. "Want some stickers? 'Dairytown Cream Cheese: The Best!' And in glorious Citrus Orange."

"Uh, no, thanks," Laine managed.

"Suit yourself, bud. See ya." The stylish stranger slapped Laine's chest and lurched off into the restroom, fumbling with the light as he entered.

"What the hell was that?"

"Don't you know? That was The Cream Cheese Man." Marisa sprouted a toothy grin. "And it looks like he got you."

"What do you mean?" Laine followed Marisa's eyes, spotting a sticky mass of cream cheese stickers adhered to his tuxedo shirt. "Asshole."

Marisa just laughed. "Wait, wait, let me get these off you." She began peeling the decals from his shirt.

"And what a wonderful color." After a roll of his eyes, Laine squinted toward the far end of the hallway where Amarantha was laughing with a strangely familiar—no, it couldn't be!

The approaching man was immaculate. A finely-cut mane of gold framed his angelic face, the closest thing to a true halo most would ever see. He was dressed in perfect *GQ* attire: an off-white blazer with sleeves pushed up above his forearms; an open, pastel blue dress shirt tucked into his 501s; no socks in his docksiders. His every stride reeked of self-assurance, and his every gesture wove a mesmerizing web. And then his eyes: aquamarine crystals set in orbs of pristine ivory. They were threats veiled in a promise.

Yes, it was him: the beast from the vision.

Laine's heart stuttered. His right forearm crawled and burned. The world fell into slow-time. Amarantha and the man moved toward Laine through the thickening air, laughing without a sound.

Laine steeled himself.

Oh what, so now you have to run out and rescue her?

Amarantha and the beast stopped before him. "Laine, this is Donovan, the one I told you about."

Laine's hands tightened into angry fists.

"Donovan, this is Laine."

Maybe she doesn't want your help!

Donovan extended his right hand. "Pleasure."

Why was it suddenly so quiet?

Bullshit! This has nothing to do with 'honor'! It's all about you!

Laine's right forearm was throbbing with furious heat.

Why was everything so loud?

Just be careful.

Laine extended his left hand, prompting the curious Donovan to do the same. They shook as the party returned to Laine's ears in proper measure.

"Well, someone discovered our little wine stash," Amarantha said, nibbling her lower lip, "but I managed to salvage what was left of the White Zin. Is that okay?"

"Yeah, that's fine," Laine managed, accepting the proffered goblet. After a shaky sip, he thanked her.

Concern crossed Amarantha's face as she stroked his shoulder. "Are you okay, Laine?" All eyes were on him.

"Yes, I'm fine," Laine lied, "I'm just a little tired. Why

don't we go join the others." Amarantha seemed convinced; Marisa didn't. She shot him a vitriolic stare over her drink.

"Good, then let's go," Donovan sang. "We were having a pretty heavy discussion on the so-called 'occult practices' of the Druids."

Laine blurted, "'So-called'? Frankly, I don't see how any practitioner worth—"

Amarantha silenced Laine's outburst with the wave of a hand. "Not now," she whispered. "Trust me."

Trust me.

The foursome continued down the hall. Donovan spared Marisa a glance and a smile; she returned the compliment. Laine pretended not to notice, swallowing the wine deeply to combat the disgust rising in his throat.

His right forearm was still burning.

* * *

Laine's reflection doubled and distorted in the residue of a forgotten beverage. He was sitting alone in the kitchen, empty plastic cups and stained paper plates providing his only company; numb lips and occasional foot traffic his only stimulation.

He had excused himself from any further conversations after his outburst in the hallway. He should have followed the course of Donovan's "snide" comment before giving a retort. All the man had meant was that to the Druids, there was no division between the occult and the religious in much the same way that the obeahs and houngans of Voodoo made no such distinction, a fact Laine was well-aware of. But of course, there was no amending his mistake now.

If Donovan was indeed the threat, he had already won the first round by making Laine look foolish, and if he wasn't, Laine was still the fool. Either way, he had lost. "Way to strike first and true."

So now Laine was sequestering himself in the thrashed kitchen, gleaning snippets of the ongoing revelries in the next room. He couldn't blame anyone but himself for his solitude, and besides, he never was much of a party animal.

Laine didn't notice the girl's intrusion until she slammed a case of Bud on the table and said, "Hi."

"Hello," he returned. There was something familiar about the ample, turquoise-eyed Latina, but damned if Laine could put his finger on where they met.

"Is *all* the wine gone?"

Laine shrugged. "Uh, I don't know, probably."

"Damn." A purple bubble inflated and popped in front of her smooth, café au lait face. "So you don't remember me, do you?"

"I'm sorry, I'm kinda buzzed right now."

"I'm Heather," she managed around her Hubba Bubba, Bubblicious, whatever was in her mouth.

"I'm Laine."

"I know. I'm Amy's friend," she said with a puzzling degree of annoyance. "We've met a couple of times at the church."

Laine stood and shook her left hand. "Yeah, I remember now," he half-lied, "How have you been?"

She seemed relieved . . . and quite drunk. "I've been all right. Had to get away from Jimmy and his fucking stickers for a while." Heather began rummaging through the cabinets.

"Ah yes. Jimmy." Laine squinted into the living room where Donovan's sidekick was holding audience, recounting some story or other that made the crowd roar with laughter. Marisa was squeezed in next to him on the sofa, pulling away whenever he periodically played with her emerald "beak".

"You know, Amy was pretty excited to see you again."

"What?" He turned toward Heather.

She was staring at Laine with the look of one who had made a decision, then said, "Your coming tonight has made her pretty happy."

"Oh, I'll wager I'm not the only source of her joy this evening." Laine snorted.

Apparently Heather didn't hear his gripe through her bubble popping and cabinet slamming because she said nothing. Airhead. Laine might have even thought her attractive were it not for the incessant gum chewing.

"Aha! I find one!" Heather proclaimed, brandishing a bottle of red and doing a little dance that made the coils of her brown hair spring.

Laine said, "Well done," as he turned his attention back to the living room. Marisa was gone. "Listen, I have to find my girlfriend, get ready to leave. It's been a pleasure . . . ."

". . . Heather," she completed for him as though he had already forgotten.

"Right. Have fun."

"Thanks."

Laine slid into the adjacent living room where the stragglers continued their carousing. Still no Marisa was to be found.

"I'm right here," she said, her voice alarmingly close. "Boy, you must be pretty drunk. You walked right past me. You okay?"

"Yeah, fine," he smiled. "I am a little fucked up, though."

"Are you *really* fucked up?" she drawled with that wonderfully mischievous grin of hers.

"Well, I'm not *really* fucked up, but we should book if you're good to ride." Before he made a bigger ass of himself.

"I'm buzzed, but I can handle it. Let's say our goodbyes."

After inquiring, Jimmy directed Laine and Marisa to Amarantha's room, stating that she and Donovan disappeared behind closed doors about thirty minutes ago. Laine put on his best poker face, thanked Jimmy, and trailed Marisa down the hall.

"Knock knock," Marisa warned at the door.

"Come on in."

The scene inside was chaste. Donovan was sitting in the chair Laine had occupied two hours earlier, and Amarantha was sitting at the edge of her canopy bed, rubbing the trim of a childhood blanket. Even the altar remained extinguished.

"Are you guys leaving?" Amarantha whined.

"Yeah," Laine conceded, "I have to be at work tomorrow, and I'm a bit drunker than I should be."

"Yeah ya' are." Marisa laughed as she retrieved their helmets and coats from the armoire.

"So 'gotta go now, gotta fly.'" Laine pecked Amarantha on the cheek and quickly locked eyes with her for remembrance. Amarantha reciprocated before turning to Marisa.

"Donovan, it's been a pleasure," Laine proclaimed.

The beast rose from the vanity, this time offering his left hand. He learned fast. "The pleasure was all mine, Laine. I'm glad we finally met properly."

"Same here." Because Laine liked to know the face of his enemies. Or *potential* enemies. He draped his long coat over his shoulders like a cape.

"I'll give you a call tomorrow, Laine," Amarantha promised.

Bitter and drunk, Laine said, "I know you will."

* * *

It was the longest fifteen-minute scooter ride in Laine's experience. Within the first five minutes of the journey, Laine knew Marisa would remain reticent to focus on the road, so he satisfied himself by soaking in the light of the waxing moon.

Halfway through the ride, it struck Laine that Samhain —Halloween—would fall on a Friday and a full moon this year. Was there a more auspicious night in which to consecrate his pupil? Beneath Selene's full, glowing face a new daughter could be born. The possibility lightened Laine's leaden demeanor despite Marisa's silence, despite Donovan's questionability, despite his earlier failings. He smiled beneath the autumn moon for the remainder of the trip.

Marisa's manner hadn't changed when they entered the Sunset District flat she shared with her sister and her sister's boyfriend. She merely rolled into the garage, locked up the scooter, and once inside the house proper, went about her nocturnal ritual of greeting and feeding her birds without casting Laine a single syllable.

Laine was standing at her bedroom door, mutely staring at her back as she dabbed out her green contact lenses and squeezed saline solution into her palm. "Look, I'm going to wash up a bit," Laine offered weakly. "I'll be back."

Marisa grunted her acknowledgment.

"Fine." He walked down the short length of the hall to the bathroom and locked the door behind him.

The alcohol and the moon rush had melted away, leaving only exhaustion. Laine turned on the faucets, let the water run a short time, then stuck his hand beneath the flow, resisting the urge to jerk it back when scalded by the heat. The pain innerved him, forced him to center.

He took measured breaths as he increased the cold water to compensate, then rolled up his right sleeve.

"Ah, the spoils of war." Scrawled on his right forearm in Magic Marker and wolves' blood ink was a barbed, black tattoo: the spear of Moloch. The central sigil attributed to the dark entity was enclosed at its cardinals by four, triangular elemental glyphs meant to bind it. A long, pointed shaft with stylized thorns cut through the seal and ran the length between Laine's wrist and inner elbow. The simple Egyptian passage inscribed on his outer forearm came alive in the bathroom's incandescence, writhing on his skin. Though the characteristic burning had ceased, tension remained in the spear like the impatient coiling of a panther's sinews before the pounce.

Had Laine shaken with his right hand and unleashed the spear's power against Donovan, it would have bled the beast's soul until only despair and weakness remained. At the very least, Donovan would have found even the simplest legerdemain impossible to cast. It was the latter effect that Laine employed against his previous student; the one who had gone astray and required binding. Definitely a useful weapon in a Magick war and one its original custodians did not relinquish easily.

It was a shame that all that hungry suspense remained unused, but with the doubt that Marisa had planted in Laine's mind, it would have been unwise to afflict Donovan uncertainly. Laine hated for a good working to go to waste, but there was another way.

"*Tua-a em Tehuti tua-a em Tehuti . . . .*" Laine recited the Egyptian mantra of sealing in a sonorous loop, linking the end to the beginning until it was a drone of uncertain speech imperfectly heard. Once grounded, he broke the chant, pulled an oil vial from a pocket, and washed the ink from his arm, sending the spell's physical anchor flowing away in a whirlpool.

Laine stroked clove oil onto the spot where the spear had once been. The oil began its anesthetic effect, cooling his forearm.

"Stasis," he intoned. "Hold until I summon thee. As is my will, so mote it be." He rolled his sleeve down again, then replaced the vial and left the restroom.

As Laine approached Marisa's door, he was greeted by the scent of white jasmine incense. What was she doing? Maybe a working was in progress, and he shouldn't enter. He rapped lightly on the door.

"Marisa?"

"Come in."

Laine opened the door to Marisa's tastefully eclectic room. A dozen or so candles sputtered on the stereo cabinet, the nightstands, her altar, and her makeup table. Suspended from one corner, a back-lit Japanese parasol was illuminating the haze, and both birds' cages were covered for the night, protected from the jasmine smoke.

And in the center of the room, Marisa was kneeling on her unframed bed, wearing only a black lace teddy and surrounded by mosquito netting. She parted the drapery and smiled. "So are you just going to stand there with your mouth hanging open or what?"

"Hm. Let's try out 'What'." Smiling salaciously, Laine shut the door behind him, shrugged off his suspenders, and kicked off his shoes. He approached her patiently, cautiously, like a hunter stalking its prey.

Marisa coiled her arms around Laine's neck once he reached the bed, bending him forward for a kiss. She pulled him onto the bed until he too was kneeling, then stripped him of his tuxedo shirt.

Their pairing was like the completion of a jigsaw puzzle: an enigma made sense through the merging of their lips; their skin; their hearts. Marisa provided a purer intoxication than any wine Laine had ever imbibed, and he was going to drink of her fully. Their kisses were interrupted only when Marisa struggled to remove Laine's belt.

"Goddammit," she griped.

Laine sighed. "I swear, every time: you and this belt." He grabbed the end of the harness and freed it with one tug.

Marisa grinned. "Showoff."

Laine chuckled as he laid her back on the bed.

The netting enclosed them.

* * *

John's car rumbled to a stop at Heather Dominguez's Mission District home. The Skylark was packed with Donovan's Petaluma friends, all of them bragging at the highest decibels possible. Jimmy was in the backseat with her, obviously pissed about having to share the ride with his buddies, but since it wasn't his car, it wasn't his call. The Adam Ant song on the tape deck was the best thing about this trip; Jimmy's constant pawing of Heather was the worst.

"So, Heather," he said to her *chichis*, "what are you up to this weekend?"

Heather's migraine rattled in her skull. She did not need this shit. She wore this heavy-assed sweater to prevent exactly this kind of attention. "Hey, try looking me in the eyes, sport."

Jimmy finger-groomed his quiff cut and made eye contact. "Uh, you want to go out or something? With me?"

Heather managed to smile through her pain as everyone in the car grew silent with anticipation. "Tell you what: why don't you call me when you grow some pubes. Say, in about ten years?" She squeezed out of the car as Jimmy's jaw bounced off his chest. "Oh, and thanks for the ride, John." She slammed the car door, and Heather could hear Jimmy's friends busting his nuts through the glass and steel Buick as they pulled away. Served him right.

Once the car was out of sight, Heather stumbled up the stairs to her flat. "Goddess, please let my keys be at the top of my purse," she prayed. As she leaned against the door frame to catch her breath, she fought off the sudden urge to hurl. Man, was her head spinning.

"Thank The Goddess," Heather said when she found the keys within easy reach. That's right, she put them up top while Jimmy was breathing in her ear at the party. Getting the key into the hole was a bit of a pain, though. Why did that always happen when she had to pee?

An urgent moment later and Heather was in, locking the door and tripping for the bathroom. Once at the toilet, she didn't know whether to barf or piss but opted for the latter, singing "Goody Two-Shoes" as she did. Damn, now she'd never get that song out of her head.

Heather finished up, then grabbed the Tylenol bottle from the medicine cabinet only to find it empty. Great. Then she remembered something about water: drink a lot of it and the alcohol would thin out, relieving the hangover. Killing the light, she stepped out into the hallway. The shadows tried to smother her, kicking in a new wave of the spins.

She snapped on the kitchen light, and about a dozen six-legged dots ran for cover in the cabinets and behind the stove. It seemed no matter how clean they kept the place, the roaches always returned. Life in a barrio. She rinsed out an old jelly jar, filled it with water, and chugalugged.

Her brother Rudy appeared from his room, rubbing the sleep from his eyes. "Whatcha doin'?"

"Just getting some water, Rudy, that's all," she sighed. "Go back to bed."

"How's Amy?" he asked, ignoring her. Now the punk was going to give her a hard time.

"She's fine, Rudy, go back to bed."

Rudy flashed an impish smirk that brought a reluctant smile to Heather's face. "Mom said I could stay up if I want to."

"Sure she did. Quit lying and go to bed."

"Make me."

Ah, a twelve-year-old's defiance. "Rudy—"

"Okay, okay. Can I have a kiss goodnight?"

Heather knew the little butt wipe was up to something, but she said yes anyway. Rudy wrapped an arm around her neck, moved close to her cheek, and gave her a big, sloppy lick while embracing her like a boa constrictor.

"Aaagh! Rudy, stop!" she screamed, wrestling her brother off of her. She swung to hit him as he broke away but missed by about a foot. They both giggled, then Rudy dashed for his room, stopped short of the door, and mooned Heather before diving in.

Rudy yelled, "Psych!"

Heather cracked up. "I'm telling Mama!" she managed. It was a bluff. Heather knew that even if she did narc on him, his punishment would be light. No, just let the punk sweat it out for a while.

She wiped off the spit with a sleeve and collected herself, finishing off another glass of tap water. After rinsing her jar, she went to her room.

The lamp light hurt her head, but at least the nausea had ended. Heather undressed and slipped slowly into bed, fighting to find a comfortable sleeping position. The headache subsided for all of three minutes before returning with a fury. She squeezed tears from her eyes.

The first time Heather had a hangover, Amy was there.

Amy, Heather, and their friend Saffy had snuck into Amy's mom's liquor cabinet one night and got blitzed. Dear, charmed Amy went through it all with flying colors while Heather and Saffy barfed and reeled. By the next day, Heather was straight enough to face her mom. Yeah, they still got busted, but it wasn't too bad because at least Amy went through it with her.

They had grown apart over the three years Amy hung out with Laine, and now Donovan was back in the picture to complete the split.

Fucking Donovan. She never did like or trust that pretentious twit, and now Amy was all sprung over him. Whatever.

Before Amy's emancipation from her birth mom, they had been like sisters. Now Amy had her favorite witches to play with. She didn't need Heather around anymore. Not anymore.

"Fuck it." Heather turned over on her side and shut off the lamp.

Funny how warm tears could be.

* * *

Laine's room still bore the stale scent of patchouli and dragon's blood. He threw open the window as he tore out of his clothes. Leave it up to work to ruin a perfectly good weekend. He wouldn't be running late if Marisa weren't so damned persuasive. Oh well, if you had to be tardy—

He was culling through the closet for his gray shirt when the phone rang. "Laine here."

"Hey."

"Hey, Amarantha. What's up?" Laine's watch said it was 2:15. Forty-five minutes left.

"Oh, nothing. I just wanted to thank you for coming out last night."

"No problem. I wouldn't just flake on you. It was my pleasure."

"Did you and Marisa make up?"

"All night," he said with a smile, "But I'm running behind, so if I can call you later—"

"I'm sorry, I'll make it quick. I just thought you should know I was talking to Donovan about stuff last night—well actually this morning—and he asked me to go with him. Steady."

Laine froze. "I see. And you said?"

There was a pause. "I said yes."

Any joy that lived in Laine was strangled to death by the knotting of his guts. He dry-swallowed as his right forearm taunted him with a slight burning. The bastard got two for one.

"Laine? Are you still there?"

MONDAY, SEPTEMBER 29TH

Autumn, the Reaping Season. Such a dark title for so beautiful a time of the year. As Amarantha and Heather walked up Hyde Street in San Francisco's Russian Hill district, Amarantha found herself enthralled by the glamour of it all: the receding sunlight bathing the well-tended lanes in amber, lending a romantic air to the couples that strolled by; the raucous cable car that drew itself up the shallow grade; the rows of trees whose leaves never turned colors as they did back in the South-Central U.S. This was Amarantha's time; this was her city.

"Amy," Heather whined, "how much farther is it? It's colder than a witch's tit out here."

Amarantha sighed at Heather's vulgarity. "We're almost there, just relax. In fact, I think this is it."

The duo stopped in front of a café with the words *Russian Hill O' Beans* emblazoned on the windows in gold leaf. The display featured paper filters and French presses arranged in an almost Stonehenge fashion on a plot of roasted coffee beans. Company mugs and home espresso machines shamelessly promoted their elevated prices.

"Oh yeah, this is it. Just as Laine described." Amarantha smiled as she entered the spacious shop, its air filled with heavy aromas and chamber music. To Amarantha's right were racks of small Mason jars filled with various coffees, teas, and spices for the olfactory sampling. Beyond those were wooden shelves teeming with larger jars for actual purchases. The long vines of yellowing creeper plants slithered along the trims and corners of the off-white walls and coiled around framed sheet music from a century ago.

As Amarantha moved farther in, she heard a slam and a jingle. She turned to find Heather with an embarrassed grin on her face, holding the door open against a serving table that had gone unseen. "Now who put that there?" Heather griped.

"My boss, who else?" Laine's voice called from the prep area at the back of the cafe. "And I agree with you: it's the worst place to put a table, but he bought six sets before realizing they wouldn't all fit. Typical of him." He smiled his smile, summoning them in. "What have you guys been up to?"

"Roaming Polk Street, mostly Fields Bookstore and Zee Continental." Amarantha gave him one of her rib-crushers, and found Laine was no longer saddled with the dread that rode him on Friday. She released him and smiled at the espresso maker. "Wow, is that a manual machine?"

Laine nodded. "Yup. None of that Haight Street push-button crap here. All hand-cranked."

"So you know how to work this thing?"

Laine stroked the copper and brass skin of the machine like a lover. "You kidding me? I've been called the best latté maker in The City—well, by default anyway."

There was a boast. "Let's see you do your thing then."

"Done. Heather?"

Heather rubbed her chin. "Can I get a pastry too?"

"Sure."

"Can I go to the bathroom first?"

"Sure," Laine repeated. "Straight back, up the stairs, through the office, to your left."

"Thanks." And Heather was off.

Once alone, Amarantha noted, "Well, you're in a good mood, Laine."

"A weekend of carnality will do that to you." Laine was grinning ear to ear as he adjusted his eyeglasses and prepared her drink. "Unfortunate side effect."

Amarantha blushed at his rakish attitude, and it hadn't gone unnoticed by her mentor.

"Aw. Athena, Athena, as chaste as the dawn," he japed, nodding at her flushed cheeks.

"Oh, be quiet you. You know—"

"Yeah, I know."

Laine's Tantric teachings had been strictly theoretical, but the lessons did stir the natural curiosity in her. Sex was one of the few mysteries Amarantha still hadn't explored, at least not properly. It had always been the wrong time or the wrong guy. Either she was too young or they were too eager, and the eager ones always got angry when she denied them.

But now there was Donovan. The way that he looked at her, spoke to her, and touched her cheek always set her blood afire. All things in nature had a proper time for expression, and her time felt near. When it was The Goddess' will, she would gladly accept Donovan—the right man—in her bed.

"Subject change," Laine declared, snapping her from her thoughts. Had he been skrying her again?

With Amarantha's latté now completed, Laine said, "Samhain: let's go over the details, shall we?" He grabbed his green subject notebook from under the register, set her beverage down on a table, and joined her. "Oh, did you want a pastry as well?"

"No, thank you." She sampled the parfait-styled drink, and wiped the thick froth from her lips. "Very good."

"Told you." Laine's smug smile melted away as he

thumbed through the pages of the notebook between them. "Okay, I won't need any personal fetishes because of the nature of the rite. In fact, since you will officially be free from my 'oppressive rule', you can have your old personal items back."

Laughing, Amarantha said, "That's okay, keep them."

"Very well." Laine flipped the page.

"Did you want to do it at my place?" Amarantha downed more of the latté.

"Well, you do have the space for it. My room might be too small. I'm thinking either your bedroom or the dining room, depending on if Joanie is around or not."

"I think I can get her out of the house for the night."

He nodded. "Also, I originally wanted to perform the ritual skyclad, but now with Donovan—ugh, and Marisa would have a shit fit, pardon my French." Laine shrugged.

"We could still do that," she assured him.

Laine cocked a brow. "Are you positive?"

"Yes. Donovan won't mind. He *is* one of us." Another point for him. He knew how important Laine was to her, both as a friend and a mentor. Besides, nude rituals were common in Pagan practices.

Unfortunately, it wasn't the same situation for Laine. Amarantha didn't need to skry him to know what he was thinking right now: Marisa *would* mind. "You know, you could just not tell her about it. Witches' business."

Laine grimaced and removed his glasses. "I don't know. Love, man." He shut the notebook, sighed, then leaned on the table between them. He had a faraway look in his eyes; a gaze that transcended the present.

"Everything is far more intense through the lens of love, you know?" His tone was trance-like. "Whispers twist into poetry, a room can transform into heaven, and a song can become the soundtrack of your soul.

"But by the same token, all the pains of life are also magnified by love: words can envenom you; a song can bedevil you; a room, haunt you with its echoes, and there is no escaping the agony of the heart. I never want to be the cause of that kind of pain, and I never want to live it."

Amarantha had never seen nor felt Laine like this before. This wasn't just about the ritual or Marisa or herself, but about the weight of . . . everything. Old souls were often sheathed in young people, and those with wisdom bore a heavy burden whether they were a "mundane" or a mage. It was understandable why Laine wanted to retire. He needed to let go and simplify his life; needed to just love Marisa and just make art. Now that that possibility was near, Laine was just a man.

Taking her hands in his, Laine returned to the present. "You know, in certain folklore, it's said that our kind should never fall in love for fear of losing our powers. I say bullshit, take the ride. Even if the lore is true, it might be worth the sacrifice." He released her hands and leaned back into his chair. "Know that I extend my heartfelt blessings to you and Donovan. As long as he doesn't cross myself or mine, of course." Smiling, Laine waved a parental finger at her. "Don't make me regret it."

"I shan't, my kin, and neither will he. Blessed be, Laine."

"Blessed be, Amarantha." Laine reopened his notebook and pushed his glasses back up his nose. "As for now, while we still have our—wait a minute. Heather's been in there a while."

"If I know her, she's probably painting her lips," Amarantha quipped with a roll of her eyes. "Speaking of, could you do me a favor? Could you be nicer to Heather?"

Laine's expression of confusion was pure gold. "Be nicer to . . . ? I *am* nice to her."

Amarantha held up her hands. "I know it's just how you are, but you can be a little intimidating, and you kind of freak her out."

Laine chuckled. "Huh! Really?"

Amarantha stirred her coffee intently, blending the layers of milk and espresso. "Yeah. She compared you to Darth Vader the other night."

Laine cracked up. "Wow! I'll take that as a

compliment!"

"I don't think that's how she meant it, though. She's one of us, and I just don't want her to feel—"

He looked astonished. "Wait, what do you mean she's 'one of us'?"

"Well, yeah. It's been a while, but we've done moon callings and spiral dances together. She interviewed Anton LaVey once, and—"

"Whoa, whoa, whoa!" Laine's voice leapt with both excitement and concern. "*The* Anton LaVey? Of The Church of Satan?"

"Yes, but it was for a school report, that's all. She's not a Satanist."

"Hm. Must've been some class."

"Heather was in the gifted student program at Wash, and she was able to graduate early partly because her report was so good."

Laine clearly wasn't recalling why Heather was so special to Amarantha beyond friendship, but she knew just how to jog his memory. "Hey, Laine, remember when I told you the story of The Three Girls and The Ouija Board?"

Laine considered her, visibly sifting through his memories. Finally, he said, "Three girls with a Ouija board: a dark and stormy night and a slumber party with strange happenings that affected each girl differently. One girl turned to Magick, using it for good; the second girl turned to Magick, using it for evil; the third girl was afraid of the Magick and ran away."

Amarantha leaned in close this time. "And that third girl is now in your bathroom putting on makeup."

Laine's face went blank. "That was Heather?"

"That was Heather." Amarantha smiled, finishing her drink with satisfaction.

Laine expelled a breath, then stroked his lower lip. "Intriguing. Does she still practice?"

"Well, at first she was really interested, asking lots of questions and so on. Now I don't know. You could ask her."

"I could. Maybe I'll run her through a 'Yoda': find out

what she's up to on the under."

"Sure, just don't talk like Yoda."

"Speak like him, I will not," Laine said in a perfect impersonation.

They had just finished chuckling when Heather reappeared from the restroom. "Sorry I took so long. My lipstick needed fixing."

Though his face was passive, Amarantha knew Laine was laughing inside.

"Well, it took you long enough," she chided. "Now I have to go. Give Laine your order. I'll be back."

Amarantha shot Laine a sidelong glance as she rose, receiving a slight nod of acknowledgment, then departed.

* * *

Heather's mom always said "it's none of your business what people say about you." Well, she probably never walked in on two suspicious-acting witches before. And now Amy was leaving her alone with Laine? Shit.

Laine was already up and heading for the kitchen. He pulled a saucer from the stack beside the machine and asked, "So, Heather, what kind of pastry would you like?"

She checked out the tray in front of her. "A bearclaw."

"Done," Laine said, removing the cake with a pair of tongs and laying it on the saucer.

As he set the bearclaw in the toaster oven, Heather didn't feel creeped out by Laine like she normally did. Under his green apron, he was wearing a perfectly normal pair of black slacks with matching suspenders, a white dress shirt, and a red "power" tie. Equally surprising was the pair of silver prescription glasses—absent during Amy's party—on his face, proving he had human flaws after all.

"What kind of drink did you make for Amy?"

"A latté. Want one?" Laine waved what looked like a tall parfait glass.

"Yes, thank you."

Laine was crafting the drink with care and expertise,

pouring the hot milk, layering in the espresso, and topping off the whole thing with fine foam and a spank of chocolate powder. It almost looked too good to drink. Almost.

"Wow, that's hella pretty," she flattered. "It's like a work of art."

"Thank you." He barely looked up as he placed the drink on another saucer and brought out her pastry.

"No, really, that's a cool skill. I kinda' thought you were like—"

Laine paused and pointed at her with a black lacquered fingernail. "Evil incarnate? Darth Vader, perhaps?" he growled in a horror movie voice.

Oh shit! Did Amy have to squeal on her? It was just a joke. "I didn't mean to—"

Laine laughed. "Don't worry about it. You're not the only one who's said something like that. When you're a tall, Black, *Star Wars* geek, you give off the vibe." There was actually a smile on his face, and it wasn't scary at all.

Heather relaxed a bit. "Ah. I like fantasy myself. You know, *Excalibur*, *Conan the Barbarian*, *Red Sonya*—"

"Oh, I love *Excalibur*!" Laine oozed. "It's one of my favorite movies. And I loved the first Conan flick. The second one sucked though, despite Grace Jones."

"Me too!" Boy, she did *not* see that one coming. Heather's mouth was so wide open, she could have shoveled in the whole bearclaw in one gulp. "I mean, I agree."

"So I trust I didn't put you off at Amarantha's party," he said, sitting down at a table with her. "It's just that I don't like crowds of strangers, and I like to keep a low profile until I know where a person's coming from. I also didn't recognize you at first because, well, I was pretty plastered. You understand, don't you?"

"Yeah, I think so. That must make your job here hard, though." The drink was as good as it looked.

"Not really. I mean, I get along with people, I just don't like them." His smile made her smile. "By the way, Amarantha mentioned that you might be looking for a job.

We have an opening here."

"Really? Making coffee?" She chewed a chunk of the buttered pastry.

"My boss Mohammed just got a new computer, and he's been looking for someone who can work it. Someone to file, take notes, that sort of thing."

What didn't Amy tell this guy? Still, it was very tempting. "*I* have office experience. What kind of computer is it?"

Laine shrugged. "Macintosh, I think. I don't deal with the office stuff that much. I just work the register and take orders from our clients. Anything having to do with the office, I don't like to screw with. So what do you think?"

It took Heather all of two seconds to agree to fill out an application. What could it hurt? "Can I bring this back to you?" she asked after receiving a copy.

"No problem. The pay starts at six an hour, but he's usually pretty good about raises." Laine excused himself to answer the ringing phone.

"Well, looks like Christmas is taken care of," Heather said to herself. It would be nice to finally buy gifts for Mama and Rudy. She folded the application in quarters and slid it into a bomber jacket pocket.

Laine slammed down the phone.

"What's wrong?" Heather asked.

He tore off his glasses and wiped his face with the palm of his hand. "That was Mohammed. Applied Biosystems is placing an order this week, which means I have to order more beans and work some overtime." He threw his hands up, then returned to his seat. "They're our biggest account, and they'll want somewhere between fifty and eighty orders of coffee. We make each and every one of them by hand. Forty little man-weighed packets in each bag, sealed and marked."

Heather shook her head. "Damn, no wonder you hate people."

Laine stared at her for a pause before cracking up. Heather joined him.

"Hey, Heather, can I ask you something? Confidentially?" Laine's face was all serious.

After swallowing some bearclaw, Heather said, "Sure, I guess."

Laine glanced over his shoulder, then leaned on the table. "What do you think about Donovan?" he asked, his voice just above a whisper.

Heather finished her latté. "Donovan . . . . What about him?"

"You've known him for a while, right? Will he be good to Amarantha?"

"Well, I hate to admit it, but Donovan's not as bad as some of her former boyfriends. I don't know what she's told you, but Amy doesn't have the best track record in that department." It was almost as bad as Heather's.

"Really? That's surprising."

"Yeah, her last four guys were dickheads. At least we've known Donovan for a while."

"How long?"

"Six or seven years? We all met at the church." She dug through her purse for her pack of grape Bubblicious. "Want some gum?"

Laine waved away her offer. "That long?"

"Yeah, but he was way different back then. Just a scrawny kid with a mouth full of metal that kept to himself." Heather unwrapped the chunk of gum. "We used to call him Vampire Boy until he cried about it."

Laine chuckled, "Why?"

"Oh, because when he had his headgear on, he used to breathe through his teeth." She imitated him with a *ssk-ssk-ssk* sucking sound, then popped the gum in her mouth.

Laine lost it. He laughed so hard he had to cover his mouth to keep the noise down.

"Yeah," Heather continued, "so he pops up a couple of years ago all handsome and chromeless, and Amy's been whupped over him ever since. The thing is, something about him bugs me more now than it did back in the day, but I can't put my finger on it. Maybe it's because he's a witch now."

"And other witches scare you?"

Heather smiled and said, "Depends on the witch, I guess. You don't trust him either, do you?"

Just then, Amy returned from the bathroom. She had an I-told-you-so expression on her face when she saw Heather still smiling. "Well, I see you two are getting along."

"Yeah, Heather's hilarious," Laine covered. "How did that go again?" he asked Heather.

Damn, busted!

"Oh yeah, what do the letters in NASA stand for?" He paused for effect before answering, "Need Another Seven Astronauts."

Good thing Heather had heard that joke before, otherwise she would have blown it. Instead, she smiled.

"Okay, that was tasteless," Amy commented.

Laine added with a lick of his lips, "Unless you're a cannibal." Heather laughed when Amy went pale.

The café phone rang like it was timed. Laine answered it, and after a few hushed words, it was obvious his girlfriend was on the other end. "Hey, Marisa says 'hi.'"

"Hello," Amy replied, then said to Heather, "I have to pick up more stuff for my classes. You ready to go?"

"Oh. Sure." Heather grabbed her leather bomber jacket from the back of her chair.

Amy had begun to bus the table, but Laine turned around and stopped her.

"Leave it. I'll get it," he said, cupping the phone. The tangled cord stretched as he went for the dishes. "You guys leaving?" he whispered.

"I've got to go," Amy whispered back.

"Hold on a minute—" Laine retrieved their dishes while wound up in the telephone cord like something from a Bugs Bunny cartoon. Heather was about to laugh when one of the Irish coffee glasses slid off its saucer.

It fell to the floor in slow-motion, disintegrating into shards of blood-red light. It was the only sound she heard.

"Aw damn. Marisa, let me call you back."

She drew shallow, spasmodic breaths as she caressed her raw wrists . . . .

"Heather, are you alright?" Amy asked from far away.

. . . and pulled herself into a fetal position.

"What's going on?"

"Nothing, Laine. It's nothing. I better take her home. Come on, Heather, let's go."

Heather felt Amy's gentle hands guide her from her seat. "I'll be okay," she managed.

Forget the glass. Forget the glass. Forget . . . .

* * *

"Okay, what next?" Laine asked, shaking water from his hands.

Marisa twisted the red cap off the bottle of Kikkoman. "Are they all washed?"

"Yup."

Marisa slid Laine the wooden cutting board. "Okay, start chopping."

Laine picked out one of the knives from the kitchen drawer while humming Translator's "Everywhere That I'm Not" with Marisa's stereo. Not sure which bowl of vegetables to start with, he grabbed the green onions.

"No, start with the ginger."

"Ah. Why?"

Marisa was shaking soy sauce into the wok. "Because it'll take the longest to fry."

". . . So it should go first. I get you now. I think." Laine picked up the vaguely human-shaped root and examined it. The "head" seemed as good a place to start as any. Once done, he showed Marisa his handiwork. "Is this enough?"

Marisa's eyes bulged. "More than."

Laine shrugged, grabbing the mushrooms.

"Actually, do the broccoli next."

He grabbed a sprout and started cutting.

"No. Not like that," Marisa admonished, "Lengthwise, like this." She took the knife and began vivisecting the poor plant with rapid strokes, slicing ever-closer to her fingers, but never quite touching them. "Now what's wrong with you?"

Laine had been unaware of his grimace. "Man, you freak me out when you chop things up like that."

"That's how you're supposed to do it."

"Yeah, I know. I just hope your fingers don't end up on the menu."

Marisa gave another exasperated sigh. "Look, I'll tell you what: since you're so squeamish, why don't you go set the table instead."

"Aw, but I wanna learn how to cook."

Marisa scowled, her patience all but gone.

"'Set the table.' That's a great idea." Laine slinked away. This should be simple enough, at least. After all, the only utensils involved would be chopsticks.

Laine gathered some dishes and took them into the dining room. After setting the dinnerware, he picked up one of Marisa's birthday roses from the centerpiece, then went to a window. Peering through the blinds, Laine followed the slow course of the stars in the Stygian sky above and pondered.

It was a difficult thing for Laine to let Amarantha go like he had; like he would do in a month, but he had to prove to himself that he could. She had become so integral to Laine that he feared that Marisa might be right. Not about his supposed infatuation but his overprotectiveness. He felt like a widower giving away the hand of his only daughter, and he had to be strong enough to just let go.

Contrarily, he had to trust his instinct. He had to trust the vision that made him ache still. Laine had never gone wrong by heeding an omen, particularly one so inexorable, but now his motives seemed questionable to himself as well as Marisa. The only person that seemed to be as "crazy" as he was Heather.

What had happened to Heather in the shop earlier that day? He broke a glass, and she suddenly went all catatonic. Taking a deep breath, Laine extended his consciousness through time, slipping mentally backward to perform a retroactive skry.

* * *

Firmly in an astral facsimile of the cafe, I moved through the phantom space. I saw myself, Heather, and Amarantha as a static imitation of what was.

"When I broke the glass," *I recalled before kneeling next to Heather's echo. I touched her shoulder and established an empathic link. Emotions emerged in a wave of helplessness and fear, but no details as to why came forth. Whatever affected Heather had been repressed so vehemently that she had probably forgotten its origins herself, at least consciously. The splintering glass smoked it out of her, but it still wasn't fresh nor clear enough for me to read, not without knowing more about Heather.*

"Dinner's ready," *Marisa announced from behind me. I stood and turned in the cafe to face Marisa's dining room table.* "I didn't put much oyster sauce in it, so here's the bottle if you want more."

* * *

Laine shook the remnants of the vision from his head, then took a seat at the table, placing the rose beside his plate.

Removing his glasses, he and Marisa dug in. They proceeded quietly at first with Marisa watching him eat, and Laine just watching her. He never tired of looking at her. In fact, all she did was make him hungrier, though not necessarily for food.

Finally, Laine broke the silence. "I was talking to Mohammed today, and he's made me manager of the shop."

Marisa smiled brightly. "Really? Yay!"

"I know, can you take it? And I've only been the supervisor for five months. Apparently, Peter's off to bigger and better things, so I'm up."

"Aw, you take better care of that store than they do anyway. So is the cheapskate gonna give you a raise?"

"Yeah. There's just one thing though."

"Uh-oh," she said onto her food. "It's always something."

"Yeah. I'm going to be working some shitty hours. He only brought it up now because Applied Bio placed a big order today. Between my promotion and your weekend job at Pier 1, it's going to be tough making time." As if their relationship needed more strain.

"We'll figure something out." Marisa didn't have to look up from her plate. Her voice belied her sincerity.

"Yeah, we'll work it out." This could prove fortunate. It would mean fewer confrontations with Marisa and an easier task of keeping her out of harm's way if things did get FUBAR with Donovan.

"Well, you know," she started, tentatively, "if you do get that raise, it means you can move in here."

Laine's gut knotted as he put down his chopsticks. "You mean with Kelli and Mark? Yeah, right, what you said. We barely get along as it is." They thought Laine's frequent weekend visits warranted his contribution to the rent, but according to Marisa, Mark had been far guiltier of that transgression when he first started dating Marisa's older sister. Such puerile nonsense. The two couples had been in a state of silent contention for months, and no amount of bribery would change that. They simply didn't like each other.

"We could always get our own place," Marisa offered.

"That we could." Laine was not in the mood to discuss this right now, and Marisa knew it. It showed in the way she pushed tofu around on her plate.

After a pause, she smiled. "I know it's a ways off, but my mom has formally invited you to join us for Thanksgiving this year."

Laine froze in mid-bite. "Are you kidding?"

"No. I talked to her this afternoon right after I got off the phone with you." Their eyes locked. "You want to come? You'll finally get to meet the rest of my family."

Laine cocked a brow and smirked. "Wow, you guys plan early. They gonna size me up for the kill?"

"Actually, I think my folks are finally accepting us. Weird, huh?"

Exactly the word Laine would use. The only thing he found more discomforting than Marisa's flat-mates were her parents. He had this "paranoid" notion that they didn't like him much, with his being Black and all, but now he was being invited to a family function. It looked like times had changed.

Laine wiped the rice from his lips. "When you go in to work tomorrow, tell your dad I'll have to check and see what's happening with my family then."

Marisa's face was expectant.

"Otherwise, yes, I gladly accept their invitation."

Marisa's smile lit the room. "Really?"

"Sure. Why not?"

Marisa hopped from her chair and rushed to his side of the table. "Oh boy," she chirped and kissed him deeply.

Just like that, all the day's tensions melted away. Laine rose from his seat and held Marisa tightly, not wanting to let go. Ever.

"Wait a minute," she laughed, "Let's go to my room."

"Forget that." Laine yanked off his tie. "Right here, right now."

"Kelli and Mark—" Marisa managed between kisses.

". . . Aren't here. Let's go." He practically tore the shirt off his back while she tried to be sly about moving the dishes aside. Laine leaned Marisa back onto a clear spot on the dining room table and tugged eagerly at her black stretch top, muting her with his lips.

Then there was the sound of a door closing.

Laine and Marisa looked up into the kitchen and saw the slack-jawed faces of Mark and Kelli, the groceries in their arms just barely so.

Laine had to think fast. "Say," he bellowed theatrically, looking around in mock confusion, "this isn't the bedroom!"

They hopped off the table, adjusted themselves, and staggered for Marisa's room, grinning all the way. Hell, Laine even felt his face flush, a rarity to be sure.

On the verge of hilarity, Marisa said, "Oh yeah, there's plenty of stir-fry left if you guys want it."

Shutting the door behind them, Laine and Marisa stood in the middle of the room, smiled stupidly at each other for five seconds, then burst out laughing long and hard.

* * *

Amarantha butted her hip against the doorbell again, the bags of cooking supplies steadily sliding from her grasp. What was taking Joanie so long? Amarantha told her about the shopping spree before she left that morning.

Terra was scratching and crying at the other side of the door.

"Terra? Go get Joanie. Hurry." The cat's calls retreated into the bowels of the Victorian.

Amarantha used the moment to steal a glance at the space above the front door. Her olive branch and shield sigil was still there, scrawled in chalk and psychically guarding the eastern entrance of her house. Three other glyphs—over windows in her room, the dining room, and the bathroom—secured the remaining cardinal points. They shouldn't need recharging for a while.

Footsteps approached, and the front door opened.

"Took long enough," Amarantha whined as she handed her mother two of the four bags.

Joanie shuffled toward the kitchen in slippered feet. "Couldn't reach your keys, huh?" Her voice was dull and drowsy, still stained with sleep.

"I kind of had my hands full." Amarantha booted the door closed behind her, then followed Joanie down the hall. "Any messages?"

"Heather called an hour ago. She sounded kinda rough, like she used to sound. We chatted for a bit, but you should call her back."

"Yeah, she probably had a hard night," Amarantha offered, "I'll call her in a minute."

"Good." Joanie dropped the bags onto the kitchen table with a *clunk*.

"Careful. This stuff wasn't cheap, you know." Amarantha dove into one of the heavier sacks.

"Sorry. So what did you get?"

"Books, flour sifter, garlic press—oh yeah, did a William-Sonoma package arrive yet?"

Joanie yawned, "No, sorry."

"It should be here by next week. If I'm in class, just sign for it."

"Okay." Joanie scratched her mop of graying hair.

"I'll go call Heather first, then I'll come back and put these things away." Amarantha grabbed a couple of her new books.

Joanie's eyes swept the white and tan bags. "You sure you don't want me to—"

"No! No, that's okay. I'll put it all away. You must be tired from all the cleaning. You wouldn't even guess there was a party here." Amarantha kissed Joanie on the cheek. "I'll be back in a minute." She left the room, smiling.

Reaching her door, she found the last evidence of Friday's soiree: an orange cream cheese sticker stuck to the jamb. "Oh Jimmy, Jimmy, Jimmy . . . ," Amarantha sighed as she removed it.

Amarantha sat at her vanity, discarded the sticker in the nearby wastebasket, then picked up her blue Princess phone and called Heather. It rang once.

"Hello?" Heather still sounded ragged.

"Hi, it's me. How are you feeling?" Amarantha's old chair gave a painful creak as she settled into it.

"Embarrassed."

"Don't be. You know I understand."

"Yeah. How did shopping go?"

"Great," Amarantha said, thumbing through *The Joy of Cooking*. "You have to see the stuff I got. Are you coming over?"

There was a pause. "No, I have to watch Rudy since mom stepped out for a sec. Actually, I wanted to ask you something else."

"What's that?" Ooh, *there* was a nice recipe.

There was another pause. "Did you tell Laine about that Darth Vader comment I made the other night?"

Amarantha closed the book. "Yeah, sorry."

"It's cool. He thought that was funny. What about my looking for a job?"

Amarantha was getting the picture. Apparently, Laine had skryed Heather. "Actually, yes I did mention that you wanted a job," she lied, not wanting to scare her.

"Oh. Okay."

"Are you going to apply?"

"Yeah, I think so. I just hope Laine doesn't think I'm some kind of basket case."

"Laine would never—" Amarantha's phone made a call-waiting beep. She sighed, "Hold on," then clicked over to the other line. "Hello?"

"Hello yourself," Donovan's melodic voice returned.

Her blood rushed. "Hello, Donovan. How are you?" She nibbled her lower lip.

"Better now. I wanted to ask you something."

"Um, can you hold on a second?"

"Is this a bad time?"

"Oh, no, not at all. I have Heather on the other line. Just let me—hang on a second." She clicked back over.

"Donovan?" Heather asked when reconnected.

"Yes. Can I call you back? It's long-distance and all."

"Sure, no problem. Talk to you later." Heather hung up abruptly.

Amarantha frowned, then drew a deep breath before clicking back to Donovan. "Hello?"

"Hey, look if this is a bad time—"

"No, not at all. I'll have Heather over later. So what's up?"

"I've missed you."

Be still her heart. "I've missed you too, but you just flew back to San Diego yesterday. Why did you have to leave so soon anyway?"

"Aw, part of the settlement agreement. I have to spend some time with my dad. Visitation stuff."

"When are you coming back up?"

"Not until the end of the month, for Samhain. Is that okay?"

That was more than okay. "I'd like that. A lot. So is that what you wanted to ask me?"

"Not exactly. I was thinking just because I won't be home until Halloween, it doesn't mean I can't see you. Jimmy's throwing a party at his folk's place in La Jolla this weekend, and I was thinking you could come down, and—"

"Yes!" Amarantha enthused, "But there's just one problem: I just bought a bunch of cooking supplies for school, and I don't have the money for a ticket to San Diego."

"*No problemo*," he assured, "My dad can book you a flight in no time."

Amarantha stood up with excitement. First, the books slid off her lap, then the receiver slipped from her shoulder when she tried to retrieve the books. The tangle of items clamored on the hardwood floor.

"Damn it!" Amarantha blushed at her own curse as she unknotted the mass of paper and cord. Finally collecting herself, she sat back down and returned to Donovan. "Are you still there?"

"I am. I don't know about my ear, though," he joked.

"I'm sorry. I'm so sorry."

"So I take it that's a 'yes'?"

"Definitely," she sighed.

"Great. I'll arrange everything and get back to you later."

"That would be great."

"I love you, Amy."

There was that flutter again. "I . . . I love you too."

"Until later then. Remember, I'm always with you. I've

always been."

"Blessed be." The receiver went silent, and after a short lull, Amarantha fell backwards onto her bed. "Yes!"

"Amy?" Joanie's worried voice called from the hall.

Amarantha yelled back, "I'm okay. I just dropped something."

"I thought I heard a scream."

Amarantha sat up. "It's okay. I'll be out in a minute." She couldn't stop grinning. She felt like she had just drank one of Laine's lattés and could do anything right now.

Looking around her room, she spotted the Parrish prints leaning against her wall. They should help divert her anxious energy.

Amarantha opened a nightstand drawer and pulled out a hammer and some nails. She took everything to the spot on her wall next to her door, then examined the two prints, selecting which one to hang first.

"Perfect." *Ecstasy*: a lone woman standing on a rocky precipice, blown by the amber breath of an autumn wind. She sat the print down and began hammering in a nail. In her enthusiasm, Amarantha miscalculated and hit her finger with a solid *thud*, breaking the skin.

"Ow! Well, that wasn't stupid." She sucked the pain from her finger, walking in an aimless circle for a moment before looking at the damage.

The blood flowing from her split skin mesmerized her, its sticky trickle the center of her attention.

Remember, I am always with you.

Amarantha went to her altar where Donovan's roses lay only slightly wilted and dry. Beside them were empty oil vials, cleaned and saved for future fragrance storage. She picked up one of the bottles and removed the lid.

I have always been with you.

Squeezing the injured finger firmly, Amarantha watched the little rivulets of blood fall into the vial. She stroked the digit against its rim to catch every drop, and once the vial was filled, the bleeding stopped of its own accord. She set the vial upon her altar.

"Oh, look at this mess," she said of the fallen hammer and nails. The hardwood floor was surprisingly undamaged though.

Reclaiming her tools, Amarantha went back to the wall space, repositioned the nail, and tried again, this time without mishap.

FRIDAY, OCTOBER 3RD

"You mean she's gone already?"

"Yeah, Amy left a couple of hours ago," Joanie told Heather. "She caught the 4:20 flight."

Heather knew she should've called Amy sooner, but she was so busy with copying and dropping off her résumé that day, she didn't have the time. Besides, what would Heather have said to her anyway? Amy, don't go! Your boyfriends always suck! Yeah, *that* would've worked.

"She left me Donovan's number," Joanie offered, "I'm sure she wouldn't mind if—"

"No, that's okay. It wasn't important." Not anymore. Now it was too late. "I'll see her when she gets back. Sorry I woke you, Joanie."

"That's okay. Tell Margarita I said hi."

"I will. Bye." Heather set down the receiver and leaned back on her bed. Yeah, it was too late by far. Amy was nearly on the ground in San Diego, ready to get all dressed up and party with Donovan.

pale shadows

It was way too quiet in the house, and Heather was half-expecting Rudy to ambush her from out of nowhere, but the attack never came. The only other time he was this quiet was when he was either reading comics or drawing them. That was just fine. She wasn't in the mood for one of his Hulk Hogan imitations anyway. She'd rather pick her noise.

Heather clicked on her clock/radio. KITS was playing The Police's "Don't Stand So Close to Me '86": they should've left that song alone. She turned the tune down and searched her canvas book bag for the folder containing the rest of her résumés and applications. With Bubblicious and a Bic pen in hand, she looked over her employment options.

"¡Hola!" Margarita Dominguez stood in Heather's threshold bearing two bags of groceries and a large smile.

"Hola, Mama," Heather returned. Her mom sat the bags down on the bed, then kissed her daughter's cheek. Heather hugged her back. She smelled like the fresh produce del mercado. "Joanie says hi."

"¿Estás mejor?" Mama asked as she removed her overcoat.

"Sí, mucho." she returned. "¿Y tu?"

"Sí. Gracias, mi dulce."

"¿Mama, por que llevas tu abrigo? Hace mucho calor."

"Hmph. ¿Haz ido por una caminata? Hace frío en la noche." Mama planted her hands on her broad hips and looked toward the kitchen. "¿Dónde esta Rudy?"

"Dibujando."

Mama pursed her lips. "Who mopped the floors?"

"I did. El lavó los platos."

Just then, Rudy staggered in from the hall, looking like a borrachito. Heather saw it coming.

"Rudy, how many times do I have to tell you not to lie around in your school clothes?" Mama jabbed a finger toward his room. "Off! Now!"

Rudy groaned and shuffled back to his room.

"That boy, I swear: qué caraduro."

Heather smirked. "Sí, creo que es hereditario."

56

Mama smirked back. "Okay, that's enough out of you." She retrieved the bags of groceries from Heather's bed. "I better get dinner started."

"I'll be there in a minute, Mama. I just want to go through these."

Mama glanced at the stack of applications. "*Ay bendita,* look at you! Find anything good?"

Heather sighed. "I don't know. It's hard to tell. It's all seasonal work. There were a couple of promising positions, but there're also a lot of people more experienced me." Heather looked up into her mother's eyes. "But I'm sure I'll find something before the holidays."

Mama kissed Heather again, filling her nose with spicy fragrances. "*Yo sé, pero no te molestes. Estamos bien.* I want you to do good for you. Trust yourself. You're stronger than you think."

"I know, Mama. *Eso tambien es hereditario.*" Heather smiled as her mother left the room with uncompromising steps. Her mom never took any shit from anyone, always said what she meant, and always meant what she said. Mama was the strongest person Heather had ever known, and she hoped that those traits were as hereditary as she claimed.

Heather spread out the applications and looked them over until her eyes stopped at the one for Russian Hill O' Beans. Heather didn't know if Laine had forgotten about what happened on Monday or not, but as she looked at the blank lines, questions arose. Laine had bitched about Donovan under his breath at Amy's party, and it was clear on Monday that he didn't trust that asshole. Laine was probably the only person who could have convinced Amy not to run off alone to Vampire Boy, yet he did diddly-squat. Didn't Amy always say that he was her protector?

She drew little scribbles on a piece of scratch paper with the ballpoint pen, testing the ink flow. There was more than enough to fill a job application with. Yeah, she would submit it, but whether she got the job or not, Heather would get answers from Laine.

pale shadows

Jimmy's dad Professor Baum was a verbose and droll old hippie. He was perspiring profusely as he gobbled down a bowl of Chex Mix and rambled on about—what was it? Oh yeah, non-sequential time, something to that effect. Neither Amarantha nor Donovan contributed much to the conversation except for quiet and polite attention. They were afraid of adding fuel to the professor's verbal fire. And all this just because Donovan mused about how time flies.

Amarantha cased the crowded rumpus room for some means of escape, but all the fellow revelers were strangers to her, and Jimmy was currently preoccupied with the attractive redhead in the seafoam sundress who was draped over his shoulders. To think he wasn't even drunk yet, and he was already up to his gags.

Amarantha fanned herself with the paper napkin she'd been using as a coaster, but the gesture was redundant considering how well the air conditioning was working. It was probably the room's opulence that was wetting her palms. A massive projection television was running a LaserDisc copy of *Blade Runner*, but she couldn't hear it over the compact disc player. The cherry-red leather furnishings and chocolate-brown walls made Amarantha feel like she was inside a piece of See's candy.

Speaking of candy, Donovan could make for a nice dessert. He looked somehow soft tonight. He didn't wear makeup like Laine sometimes did, but Donovan was still close to androgynous. His jeans were snug, his white Lauren shirt was loose, and his face was oh-so-angelic with a gentle light in his eyes and a crown of fashionably mussed hair.

"Eternity can't be measured chronologically, man, because eternity is not a temporal state, but a state of consciousness, dig?" Professor Baum brushed rice cracker crumbs from his blue linen blazer. "Specifically, it is the state of being in which the consciousness is focused on the interminable Now, see. You lose sense of 'beginnings' and 'endings'." A smug grin stretched the voracious scholar's face. "That's why my classes seem so long."

Not to mention his party conversation. Amarantha took a sip from the punch Donovan had given her earlier, then wiped her brow.

"Whoa, whoa, whoa! What's going on here?!" Jimmy had finally taken notice of Amarantha and Donovan's plight. He adjusted the black jeweled bolo tie around his upturned collar and plowed his way through the crowd to intervene. "Is this guy bothering you? 'Cause if he is, I can have this yuppie scum forcibly ejected." Jimmy's eyes smiled over his Mock Tortoise Wayfarers as he threw an arm over his dad's shoulder. "We're trying to have a classy soiree here."

The professor sat the empty Chex bowl on a nearby oak end table. "Okay, okay. I guess I've chewed your ears off 'long enough.'" He did that quote thing with his fingers. The pun drew a low groan from Donovan's throat, while Amarantha bit her lower lip and just shook her head.

Jimmy wafted his dad away. "That's right, off with you. You've got your own party to go to."

"Yes I do," the professor confessed. "So you kids have fun."

"Yes, sir. We will," Donovan assured, smiling.

Jimmy was in rare form. "Yeah, that's right. Go, and hey, don't trust anybody over fifty!"

"Yeah, yeah, yeah." Professor Baum left through a part in the shifting crowd, his auburn ponytail swinging behind him.

Jimmy sighed. "Sorry about that. My old man . . . ." He opened and closed his hands like long-winded sock puppets. "You guys alright?"

Amarantha smirked. "We'll be fine. I think the pain is receding. It's easy to see where you get your sense of humor from, with the exception of the cream cheese stickers." Donovan laughed.

Jimmy went all loose and let his eyes roll toward the high, wood-paneled ceiling. "Aw c'mon, Amarantha, are you still mad at me about that? I was wasted! Isn't there some way I can make it up to you?"

"Well, a fresh drink would be a good start," Amarantha admitted coyly, handing Jimmy her empty Dixie cup. She shared her smile with Donovan, who seemed quite amused by their little exchange.

"Fair enough," Jimmy said, taking Amarantha's disposable dinnerware from her. "A little hair of the dog? Jesus, I do sound like my dad. How about you, D? Ready for something more exotic than Hawaiian Punch?"

Donovan stretched for the sky. "I think it's about that time. Nothing too exotic, though. I'm driving."

"I'm on it." Jimmy caught sight of the redhead he gave the piggyback ride to earlier and said, "Anise, hold up . . . ." And Jimmy was gone.

Amarantha absorbed the rumpus room's affluence again. "I didn't know Philosophy paid so well," she observed over the volume of Prince's *Parade* album.

"Actually, he teaches law at USD. Jimmy's stepmom is a lawyer." Donovan smirked. "Guess how they met?" A red balloon sprung past him. He batted it back into play.

"Naughty, naughty." Amarantha's lower back told her it was time to sit.

"Well, lucky us. There's space on the sofa now," Donovan announced, his sly expression revealing that Amarantha had just been skryed. Impressive that she hadn't felt a thing. Usually Laine was the only person who could psychically slip past her defenses. "Shall we?"

Amarantha sat down and at once understood why flies loved butter. "Ooh, this sofa's sooooft."

"So you said Joanie was yours *and* Heather's Big Sister before she fostered you both?" Donovan asked as he sank into the couch cushion. "I didn't know they could do that."

"Well, it's very unusual, but since Heather and I were already friends, and she was already assigned to Joanie, exceptions were made." Amarantha tapped the returning balloon to Donovan.

"Because of the drug stuff?" He flicked the red sphere back to Amarantha.

"Yup. My birth mother Alice liked to party. I mean, she *really* liked to party," she began, swatting the balloon toward a circle of kids sitting in front of the unused fireplace. "She used to hang around with a pretty affluent crowd, and I was her little debutante. My 'family' was an ever-changing sea of rich addicts and trust-fund hippies, and before long, she was deep into drugs too. Our real family blew the whistle on her, but rather than sending me to Arkansas to stay with my dad, I was granted the option of a foster mother: Joanie. I was emancipated from my birth mom in '84."

"*That*, I remember. So why didn't you stay with your dad?"

"He left us when I was two, so neither of us felt comfortable with that arrangement."

"Some girls have all the luck," Donovan quipped. The red balloon bounced off the back of his head. He volleyed it to Amarantha, who served it back to the circle.

"Funny thing is, Alice and I get along much better now that we don't live together. And she did keep me away from all the drug stuff. In fact, if it wasn't for her, I probably wouldn't be . . . a practitioner." Amarantha whispered the last part mysteriously.

Donovan nodded knowingly. "Ah, so *she* is the source."

"Oh yes. Her and The Other Mother," Amarantha glanced skyward.

"So why was Heather staying with Joanie? I still don't know her story."

"I'm sorry, but that's her tale to tell," Amarantha said as she considered the carpet's woven labyrinth of crimson and beige. A balloon burst.

"Fair enough." Donovan cased the room. "What's keeping Jimmy with those drinks?"

"Probably Anise. So you haven't lived with your dad for, what, two years now?"

Donovan's mouth tugged into a crooked smile. "Almost three."

"How is the visit going?"

"Aw, you know him. He's a total hard-ass—pardon my French."

Amarantha smiled through her blush.

"He subscribes to *Mercenary Magazine* and thinks *Rambo* is the best movie ever, so you can imagine where his head's at. His girlfriend's nice enough, though, and his real estate gig is paying him well."

Jimmy finally returned with a glass of white wine in each hand and Anise once again riding him piggyback and laughing. "Here you guys go: vino." Jimmy leaned forward. "I hope it's to your liking. Wait, have you met An —"

A passing preppie bumped into Jimmy, spilling half of Amarantha's beverage on her lap.

"Oh shit, I'm sorry, Amarantha," Jimmy apologized as he slid the redhead from his back, gave Donovan his drink, and grabbed a handful of paper napkins from an end table.

Amarantha was more surprised than angry, but Donovan's face was drawn tight. "Jimmy—" Donovan griped as he stood up.

"It's okay," Amarantha reassured Donovan on Jimmy's behalf. She took the napkins and swabbed the puddle of wine in her lap. "Luckily it's a white. Can you point me to the nearest bathroom?"

Jimmy stammered, "Yeah, just head back towards the front door and make a left at the foyer. It'll be on your left."

"Meet me back here?" Amarantha asked Donovan.

"Yeah." Donovan was still visibly angry, but he leaned forward to kiss her nonetheless.

Amarantha smiled as she left for the water closet, and once inside, it was easy to see why she had to wait in line for so long.

"Goddess, look at this bathroom," she admired. The décor was all glossy black tiles and brass fixtures. Two onyx basins were embedded in black marble counters with gold veins, and even the towels were in on the dance of colors.

Amarantha's drinks finally caught up to her, so she relieved herself and washed her hands before drying off her dress with a fresh hand towel. "Good as new," she appraised in the mirror.

Then that sensation she'd heard of so often it was cliché, the one about someone walking on your grave? She felt it now. A mind familiar yet alien had tailed Amarantha through the currents of psychic chaos, and it was awaiting her outside the bathroom door.

She set her jaw, went to the entrance, and slowly twisted the lotus-shaped doorknob.

The girl behind the door was the same height and build as Amarantha, but with hair as black as a Nihtheim night and eyes as azure as a summer sky. What simmered behind those eyes was haunting, rabid, desperate. A chill touched Amarantha, but it wasn't cold enough to back her down. No, she just let the black-laced witch consider her in silence, at least for now.

"You are Amarantha Powell?" the woman declared more than inquired.

Amarantha nodded, shrugging off the woman's invisible shoves, pushing back with her mind in kind.

"I am Lillian Crane. Donovan Walsh is my consort. I am not done with him. You have no place here, sister."

Amarantha said directly, "Really? I differ," as she stepped past her and into the hall.

"You tread in waters deep and still, but a storm churns beyond your will." Lillian became incredibly large; her voice, immensely bestial. The witch reached out to touch Amarantha's cheek, but Amarantha dodged her hand as if it were full of angry vipers. "If you would not drown, little one, then you shall relent."

Not a bad trick, but Amarantha possessed more potent Magicks. She inhaled an astral wind as the words *Athené aigis athanaton* vibrated her bones in a sustained hum. She fixed her mind's eye on a vision of her Magickal self clad in Athena's armor. The Gorgon breastplate and shield weighed upon her as she stood at the ready, and her eyes burned beneath her crested Corinthian helm. She struck the floor thrice with her spear.

Befana Delafey exhaled venom. "On the Day of the Geniae, where were you? During the Panathenaea, where were you?" She took a step forward; Lillian took two back. "How dare you threaten me with my brethren's storms? How dare you petition me? You are no sister of mine, 'little one,' not even a daughter." Befana took another step and struck the floor thrice more. "Flee!"

Lillian staggered, her spell broken. Now she knew what glamour was. She stammered, "Amarantha, I only meant —"

The party's roar slammed into Amarantha's ears when Donovan pulled the sable witch away and pinned her shoulders against a foyer wall. Prince's "Girls & Boys" blared from the stereo, smothering the couple's words. The exchange was brutal, passionate, but no one else at the party seemed to notice. It made sense: witches' business.

Lillian swatted away Donovan's grasping hands, made some final, unheard declaration, then glanced at Amarantha as Jimmy emerged from the rumpus room.

And then came what Professor Baum had described: the eternal instant. The one in which Amarantha was drawn into Lillian's diamond-blue eyes like light into a prism of sorrow. Lillian's woes became Amarantha's, and she felt her soul wrung for tears without knowing why.

Then Lillian Crane vanished behind a veil of celebrants and kicked balloons as if she was never there.

Donovan punched Jimmy in the chest with two fingers. "What the hell's going on, Jimmy?" he growled.

The hipster blanched and fidgeted with the bejeweled crucifix dangling from his left lobe. "I . . . I'm sorry, man. I invited her before you told me Ama—"

Donovan held a punishing finger up and said, "Follow her, Jimmy. Keep her out of here!" Everyone heard that.

"I'm sorry," Jimmy whined before watching Ama-

AN AUTOBIOGRAPHICAL NOVEL

rantha rejoin them in the foyer. "I'm so sorry."

"It's okay, Jimmy," she reassured, but Donovan was still miffed.

"Just go." Donovan took a deep breath and grabbed the two fresh glasses of wine from Jimmy before his friend slinked out the front door to make sure Lillian remained banished.

Donovan turned to Amarantha, a weak smile on his face. "Are you okay? What did she say? What did she do?" he asked sincerely.

"Just a hollow threat. Donovan, who was that girl?" She didn't take her eyes from his.

"That was Lillian."

"She told me that much." Amarantha crossed her arms and leaned against a foyer wall.

"She was a pupil of mine for a while," he said, offering her a glass.

Arms still crossed, Amarantha asked, "Was she also your lover?"

All pretense left his manner. "Yes."

"I see." She accepted the wine glass from Donovan and took a deep sip.

"Look, Amarantha, don't let her bother you. Lillian and I—well—our relationships, both romantic and Magickal, were doomed from the beginning. She's one of my failures."

"As in you have many?"

Donovan sighed. "I'm sure Laine has told you that every mistake is a lesson that leads to success. As a teacher, he must have failed at least once."

"Yes, he has, with his first student Karina, but he wasn't —they weren't a couple."

"Lillian and me—" he started angrily, but then he caught and calmed himself. "I broke up with her a year ago. It's history." Donovan set his glass down on a nearby coaster and touched Amarantha gently on the shoulders, his blue eyes and golden hair radiant. "Look, Amy, you are far stronger and wiser than Lillian will ever be. Laine has done well with you. I can only hope to do so well.

"But do know this," he said, leaning closer, "As long as I live, no harm will ever befall you; no want will you ever know; no whim will ever be denied. Don't worry about Lillian. She won't bother us again."

Amarantha surrendered into Donovan's embrace. Ah, how right it all felt. So Amarantha would have to consider Donovan's former pupils, both fallen and exalted. So what? It was all worth it in the end. Even with the threats and the noise and the doubts, this one eternal instant was right.

"I swear to you by The Goddess, no one will ever get between us." Donovan's warm, soft lips touched Amarantha's forehead. She held him tighter and kissed him till she thought her lips would bruise.

"As you will," she whispered, "so mote it be."

* * *

I was ridden by Neteru; I rode Neteru. We shattered glen and dell in our fevered dash through one of Nihtheim's many forests, the cool shadow of my airborne Queen cloaking us. The wildebeests cheered our passage, for never had they known their liege to be so carefree, so full of mirth. I had never felt such joy as I did when my Queen and I burst out of the forest.

Elysium Valley was blanketed by a rolling field of Janus flowers that oscillated in the wind between midnight-violet and dawning-gold and exuded a perfume of honeysuckle and jasmine. Settled upon this steppe as well were the truncated Watchtowers of Knowledge, homes to all of my grimoires on this plane and keepers of arcane lore. They were resplendent against the background of looming mountain ranges, their sandstone flanks touching the bottoms of the granite clouds.

There were many jagged slopes and craggy peaks along our route, yet we bounded and sailed over them all without contest until we reached the final summit.

A spire of gold-rutilated emerald overlooked one of

Nighthome's shores. This was an aesthetic keep. It hosted no manuals on history or ethics or The Art, but instead was a tribute erected in honor of my union with the Queen. During Nihtheim's brief daytime hours, the aloft edifice captured the sunlight reflecting off the sea and shared it with the inland.

And I rose from my quadruped form of a pard to the bipedal stance of a man. And my Queen, Seawing, shed her feathered garb and descended to my side. We embraced, and I danced inside her until spent.

I later awoke atop our spire to find my Queen was not with me. Seawing trilled from above. My Queen had risen again, dancing in a Dervish spiral beneath the dusky sky.

Then something changed.

My attention was trapped, and my heart chilled as my Queen followed a widdershins course around Sol with an elusive purpose, circumscribing the star. She ignited, and the comet that was her flaming form shook the air with a clamorous roar. Wildebeests began crying, not out of joy, but out of mortal terror.

My Queen uttered a tortured, metallic screech and plunged into the core of Sol. Tenebrific clouds were thickening and slithering overhead; wildebeests died of fear; the sun dimmed. Silence.

Then the sky shrieked once more: the sky and my Queen. Falling fast and all aflame, Seawing tumbled straight toward me from the false eclipse she had created. She neither heard nor heeded my screams as she fell upon me with murderous intent. I would die unless she did first.

My claws had just reached her heart when she broke through skin and organ and bone, crushing the last of my breath from me.

I fell.

* * *

Laine arrived, sickly and grave. The last vestiges of adrenaline slipped away from his prone body, leaving the shakes as a memoir.

It was uncommonly dark. Had he been buried alive? Was that the reason for his paralysis and asphyxiation? He raised his head from the pillow that was deadening his senses, only remotely amused, but the crushing weight was still upon him.

"Laine, are you okay?"

He turned his head toward the voice. It all suddenly came back to him: Marisa had been concerned about his workload and stress and generously offered him an oil massage. It was her nude form that was crushing him now. The nightmare was over.

"Are you okay?" she asked again.

Laine nodded weakly.

"What happened? You tensed up all of a sudden."

"Nothing. A vision."

"Was it Amarantha again?" There was that jealous sting in her voice. What could Laine tell her? That they were doomed to mutual destruction? No, forget it, call it a day. They weren't broken yet.

He touched Marisa's bare thigh, signaling her to get off of him so he could turn over. Once on his back, he rested a trembling hand on his face.

"Laine, was it Amarantha?"

He decided. Goddess, help him.

Laine nodded. "Yes, it was Amarantha."

* * *

Heather approached Russian Hill O' Beans, her completed application secured in a book bag. She peeked through the front door and saw Laine hunching over a pile of boxes next to the grinder, his back to her.

Heather stalled. What the hell was she doing? This guy pulled thoughts out of brains like Doritos out of a bag. This was the man that enhanced and refined Amy's already impressive talents; the mage Amy followed loyally.

Then there was that question again: how could he let

Amy go hundreds of miles away to a witch he didn't trust?

That was it. Taking a deep breath, she swung open the front door . . . right into the mystery table set. "God damn it!" she cried when wood collided.

Laine looked over his shoulder. "I should've recognized the knock. Come on in."

Heather shrugged and sighed as she entered the café. A particularly moody dirge was playing on the radio, doing absolutely nothing for her confidence. The rest of the table sets—so clean and orderly the last time she was there—were now crooked and covered with un-bussed cups and saucers. It looked like a minor storm had hit the store.

"I just came to return the application," she announced, "if the position is still open."

"It's still open. Set it down next to the register." He didn't even spare her a glance. She followed his instructions, then stood beside him.

No bullshit about those coffee orders. A pitcher containing carefully-weighed coffee grounds was sitting on the scale in front of Laine. Like a machine, he dumped the coffee into a small plastic bag and set the packet in a box. Scoop, weigh, bag, box, over and over. From the count, she could see he was nearly halfway through this lot.

"What happens to the bags next?"

"Diana comes up and grabs a box, takes it in back, and hand-seals them with these little cheapo sealers we have. 'Hours of family fun.'" There was nothing funny in the way he said that.

"So what happened to the shop?" Heather asked, frowning at the wreckage.

"Morning rush." He stopped shoveling and faced Heather. "Are you okay?" He looked like she should be asking him that.

"I'm fine, considering. Thank you."

"Care to talk about it?"

"Not really."

"Okay." Laine nodded slowly as he returned to his work.

"So you know," she started cautiously, "Amy's in San Diego with him."

His jaw clenched, but he kept bagging. "Yes, I know."

"Have you even talked to her about Donovan?"

He nodded. "Before she introduced us."

"And you let her leave, anyway? I thought you were supposed to protect her?"

Laine stopped scooping and stared at Heather again. "You're her friend too. Why didn't *you* stop her? Look, I am Amarantha's mentor, not her master. I can not tell her what to do, only guide her along the path." He turned back to his work, filling the last Mylar bag with coffee grounds. "I didn't say anything for the same reason you didn't: it would have been an offense to free will. Besides, I don't think she would've listened anyway. To either of us."

He was right. Heather just didn't want to admit it to herself. "Poor, stupid us. So now what?"

Laine stroked his lower lip. "Hold on a minute. Hey, Diana!"

Footsteps sounded from the back office, and a punky Latina sporting a Sony Walkman stepped out from the hall. "What's up, Laine?"

"Diana, this is Heather, our new secretary," Laine introduced.

Wait, new secretary? She got the job?

Laine winked. "Manager's prerogative. Heather, this is Diana, one of our wage slaves. Diana got suckered into working this fine Saturday morning the same as me."

Diana smirked. "Fuck that. I got bribed with OT."

"Ah. Of course you did. In that case, watch the shop. We're going on an extended lunch break." Laine tossed some keys to the coffee-smeared girl.

Diana caught the keys easily, then said, "No problem. When will you be back?"

"A couple of hours. The orders will hold until I return." Laine pointed his chin at the headphones slung around Diana's neck. "And you might want to take those off."

"Hey, I heard you, didn't I?"

"It's not me, it's Mohammed. If he comes in, you won't have to hear him gripe." Laine put on his Darth Vader voice. "'He is not as forgiving as I am.'"

"Gotcha. See you in a couple." The punker chick grabbed the box of coffee and ascended the stairs to the office.

"She seems cool," Heather offered.

Laine stood and tugged his way out of his dirty, green apron. "Diana? She's great. One of the few 'mundanes' I don't loathe." Heather shared his smirk. "Let's go." Laine headed to the hall closet.

"Wait a minute, where are we going?"

"Dyansen Gallery down on Beach Street," he answered, pulling on his blazer.

"What for?"

"I think you deserve deeper explanations, and I'm going to give them to you . . . in front of some Erté. Let us go."

"Air what?" Heather shrugged as she followed Laine out the door. Looked like there was some small hope after all.

* * *

Laine shut his eyes and drew an indulgent breath once he crossed the gallery's threshold. The scent of perfumed patrons and linseed oil mingled in the air, bringing a smile to his lips. He was relishing the passage of fan-spawned breezes and attractive sales staff as the inspirations of dozens of artists brushed his mind.

Laine opened his eyes: the spacious gallery was filled with black-lacquered pedestals carrying the dreams of humanity as their burden. Here was a huge chunk of crystal, carved and frosted on its inverse with a relief of a nude maiden; there was a modern interpretation of a classic Noh drama on stretched canvas.

Laine had intentions of returning to this refuge since dawn. Along with Nihtheim, here was one of the few places that gave his spirit respite, something it sorely needed. In

71

this edifice, all the pains and trials and dark remembrances were swept away by strokes of round sable. Home away from home, this place.

"Hey, Laine!"

"Oh hey, André, how you doing?" Laine gave a nod of recognition to one of the immaculately dressed sales staff who had the kind of tan that one paid good money for.

"Here for Nagel again?" André asked around his thick Italian accent.

"You know me too well. I came with a friend this time." Laine turned to introduce Heather only to find she had disappeared. He scratched his chin. "Hmm. It seems my partner has wandered off."

Laine spied Heather standing farther back in the gallery, visibly entranced by the artwork she viewed. She had discovered the graceful renderings of Erté, and as far as he was concerned, anyone who liked Erté couldn't be half-bad. The Bob James/David Sanborn track playing on the gallery PA concealed Laine's footfalls as he stepped up beside her.

"This is 'Air What,'" Laine joked.

Heather started at his sudden arrival, then smiled back, recalling her earlier query. He rotated the lazy Susan-like pedestal bearing the sculpture.

"He's a French artist who did all these great pieces for *Vanity Fair* back in the '20s. He's one of the major artists who defined the Art Deco look. He and Patrick Nagel are also my main artistic inspirations. All these prints around us," he said, gesturing at the walls, "are serigraphs of Erté's work." He paused to take in Heather's reaction. She seemed intrigued, soaking up the information. When he spoke again, Laine's voice was lowered. "Actually, in a way, it's kind of pathetic."

"His works?" Heather asked, visibly stunned. "I think they're gorgeous."

Laine looked around for eavesdroppers, then said, "Oh no, nothing like that. It's just that half the people here are on a death watch. Erté is still alive and still creates, but he's about ninety-four years old now." Laine nodded at an ornate table mirror entitled *Femme Fatale*. "Most of these brass sculptures are recent creations, and all these art collectors are just waiting for him to croak so they can cash out."

Heather scowled. "That sucks."

Laine nodded in agreement. "That's Capitalism. They keep throwing these tributes to him while they circle like starving vultures. But at least he's getting recognition while he's still alive."

"That's true. So you said he's one of your main inspirations: do you paint?"

Laine groaned, never taking his eyes off the piece before him. "Not really. Not yet. I have some acrylics that I've been playing with, trying to get used to the medium, but when you've spent your entire life sketching with pencils, something as permanent as paint can be intimidating. I haven't completed any pieces yet."

"I know what you mean," Heather agreed. "I did some watercolor stuff a while back."

"Watercolor? Really? Hell, I can't use that stuff. The diluted paint just gets everywhere. So hard to control."

"Well, I'm probably not as good as you, but it's fun messing around with it anyway. I think it's kinda like Amy, you know? Don't try to control the paint, just guide it."

"Wow. That's a good way of looking at it." The purity of her conceit touched Laine. He had forgotten the flavor of the muse's kiss; the revelry of deep-night scrawlings; the smooth bliss of India ink; the exhausted joy upon display. His works now felt born out of labor, not love. Gone was the fun.

Laine rediscovered his voice, somber and low. "So what do you want to be when you grow up, Heather?"

"I want to be a doctor or at least an RN. I like the idea of healing people, you know?"

"Noble profession. What's in your way?"

"*Dinero*. School is fucking expensive," Heather growled. "Hopefully with this job, I can join NEC; become a Medical Assistant."

Laine turned to Heather and gave her a quick eye-lock, modulating his voice for emphasis. "I believe you have a good chance at that, Heather. *You* just have to believe it." He broke the lock. "Patience and diligence are tools. Use them. Manifest."

A slow, wide smile slid across her blushing face. "That's kinda what my mom says. Thank you."

"That's why I'm here."

Say something, stupid.

"What was that again?" Laine asked.

"Me? I didn't say anything."

"Oh." Heather hadn't, but it was definitely her voice.

She shook the confusion from her face. "So you gonna do something about Donovan?"

Laine snorted. "I couldn't even if I wanted to."

Heather planted her hands on her hips. "So what's in *your* way?"

Funny girl. "An oath," he sighed. "I've sworn to Amarantha that I wouldn't intervene unless something goes wrong, and Donovan has done no wrong. All I have are bad dreams and frail suspicions. No, I can't go back on my word, especially with her consecration so near."

"So all you can do is wait it out, thumb in ass?" Her voice was equal parts frustration and outrage.

Laine crossed his arms and drummed a bicep. "You know, you have a very colorful take on the English language."

Heather said with pride, "I get that from my mom too. And anyway, what about you and Amy with your 'thou arts' and 'for sooths'?"

Laine laughed and shrugged. "What can I tell you: I love dictionaries. Besides, such sweet prose is par for the course with our kind. As for Donovan, you're right: I'm restraining my energies unless he moves against Amarantha or myself."

"Donovan," Heather said dryly, then she smiled as she did her little vampire-sucking gag. The joke loosened the remaining umbrage that embraced Laine, allowing him to laugh deeply. He stopped when he noticed something bewildering about Heather's giggles.

"Whoa, wait a minute," he said, "what the hell was that?"

Catching her breath, Heather asked, "What was what?"

"That laugh—" Laine mimicked her giddy *tee-hees*.

Heather lost all composure. "Laine, stop it!" she gasped between *tee-hees*. "I can't breathe!"

Oh goody. He smirked maliciously as he continued the ribbing, stopping only when her face shone crimson.

"Eat me, man!" Heather was beginning to regain herself. "You are so fired!"

"Yeah, right, what you said. Anyway, as far as Vampire Boy is concerned, my hands are tied."

Heather wore the same familiar expression she had at the party: she had just made a decision about him, and it was an important one. "Um, Laine, I have an idea."

"Okay."

Heather's demeanor was assertive. "You took an oath, but I didn't. I can be your eyes and ears. I can watch Amy and Donovan, let you know what you don't know."

Laine stroked his lips. Here was a girl he scarcely knew saying she would act as a liaison—as a spy—between two potential adversaries? "I don't know, Heather. You'll be caught in the middle of something you might not be able to handle."

Heather rolled her eyes. "I'd only be telling you what I find out. It's not like I'd be taking any risks. Amy tells me everything anyway, stuff I'm sure she doesn't tell you."

That was undoubtedly true, considering Laine was oblivious to Amarantha's boyfriend troubles. He had always assumed that with her looks, Amarantha could pick and choose any Prince Charming that came along and tickled her fancy. Then again, maybe that was the problem.

Heather added, "You want to protect her, right? Me too."

The logic of her offer was strong; the morality, sound. Who better to keep an eye on you than your lifelong friend?

And Heather was right: she was in the best strategic position.

"*If* we were to do this," Laine said tentatively, "you would have to be better prepared for any contingencies. Good intentions won't help you if the curses start flying."

A smile was already growing on her face. "Then teach me to handle it. I'm familiar with a lot of the basics already."

"So I've heard. The first step would be to see how much more you need to know." Laine stroked his chin and said, "I'd have to teach you enough to give you a back door, at least. You probably wouldn't be able to fight with it." Laine sighed, "Okay, Heather, you're on. Bring to my attention whatever is going on with Donovan and Amarantha, and I'll provide your tutelage."

Heather let out a "Cool!" as Laine moved toward one of Erté's alphabet prints, this one of a blue-skinned maiden standing in the concavity of a waxing moon: the letter D.

"If our instincts about Donovan are flawed, then no harm done, and the issue is dropped. If we're right . . . well, run fast. I'll do the rest."

"I understand."

Laine had to force himself to smile comfortingly. This wasn't the ideal way to tutor. They had less than a month to work on a vocation that should never be rushed. Hopefully, Heather was as seasoned as Amarantha had claimed.

*　*　*

Donovan had proven himself quite the gentleman after the previous night's party. He and Amarantha drove to his dad's home, and upon arrival, he tucked the exhausted Amarantha into a guest room bed and slipped away, never taking advantage of the tipsy girl. That morning, Amarantha awoke to find a dozen pink roses littering the bedding and the aroma of a hot breakfast filling the elegant home. The smell had lured Amarantha into the dining room where her vegetarian meal awaited, but the spread was so abundant that she surrendered by the second bagel. Instead, she had searched the Colonial-style house for Donovan but came up empty-handed.

Now, Amarantha was basking poolside in her red and white one-piece, writhing beneath the smoggy, afternoon sun. A glass of fresh-squeezed OJ and one of the roses were sitting on the deck beside her as she flipped through the copy of *LaRousse's Gastronomique* she had packed for the flight. Yeah, she could get used to this.

Amarantha felt Donovan's eyes on her. His gaze caressed her in a most ungentlemanly fashion as she shifted in the deck chair, peeling her sweating skin from the recliner's vinyl bands. She let him watch without comment.

"Did you enjoy breakfast?" Donovan asked from the sliding glass door behind her.

"Did you enjoy watching me?" Amarantha faced him, giving him her sly eye. If he was embarrassed by his voyeurism, he was doing an excellent job of concealing it.

"Very much so, thank you. May I?"

Amarantha gestured toward the identical deck chair beside her.

Donovan was in a pair of deep blue jams and a silk shirt that Amarantha thought was far too nice to lounge in. "Sorry I disappeared this morning." He took a sip from his iced tea. "My dad had me run some errands."

"That's quite all right. It usually takes me a while to get up anyway."

He smirked. "Hmm. I'll have to make a mental note. Oh, and I asked Jimmy to keep an eye out for your earring."

"Thank you. It's a really important piece to me. Just bring it when you come back to The City. I'll need it for Samhain."

"Deal," Donovan said. "Speaking of, I hope this isn't inappropriate or an imposition, but I was wondering if you're open to an idea."

"Oh really? And what might that be?" Here it comes.

"This is for both of us. When I get back to San

Francisco, I was wondering if you would perform a ritual with me. One of bonding?"

"A bonding?" Amarantha played with his words in her mind till she reached his true meaning. "Wait, you're talking about a handfasting, aren't you?"

Donovan just shrugged and grinned.

"Boy, you don't play when it comes to boons, do you? You're talking about a Wiccan wedding."

Donovan seemed to get some of his bravery back when he said, "Yes, I am. I was thinking if we're going to be learning from each other, teaching each other, a ritual formally binding our energies makes sense, and what better way than with a handfasting?"

Amarantha squirmed. "Absolutely, but I can't do that, not yet. I'm to perform a ritual with Laine that night. It'll be a full moon on Samhain, and—"

"I know. That's why it's perfect."

"Yes, but Laine will be performing my Wiccaning. After that, I'll no longer be his pupil. It's important to both of us."

Donovan suddenly brightened. "How about this: why not have Laine perform our handfasting? It would be perfect. Almost like a father giving away the hand of his daughter—so to speak." Donovan wiped condensation from his glass and licked the dew from his fingers. "Besides, handfastings aren't like mundane weddings: they only last a year and a day with the *option* of renewal, so hey, 'Satisfaction guaranteed or your money back.'"

Admittedly, Donovan was right: The three of them pooling their powers together—marking the changing of the guards—would be an unprecedented event for all of them.

And Amarantha did love Donovan enough to seriously consider his offer, but the problem was Laine: he probably wouldn't go for it. Despite his noble intents, he had no trust in Donovan. That was something he couldn't conceal when they had spoken at the café.

Still, Laine was open-minded enough, and this one

event could change his views of Donovan. Then they could all live happily ever after: Laine and Marisa; Donovan and Amarantha. It could erase all differences and doubts.

So why did this feel so ill-fated? Amarantha needed more time to work it out. She needed her looking glass.

"Donovan," she started quietly, "I can't promise anything, but I'll talk to Laine about it. He might accept the offer, however, if he doesn't, I'll have to honor our previous arrangement. I must perform The Wiccaning. Is that okay?"

The cheer had left Donovan's face again, leaving only —what? Introspection? Planning? Finally, he said, "You're right. Talk to him, though. See what he says and let me know. I won't stand in the way of any plans you may have." His caress was as soft as sunlight.

Amarantha smiled and kissed him tenderly. "Thank you, Donovan. Who knows? Laine might just surprise you."

Heck, he might just surprise them both.

pale shadows

SATURDAY, OCTOBER 18TH

I became Befana Delafey: I became the spirit of the shell; the force in the form; the body of light.

Before me was the looking glass, stained in ritual with a decoction of mugwort in preparation for my passage beyond. Behind me was sitting the burden of my flesh, stable and sure and awaiting my return.

I looked beyond the glass toward my world: a world pleasant and calm; a world where answers lay; a world that was subject to my will.

I stepped forward, breaking the mirror's cool surface with my toes, my hips, my torso.

I was home. I was beyond.

A sweet wind touched me like the first kiss against a newborn's skin. The sky went on forever in blue washes and spectral ribbons, and a wedge of long-winged birds were swimming and whistling above the gentle haze that enveloped me. The soft, damp earth cushioned the arches of my feet and released a woody, cedar scent.

pale shadows

Every breathing, sentient being had this: a realm within them that was untouchable and beyond judgment. Most people would never find these halcyon kingdoms of the soul, and many that had succeeded did so only because of great duress or trauma. There were tales both legendary and infamous of those who were seduced to these netherworlds, never to return to the inland of sanity. Such was the power of Maya over the unprepared mind.

As I pondered, a rustling from behind brought me to. Between two Parthenon pillars—one onyx, the other ivory —shone my silver unicorn, radiant beneath the pale shadow of the sun. It lifted its majestic head, its horn braided with ribbons of autumn hue, and he caught my glance, drawing me into its vast, black eyes toward an unseen mystery. The depths of its ancient eyes made me recall some long-forgotten tales of the perils of a unicorn's gaze, but still I reached for the occult secret therein.

Just as I was to claim it, the creature blinked, and the enigma went away unattained. Aloof, my unicorn turned away, passed between the pillars, and vanished into the glade beyond like a half-tasted memory.

I followed obediently, wading my way through fragrant creepers and fog-touched bramble. Such a long walk for so short a distance.

The glade opened gloriously onto a pool of shifting colors that looked like something from a mad fever dream. The drinking unicorn was standing upon the pond's surface, lapping liquid confusion from its bearded chin. How then was I to follow it; to accept its veiled invitation?

Of course. The pond. It had led me to the pond.

As I considered the unctuous breaks of my reflection, I knew that this pool wasn't meant for human consumption. Not in any expected fashion.

I knelt and dipped my hands in, letting the plasma flow between my probing fingers. Slippery. Then, with nary a thought, I cupped my hands in the pool and splashed my eyes with the elixir, blinding them, burning them.

After a moment, I blinked away the excess fluid and

took in the glade around me: colors had lost their luster; the fog had slipped away revealing a muted night sky; the pond was now just a pond. My unicorn was still standing upon the pool's center.

So then would I. I stepped onto the aquafirma, intent upon communing with the divine beast. "Closer, closer," it beckoned silently, and then, "Stop."

We were no longer alone. Our flanks were occupied by two figures rising silently from the pond.

Near the sunrise shore, suspended just above the water's surface, was an angel dripping with white brilliance. I felt its reassuring smile as it extended a flaming hand toward me.

Near the sunset shore, likewise hovering, was a black-cloaked figure accompanied by two pitch hounds. It too offered a hand, but this one filled me with dread as albino serpents bound its wrists and fingers like reptilian manacles and rings. There was no smile. No face at all.

Then the surface broke beneath me. As my limbs flailed in panic, I was engulfed by deep and still waters. I pulled myself to the surface of the lowland basin with desperate strokes, coughing and clawing for air and safe purchase.

The angel: my salvation now depended on him. As I drew closer to the seraph, his radiant smile grew, and his glamorous hand grasped mine, rescuing me from a watery demise.

Now ashore and safe in the angel's blinding embrace, I squeezed the last of the fluid from my eyes and gazed back onto the pond. Both my unicorn and the dark sentinel were gone.

* * *

The city had slipped three weeks deeper into autumn's maw. The climate swallowed its inhabitants whole and chilled those who traveled in its breath unprepared for the sun's deception. Amarantha took a long look at the blustery day beyond the window at For Heaven's Cake, stirring her

Earl Gray tea and settling deeper into the folds of her sweater.

The stew of slow-boiling clouds broke for an instant, filling the front of the café with sublime light. The denizens of Haight Street were passing before her, exchanging greetings, stapling up band fliers, and bumming change. She watched them all go by as they enacted their dramas and lived in their worlds, and to Amarantha, their lives seemed so simple; so free of profound discord and indecision.

Yes, she was envious of them.

"I've got the cream and sugar," Heather announced, returning to the table with her latté. She sat across from Amarantha, took a careful sip, frowned, and shook her head. "These are okay, but Laine makes them better."

"True, true. I don't even bother ordering them here anymore," Amarantha agreed.

She returned her attention to the day outside, noting that the wound in the clouds had healed itself. It should always be so easy to find solutions in the wind.

Amarantha still couldn't decipher her vision walk. She had run myriad interpretations through her mind, none of them being very fruitful. Who was the angel? Who was the shrouded? Herself? Laine? Donovan? Was it even someone she knew or no one at all? And where did her unicorn go?

Amarantha had been up till 3:30 that morning trying to piece it all together, ultimately succumbing to exhaustion and awakening with the conundrum still plaguing her.

That and Samhain. After all, that was why she did the midnight pathworking in the first place: to gauge Laine's response to the boon Donovan had requested; a request she still hadn't discussed with her mentor.

"Amy, are you alright?"

Amarantha turned to her forgotten companion. "Oh, yeah. I've just got a lot to think about, that's all."

"Samhain?" Heather smiled, bobbing her head to the Romeo Void song filling the air.

"Yes." Amarantha blew steam from her mug.

"Don't worry about it. I'm sure everything will be cool."

"I hope so," she murmured to herself. An idea suddenly struck her, carrying with it some modicum of courage. "You've been spending a lot of time with Laine lately, right?"

Heather stopped in mid-sip, strangely unbalanced by the question. "Not really. I mean we work together, so I see him then," she said collecting herself. "And after what happened to me at the cafe, I asked him to give me some meditation tips."

Amarantha's mouth fell open. "Are you practicing again?"

"Nah, it's just breathing exercises and some visualization. Nothing hardcore, just a refresher. It's not like Laine has the time."

"True. Has he mentioned Samhain to you at all?"

"Not much, but I guess he figures that's between you two, and it's none of my business—which it isn't."

Heather's broad smile did little to raise Amarantha's mood, but she returned the gesture nonetheless. "It's just that I wanted to know if he was in good spirits, that's all," she said out the window.

"As good as Laine ever gets, I guess."

Amarantha frowned. "Donovan asked if he could participate in the ritual. You know, make it a joint ceremony. I don't know how Laine will—"

Something strange happened to Heather's face: something so quick Amarantha almost hadn't noticed. Heather's jaw dropped slightly, swiftly, then set itself into a tight resolve before she glanced away.

"What, Heather?"

Heather pursed her lips, then advised, "That definitely sounds like something you should talk to Laine about."

"Yes, you're right, of course. Forget I said anything." Amarantha used to know Heather's feelings about The Art, but something about her response seemed odd. It was like she wasn't as scared anymore.

Heather smiled and shrugged. "Forgotten."

Butterflies fluttered inside Amarantha as she sipped her cooling tea.

Heather's sudden howl of excitement shattered Amarantha's somber reverie. Billy Idol's "Blue Highway" was playing on the café's radio, its volume nowhere as loud as Heather's as she tore through the chorus.

"Oh Goddess, Heather." Amarantha buried her face in her hands and blushed. When she finally stole a peek, Heather was radiant with embarrassment and something else. Everyone in the café broke out in polite applause.

"I'm sorry," Heather squeaked, her body still bouncing to the beat.

"Oh no, that's okay. Actually, you were pretty good."

Heather's face became a deeper crimson when the cashier turned up the radio for her pleasure. "Oh God! Thank you!" They both laughed insanely.

"You know, Heather," Amarantha started after they had settled down, "I think the Goddess' touch goes well with you. It always has."

"What do you mean?" Heather's face was frozen with panic.

"I know what glamour looks like, Heather. Laine *is* training you, isn't he?"

Heather let out a long sigh. "Aw shit, Amy. I didn't want to say anything because I didn't want you to think I was glomming on your mentor or trying to steal him away. It's just he's been helping me work through stuff, you know?"

"I'm not mad," Amarantha said into her mug.

"Really?"

"No! I'm proud of you!" She touched Heather's hand. "I know Magick kinda scared you, and I've always wanted him to teach you too, but he only takes one pupil at a time, and now he's going to quit mentoring, so I didn't think he would."

"Oh, thank The Goddess! It was killing me not telling you."

Amarantha grinned. "So how does it feel to be back in the fold?"

Heather was stirring her latté as she thought of an answer. "Amy, you remember *The Vampire Lestat*: how he described everything when he first received the Dark Gift? I mean, he could see the blood flowing under people's skin and smell things from blocks away? That's what this is like," she whispered, tapping the water-worn tabletop. "It's like people and things are made of glass, and if you look at them just the right way, you can see beneath the surface of it all."

"I know," Amarantha confirmed. "You just have to know how to look."

"Yeah." Heather sighed as she leaned back into her seat, her blue-green eyes far away and deep. "And it's not like learning anything new. It's more like I'm remembering things that I forgot. Like when we were kids: all that stuff we could do because no one told us that it was impossible." She shook her head in awe. "It's really weird. It's like remembering how to play Pretend and then making it real."

"Essentially that's what we do: take the worlds inside and evoke them. 'As above, so below. As within, so without.' It's creation." Amarantha leaned in close this time. "But never forget that nothing happens in a vacuum. We *are* bending accepted laws of 'reality', and there's always some reaction to that."

Heather snapped her fingers and nodded knowingly. "Karma. The Threefold Law. 'What you send out shall return to you threefold.'"

"Exactly. Cause and effect apply in all the worlds, and without the proper moral or ethical framework, you're just asking for trouble. *That* is where the Rede of Chivalry comes in. *That* is where the truest and hardest tests lay. But I'm sure Laine will teach you all of that."

Heather nodded her understanding, and the twosome finished their drinks in silence.

The Rede of Chivalry: even those revered codes of ethics were no insurance of an untroubled life. The rules were well-defined and well-meant, but they could often lead to dilemmas of their own, despite—or maybe because of—adherence. Sometimes you had to choose between obeisance and disregard to do what you felt was right. What if the only good was to do harm? What if betraying a trust was the only way to save a friend? Consequences, always consequences, especially for their kind and with few promises.

Amarantha's mind bent toward the vision of the serpents threading through the shrouded one's fingers. That part of the enigma was clear at least. Serpents were an ancient symbol of wisdom and truth, were they not? And truth often wore a grim guise. Yes, an angel had rescued her, but from what exactly? Amarantha should have been grateful for his hand but felt otherwise.

"You know what, Heather?" Amarantha started, "I need to pick up some things for a working, anyway: would you like to go to Curios & Candles with me? Get some supplies from Jeffrey?"

Heather's eyes lit up. This would be the first time they would both be going to the Magick store as Wise Women. Without pause, Heather snatched up her book bag and said, "Let's go! My treat!"

"Oh, but Heather, you paid for the drinks and—"

"What's the fun in having a job if you can't spend the money? C'mon, my treat." Heather gasped before adding, "Ooh, we can hit the Esprit outlet afterward!"

Knowing her longtime friend wouldn't take no for an answer, Amarantha quietly acquiesced and gathered her things as her mind settled on more solemn matters.

Perhaps the angel's deed was well-intended, but Amarantha had to embrace this hallowed adage: the truth will set you free. So she would seek out that truth through ritual. Nothing too flamboyant, just a little contact with the other side.

Yes, the working must be subtle yet potent: subtle enough to elude an angel; potent enough to rend a shroud.

* * *

I, Nihthasu, was standing above the windswept valley of Elysium once more. It was time for answers.

Moonlit fog was racing around me in enraged herds, striking vast sparks with each hoof touch. I descended onto the back of one of the diaphanous steeds, was carried beneath the surface to the surface, and set down gently upon the solid earth.

The haze was omnipresent and pulsing with smothered light. I moved through the thick air that seemed charged with dissuading my passage. This fog was not summoned by me.

I arrived. The monolith before me was rendered in shadow with only a liquid iridescence to describe it. Looking up its long flank, its true nature was revealed to me in candlelight-gold: a large, crook staff motif served as the sole beacon, marking the size, place, and purpose of this structure. A Tower of Knowledge: A keeper of answers.

I spoke the words; the doors were opened. A vagrant wind invaded the chamber and stole away just as swiftly, but failed to relieve the dank scent of desecration. Torch flames were twisting within this austere monument, and a lone pedestal bore an ancient tome.

I stepped up to the grimoire and unlaced its leather binding. After a stroke upon its silver tracery, I pressed my thumb against the flat edge of the pages and let the leaves fall where they may. They stopped their cycle, and I read its portent.

It was a dissertation on sacrificial God-King figures of different lands: the many guises of The Horned One; The Solar Deities; tragic heroes like Arthur Pendragon; religious icons like Jesus Christ. Virtually every known psycho-dramatic belief system had a sacrificial god, and the inevitability of this Great All-Father archetype ascending for a greater good was almost cliché.

In this mystery, in this realm, I was the God-King, and I too was meant to die. The knowledge of my demise did not dishearten me, though. I had anticipated this; indeed, counted on it. It would enable me to live at peace with my

pale shadows

Queen and end my Magickal toils.

But what form, my death?

I closed the tome, again touching its embossed, leather cover. No, the answers weren't on these pages. The vectors of death were external, and the signs would come from without.

The abattoir smell rose again intensely, and a grist of flies trespassed the tower and gathered around my head. I emerged into clean air, but the disharmonic drone remained as the river of winged pestilence drew my attention upwards.

Where once shone the tower's beacon, the instrument of my demise was revealed in a column of six glyphs scrawled in bloody offal and animal feces: Qliphoth!

* * *

The staccato circus of images on the RCA awoke Laine as he sat in the lotus position on his bed. The TV's erratic flicker had hastened his return from Night Home, and now distracted, he watched the screen transmit at thirty frames per second.

Reagan promised tax reforms; Museveni spoke; Aquino smiled; little Kevin Collins still wasn't home. The entire Cola/Cold War world was served up with MTV jump-cuts and dancing pastel hues. Despair and deception in living color and stereo.

Laine punched the television off, and his eyes soon dark-adapted. Reaching into his trouser pocket, he retrieved his lighter, sighing as he contemplated it. It was a profile of a panther bust with blue rhinestone eyes, and its matte, obsidian skin was cool to the touch. Another gift from Marisa.

He searched among the new issues of *Love & Rockets*, *Samurai*, and *Warlock 5* comics beside him for the fresh pack of Gonesh #6 incense. Thumbing back the pard's ears, Laine ignited a stick-tip in the flame that had erupted from the panther's skull, then went to his altar and lit a black candle with the burning incense before placing it in its holder.

Laine smoothed out the wrinkles in the black satin altar cloth, satisfied with the symmetry of the items upon it: a copy of Aleister Crowley's *Magick: In Theory and Practice*; a deck of *Magickal* tarot cards; a falcon athamé; a silver goblet; a brazier with an unburned charcoal disk. A practitioner's altar was a reflection of that mage's paradigm; a microcosmic representation of the magician's worldview. It appeared that Laine's world was growing oh-so-black.

There was nothing worthwhile in the Strathmore sketchpad laying on his bed. Indeed, his lack of inspiration was what prompted Laine to slip into Nihtheim in the first place. It was a quest for an artistic spark as well as answers. He was granted only one of those boons: the heavier of the two.

The Qliphoth weren't demons in the mundane sense, but were astral embodiments of humanity's imbalances; their weaknesses and cruelties. For the past seven years, Laine had battled and bent many of the Qliphoth's malefic ranks and then employed them to do his bidding in his campaign of spiritual balance. It was his "alliance" with those sunless corps that had allowed him to acquire the spear of Moloch. That acquisition may prove costly indeed, for now it seemed they wanted Laine's blood on their tongues.

So mote it be. The invitations were out. Besides, he still had the spear.

Laine pressed "play" on his cassette deck. Andreas Vollenweider's electric harp displaced the dead silence as he walked to his window. A late cloud cover was plunging San Francisco into premature night. A little more humidity and he could probably make the stallions race the skies; help clear the air and add a little excitement. But not just yet.

Then the phone rang. "Hello?"

"Hey, it's me."

Were he and Marisa supposed to meet that evening? "Look, I'm sorry I didn't call. I have a training session

91

tonight."

"Amy?"

"Heather."

"That's cool. Nothing's happening at Wolfgang's tonight, so Tori and I are going out for drinks."

When Laine visualized Marisa wearing one of her dresses and looking the way she could look, his stomach churned.

"So Tori was telling me about a couple of parties happening on Halloween that we can hit. Our old friend Kristin is—"

Shit. "I thought I told you I was performing a ritual with Amarantha."

"No. You didn't."

"Yes, I did. At her party? The Wiccaning? She'll officially be a Wise Woman?"

"You didn't say on Halloween."

"I thought I did," he repeated, knowing it was moot. "Look, it's no problem though. I'll perform her ritual, and then we can spend the rest of the night together with your friends, all right?"

"Don't inconvenience yourself," Marisa said in petrified tones.

"C'mon, Marisa, I said we'd do something afterward, and we will."

Laine heard her huff sharply. "Laine, don't even worry about it. Do your thing with Amarantha. I'll go out alone if I have to."

There was a long, expectant silence. What could he say? Despite her frequent bouts of Libran indecision, when Marisa's mind was set, there was no changing it. So much for her promise at the party.

After a while, Marisa said, "Look, if you're not going to say anything else, I gotta go. Tori's here."

"I'll call you tomorrow, okay?"

"Yeah, right, what you said. Good night." A hollow click; dead air; dial tone.

Laine cradled the receiver, outrage roiling inside him.

The music was an annoyance now, and Laine thought the boombox to be a tempting victim for his anger, but instead, he jabbed the stop button and leaned on the soundless television.

"Of all the fucking demons and foot soldiers I have battled," he hissed lividly, glaring at Trump, "Of all the crucibles I've endured, this bitch tests me in—"

What was that thin, buzzing sound Laine was hearing? A static discharge?

A low, familiar chiming drew Laine's attention to Amarantha's gift basket.

The bell earring.

Laine tossed Trump onto the relative safety of his bed and loosened the top of Amarantha's potpourri basket with a twist.

The ringing grew.

Within the basket's shadow . . . .

The ringing grew.

Was there something inside the basket besides Amarantha's . . . ?

The ringing grew.

Something black and slick swimming amongst the petals . . . .

His phone rang.

Laine's fingers found nothing but rose petals, a lock of Amarantha's hair in a tissue, and the earring.

"Interesting," he whispered. He'd have to log that in his journal.

The phone rang again.

*　*　*

It was chilly before: now it was dark, windy, and fucking freezing. Heather zipped her brown bomber jacket up to her chin and watched the crowd filing out of the Galaxy Theater across the street. Van Ness and Sutter was where Laine wanted to get the news, and Heather wasn't one to question his motives. Not anymore, even if they did always meet at the least convenient locations possible.

She glanced at her Swatch: 7:31 pm. He was only a minute late, but in this weather—

Heather heard rustling to her right and looked down just in time to see a dirty sheet of newsprint slap and wrap itself around her ankle.

"Shit," she said as she shook it loose and continued her wait for Laine.

The traffic suddenly fell silent. At the bottom of the grade, Heather saw a cyclone of newsprint floating silently toward her. A black banner twisted in its eye, swirling under the salmon glow of the streetlights. *San Francisco Chronicle* pages were following the specter like obedient minions, and Heather's neck hairs stood as the banner took on a human shape.

It was Laine, and it wasn't. He was invisible where light didn't fall, and his feet never quite touched the sidewalk. One by one, the newspaper sheets fell to the ground in a path behind him. So this was real fascination, or glamour, as Amy called it. Heather *had* to master that spell.

Laine stopped just out of arm's length, his blood-red tie waving to the side against his black suit and white dress shirt. Boy, he looked a lot taller than six-foot-three, as if that wasn't tall enough. "What have you heard?" he asked.

"Wow, it looked like you were floating down there!"

"Old trick. What have you heard?"

Right, business first. She sighed. "Well, Donovan's coming back around Halloween, but that much you know. However . . . ."

She expected Laine to take the bait and ask for more, but he didn't. His expression reminded her that she had volunteered for this task. She'd have to come through.

". . . However, Amy mentioned something about doing a joint ritual with you and Donovan. She wanted my opinion."

Laine grunted. He did that a lot. "Was that it?" he asked directly.

"Mostly. So what do you think?"

"I think that if that's what Amarantha wants, she'll have to ask me herself. Otherwise, she's not as ready as I thought."

Heather nodded. "That's what I told her, sort of."

"Anything else on Donovan's ex, Lillian?"

Heather shook her head. "No, nothing."

Laine frowned hard and said, "Then we'll consider her out of the picture." He slid a finger up the bridge of his nose. Guess he forgot he wasn't wearing his glasses.

Heather smiled at a memory. "Amy said I was glamouring. She noticed the change."

"Not surprising. You'll grow brighter and more magnetic till you learn to turn it off. We wear our minds."

"Yeah, but that's the scary part: I thought Amy was gonna' skry me and blow everything, but I think I covered it okay."

Laine smirked a little. "Well done, but you have nothing to fear though. Your motives are pure. You're simply watching out for her."

Heather saddened. "I don't feel so pure."

Laine simply nodded. "Sometimes you have to do questionable things for the greater good. It's not always easy, but it's part of what we are. If you don't believe you can handle it, it's not too late—"

"Oh give me a fucking break, Laine. You know we can't stop now. We have to go all the way."

Laine grunted again, this time smiling with pride. She must have passed another test.

"Very well, Heather." Laine's ring-spangled fingers glittered in the red neon of a pizza parlor window as he fixed his crooked tie. "Shall we go?"

Now how could Heather resist?

* * *

The Mission was the oldest district in San Francisco, and Laine could always tell. Beneath the class neglect and community spirit was an ancient and pure well of untapped energy, perhaps the same energy that had brought the missionaries here so long ago. The landfill shorelines and cement sand dunes had disrupted The City's natural mana flow elsewhere, but here, where ancient lagoons and bedrock mingled, the energy flowed purely. Here on Shotwell Street beneath the towering junipers and stalwart cathedrals, Magick wrought would last for as long as this realm floated in the bay. Laine inhaled a heady draught of dog urine and *pupusas* and was cleansed.

"God, Laine, you really like this dump?" Heather quipped.

"Oh yes."

"Why? There are drunk farts, fresh bullet holes, and stale hookers everywhere. This place sucks. The best thing about The Mission is the food, and if you try to get some at night, some dickhead starts yelling shit. '¡Ay, qué guapa!'" she hollered, swaggering like a Latin pimp. "'Hey, *chichis*, nice sweater. What's in it?'"

Laine smiled at his young charge. "I sympathize, truly, but . . . you just don't see what I see, Heather. Perhaps you will soon."

"Whatever. Just remember: you're the one who's not wearing their glasses."

Laine laughed despite himself. "*Touché.*"

By this, his third visit to Heather's home, Laine had grown accustomed to the flat's precarious stairway even though it groaned beneath each footfall. He ran his fingers along the aged steel-lace handrail as they topped the climb, and Heather fumbled for her house keys. They finally entered.

As Laine shut the door, he was enveloped by the comforting darkness of the hall. There was the lone sliver of light breaking from one of the rear rooms, probably Rudy's.

Heather touched his arm and said, "Hold on a second. Mama, I'm back." She knocked on the door beside her and slowly pushed it open.

Parents: Laine still had a problem meeting them

whether they were Marisa's or, in this case, Heather's. On his last two visits, he was fortunate enough to not have to face Heather's mother since she had been out, but tonight the inevitable meeting had come.

"Mama, this is Laine. Laine, my mom Margarita."

Laine peeked into the dark, converted living room. Only the blue-white glow of the street lamps outside confirmed that the room was even occupied. Heather's mother was reclining beneath her bedsheets, watching the Latin television show beyond her toes. Her strobing silhouette spared him a glance, sized him up, and said "Hello" in a discomforting manner.

"Um, good evening, Ms. Dominguez," Laine said respectfully, then he slipped back into the hall. Goddess, he hated that.

"Mama, Laine and I are going to my room. To talk. Do you need anything?"

Her mom responded in Spanish so quickly that Laine's high school lessons couldn't keep up.

"No problem." Heather shut her mother's door and led Laine to her room. "You'll have to excuse my mom. She just went through a hard breakup, and she's just very protective about me when it comes to boys."

"I almost took her mood personally."

"Don't. You want some tea? I'm sorry, but it's just Lipton's."

"That's okay. I could use the caffeine anyway."

Heather led Laine into the kitchen. When she shut on the light, a fleet of roaches fled the scene. Laine was embarrassed for her.

"Sorry about that," she muttered.

"Don't worry about it. I have the same problem at my place. Vermin will outlive us all. So what about your father? Was he the protective type too?"

"I don't know. I never met him."

"No? Maybe you're better off," Laine said. "You know, the last time I saw my father, he was still dressed like Sly Stone. That was just a couple of years ago. Nothing to miss there."

Heather brightened. "The only good things I got from my dad were the eyes and the complexion. *Soy de Puerto Rico como el coquí*, but Dad was Irish."

Laine only caught about half of that, but said, "Aha, I was wondering about that."

"And Mama's a lesbian, so it's not like she misses him."

"Aha, I was—what?"

Heather tee-heed and nodded.

"Wait, now how does that work? Let me rephrase: what about Rudy?"

"Different fathers," Heather was twirling a teabag around her finger. "Mama wanted a matching set."

"So did my mother. I wasn't planned, and my sister has a different father. He didn't stick around either."

Heather was still except for her quivering lips. "Rudy's dad and Mama stayed together for a while. Then the abuse started. One night she had finally had enough and went after him with a hammer. I . . . saw the whole thing." Heather looked like she was on the verge of another episode, but she returned behind her eyes and added, "She didn't kill him or anything, just made sure he knew who he was fucking with. While she was away for court-appointed evaluation and counseling, Joanie took me in. That's when Amy and I became friends."

Laine shook his head softly. "I'm so sorry." Now he had the missing piece.

"Some world, huh?" She went back to tending to their tea. "So what about your mom and sister? Are they witches too?"

Laine chuckled. "Hell no, just very open-minded Baptists. My mother's side of the family has always been pretty intuitive though. My aunt figured out what I was almost as fast as I figured out Amarantha."

"Yeah, how did you figure out Amy?" She dropped the bag into a Laurel Burch mug.

"She never told you?"

"Nope," she replied, taking a seat at the kitchen table.

Curious, that. "Okay. Well, she and I had a mutual friend from high school three years ago. I was already out, but our friend was a senior. Amarantha—"

"Uh, Laine," she interrupted, "please sit down. You're making me nervous."

"Oh. Sorry. I'm prone to lurk and hover." He slipped out of his trench coat, draped it over an arm, and joined Heather at the Formica table. "Anyway, I went to visit our friend and there she was with Amarantha. I told Amarantha how attractive I thought she was, she told me that she used to model, and I said I could use one for some paintings. So we exchanged numbers.

"Now I sensed that there was more to her than just beauty, and I was eager to find out what, but every time we'd schedule a meet, something would come up. After a while, I was about to give up on working with her, but I gave it one more try and called her again.

"We were talking about not-much-at-all on the phone while she was folding laundry when suddenly she says, 'Oh, this is interesting.' 'What's interesting?' I asked her. 'I've just found someone's book in my basket.' 'Oh yeah?' I said, 'What book?'" Laine paused for effect.

"Well, what book was it?" Heather asked anxiously.

"*The Necronomicon.*"

Heather's jaw dropped. "Get the fuck out of here!"

"I shit you not. And yes, I knew that *The Necronomicon* was a work of fiction, but the fact that *she* knew was surprising. That was just the first of her many surprises. When she showed me her box, I almost—"

Shock slapped Heather's face. "Her what?!"

"No, not *that* 'box'! Goddess, woman!" After a good laugh, Laine added, "The one under her bed. The first time I went to her flat, she showed me her box of Magickal tools."

"Oh yeah, that one," Heather said, still tearing up.

"Anyway, that's when I took her on as a pupil. Then two years ago, she went away, vanished. She left to see her family in Arkansas, and just like this year, she did so abruptly, unceremoniously. After about two weeks I started to question if she really was meant to be my pupil or if I should find another. So one evening I meditated, mused, and Magicked and asked 'the forces that be' whom, if not Amarantha, was my true successor."

"What did 'they' say?"

"'They' urged me to go to North Beach on a night when the mist beckoned. There and then was where I would find my true pupil. And so I eventually did.

"Following my instincts' quiet tugging, I walked for a short time through the tourist-stricken streets until I came across a figure in the crowd ahead of me. I recognized my true student among the 'mundanes' even with her back to me. It took no bravery to tap the stranger on the shoulder."

"It was Amy?"

"It was 'Amy'. I was only slightly surprised when she turned around. She had just returned home that same day, and at that moment, it felt as if she had never left. All of my doubts about her melted away."

Heather sat stunned and slack-jawed for a pause then asked, "Okay, fine, but why her? Why is *she* so important?" The taint of frustration in Heather's voice belied her envy.

Laine sighed, but the tea kettle's shrill alarm summoned Heather before he could reply.

"Wait a minute," she said as she rose.

Laine used the lull to examine the pictures on her refrigerator. A shrine to youth: there were baby photos of Rudy; shots of Heather blooming into adolescence; prints of Margarita smiling and well-tanned in some tropical locale. Conspicuously, but not surprisingly, there were no shots of Rudy or Heather's fathers.

Heather took her seat across from Laine, setting down their steaming mugs and a box of C&H sugar. "You were about to say?"

"We've developed quite a rapport, Heather," Laine resumed, "so let me answer that question with another: when you skry me, what does it feel like?"

Heather visibly mulled over the question. "I don't know.

It feels like a reminder; like a voice telling me something I already know, somehow."

"And yet you've never faced the voice?"

"No. It's gone pretty fast. I don't have any control over it."

"Hmm. Well, in Amarantha's case—and mine—we have kissed the lips that speak the words, and witches like us are rarer than you'd think."

"The Goddess?"

"I use 'Goddess' in the collective sense, but yes. You're familiar with Shamanism?"

"Yeah, they have totem animals: spirit guides in the form of sacred animals."

"Right. In Hermetic practices they're called Holy Guardian Angels; in psychology, The Genius or Higher Self. Same actor, different masks.

"What it really is is the Holistic Self: the part of us that remembers what has been forgotten, knows what has yet to be considered, and lives the life unlived. It is The Self seeking completion, and it is this Self that utters The Calling."

"Damn!" Heather's tea had been forgotten.

"Quite." Just speaking of The Art sent a charge creeping across Laine's skin. There was an astral blooming above his head and between his eyes, and with them came the familiar, euphoric warmth.

"Do you have a headache?" Heather asked.

"No, no. Quite the opposite. My head has never been clearer. You should drink your tea."

"Okay." Heather's mouth pulled to one side of her face, suspicious.

"In any event, it is common for The Undiscovered Self to take the form of the gender opposite your 'self,' so in my case, yes, it was The Goddess. Could be a man in yours."

Heather snorted into her cup. "Don't count on it."

Laine silently sipped his tea then added, "Well, it was a Goddess in Amarantha's case as well. The forms can be as varied as the people who see them. The point is soon,

101

Amarantha will no longer be 'separate' from her Higher Self, but shall become one with it."

"Wait, you're saying she's going to be a Goddess?"

"Yes, after a fashion. That's what The Mysteries are about, but hang on—" He dug through his overcoat pockets until he found what he sought. "Here we go."

"Damn, is that a book in your pocket, or are you just glad to see me?"

"Ha-ha." My, weren't we a comedian tonight? "*Moon Magic* by Dion Fortune." Laine was displaying the book like Miss Mary Ann in *Romper Room*, getting more laughs from Heather. He flipped through the pages until he reached 56.

"'It was my task to bring certain new concepts to the mind of the race; not to its conscious mind, but to its subconscious mind, and this is done by living them. One who had knowledge once said that an adept must not merely tread the Path, he must *be* the Path, and this is true.'"

Laine closed the tome and then returned it to its pocket. "So in essence, if the pantheons of Gods and Goddesses represent states of human consciousness, then we of The Art are the embodiment of these states, and our task—The Great Art—is to elevate the consciousness of humanity. You got all that?"

"Oh yeah, I get it."

"Good, 'cause I don't know if I can say that again." He feigned exhaustion. "But you know what? All this is academic, and none of it will matter until we strengthen your astral body." Laine rose from the weathered chair and summoned Heather with a gesture. They carried their mugs with them as she followed him to her room.

Heather's room was as sparsely decorated as Laine's, although larger: dresser with mirror; nightstand with a lamp and clock/radio; one poster of Adam Ant; another of Billy Idol. The rest was peeled paint and scarred wood. On the low dresser were the first signs of her Magickal life: a makeshift altar. She grabbed a small brown paper sack from its top.

"I picked up some frankincense at Curios today. Can we burn it?"

"Well, it's a bit solar for my tastes, but sure, why not."

Buoyant, Heather lit a charcoal disk and watched it sputter and smoke on a brass plate. Laine switched on her lamp and then walked to her door and shut off the overhead as Heather dropped what looked like amber pearls on the smoldering disk. The resin spat and bubbled. "I like the way the charcoal sparks."

"Me too. Move back."

Heather scooted a meter away from her dresser and sat cross-legged and erect. She closed her eyes and took even breaths, grounding.

"Good. Very good. Now, remember how we begin?"

"Yes. 'Always start from zero.'"

Very good indeed.

* * *

Amarantha found the long, rectangular box easily in her darkened room. She slid open its drawer as she moved toward her veiled altar in the corner. It was time for a little illumination.

The bulb of the long-stemmed match snapped against the box. It sparked but didn't catch. Two, three, four strokes later, the match lit. Spheres of light spread as she set fire to the wicks of the newly-purchased tapers. A puff of breath and the match was out.

All the candles' flames fluttered, stretched, and died.

The second match lit more swiftly, but now the candles wouldn't light. Their wicks glowed as if to taunt her, and it took over a minute of coaxing before the new flames became consistent.

Amarantha set the box down, resolve now waning. She was no fool. There was no need to check for hidden drafts in the windless room. No, there was a perfectly good reason for all this, but she still needed to finish bringing her tools to play; to complete the act.

She extinguished the victorious match and discarded it, then opened a dresser drawer to retrieve her Nag Champa incense. It wasn't there.

Amarantha suppressed the anxiety welling in her long enough to go through all her drawers, throwing their contents everywhere.

"Oh yeah. Curios." Amarantha took a deep, calming breath as she dug through the brown paper bag on her daybed and pulled out the new pack. Returning to her altar, Amarantha removed a stick from its packaging and touched it to the burning wick.

The incense wouldn't light. Not even a sputter.

"Then that's it." Amarantha set the slightly-charred incense on her altar and then blew out all the candles.

There would be no audience with the asps. There would be no conversations with the unicorn. Even if the incense had lit, it wouldn't have helped anything. This ritual would not succeed. It was not meant to, at least not now.

In the dark, she went to the corner of her brass bed, grabbed the vinyl edge of her childhood blanket, and rubbed it frantically.

I am always with you.

* * *

My reflection wasn't in the mirror. There was just the black emptiness waiting for my light. All things began with the breath, I've been told, and so I breathed.

Inhalation: I swallowed the world outside and digested it. All its colors, all its flavors, and all its textures were broken down by my mind into their simplest elements. The whole of existence was suspended between my breaths.

Exhalation: the world emerged from my parted lips. Seven links of fire fueled my inner light, providing me with the material for my recreation.

"When you feel ready, mold the light."

Inhalation: I filled my vessel to brimming, not afraid of

spilling the light that I was.

Exhalation: and then I poured the light in a thin stream onto the mirror; into the mirror. It pooled and gathered in the dark behind the glass like spilled milk on a black lacquer table.

"The details aren't important. Just mold the light into a suitable size and shape."

Inhalation: I caressed my shoulders, neck, and head into being with my mental hands.

Exhalation: the small of the back; the size of the boobs; the turn of the hips followed. I stared at my reflection in the mirror, yet it wasn't my reflection at all.

Inhalation: I am further strengthened.

Exhalation: She is further strengthened.

"Once the body of light is complete, wear it."

Inhalation/exhalation: I followed the glowing stream, slipping swiftly yet surely into the mirror and my astral form. Now came the tricky part.

"Take it slow."

Inhalation: I did as he bade. I slowly turned around and "put on" the body of light. I wore its feet, legs, hips, torso and arms, neck and head.

And then I opened my eyes.

Exhalation: on this side of the mirror all was black and vast. I would build a temple here someday, but not this eve. Through the mirror's "other" side was my room where my body was sitting, appearing to be somewhere between sleep and death. That was the trick: not panicking at the sight of my own empty body. I'd failed that test before.

"Don't try to walk or interact with anything. Simply be. Hold your consciousness still."

Inhalation: a trickle of liquid light was tethering my heart to the heart of my flesh, keeping me from straying. The only time that thread could be severed was in death. Knowing this kept me calm and centered in my body of light.

Exhalation: beyond my mortal body, a soft gray figure with a brilliant, platinum crown was standing. There was something strapped to its right arm. Maybe it was his arm. I couldn't tell, but whatever it was, it was the darkest thing in the room. I did know that the figure was Laine's.

"Remember your breathing."

Inhalation: the room lightened, and the walls thinned. I could see into my hallway.

Exhalation: as I settled even deeper into my astral body, my eyesight sharpened, and I saw a ghost moving down the hall from the front of the house. It stopped at my bedroom door.

Sharp inhalation!

* * *

Then pow, Heather found herself back in her room, staring wide-eyed at her reflection in the mirror. There was this sensation like when she'd wake up in the middle of the night and couldn't tell which direction she was lying in. The incense smoke didn't help matters.

"What? What happened?" Laine asked. He looked just as shocked as Heather was.

"Somebody's at—" There was a knock at Heather's door. She almost shit herself right then. "Hello?"

The door creaked open, and Heather's mom poked her head into the smoke-filled room, a big smile on her face. "Whoo, *tienes que abrir una ventana. Podía ver el humo desde mi quarto,*" she said, swatting at the clouds. "*¿Es incienso eso?*"

"*Si*, Mama."

"*¡Por supuesto huele como un iglesia aqui!*"

Heather and her mom giggled while Laine stood there totally confused.

"My high school Spanish is a bit rusty," Laine confessed after Heather's mom left the room. "What did she say?"

"Mama was wondering where all the smoke was coming from, so I told her we were burning frankincense. Then she said, 'No wonder it smells like a church in here.'"

Laine laughed and coughed while Heather threw open a window.

pale shadows

TUESDAY, OCTOBER 21ST

"**A**my? Hey, you in there?"

Amarantha blinked absently as she looked up into Brandon's mask of concern. It took a moment for her distant mind to return to the here and now of the cooking class.

"Oh. Brandon." She glanced around the nearly empty kitchen, the scent of fresh potato gnocchi and pesto sauce loitering about her head. Four remaining students single-filed noisily from the immense classroom, lugging their notes and wares. There was the sudden, sobering slam of a large cookbook: Chef Cashman's cookbook, and judging from the look in his eyes, he was far from pleased with Amarantha right now.

"Oh crap," she sighed.

"Huh. That's putting it mildly," Brandon said with a wry smile. "Are you okay? You've been vegging out for over ten minutes now."

"The steam . . . ." she whispered. Amarantha was

109

following the class just fine till the gnocchi started boiling. The steam had mesmerized her, insinuating dire thoughts that had now, upon awakening, gone to the place mist went when it died. Now she was stranded with a soul in suspense and a teacher enraged.

"What did you say?"

"Nothing, Brandon. I'm sorry. Thank you."

"Yeah, okay. Look, let me help you with your things," he offered, putting her materials in her backpack. "I can fill you in on whatever you missed over lunch."

Amarantha crept timidly along the rows of counters with Brandon following closely behind, carrying the bulk of her school books. As she got within two yards of the door, Chef Cashman sidestepped, blocking her exit with his corpulence and twisting strands of his graying beard. Here it was: her comeuppance.

"I appreciate that you're new to my class, Miss Powell, but I trust that you will be far more attentive in our next session," he admonished with his deceptively youthful voice.

She stared at the front of his stained smock. "Yes sir. Sorry."

"Good. Because I wouldn't want to report on your 'short-attention-span' problem. I get more than my job's worth of that nonsense."

Amarantha's jaw clenched. How dare this . . . . "Yes sir," she choked out.

"Fine. Go to lunch." Just as ominously as before, Chef Cashman sidestepped from in front of the door, still preening his beard. Eyes averted, Amarantha walked out.

Brandon hissed in a breath. "Damn, Amy, Cashman was pissed."

"Whoopie doo."

"Well, you might want to watch your step."

"'Yeah, right, what you said,'" she quipped, staring at her LA Gears.

"Hey, just trying to help."

Amarantha couldn't miss the hurt in his voice. "I know.

I'm sorry, I shouldn't take it out on you. I . . . haven't been sleeping too good."

"No problem. I understand."

No, he didn't. There was no way he possibly could.

Brandon then did exactly what Amarantha hoped he would do: changed the subject. He was babbling about something or other related to class, while Amarantha responded in grunts when appropriate. She hated to be rude to him, but her brain was so exhausted that her attention kept slipping into more personal topics.

None of her ritual attempts had been working. It was as if she was caught between one force that was frustrating her efforts and an opposing one pushing back to protect her. Funny thing was she found the protection as infuriating as the threat. Both had cost her ease, leaving only sour dreams when she *could* sleep.

Whose protection was it? Not Laine's or Donovan's. She knew their touches far too well, and if either of them were increasing their auspices, she would know. And while Heather's progress was astonishing, she still wasn't potent enough for so profound an effect.

Was she? No, Amarantha would recognize her best friend's touch as well. Even if Heather had undergone some grand, archetypal change, some footsteps remained when the tide went low; some psychic imprints were never swept away.

And what or who was the threat? That list was almost the same. Lillian was still a possibility. What Laine had envisioned was a possibility. Heck, bad astral tides and Samhain worries were possibilities.

Amarantha loathed the feeling of helplessness all this created. True, Laine and she had often joked about her infamous "Libran indecision", but this lack of control would not do. With her Wiccaning just ten short days away, Amarantha needed her rest and focus.

Angry winds were shaking the walls as she and Brandon followed the patches of sunlight leading to the exit. "Earthquake weather," he offered.

Amarantha nodded. "Or the start of a huge storm." Nature exerting its will: now that idea pleased her. She removed her *toque blanche* and handed it and the rest of her books to Brandon. "Watch these for me, please."

"Sure, but where are you—"

Amarantha pushed her way through the heavy doors and stepped out into the wind tunnel that was the corner of Turk and Polk streets. The air ripped through the layers of her uniform and chilled her skin. Her arms thickened with goose-pimples as she opened them in a gesture of supplication.

Or the start of a huge storm. She thought of Laine and wondered if any of this was his doing, as had been the case in January.

Amarantha shut her eyes, languidly removed the barber's pins from her strangled hair, and let her golden tresses fall. Her lungs cooled and cleared with each deep, grounding breath she drew; her cheeks blushed from the biting breeze and whipping locks. Teeth chattering, she vibrated her affirmation to Athena and drew down The Goddess' strength from the furious sky above until the exhaustion and incoherence that three nights of insomnia had caused her was just a memory.

Ah, this is what she was. Not a pawn, not a child, but a Wise Woman capable of petitioning the gods; capable of controlling the very world around her; capable of making the right decisions and of accepting the consequences of the wrong ones. She was alive again. Amarantha was large again.

She calmed the winds, and the city subsided into a haunting stillness until the sky was torn by the wail of air raid sirens. Twelve o'clock noon, Tuesday.

Amarantha opened her fiery eyes, almost blinded by the curtain of her own tangled hair. Beyond the blonde veil, a familiar man was holding a bouquet of six red roses nestled in baby's breath and euphorbia. She smiled as Donovan Walsh presented his gift to her, bowing his head in reverence.

* * *

Laine waited for the last traces of the air raid siren to die out before he walked into Russian Hill O' Beans. He would miss the crisp autumn air that alleviated some of his clinging malaise.

"What the fuck took you guys so long?" yelled Diana as she glowered over the display racks. "Some yuppie bitch just went off on me because I didn't have the right change!"

"Diana, relax. We had to get the decorations for Halloween." Laine tossed the bundle of coin rolls at her, not bothering to see if she caught them. He knew she would. "Are you happy now?"

"No."

Laine threw a bag of Gummy Bears and cleared his throat when it got halfway to Diana. She caught that too. Damn, she was good.

A glowing smile popped onto Laine's co-worker's face. "Okay, now I'm happy."

"I thought you'd be. Any new orders?"

"Just one French Roast," Diana said as she broke open a dime roll. "They don't need it until tomorrow."

Laine coughed. "Might as well do it now."

"What? Why?"

"Because we're the dealers, and they're the addicts. 'Movers and Shakers: The Coffee Achievers,' remember? Besides, you know Mohammed's going to make us do it anyway." Laine's throat was dry, scratchy. He removed his glasses, coughing uncontrollably.

"You okay?"

"I don't think so," he managed around the tickle in his throat.

"C'mon, can we torch the order?" Diana produced a yellow Bic lighter from a black jean pocket. "We can say we dropped it in the oven while heating up scones."

"'The Ranger won't like it, Yogi.' Just weigh the coffee, please? Thank you, Ms. M." The shop slid sideways. "I'll be back in a minute."

What was this? It sure wasn't the stomach flu. Maybe a fever, but Laine's head was cool. Damn, what did he eat? Maybe it was that mint It's-It.

The café rolled the other way as Laine topped the steps leading to the office and restroom, forcing him to await his vertigo's end against a coffee-stained wall. He hooked the latch on the bathroom door as he removed his pants and sat in anxious silence.

The window facing the alley was transmitting a sunbeam as soft as down. Laine leaned on his bare thighs and stared at the corroded drainage screen between his feet, wondering where the conduit led.

Tremors ran through Laine's limbs, rattling the toilet seat and jangling his belt buckle. The feces would not come. He sniffed forcefully at the mucus spilling from his nostril, finally wiping it away with his hand.

A pigeon coo invaded the brief hush as Laine looked at his slick palm.

"What the hell . . . ." Smeared into his love-line, his lifeline, were two broad strokes of tacky blood.

"Goddess." Laine smelled iron.

Then the real pain came, slamming his tortured body back against the john. A constellation of magenta sparks exploded behind Laine's eyes as he reflexively kicked and bludgeoned the blood-hued walls.

"Stop it!" he growled, "Stop it now!" The contents of his stomach liquefied and congealed, then erupted from his lips in flaccid spurts of phlegm and bile. His bowels squirmed and contracted, expelling his waste in wet, noisy chunks. He wanted to scream. He needed to scream, but he needed to laugh more, and so he did. The shadow of a fleeing pigeon eclipsed the five-foot-square room.

Laine rolled his head, then locked it and his mind. He mentally swam upstream until he reached the source of the river of pain.

Right there. Nihthasu's opponent was right there. "You're mine."

So what do you believe in, Amarantha?

* * *

And I touched him and instantly recognized that sickly-sweet veneer. Pity, it was *Donovan.*
"All mine."
I reached out for my target's astral heart and squeezed, but not enough to kill. Just until I heard Donovan's long, psychic scream, and my pain finally fell away. Only then did I release my grip.
"All mine."

* * *

Laine gasped and gulped the fetid bathroom air through his teeth. His carotids were pumping like agitated worms, filling his head with the thunder of his own heart. Soon, the adrenaline dissolved, leaving Laine almost empty.

Almost. His right arm felt like it was bleeding ice water. A flip of the sleeve revealed nothing, but the numbness and angry tension were real. "Ah yes. The spear."

* * *

Amarantha held the flowers to her breasts, wishing they were the man before her now.

Donovan gently rent the tapestry of Amarantha's hair, gesturing the knots away and bringing her face out into the sunlight. "Oh yeah. Here. I found this in our guest bathroom." He placed the bell earring in her palm and closed her hand around it.

"Thank you. I wasn't too worried though. It always finds its way back to me."

"That ritual was the most incredible thing I've ever seen," he half-whispered as he resumed grooming her, "but you should be more cautious about your audience." Donovan gave a slight nod past her shoulder.

Amarantha did not need to look. "That would be Brandon. He has a crush on me, but he is not considered. Just a young soul trying to appear old." Amarantha looked up into her beloved's aquamarine eyes, smiling. They belied a hint of his fear.

"You're still 'up there', aren't you? You're still connected."

She took one of Donovan's hands and guided him away from the school doors, out of sight. The couple stopped next to a row of Vespas and Kawasakis parked on the sidewalk, their presence mildly perturbing a cluster of feeding pigeons.

"We're about to set our clocks back an hour, Donovan, not a week."

"I know, I know, but my dad was driving me crazy, so I flew up today." Donovan tried to take Amarantha into his arms, but she took a single, fluid step back from his reach.

"Your impatience will get the better of you someday," Amarantha teased, "After all, we have all the time in the world." She was enticing Donovan and felt no guilt about it. Despite Lillian's difference, this consort was hers, and Amarantha would use all of her glamour to keep it that way.

Donovan responded with a smirk. He knew this game well enough. His body settled as he recaptured his escaped composure.

"You haven't allowed me time to properly prepare for your arrival," she continued. "The house is still a mess, I have to get ingredients for—"

"—You haven't spoken to Laine yet about the hand-fasting . . . ."

Amarantha's heart sunk, and she turned away from Donovan. "No, I haven't. I don't know if it's these feelings I have or these dreams I've dreamt, but I'm afraid to ask him." She met Donovan's skrying gaze. "Laine has never denied me anything and has always shown me a gentle hand. He is more than just my mentor: he's also one of my best friends." Amarantha shook her head. "But these

116

dreams, these feelings—"

"Well, maybe you're just looking at this the wrong way, Amarantha. What if these dreams are not omens; these feelings, not portents?"

"What then?"

Donovan took a step toward Amarantha, cupping her face in his strong, comforting hands. "They are just feelings. They are the symptoms of your confusion, not the cause. Amy, in ten days your entire life is going to change. You will no longer be a student with a mentor picking you up whenever you stumble. You will be on your own, and that frightens you.

"But Laine believes in you, or he wouldn't be bothering with your ceremony. And I believe in you because I've seen what you can do. I have watched you for many, many years, and now is your time." Donovan's fingertips left warm trails on Amarantha's face as he released her. "So what do you believe in, Amarantha?"

He was right. Amarantha's old life had to die before her new life could begin. A joint ritual would simply be the completion of an ancient and natural cycle. A laugh sprung from Amarantha's lips as she considered Donovan.

"You're right, Donovan. It's not Laine I've been afraid of, but my future. I will speak with him tonight. I can see no logical reason for—Donovan, are you okay?"

His face had taken on a sickly pallor made all the more horrific by his smile. "I'll be fine. Airport seafood: not a good breakfast choice."

Panic displaced pleasure. "Are you sure? Do you need to sit?"

"No, I'm—" Donovan grunted in pain as his knees collided with the concrete sidewalk.

Amarantha grabbed for him. "Donovan!"

He was hunching over like an ailing mongrel, clutching at his flanks and breathing asthmatically. The roses fell to the ground as Amarantha crouched beside him and pinned his arms to his sides, halting his attempts to tear out his kidneys.

"Somebody help me!" her voice cracked.

A rattling sigh sounded from her lover's throat as a thick stream of blood spilled from his nose and crafted a macabre pattern around the flowers. His face was distorted in abject agony.

"Oh, Goddess!" she pleaded, holding Donovan tighter. *All mine.*

And that's when she felt it: Laine's unmistakable psychic touch. Shock and recognition threw Amarantha backward, upsetting the pigeons and sending the flock swirling around them in a frenzy. Filthy quills rained upon Donovan's shoulders like an angel's ruptured wings.

She wept, too terrified of Laine's eventide caress to help her suffering love.

For the first time, Amarantha feared her mentor.

* * *

"A silver chalice filled with pain; a simple cant and all was drained, 'til emptiness alone remained."

The last swallow of potion warmed Laine's throat and gut as it slid and settled. He smiled darkly as he set the spent Irish coffee glass in the sink and considered the ball of tissue in his fist. There was no further trace of the nosebleed he had suffered, nor of the intestinal distress he had endured. Just the tepid mix of peppermint, lavender, and honey calming his stomach. Even the spear had subsided. "Lesson learned; class dismissed."

"So you say Donovan attacked you, huh?" Diana was sitting at one of the serving tables, fraying the Gummy Bear wrapper into cellophane tassels. "What, did he cast a 'spell'?"

Laine nodded. "Indeed."

"And he did it because he wants Amy's power for himself?"

"Indeed." He dropped the balled-up tissue into the kitchen garbage pail. "He's what we call a psychic vampire. He feeds on the energies of others, and Amarantha has a lot to feed on. I'm the only thing in his way."

"Vampire, huh?" Diana tossed her Gummy Bear streamers at Laine in a feeble attempt at levity. He locked onto her with a withering gaze, but Diana just smirked. "Well, how did he do it? I mean, isn't he supposed to have some of your hair or a fingernail or something?"

Bothersome girl. "Usually, yes, but once we're skilled enough, we can draw links to people on sight. We don't need hair or photographs to establish connections. All we need is a steady gaze and a firm handshake. That usually does the trick."

Laine looked at his right hand: the hand rendered impotent by conscience and doubt. True, he had hit his mark, but he had displayed mercy too. Donovan had not felt Laine's full fury. Would it be enough?

"How do you know it wasn't just a flu bug?"

Laine sighed. "Bother, Diana . . . ."

"No, really, it could've just broke while you were in the bathroom."

"I know the difference."

"How? How can you tell?"

"What flu passes so quickly?" Again, Diana ignored the gaze he threw at her.

"Look, I'm sorry, but it sounds like a big mind-fuck to me. Maybe this shit happens because you guys psych yourselves out to make it happen. I mean, where's your proof?"

Laine snatched up the garbage pail, shaking it as he roared. "You want something you can touch?! You want something to defy your comfortable ignorance?! Here!" He charged toward Diana and slammed the pail on the floor between them. Blood-soaked tissue wads popped out over the rim and fell like grisly snowballs onto the polished floor. "Here's your proof, then," he hissed, "Sleep well."

Diana barely glanced at the litter. The fury in Laine's eyes had apparently muted her. Neither of them moved nor spoke, and the very air around them rumbled with silence. He breached the stillness by retrieving the scattered garbage and returning it to the can. Once done, Laine regarded his friend gently. "I'm sorry, Diana. I didn't mean to scare you."

"You didn't," she lied. "I've just never seen you go ape-shit before."

"Trust me, you haven't seen ape-shit. You don't want to."

"So what are you—"

The inevitable phone ring.

Laine shoved the garbage pail back beneath the sink, then turned to the off-white phone. A deep breath—two more rings worth—then he lifted the receiver. "Russian Hill 'O Beans: Laine speaking . . . ."

Dead air.

"Hello?"

Pause. "You promised, Laine. You swore." Amarantha's thin voice came from somewhere bleak and distant.

"What did I promise, Amarantha? What did I swear?"

"Don't do this!" Her voice pitched into near-hysteria. "You swore you wouldn't hurt him—"

". . . Unless he hurt me first. Donovan started this, not I."

"I was with him, Laine," she asserted. "Your name was on his lips; your presence was all over him! I heard your voice!"

"I followed my pain to its source, and there he was."

"I can't believe it," she said, slipping away again. "How could you do that? How?"

"Amy, listen to me: have I ever lied or broken an oath to you before?"

Amarantha's long silence was awful. To the best of his knowledge, Laine had never led her trust astray. Why was the answer absent from her lips?

"No," the reply came in sobs. "No, you've never lied to me. Before." The connection broke.

"She's gone?" Diana asked.

Laine nodded. He cradled the receiver, then buried his face in the crook of his elbow. Why? Why was it all slipping away?

The abused door chime announced Heather's entrance. Her pride at not slamming into the table washed over Laine in waves. "Cool. Hey, Laine, I just saw this little Black kid with a Darth Vader costume down the block." A Headlines shopping bag rattled in her hand. "You got any old pictures of yourself, 'cause—what's wrong? What's going down?"

Laine peered into the expectant eyes of his only ally in this conflict. He didn't need to utter a single word. She knew what was coming, but he spoke the obvious anyway.

"It has begun."

*　　*　　*

Everything had changed.

Where once he would have known his foe's intentions, Laine was blind. It was an ancient ploy, to be sure: to get one's opponent to act rashly and strike in a most untimely and unseemly fashion. Laine had attacked Donovan in Amarantha's full sight, and that was all she saw. He was losing ground; he was losing his pupil; he was losing faith.

Laine Douglas's soles crunched on playground sand as he topped the southern steps of Alta Plaza Park. The steps themselves were historical, having been damaged in a famous car chase in *What's Up, Doc?*, but that wasn't its draw for Laine. A lifetime ago, it seemed, the Pacific Heights park was a source of recreation for him and the rest of the students of Rooftop Alternative School. Many a lunch hour was enjoyed there with his pre-adolescent peers; many a fond memory was forged. It was those ghosts that anchored his despondent soul to this place.

Even in those early years, Laine sensed that there was more to the world than what was taught or seen or sermonized. There were possibilities beyond this veil of sensation; a truth to the myths that were written of, but what? And why those old feelings of alienation? Why had his blood told him he inhabited a world in which he didn't belong? What was more than this?

Rooftop had dropped the hint. It was the mid-70s, and the paranormal was almost mainstream. Transcendental Meditation, Bigfoot, the Bermuda Triangle, ESP, UFOs, and all the world's unusual phenomena were popular fodder, and Rooftop was an open-minded school.

The year they introduced psychic studies to the curriculum was exciting, to say the least. Laine's fellow students constructed peg boxes, colored cubes, and drawings of waves on index cards in preparation for the battery of tests. Laine tried them all: he dropped marbles down the peg-boards, attempting to predict which slot they'd settle in; tried gleaning which color of the cube was facing up in the enclosed box; struggled to skry the waves or the triangles or the squares from the index cards his peers were holding.

Laine failed at almost every exercise and proved no better than average. Some of his classmates' results were astounding, but despite his own intellectual prowess, Laine's abilities were quite mundane. He possessed the Magickal will but lacked technique. There were only two exceptions.

The first was during a breathing exercise where they were told to visualize a warm liquid slowly filling their bodies to relax them. Once filled and utterly relaxed, they were instructed to see themselves at the bottom of a flight of stairs. Counting the steps as they ascended, Laine and his classmates exited through a door at the top into whatever destination they liked.

Laine visited his cousin's new South San Francisco home. He hadn't been there yet, but he would see it that weekend. When Laine did in fact visit his cousin, the house was identical to his vision. Laine's first astral journey.

The second success was in the school's auditorium. Rooftop was literally on the roof of Pacific Heights School, and its entire staff and students fit quite comfortably in the hall. On the stage was a large mason jar containing a purple marble. All were instructed to close their eyes and see the marble move with their minds. Within three minutes, all in attendance heard the clinking of the marble as it threw itself against the inside of the jar.

Laine's first proof of "reality's" plasticity had only stoked his appetite for a proper teacher. More lessons would come, but not for years and not from any earthly agent. Not until adolescence had pushed Laine to the point of desperation. Ever since then, though, Laine had easily walked the hidden trails that few traveled; understood the truths that few knew existed; became what few believed in. He had rent the veil. He had "created change in accordance to one's will."

But now, being a mage wasn't enough. It wasn't enough to save Amarantha or thwart Donovan. It wasn't saving his relationship with Marisa, nor was it easing his indelible dread. So what was he supposed to do? What was he missing?

Laine looked up at the silhouettes of the transplanted trees, their gnarly fingers interwoven into a clumsy handshake. Wrens flew like black fléchettes about the towering flora, screeching their evensong. He had heard once that the cants of birds were ever-changing, ever-varied, ever free. Laine doubted that. Right now, to his ears and heart, their dirge sounded as fated as his life.

*   *   *

Amarantha Powell lit her white tapers and ignited her White Lace incense with ease. Perhaps it was because of Donovan's slumbering presence in her room, perhaps not, but all was calm and quiet and as it should be.

Except for her unease. Amarantha sipped her cooling cup of Red Zinger tea with false ginger as she watched her love dreaming on the bed before her. The sleep of the innocent?

No, it couldn't be true. Laine must have lied or at least been mistaken. Donovan had been entirely oblivious to Laine's claim of an attack, perhaps even incapable of such foulness. Laine was far too powerful to have been stricken the same way Donovan had been earlier. He would have never let his protections lapse enough for such a hex to affect him. It simply wasn't Laine's way.

Then again, Laine had freely admitted to having assaulted Donovan using an old turn-back spell all of their kith and kin learned early on. And yes, it was true that Laine had never betrayed her confidence before, but was he the same man she had pledged her alliance to; whom she had entrusted to watch over her? Had his hatred of Donovan twisted his ethics so far that he'd defy the Rede?

Amarantha knew Donovan would eventually ask about her suspicions, and she would have to answer him earnestly. All she had was Laine's admission and roughly a week's time with which to balance the scales. She disentangled her mind, then emptied her coffee mug, wishing that teabag dregs were skryable.

Goddess, everything was changing.

Terra fidgeted for comfort in the open vanity drawer next to Amarantha's shin. She grasped the scruff of the cat's neck, intending to place her familiar on her lap, when a shard of cold metal snagged on the friendship bracelet Heather had given her a year earlier. Amarantha secured the cat and then examined the object clinging to Heather's token.

A bemused smile of recognition tugged at Amarantha's lips as the jagged remains of a brass cross dangled before her. She carefully pulled the pendant from her bracelet as she slid the drawer closed with a foot.

She'd almost forgotten that she had the thing. It was just the upper half of a barbed and broken cross, its lower piece obviously still buried in her drawer. As struck as Amarantha was when she had first laid eyes on it, its costume-jewelry origins were quite obvious to her now. The piece was of little value to anyone except herself. Funny how so little a thing like a cheap crucifix could prove so pivotal to her life.

They were twelve-year olds: Amarantha, Heather, and Saffron. The trio was quite close in those days, and Wicca was as regular a part of their friendship as sleepovers and gossip. It was during one of those slumber parties that Saffron unearthed her older sister's Ouija board.

That night, the wind howled through the chimes outside Saffron's window, creating a clamor more frightening than Jacob Marley's chains. Each girl had a different colored candle before them: Amarantha's was white, Heather's was silver, and Saffron's was black. Saffron made up a chant that was more silly than scary, then the three girls placed their fingertips on the plastic pointer. They left it up to Amarantha to ask the spirits a question, so she did: would they be friends forever?

After a brief wait, the pointer moved, not to the words "yes" or "no", but toward the alphabet beneath them. The window revealed the letters T . . . R . . . E . . . E and stopped.

Tree? That's all it had said. The three girls began their round of accusations and denials, each one blaming the others for pushing the planchette across the board until they finally agreed that the message was too strange to be fake, so instead, they tried to figure out what the spirits wanted. That was when Heather hit upon the solution.

On nearby Ocean Beach, there was a creepy old tree they used to call "the crying tree" because it always looked so sad with its bare boughs and weary posture. Saffron insisted that they go see the tree, tonight, right now, and so with nothing on but sandals, nightgowns, and long coats, the girls ventured out across The Great Highway to Ocean Beach in search of "the crying tree".

Amarantha was sand-blasted but enthralled. She could barely make out Heather's windswept form trudging ahead like a clumsy Cimmerian warrior against the slate and onyx sky before her. Saffron was keeping pace with Amarantha, sniffling and gritting her teeth, her copper hair laden with ocean mist. They began cresting the dune that Heather had already vanished over, and upon reaching the top, they stopped for a breather.

That's when they heard Heather scream. Twice.

Amarantha and Saffron dashed down the side of the

dune so swiftly, they almost fell. As they closed in on the crying tree, Amarantha could see a middle-aged man scurrying away from prone Heather's position. She was screaming wildly and shuffling away from the tree on her butt. Amarantha got to Heather first and tried to calm her friend down while Saffron ran after the gangly stranger. Heather's foot had a bloody gash, but she seemed otherwise unharmed. That didn't stop her screaming though. Heather was hysterical, swearing that they were all "going to Hell."

Saffron returned to tell them that the guy was some brain-fried old hippie, and he had probably been more afraid of Heather than the other way around. Once she saw Heather's injury, she and Amarantha acted as crutches for their friend till they made it back home and bandaged her wound.

That following morning, Amarantha awakened and headed to the bathroom only to find Saffron already there. Her back was turned to Amarantha, but it was clear that she was staring at something with great intensity. Amarantha's greeting startled Saffron, and the teen spun around, concealing something behind her back. Knowing she was caught, Saffron displayed the item that so captured her attention: a large, Gothic cross crafted to be worn inverted. She said she had found it when she went after the hippie the night before but didn't mention it because, well, it was meant for her. Amarantha asked to see the pendant, assuring Saffron that she had no intention of keeping it. Saffron placed the cross on Amarantha's open palm.

It immediately broke cleanly in half with a metallic *ping*.

Saffron was incensed, accusing Amarantha of breaking it on purpose. Amarantha shrugged as she denied it, which only made Saffron angrier; so angry that she threw the second half of the cross down at Amarantha's feet.

She's had the stupid thing ever since.

That had been the beginning of the end of her friendship with Saffron. Over time, it became clear that they had differing ideas on how The Art should be used, so they parted company. Saffron had followed a path of cruelty and self-destruction while Amarantha walked the nobler lanes of Magick.

But that's how it was sometimes, wasn't it? Some friends you kept with you forever while others faded away into the fog of memory. Amarantha had always believed that Laine would be one of the former. Now, she wasn't so sure.

* * *

It took five finger-pricks of the sewing needle to finally make Heather Dominguez wince. She gently sucked her injury, the sound echoing through her quiet, chilly room. Breaking out her old Singer would be easier and faster, but something as Magickally important as this ritual chemise should be done by hand. How else could she imprint it with the proper energies?

Who was she bullshitting? She was way too distracted and negative to do that anyway, especially with her monthly in full effect. Thank The Goddess that was almost over.

Heather set aside the project and rubbed her sore back. Two hours of sitting cross-legged proved to be a bigger bitch than she expected, even on a bed. She put her feet on the floor and stretched the aches away.

It has begun. That's what Laine had said, and now Heather was in the middle of a witch war. As much as she was starting to believe in her abilities, the very idea scared her shitless. Donovan had hexed Laine. *Laine!* He was the only thing standing between Heather and Vampire Boy, and he was attacked. If Laine fell, she didn't have a chance against Donovan and Amy if the two of them figured out what she was up to. Hopefully, Laine had some secret plan in mind to deal with all this.

Sometimes you had to do questionable things for the greater good: yeah, no shit.

The world seemed haunted-house quiet; *Friday the*

pale shadows

Thirteenth quiet. She had lit the fat, musk-scented votives on her altar earlier along with some Nag Champa incense, but their warmth and tranquility were lost on Heather.

The sound of breaking glass and laughter shot through Heather's bedroom window. She jumped and gasped. She hadn't felt this afraid since the bad old days when she first played with Magick.

A second shattering of glass drew Heather to her window. Two homeboys were on the street below pulling long fluorescent bulbs from a skinny cardboard box. One of the pair hooted while the other made like a ninja and smashed the spent fixture against a concrete wall.

A single blink of her eyes sent a teardrop rolling down Heather's cheek. She hadn't realized that she'd been crying. Wiping away the tear with a bare forearm, Heather sighed as she lay back down on her bed. She stared at the atlas of peeled paint on her ceiling, her mind drifting fitfully.

Another bulb shattered, and Heather felt it then: the liquor-sodden body crushing her lungs; her wrists struggling against the sofa cushions; the hot, putrid gasps against her young breasts. Goddess, her pelvis: the agony was endless.

Fearfully, she looked up at Rudy's father's flushed grimace as he shushed her softly, bucked violently. Her wrist slipped loose from his vise-like grip, snapping painlessly into the empty water glass on the coffee table. It fell to the floor in slow-motion, disintegrating into shards of blood-red light. It was the only sound she heard.

Heather was gritting her teeth against the sting of her rug burned back as her mother's boyfriend spent himself on her, his final thrust being the angriest. He pushed himself off of her, smiling with satisfaction while tears of hurt and vulnerability trailed into her ears and pooled on the coarse, plaid fabric of the sofa cover. She was drawing shallow, spasmodic breaths as she caressed her raw wrists and pulled herself into a fetal position. Light burst into the room; a fist was clenching a hammer high.

"No! Not again! Not anymore!" Heather opened her

eyes to the molten silhouette of her trembling fist haloed against the streetlamps outside. Suddenly, the trauma and fear that had haunted her for years were gone. *She* had the control. *She* had the power to make it all stop. Heather was the survivor.

Mama had told Heather many times that she was stronger than she thought; that all she needed to do was to trust that strength. For the first time in her life, she knew it to be true. If Heather could contain the memories that had hurt her for so long, then maybe—just maybe—they could handle Donovan too. Heather smiled weakly.

Yeah, everything was going to change.

pale shadows

FRIDAY, OCTOBER 31ST

SAMHAIN

A sackcloth firmament riddled with brilliant moth-holes: this will be the Samhain sky.

The moon—now at full girth in the deepening dusk—was playing a game of Hide-and-Go-Seek with Amarantha, ducking behind the immaculate Russian Hill homes. Luna's golden-harvest face would be fully visible in a couple of hours, and Amarantha was buzzing with anticipation.

Storefront lighting hopscotched the sidewalk Donovan and she traveled on as they drew nearer to Russian Hill O' Beans. The entire neighborhood was roused by the energy of the evening. The Italian restaurants were filled to capacity with costumed revelers; the cable cars had become bacchanals on rails; escorted children disguised as Transformers and Smurfs were running wild and loud and swinging bags of sweets. The blessed assurance of youth: an assurance not unlike the kind Amarantha possessed right now.

"Whoa, whoa, Amarantha. What's the hurry?"

Amarantha hadn't noticed how far ahead of Donovan she had walked. Goddess, he was absolutely appetizing in his teal and silver djinni costume. Amarantha nibbled her lower lip.

"I'm sorry, Donovan," she apologized, closing the space between them. "I just want to get this done before the moon rides high. We have much to do before Her eyes." She took his hand with silent urgency to quicken his pace. "Besides, I need to walk off that huge lunch."

"Hmm."

Once at the café's threshold, she announced, "Here we are," then turned to Donovan and caught his gaze.

He nodded. "I understand. I'll stay in the background."

"Thank you. For everything."

Donovan's grin sparkled in the night. "No one wants a fight on a night like tonight, not even Laine, I'll bet. And besides . . . ," he kissed her with rose-petal soft lips, ". . . not even he can stop us."

Amarantha blushed and opened the café door. The high-ceilinged store was packed with customers and friends and adorned with cliché Halloween trappings. Black and orange crepe streamers twisted in tandem with creeper vines. Regulars were sipping cappuccinos as their GI Joe and Care Bear children snuck chocolate bars from the plastic Jack O' Lantern at the counter. "Bela Lugosi's Dead" was drifting just above the din of clinking cups and brazen laughter.

The shop's population astonished Donovan. "Jeez, is it always this crowded?"

"No, not always, but pretty close at times, Laine says." Amarantha tiptoed up to Donovan's ear. "A few of them are probably 'like us'. Friends of Laine. There he is."

Laine was standing behind the counter with Heather, scanning a newspaper while admonishing a child who had taken one too many butterscotch discs. Across from them was a Latin girl with bleached-orange hair whom

Amarantha took to be Diana.

Amarantha closed her eyes and felt for the swirls of pale astral haze that told her the shield was ready. She didn't want to think that Laine would make it necessary, but better to be safe. She opened her eyes again and stepped up to the threesome.

"Hi, Amy," Heather greeted, chewing a chunk of bubble gum and clad in an aquamarine business suit that set her eyes aglow. "Wow, your costume came out great!"

Amarantha smiled and smoothed out her sylvan garb. "Thank you, Heather. I'm supposed to be Morgan LeFay from *The Mists of Avalon*. It was a rush job, but it came out okay."

"Oh man, I *love* that book," Heather oozed.

"I told you you would." Amarantha shifted her focus. "Hello, Laine."

He looked up from his paper with a gun-turret glance. "Ah, Amarantha. I didn't see you come in. Happy Samhain." His demeanor was like broken glass, sharp and perilous.

An easy skry showed that he too had wards up, though they were far darker and denser than her own. Shadows were moving across him like smoke from a burning pot, seeping from his right arm and smothering half of Laine's body.

Suddenly, Amarantha's self-assurance faltered. "I—we just arrived."

"'We?'" Laine stared left at Donovan, who was standing at the display racks, sniffing the contents of a Mason jar. "Ah yes, 'we'. Of course." He smiled mischievously as he adjusted his glasses with *that* appalling finger.

"So where's Marisa? Is she staying home tonight?"

"Oh, hey," he snapped, "Check out who's in the paper." Look at that: she struck a nerve.

Laine flipped *The Chronicle* around for Amarantha and displayed the page-long interview with Anton LaVey, complete with a photo of the bald-pated Satanist.

"Hmm."

"Interesting article," Laine continued, "He totally debunks the whole 'Satanic panic'. Told them that Satan worshipers aren't Satanists, Satanists are anti-Christians. Different things. He even says at the beginning of the article that he doesn't even believe in Satan. See? Procter and Gamble changed their logo for nothing."

Amarantha smiled at Heather. "Boy, this must bring back some memories, huh?"

Heather popped a big, pink bubble. "Yeah, but my interview was better." An uneasy smile curled her lips. Something was stirring behind her eyes too.

Letting it go, Amarantha said, "Laine, we need to talk about tonight."

"Hm, Zsusana Budapest is holding a ceremony at The Woman's Building," Laine reported. "We should look into that."

"Who's that?" Diana asked, munching on some Sour Tarts.

"She's an activist for female empowerment through Wicca," Heather explained. "I haven't met her, but my mom's done some workshops with her."

"She's written a few books on the subject as well," Laine added. "Wow, I really want to check that out."

"Well, maybe we can go later," Amarantha interrupted, "the four of us, but Laine, we need to talk."

Laine glanced up at her. "What? Oh yeah, just let—"

"Can I try this?"

Now what? All eyes turned to Donovan, who was holding a Mason jar labeled *Guatemalan Antigua*. Amarantha shook her head.

Donovan whispered, "Sorry," but Laine heard him anyway.

"Don't be. That's what they're there for. However . . . ." Laine produced a lapis-blue jar from beneath the counter, displaying it like an unearthed treasure. "I think what you really want to try is this:" He popped the lid. "Jamaican Blue Mountain. Forty bucks a pound. Smoooth."

"Yeah," Donovan enthused boyishly.

"Yeah? Okay, just don't tell my boss. Diana, could you make him a Melior of 'JBM' please?"

Diana huffed. "Well, why can't you just—"

"By the way, you have customers." Laine waved at the sinewy redhead standing behind Amarantha. "Hi, Claire. Nice Bo Peep costume."

"All right, all right. As if I didn't have enough to do, pain in the ass . . . ." Diana grabbed the jar and cocked her head toward Donovan. He followed her apologetically into the thinning crowd.

Laine smirked. "I love that girl." He turned his attention to Heather. "Can you tell Mohammed I'll go over the invoices with him in a minute?"

Heather's eyes darted back and forth between Amarantha and Laine. "Um, okay, I'll see you in back. I'll see you later Amy."

"We'll catch up with you later. Don't work too hard."

Heather gave a slow, suspecting nod, then headed for the office.

Laine asked, "So now that there's no one here but us witches, what do you wish to discuss? You are ready for tonight, aren't you? You've had more—"

Making certain that the three remaining customers were preoccupied, Amarantha spoke to Laine with her dreaming voice, "I have made a decision regarding tonight, milord: as much as I know it will pain you, I shall not be performing the vespertine rite with you. I'm doing one with Donovan instead."

Laine removed his glasses, folded its arms unto itself, and gently set them on the shelf behind him, out of harm's way. "What?"

"I am performing a ritual with Donovan tonight."

His eyes narrowed. "'As much as you know it pains me,' hmm? Interesting choice of words, Befana."

"Milord, I thought about what you said a moon ago: I'm going to take that ride, the same as you have with Marisa."

The scowl Amarantha expected to see—even wanted to

see—never came. Instead, a slow, cagey smile spread across her mentor's face. She was at a loss. Why wasn't he upset?

"As is your will, Befana, so mote it be."

Amarantha saved face. "You're not angry?"

"Angry?" he said, eyes wide. "Sweet Befana, know you not that I could never be angry with you? You are my pride. I am incapable of such animosity toward you. Disappointed perhaps, but—"

"Not angry?"

"No." There was a sweet sincerity in his whispers; a sincerity that supplanted her certainty with dread. What did he hide? What did he know?

"Well, milord, I am pleased," Amarantha forced out.

"There is still the matter of my disappointment, however," he said with gravity. "I have invested much expense and time toward the materials and energies necessary for your Wiccaning, and you know how much I hate wasting rituals." Retrieving his glasses, he asked, "What will become of all that now?"

An obvious yet inspired consequence dawned on her. Amarantha smiled confidently as she took her elder's cold right hand and said, "Milord, those things need not be wasted."

Laine cocked a brow.

* * *

". . . Sen we branch out; have Russian Hill O' Beans all over America. You know we ze only cafe in ze seetee sat grinds each cub of coffee?"

"Yes, I do," Heather mumbled, her hands propping up her head.

Mohammed tugged the bottom of his tan V-neck sweater over his paunch. "Efter eet catch on, sen we go eenteruhnational. You know, I shevved one morning, and got idea for eh new slogan:" he said with a thick, Arabic slur. "'Russian Heal Coffee Around Ze World!' What you sink?"

"I . . . I don't get it."

"You know, like rushing coffee around ze world, exceb Russian *Heal* coffee around ze world. You see?"

Right. Heather nodded absently. "Okay, now I get it," she mumbled.

This wasn't fair. Heather was supposed to be one of them now; supposed to be out there with Laine and Amy. She thought Laine trusted her, but he had just shooed her away like she was an annoying brat. Now she had to sit at the kiddies' table and listen to laughing boy's spiel? It wasn't fair.

The plump little entrepreneur gave a gap-toothed grin as he tapped out a beat on the other desktop with his stubby fingers. "Now, once ze wearhouse ease feeneeshed, we move ze offeece ser and use sees room excu . . . excli . . . how you seh?"

"'Exclusively?'" Heather mumbled.

"'Exuhcluseeve'. Sank you. Exuhcluseeve for backing. Ah, I can't wet." Mohammed was so happy, he was practically dancing. "Oh man, now I go to restuhroom." Oh, that's why he was dancing.

"Yeah, tea can do that to you." Heather nodded at the four glass tea bulbs sitting next to her boss's arm.

Mohammed's chair creaked painfully as he rose and ambled for the bathroom. "I'll be beck," he assured her cheerfully in a cheesy imitation of Schwarzenegger.

"I live for the moment," Heather mumbled.

What a dork. Nice guy, but a dork. Like right now: whenever Heather was in the office and he had to take a leak, he always started whistling loudly. Like Heather was even trying to hear him piss. Dork. She thought Egyptians were supposed to be cooler than that.

As Heather packed her things for the day, Laine swaggered into the office, followed by Depeche Mode's "Flies on The Windscreen" and the clamor of a dozen mugs.

Heather jumped out of her chair. "What the fuck was

that all about?" she hissed. "I thought we were doing this together?"

"What are you talking about?"

"How you just kicked me out like that. I should've been there."

"Why?"

"Because . . . ." Damn, she couldn't think of one good reason why.

"Remember, Heather, you are best kept unseen and unnoticed for now. You had no place in that conversation." He closed the oak doors and Samhain sounds behind him. "But you do have a place in this one. Please, sit." Heather obeyed. "Where's Mohammed?"

"Whistling Dixie on the can."

"Good. With all the tea he drinks, you'd think it was Ramadan." Laine sat in Mohammed's seat. "Now listen: there's been a change in plans."

"What kind of change?"

"Amarantha has decided not to perform our Wiccaning tonight. She's performing a ceremony with Donovan instead."

Heather's jaw fell open. "Holy shit. We gotta stop them!"

"No, we don't." What the fuck was he smiling about?

"What do you mean 'no we don't'? If we don't stop this now, it's game over!"

"Heather, please . . . ." Laine pointed her back into her seat, then leaned in close. "Believe me, I am quite thirsty for that bastard's blood." He leaned back and threw up his hands. "But as I've said before, I'm her mentor, not her master. Besides, tonight's not the night."

Heather sighed. "I don't get it."

"Heather, what would've happened as a result of Amarantha's consecration?"

Great, another riddle. "She'd be a solo practitioner, but I still don't get it."

"Yes, you do, Heather," he said, using the guiding voice she'd heard so often. "Just follow it through. What would be the result?"

She emptied her mind; grounded herself. "Well, she'd probably side with Donovan, and you wouldn't be able to touch him then. Not unless she asked you to, which she wouldn't."

"And . . . ?"

"You'd have to take them both on."

"Exactly. Amarantha still has a karmic bond to me, and as long as she remains my pupil, I can strike on her behalf. I have no interest in fighting both of them, and this hasty decision works to our advantage. Besides, this also gives you more training time."

"Okay. So any more 'good' news?" The toilet flushed.

"As a matter of fact, there is. Amarantha made an intriguing suggestion: one that may answer our needs. That is if you're up to it."

If she was up to it? That didn't sound good. "What exactly did she suggest?"

Even Laine jumped when Mohammed opened the bathroom door, still whistling. He stepped out of sight again to wash his hands at the utility basin.

Laine leaned in close again. "Since I went through the trouble and expense of putting together her ritual, Amarantha suggested I perform it for someone else."

Heather smiled. "So you want me to help you do a ritual for Marisa?"

Laine's face fell. "No. No, she suggested you."

Pow! "Me? But I'm not a—"

"You're ready enough, and I can easily alter the rite. You'll just need to bring me some personal favors or tokens, that sort of thing."

Heather never imagined this moment would come. "Wow. Okay, like what?"

"Hair; jewelry; bubble gum; anything you have a strong link with."

Heather was mirroring his grin. "I just finished my ceremonial shift—"

"Bring it. What time is good for you?"

"Uh, is 9:00 okay?"

"That should be perfect. The moon will just be coming in through my window." Laine pulled two noisy items from his apron pocket and handed Heather a slip of paper. "This is my address and your ritual notes," he explained as Heather examined the digits and flowery paragraphs. "Watch your step though: my neighborhood can get a little rough, especially during a full moon."

Heather slipped the scrap of paper into her nearby book bag. "No problem. I live in The Mission, remember?"

"Of course." Laine handed her the second item: a small bag of Reese's Pieces. "Happy Halloween."

*　*　*

Heather was humming "West End Girls" as the elevator in Laine's apartment building rattled and bumped to the eighth floor. A pleasant ding and the door opened.

Was the building even occupied? The halls were dead silent except for her nervous whistling and wary footfalls. She looked out the row of windows to her right, staring down into an open courtyard. The patchwork of peach and gray paint was almost black because of the shadows, and it was like the entire place sat inside of the night's belly. Man, did the heebie-jeebies set in.

Apartment 807: the door was propped open by its bolt. She shoved the heavy barrier open wider and stepped into the pitch dwelling.

"Laine?" Her voice bounced in the silence as she stepped into the short passageway. The only response was the door slamming shut behind her, just like in the horror movies. "Hey, Laine, it's me. I brought those tokens you wanted."

Laine's muffled voice asked, "Heather?"

She followed the sound coming from the hall on her right. "Yeah?"

A door on her left cracked open. "Could you wait in the living room? I have a couple more things to do." She couldn't see Laine.

"Sure. No problem. Are you okay?"

"I'm fine. I'm just banishing. Wait in the living room." Laine pointed Heather toward the other end of the hall, then slammed his door shut.

"Okay, *now* I'm scared," she grumbled.

Heather removed her duffle bag and heavy long coat as she crept to the living room, and once there, turned on a table lamp and took in her surroundings: a flower-embossed couch; a glass coffee table; two love seats, and, ooh, a big color TV with cable!

"'I want my MTV.'" She kicked back on the plastic-covered sofa, zapped on the set, and helped herself to a Pippin apple from the fruit bowl in front of her.

Elvira, Mistress of the Dark was on MTV—cleavage and all—hosting a Halloween special from Salem. Heather laughed. She would've dressed as Elvira this year, but figured forget it, she didn't want the male hassle. Besides, that costume had sold out fast, and Heather barely had time to finish sewing her hooded shift, much less a black satin dress.

After about fifteen minutes, Heather surfed past a scrambled soft-core channel, CNN, a Max Headroom/Coca Cola ad, and a full-contact karate match on ESPN. Bored, she shut the TV off and returned to the remains of her apple.

Two muddled voices were coming from Laine's room, one his and one not. Whom or what was he talking to?

Heather left her bag and coat on the couch, adjusted her shift, and headed slowly down the hall to see if she could understand the conversation. Nope, the voices were too garbled, and the mottled walls were too thick.

Suddenly, the door popped open, scaring the shit out of her. Busted! Someone angry and unseen shoved past Heather, nearly knocking her on her ass.

"Hey, what's your fucking—"

"You say you brought the tokens?" Laine's spindly arm poked out of his doorway again, palm up. He sure as hell hadn't pushed her. He hadn't even left his room. Whatever that thing was, it was gone in the shadows.

"Um, yeah," she stammered. Heather placed the ball of Kleenex in Laine's hand before it snapped back into the room. "There's some of my hair and my class pendant."

"Thank you," he half-whispered. "You can come in now."

"Uh, okay." Pulling her linen cowl onto her head, Heather stepped into the room, her eyes kept low. Before she could even cross the threshold right, Laine's voice ordered, "Look at me." Heather obeyed.

Goddess! She was blind!

*   *   *

Amarantha lit the final candle, keeping the darkness at bay. Rising at the living room's northern quarter, she blew out the fireplace match with a silent puff, and then went back to the center of the circle of ice-blue incense dust.

Each of the tapers around her marked a cardinal point on the nine-foot-diameter blue ring, symbolizing the balance of the elements. Moon Goddess fumes were thickening the air like London fog, providing a physical curtain that separated the moonlit world outside from the hallowed place. The hardwood floor was warm and smooth beneath her bare feet, and her ears were soothed by the brassy bellow of French horns heralding through the smokescreened walls.

Amarantha closed her brown eyes and clasped her hands together into a steeple of contemplation, her index fingers pressing against the bottom of her chin. The image of the room resolved behind her eyes, acting as a conduit for her will. With each turn of her breath, the astral counterpart of the sacred space increased in tangibility and brilliance until the veil between inner and outer worlds was no more.

And then she saw herself: clad in a white, Dianic tunic that was trussed snug against her young form by ivy-green silk cords. Her immaculately painted face was made all the more transcendent through grounding and glamour; her ceremonial wand stance was erect with great purpose.

The second-hand stopped; the heartbeat paused; the hummingbird froze. No past, no future. Only the still, interminable river of the Now existed within the blue ring.

It was all she needed.

The burnt-orange clouds solidifying before her described a head; a torso; a presence. Amarantha opened her eyes.

A crimson and gold robe draped from Donovan's broad shoulders, its embroidery so intricate that it baffled the eyes and maddened the senses. His face was concealed behind a fine, bearded Venetian mask of autumn hues, and his piercing blue eyes cut through the smoke like a lighthouse beacon. He was The Stag King. He was The Oak God.

He curtsied before Amarantha, extending his billowing sleeves out from his side and locking into the stance. Amarantha smiled her approval.

She closed her eyes again and assumed the Tau stance, arms raised outwards. With a thought, she ignited the pale blue ring with empyreal fire, closing the breach that had allowed her consort access.

"I, Befana Delafey, do beseech The Great Pantheon to bear witness and bless this vespertine rite. I, who have faithfully followed your wisdom, do ask a boon of thee: that Athena's touch should alight this handfasting."

Befana looked upon The Woodsman in The Mist. It was time The Maiden became The Mother; The Girl became The Woman.

"*Athené aigis athanaton.*" Befana pushed away the amber smoke with a gentle flourish, dissipating it into a dome of sapphire clouds that rippled like swift brook water. The artic-blue ring around them flared into an electric equator. The two witches were standing in the center of a pristine bubble of infinite possibility.

"By my right as a daughter of Athena and a Maiden of The Sacred Hunt, I do proclaim this place consecrated in

The Great Pantheon's name." Befana considered the genuflect man before her. "Milord, you have my leave to rise."

"Mistress." The Stag King rose and moved closer on ghostly feet, stopping just short of the brazier and chalice between them.

"I, Ranger Deorcloven, defer to The Lady's gracious manner and great wisdom. I, who have labored well and danced finely, learned secrets great and knowledge grave, do come with a penitent mind to fasten with thee if it pleases The Mistress."

"Indeed it does." Befana knelt to retrieve the ornate silver chalice before her. The consecrated dragon-stemmed cup hummed between her fingertips, and the Cabernet's dark surface hinted at the fire in her eyes.

She stood and centered. "This chalice, hewn by artisans and blessed in ceremony, is the vessel through which this handfasting shall be made truth. I beg thee, good Ranger, grant me my boon and drink of its sacred depths."

Deorcloven accepted the proffered chalice, but did not drink. His gaze slid earthward. "Know well, Mistress, that I offer no slight, but I question the value of my commerce. To have borne witness to your power's grandeur is to question my worthiness." Deorcloven's body joined his stare as he slipped back into supplication. "I am lacking."

Befana smiled and raised Deorcloven's sight by his chin. "You are not lacking in my eyes, Sir Ranger, nor in Athena's."

Befana retrieved a small, plasma-filled vial from her left hip. "Blood of my blood, good sir," she announced, offering Deorcloven the crimson tender. "I could offer no less to a man of your mantle."

Deorcloven received Befana's hand and gift as he stood to his full height. He didn't confirm the bottle's contents, for they both knew that would be a gross offense. Concealing the dram of blood within his voluminous robe, he said, "And with this gift am I given the right to drink from your depths." Deorcloven removed his persona and drank deeply of the wine. His splendid smile illuminated the room.

Befana confidently tugged loose the slipknot that held her cord in place and pulled it out to its full length. "So then am I bound to you, Ranger Deorcloven, in craft and in love." She tied one end of the cord to her right wrist, coiled a measure of it around the chalice stem, and then tied the other end to The Woodsman's left wrist.

"So mote it be," they spoke in unison.

The French horns melted into violins and cellos as Deorcloven handed the lashed chalice to Befana Delafey.

"And would you now honor my favor, Mistress?" he asked with a fox in his eye.

Befana smiled as she considered the wine. "Mayhaps, but like seeks like: what commerce do you grant?"

"As like seeks like, I grant like," Deorcloven returned seraphically. "Blood of my blood; flesh of my flesh; soul of my soul."

He slipped the cord from his wrist—no small feat—then untied the golden sash around his waist. His robe fell to the floor, wafting the indigo smoke. Deorcloven smiled as he refastened the cord around his wrist, standing skyclad before Befana's blinking eyes. She bit her lip at the sight of her Adonis.

His hairless torso was glistening with exotic chrisms and was cut with fine, candlelit muscles. A silver lavaliere that had been turned and tempered into a pentagram laced with bejeweled ivy leaves was hanging from his neck. His sex was haloed by a soft crest of blond hair and poised somewhere between arousal and flaccidity. No, Deorcloven wasn't lacking at all.

"So my love, do you accept my tender?"

Befana's blood was singeing in her veins. A low moan sounded in her throat. Would she indeed? It had all been leading up to this moment: the sweetened air; the anointed flesh; the nervous hunger. All things in nature had a proper time for expression, after all, and that time was upon her.

Befana slipped the cord from her wrist and shrugged out of her tunic, letting the white linen sheets fall to her ankles. She, too, was now nude. Befana slipped her wrist back into the cord as Deorcloven approached her, and with an eager look, she swallowed down the rest of the wine. Dropping the spent chalice so that it hung between them, Befana moaned, "I accept."

The Woodsman bound his right wrist with his ritual sash, wrapped a measure of it around the suspended cup, then bound Befana's left wrist. "Then we are fastened by love, my love."

"So mote it be," they said again in concert. Deorcloven's lips found hers; Befana's tongue found his.

So mote it be.

* * *

"Five are the rules; five are the tools for this Great Art of Making/From ash to pool, from breath to jewel, in this there's no mistaking."

I dry-swallowed as I watched the being before me: a black swirl of almost human-shaped smoke wearing a platinum crown. My astral eyes picked out the small stars on Laine's forehead and throat, and I could see the full, distorted moon through his body.

A cool breeze carried the divine aromas of myrrh, amber, and sage about my head, honing my thoughts like a whetting stone against a sword's edge.

Before me: "The breath of intelligence has embraced you, sweeping away mental penury; filling the sky of thought with the gale of clarity; refreshing the stagnant mind. You are the design and the designer. You are the wind."

A broken comet fell from the coal-black sky, its wake warming my cheek as it passed. Another soon followed a flinch away from my other cheek, and I felt a sense of limitless potential.

From my right: "The fire of will has embraced you, igniting the spark grown dim; innerving the flame gone cold; inspiring the despairing heart. You are the idea and the ideal. You are the flame."

A fine mist enveloped me, clinging to my sweaty skin. Five large drops as cool as Christmas rain fell from the drizzle. They touched my forehead, my right breast, my left shoulder, my right shoulder, and my left breast. Joy stole my breath.

From behind me: "The tides of intuition have embraced you, eroding life's steadfast barriers; linking shore to distant shore; filling the drought-drained heart. You are the artist and the art. You are the storm."

A single, tiny pebble tapped my shoulder, quickly followed by its brother, its sister. A downpour of granules popped and hissed upon me, mingling with the ringing of coins. I felt whole.

From my left: "The resolve of stone has embraced you, providing a resource where none appears; creating context to the mysteries of life; granting signposts to the misplaced wanderer. You are the carpenter and the tool. You are the earth."

Then there was just silence and shadows. I began to wonder if we were finished or if I was expected to say something, but no cue came. Instead, the apparition spread and swirled and ultimately swallowed me with its smoky wings.

"Desire and design, creation and completion: these are the provinces of The Elements. Each vies for dominance over the others. Each claims perfection in its own right. 'Tis not these things alone that make up existence, but the relationships between them. One note is not a song; one word is not a sonnet."

My mentor's voice was circling within and without my head, splitting into multiples and coloring the autumn air. "To whom does the fire answer? To whom does the wind cower? What gave rise to the oceans and forged the mountain towers? Who is your mother's mother, and how does she touch her kin? How do we hear our mother's voice when trapped in this worldly din?"

Here it was: I had to respond to Laine's call and prove

I had rightly earned my place. For an instant, I was afraid of what this smothering creature would do if I answered wrong. It was a very brief instant.

"The five you named are four plus one. The one is zero. Her element is The Spirit, and her tool . . . is silence. It is in silence that we hear her voice the loudest, and it is within her empty hand that we find her full caress. Right?"

Silence. Darkness.

Then the smoke that was my mentor thinned and retreated, his two spectral hands remaining to cradle my face. So warm.

"Cause and consideration, endeavor and effect, and the all-encompassing light that joins them. These are the elements of The Great Art. All know shadow, and all know silence, for there is no voice without quiet; no shadow without light."

I heard the voice from my mentor and my higher self, but where was this light? Why was I still blind?

Hidden lips cradled mine in their softness. I trembled from their touch but found no reason to break the kiss, so I returned it timidly. Leaning deeper into the delicate pressure, I was lost in its sweet rapture.

Then the kiss was gone, just as it was getting interesting. I was confused and stimulated.

Then Novocain-like waves rushed through me, paralyzing my body with a numb fire that kept burning ever brighter. My astral eyes were blinded not by shadow, but by a brilliance so absolute, I couldn't help but to absorb it. I became the light: I became pure spirit, and nothing above or below heaven was hidden from my soul's gaze. I became everything.

I thought I would explode until I heard my mentor's soothing voice ring in my head: From spirit we come, to spirit we go/Upon this earthly river flow/A journey as sour as it is sweet/Betwixt where beginnings and endings meet/This eve hath rounded the river's bend/This ritual is now at its end.

"As is our will, so mote it be." *I made no conscious*

decision to speak the salute with Laine. It came to my lips unbidden and uncoached because it should have.

As my soul's light dimmed and the darkness returned, thin fingers tugged and pulled at the sides of my face until the black cotton blindfold fell from my eyes. I blinked and then—what the—

* * *

A six-foot-three black panther was standing on human legs in front of her, its forehead marked with a silver *ankh*. Heather felt a serious scream coming on, but before it could escape, the panther gestured in peace, then slowly removed its face. Laine smiled easily as he set his ceremonial mask on the bed, the harvest moon over his shoulder showering them in its pale, pearly light.

Heather examined the cramped bedroom, and frankly, she couldn't tell how Laine pulled off the ritual without crashing into something. There was barely room for the surrounding candles, forget about comets.

"Heather?" His voice broke through her disbelief and grounded her in the here and now.

She looked up into Laine's Egyptian-drawn eyes, her lips tingling still. "Shit. I almost peed myself."

"Congratulations," he said, both his smile and his bell earring pealing in the night. "You are now a part of the tribe." He handed her a goblet of wine. "Blessed be."

Heather had no more doubts about herself, Laine, Amarantha, or what must be done. She was now of the kindred: she was now a witch.

"Blessed be." She drank.

* * *

The swells of their robes were soft and luxurious against Befana's back. She was looking up at Deorcloven through half-opened eyes, following his touches with her feverous mind. With fingers as light as a tickle, he drew invisible lines from the crests of her hips to the flat of her belly, and then closer, ever closer, to that unclaimed spot. He was blanketing her breasts with starved kisses, slowing only to circle her roseate nipples with his tongue. Her moans were unstoppable.

And then he touched it. Befana nearly drew blood from her lip.

"Trust in me," he whispered.

"I trust you." Why was he reciting Disney lyrics now?

"I have always been with you. I will always be with you."

"Shh." Befana's sex was aching with hunger, but he wouldn't enter. Goddess, his fingers: she was on fire; she had the chills.

"No one shall come between us," he whispered again, "No man, no mage. I have waited a long time for you, my love."

A finger slipped in. Befana gasped and began grinding against his hand, sliding him deeper inside and clutching his wrist for leverage. Prickly heat burned and itched every nerve in her body.

"You are mine now, Befana Delafey."

Propelled by lust, she clawed at Deorcloven's skin, raising welts on his back. With a certain gaze, she held him fast and hissed, "Then claim me."

Deorcloven entered her. Befana knew she was going mad. Her eyes were useless; her breathing, optional. He was filling her slowly at first, committing himself fully to her depths, then he withdrew for a measure, leaving her body wanting and arching. Over and over again he did this, first in a slow, cantabile rhythm, slowly escalating into a lunatic roundelay.

"You are mine," he stammered, his beautiful face blurring with motion.

"Take me. Come on!" she demanded, bucking ecstatically under him. Deorcloven's teeth clamped onto Befana's neck. His bite was as pleasurable as it was painful. Rigidity seized her as a surge of Kundalini fire began consuming the child she was with its carnal flame. The Woodsman was destroying all her ties, burning all her bridges, and leaving her maidenhood spinning in a cyclone of forgotten ashes.

At last, The Virgin was being deflowered. At last, Amarantha was a complete woman.

* * *

"I hope our little stroll hasn't worn you out." Heather and Laine were pushing there way into the back door of the cramped bus on 16th and Mission.

"Oh no," Heather assured, "it wasn't that bad. You were right about the 22: there's no way it was gonna cross Market and Church with all the Halloween stuff going on in The Castro. Anyway, I feel like I just drank three macchiatos. I'm totally wired."

"Ah, that post-ritual buzz. Ain't nothing like it."

Too true.

The 14 Mission bus was jam-packed, and Heather was already suffocating from the stink of intoxicated sweat. At one point she started swooning, but she found Laine to be a great leaning post. Personal space was a privilege, and between the staggering body heat and the bus driver's brake-happy maneuvering, she was glad Laine was firmly planted.

Glad and curious. "Alright, Laine, why aren't you stumbling all over the place?"

Laine glanced down at her. She never imagined he could smile so much. "What? Oh, old martial arts trick. See my feet?"

Heather looked at his trampled dress shoes. Man, he had big feet.

"I keep them a shoulder's width apart and my knees slightly bent. That way I'm prepared for—"

The crowded coach made a sudden stop—as was sometimes necessary, said the signs—throwing even Laine off balance. His elbow collided with a *cholo's* head, startling the young Latino. A roar of curses and hoots filled the bus.

"I apologize, good sir." Laine bowed slightly.

"No problem, man."

Heather smiled. Laine may not like people much, but he got along with them.

"Hey, what're you doin', running in front of me like that?" the jolly, Black driver yelled at a pedestrian, "You wanna see how we make Rice-a-Roni out here?"

A child on the bus screamed, "Yeah!" Everybody laughed.

Once they were in motion again, Laine asked, "So where do you think Amarantha and Donnie disappeared to?"

Heather shrugged. "How many times did you call her place?"

"Three," he growled, "and no answer."

"Well, she knew she was supposed to call us."

"Yeah, she did." Laine kept staring out the bus windows like he was expecting to see the couple crossing a street. He looked as worried as Heather felt.

"So are you meeting up with Marisa?"

He snorted. "Called her twice. Same answer."

It then dawned on Heather that Laine wasn't looking for Amy and The Vampire Boy. He was looking for his girlfriend on the crowded street. Ouch.

"Aw damn, I missed *Miami Vice* too. Heather, what's wrong with your mouth?"

Oh shit. "Uh, nothing, nothing. My lips . . . they're just tingling a little bit." Please don't ask why. "Maybe from the wine?"

Laine nodded. "Or probably just another side effect of the ritual," he said, leaning in close and speaking low. "It'll go away soon enough."

The sudden intimacy startled her. He was way too close, and he smelled way too good. Heather hid her oncoming blush as Laine stood back up, still smiling. She used the duffle bag containing her shift as a buffer between them. Time for a subject change. "So was that your apartment?"

Laine rolled his eyes. "Don't laugh, but I live with my grandparents—well, my grandfather anyway. My grandmother died in February. Our building used to be The Pink Palace, one of the most notorious housing projects in the city until fairly recently. I grew up there in the bad old days, you know. Women getting raped and thrown off the roof; drug deals and gun battles in the parking lot. Now it's an old folks' facility, but since the neighborhood is still screwed, the housing authority lets me stay there as a minder for my grandpa."

No surprise there. They probably needed all the help they could get. "So where was your grandpa?"

"Downstairs in the community room, playing Bingo and scoping chicks." They both cracked up laughing. A balloon popped in the background. "So, Heather, you sure you don't want to see Z. Budapest with me?" His voice changed into an old lady's. "It oughta be a hoot."

She giggled. "No, I can't. My mom's going to this party, and Rudy'll be by himself, and it's already later than I thought it would be."

"What? It's just now hitting 11:00," he said, checking his watch, "and Rudy's twelve years old. I'm sure he can take care of himself. He's a good kid, and this is coming from someone who doesn't even like kids."

"I thought you just didn't like adults?"

"Hey, adults come from kids. Besides, you're going to be plenty invigorated from the ritual for a while. You might as well burn off the buzz ghost-walking with me."

A pothole sent Heather rubbing up against Laine, invigorating her far more than she cared to admit. "Nuh-no, can't. Besides, what if Amy called my place?"

"Hm. Good point. I guess there's always next year."

"Sounds good to me. So what now?"

Laine double-gripped the chrome bus railing as he leaned for a better view out a window. "I don't know. I guess meet Ms. Budapest, hit The Castro—"

"No, I mean with Amy and Donovan."

Laine let out a big old sigh. "Oh, them."

"Any more good news?"

"That depends on what happened to them tonight and what he does later. I can't strike against Donovan as things stand, and—"

"But soon you will." The truth came to her with dreamlike clarity, "After you've undergone a change, the same as I did tonight. You have another ritual to perform."

Damn, now why did she do that? She didn't mean to read him, it just sort of happened, as it tended to between them. Now he was doing that Mr. Spock thing with his eyebrow.

"Hm. Interesting. And true. To control your world, you must control yourself; to change your world, you must change yourself. I still have some things to get in order and some questions that require a higher insight."

"Like what?"

"Like how to create a safe distance between them. When we're ready to act, Amarantha can't be in the way." He was looking out the bus windows again. "I won't have her hurt in any fashion. When the time comes, I'll need you to focus your abilities on protecting her while I deal with Donovan. Divide and conquer."

Heather shook her head. That could take a while unless — "Laine, what if I can help separate them? I mean, Amy still listens to me. Kind of. Maybe I can make her see how fucked up he is."

"That's a very good idea. They'll be watching me, waiting for me to strike. You should be able to slip in quite easily." Laine jabbed a finger at her. "But not just yet. We still need to bump up your abilities, starting with your astral temple: a nice safe haven where you can recharge and ground." Laine scanned the heavy traffic on the street. "Don't want you getting hurt either."

Amy had told Heather many times that we protect our own, and clearly Laine would rather sacrifice his life plans —hell, his own life—than let either of his pupils get hurt.

He'd take any and all wounds himself. Honor among witches. "As is your will, so mote it be. And what is 'mote' anyway?"

"It's that slimy stuff around castles."

"Ha, ha."

Laine was half-smiling. "You know I'm supposed to be retiring."

Guilt pinched Heather's stomach. "I know."

"Still, I am proud to have you as my student. I would have preferred training you under better circumstances, but —anyway, thanks for sharing the madness."

Aw shit, here was that blush again. "No problem, Laine. What are friends for?" She turned away quickly. Luckily a passenger dressed like Ripley from *Aliens* was getting off, and Heather stepped aside to let her pass, covering her glow.

"There you go, *amiga*," he said. "You know what we need to do next? Start up your Magickal panoply."

"My what?"

"Your tools of The Art: a pentacle, plate or shield; a goblet or a bowl; a sword or a dagger; a wand or a staff. They're used in rituals to act as the physical anchors for your astral weapons. Once you get really good with them, anything physical can act as a channel for their energies."

A sword . . . .

"You must also start a Book of Shadows to store your spells and a journal to track your Magickal progress. Traditionally, I'm supposed to provide you with an empty book upon your initiation, but again, time was short. Sorry about that. Also, you'll need a Magickal name. You may choose the name, or the name may choose you, but it has to indicate either the Magickal entity you are or the entity you wish to become. Once you've achieved your namesake, you may choose, or are granted, another."

"So what's your name?"

Goddess, he was leaning close again. "Nih-thaw-soo," he whispered. "It's Anglo-Saxon for 'Nighthaze'. The Goddess made the choice, but it is me."

"Nihthasu," she repeated. That explained the black fog during the ritual; during their lessons. "Do I get to pick the language?"

"Sure. If you need help, I can do Greco-Roman, Latin, Egyptian, Futharkic runes. Hebrew's still a little challenging for me, and I don't recommend Enochian or anything from The Goetia unless you know what you're doing. I made the mistake of reading Enochian out loud once: my entire right side suffered painful muscle spasms until I found a counter-spell. Not a good thing for initiates to mess with."

"Eww. Well, I'll let you know when I figure it out."

"No problem," he replied, distracted. Something behind Heather had caught Laine's attention. "Whoa, check that out."

Heather turned and beheld the most amazing sight: Madonna and Frida Kahlo were sitting in the back of the bus with a ghetto blaster, singing Run-DMC's "My Adidas" at maximum volume. A couple dressed as Ronald and Nancy Reagan joined in on the girl's rap, square-dancing down the aisle as the passengers applauded. Heather's laughter felt good, pure.

"See, Heather, I told you you'd understand!" Laine shouted above the clapping hands and popping balloons. "Man, I love this city! Oh shit, we missed our stop." He looked like the happiest man on Earth.

* * *

A cool rivulet of sweat tickled Amarantha's spine, caught in an air pocket between her back and Donovan's stomach. Kate Bush was singing about running up impossible hills from the stereo in the adjacent living room. Amarantha was smiling.

Candle flames flickered and leapt for air, fighting against their wick-enforced mortality. They would lose soon, dyeing the incense ring a dusky blue and transmuting their cocoon of robes into an illusory mountain range.

Wrapped up in the dark with Donovan.

Almost no blood had been spilled, but the ache of distention remained in her loins. Amarantha had long since consigned herself to pain's inevitability. Everyone had to endure it at some time or other, and pain, ultimately, always passed.

At least, that's what Laine used to say. Laine used to say a lot of things, much of it she believed . . . up till last week. She had once needed him to get this far: now she needed Donovan to go even further, in The Art and in love. If Laine wished to remain friends, that was fine by Amarantha. As far as The Art was concerned, though, she belonged to Donovan for the next year-and-a-day, and no man or mage would come between them.

Another ritual candle suicided. It must be time to sleep.

*   *   *

Mohandas Gandhi walked into a pub and ordered a Sex on The Beach: sounded like the beginning of a bad joke, but sure enough here was the Mahatma himself, sucking down his drink and tipping the keep.

"Hey, Paddy! Come on, you're up!"

"'Ahld yooehr 'ahrses!" The keep's thick brogue tripped into Laine's ears. "I 'ave payin' coehstahmers hare. And hwat can I get you, ser?"

Laine squinted and scrutinized the jigsaw puzzle of Irish regalia behind Paddy. If an ale list existed, it was well-camouflaged amongst the naval officer photos and cheesy bar legends. "Look, do you have McEwen's?"

"Yeah, we gaht McEwen's," Paddy taunted. "A pyent?"

"Yes, please."

Paddy finger-combed his white hair wordlessly as he left. Gandhi glanced at Laine, matching the mage's bemused smile. If Paddy was The Dovre Club's owner, it was no surprise he was irritable. Oddly, the establishment went relatively overlooked by the populace. Laine wouldn't have been there himself if he hadn't missed Z. Budapest's ritual next door. Damn, should've left Heather's place sooner.

The old Olympia Beer clock behind the bar said it was just hitting midnight, which in bar time meant it was about ten minutes till. Either way, it was way too early for a pagan soiree to end, but by the time Laine hit The Woman's Building, Z. Budapest was gone, and an after-party was underway. He could hear "Slave to the Rhythm" still pounding away in the adjacent hall, but Laine didn't dance, so here he was instead. Besides, the bar's eclectic patronage of flannel-clad rednecks and mohawked punks was far more intriguing than what remained next door.

Paddy returned, setting down the ale on a faded Blackthorn coaster.

"Three-fefty."

Three-fifty? Hefty price for a drink. Laine handed him a fiver and his ID in case there was any doubt about his age. "Back to your pool game then?"

"Daerts," Paddy corrected, verifying Laine's legality.

"Of course. Thank you."

Paddy nodded as he returned the ID and left. His gait was favoring one leg over the other. Unfortunate.

Gandhi suddenly turned to Laine and raised his glass. "Cheers."

"Cheers." Laine returned the gesture and gulped down a third of his brew.

Ah, wonderful. Someone had selected a U2 track on the jukebox, as if Laine didn't get enough of that at Marisa's. Knowing his kismet, Laine wouldn't have been surprised if she and Tori came traipsing through the pub door right then, doing a bit of Samhain bar crawling. It was a delusion of course, but a harmless enough one in which to find harborage.

So what was the count, six? Six attempts to reach Marisa tonight, including the two tries he had made from Heather's house to no avail. Maybe her Libran moods would swing in his favor by the time she called on him and maybe not.

What was their status? Should he stay or should he go? Shit, maybe they *were* better off apart. It would be safer for her and easier for him.

Easier: yeah, right, what he said.

Almost as bad was the fact that Amarantha hadn't called to explain her absence either. Now that certainly killed the good humor Laine had enjoyed earlier in the evening. He had no sense of where she might be or even if she were alive. He couldn't feel her at all. Wherever she was, Donovan had her profoundly hidden from skrying eyes.

No, Laine was definitely ghost-walking alone tonight. He downed the second-third of his ale with bitter relish, then rubbed his right forearm through his sleeve. At least the burden of the spear was gone. Between its necessary banishment before Heather's initiation and said ritual's success, the evening could have gone a lot worse. Besides, it was a temporary dismissal, and he could always summon it again if he needed it for Donovan after all.

Gandhi had miraculously transformed into a statuesque goth girl with Aimee Mann hair and a white satin wedding dress with matching elbow-length gloves. She swept her platinum-blonde rattail braid from her shoulder as her violet eyes danced with liquid light beneath the pub's dim radiance. Odd that Laine could have let so striking a woman approach him unnoticed, but perhaps she wanted it that way. No, on second thought, any woman that walked around in painted-on satin while tongue-twisting cherry stems had to expect some attention, even on Halloween.

Laine took a small sip from his mug, watching the new arrival via the bar mirror. Whatever her story was, he had no business "chatting up" attractive maidens anyway.

"So what are you tonight?" the beauty asked.

Of course, if she wanted conversation, there was no need to be rude. "That depends."

The maiden was swiveling gracefully on her stool. "Really? On what?"

"On whatever you're looking for."

She grimaced. "I would think that that depends on

whatever *you're* looking for, no?"

Touché. Not just a pretty face. "Okay, I'll bite: who am I, and what am I looking for?"

"You're a man looking for answers like anyone else, I guess. Sorry that I don't have yours."

"Well, if you had claimed to have those answers, I would have said you were full of it. In life, there are no right or wrong answers. Just decisions and consequences."

Her laughter was more intoxicating than the beer Laine was ingesting. "Are you a fan of Shakespeare?"

"No."

"'Nothing in life is good or bad, but thinking makes it so.' From *Hamlet*: so true. So have I proven myself honest?" Her hooded eyes glimmered, exposing her lavender contact lenses for what they were. The knowledge didn't diminish her charms or her sincerity.

"Honest enough. I am Nihthasu." Laine offered his hand for a shake; she offered hers for a kiss. He obliged.

"I am Magritte—for now," she introduced, retaining his hand.

"Magritte, huh? Are you Spanish?"

"Portuguese. My name comes from the artist. You are familiar, no?"

"Yeah. That's, uh, apples wearing bowlers and trains in the fireplace, right?"

"Magritte Fornaux" was pleasantly surprised. "Yes, that's right. You know your art well."

"You have no idea." Or maybe she did, for even now he could feel Ms. Fornaux trying to read him through his hands. A latent psychometrist: a sensitive that skryed through physical contact with people and things. She probably didn't even know there was a word for it. It didn't feel like it was a learned reflex as it was for Laine but instinctual; something she did when she met a new soul. Quite innocent enough.

Laine retracted his psychic claws and even lessened his wards a bit. "So, Magritte, what brings you to this end of the bar?"

She removed the knotted cherry stem from her thalassic lips. "Well, I saw you come in, and I thought, 'Now there's someone with a lot of troubling thoughts on their mind. He's too busy thinking about sad things when he wants to be happy.' So then I thought, 'Maybe he should come to the party.'"

"What party?"

"This one." Magritte removed Laine's ever-present Pilot pen from his breast pocket and scribbled an address on a paper napkin. Her scent reminded him of the Janus flowers of Nihtheim. "Here you go. I think you should join us. It will be fun, and just maybe you'll discover which decisions to make and which consequences to endure, no?"

More crowds. Odd thing was, while Laine didn't like strangers per se, he loved people watching. "Thank you, Magritte. I'll catch you there a little later. About 1:30?"

Ms. Fornaux toyed with the pentacle resting on his chest and smiled. "1:30. Blessed be." She bowed slightly. Finally, someone who understood that a pentacle didn't necessarily mean Satanism.

"Blessed be."

Laine admired her "feminine wiles" as she rose from her stool and walked away. "'Damn, how'd you get all that in those jeans?'" he murmured to himself, then checked out the paper napkin: 17th and Potrero, a warehouse party. Hopefully, the cops wouldn't shut it down before Laine got there.

Even more so, he hoped Magritte was right: hopefully, some of the answers he sought would be as easy to find as a party on Halloween.

* * *

"I'm finished," Rudy announced.

Heather looked down at him from her bed. "Is that seventeen?"

"Yup." Rudy got up from Heather's bedroom floor and handed her the month-old copy of *Red Sonya*. Just about caught up.

"*Gracias*, Rudy."

"*De nada*. You want *The X-Men* next?"

"210?"

Rudy nodded, his cheeks filled with mini chocolate bars. "Uh-huh."

"Sure, when I'm done with these."

"Okay." Rudy danced his way around the colored markers and comic books scattered on the floor. It was amazing how he managed to find the perfect shade of orange for his drawing of The Thing among the mess. Of course, he was getting more ink on his Spider-Man Underoos than on the paper. How did he do that with markers?

Heather slid aside the stack of Marvel comics on her bed, then set the Hyborian Age adventure on her lap. The DJ on her clock/radio was screaming about Castro Street and interviewing the seventh Pee Wee Herman tonight. It looked like everybody was out there: Sister Boom-Boom; the Royal Family; Crockett and Tubbs; Doctor Ruth. All the "flakes, fruits, and nuts." Too bad she couldn't go. Heather was still feeling like someone had dosed her with Jolt Cola.

"Is that where Laine went?"

Heather nodded.

"Too bad he couldn't kick back longer. I like him. He's cool."

"He likes you too."

Rudy's face lit up. It looked like he had a new hero. "Really?"

"Mmm-hmm. He told me so tonight."

Rudy looked happy with that bit of news. "Is he your boyfriend?"

Shit. "He has a girlfriend. I told you that already."

"Oh yeah."

Oh yeah: that summed it up. Man, this was stupid, acting all sprung after one kiss. Red Sonya wouldn't get sprung. She was a She-Devil with a Sword: she'd just chop the guy's fucking head off.

Rudy asked, "What you laughing at?"

"Nothing, punk. Keep drawing."

"You the punk. I pity the punk."

"Shut up. You so moded." Anyway, Heather had more important and realistic things to deal with. What the hell was up with—

"Did you see Amy tonight?"

What, did skrying run in *her* family too? Naw, probably a lucky guess. He was too busy filling in Ben Grimm's rocky chest.

Heather put the unread *Red Sonya* comic on the stack, then lay back on her bed. "I saw her at work. Why, you still have a crush on her?"

Rudy shrugged. "Is she still with that guy?"

"Yeah, she's with him all right."

Wait a minute. No, no, Amy didn't . . .

"So how come you hate him so much?"

Because tonight he fucked her friend. Why didn't Heather think of that sooner? It made sense.

"Donovan doesn't love Amy the way we do," she said simply, "He only loves what he can get from her."

"He sounds like a dickhead to me."

"Actually, 'dickhead' would be a promotion for him," she growled.

Rudy jumped up suddenly, threw out his chest, and started shadow-boxing the air like Sugar Ray Leonard. "Hey, you want me to kick his ass? I'll kick that punk's ass if you want." Somebody's car horn outside played "*La Cucaracha*". Heather fell into painful laughter.

"I . . . I don't think so, Rudy," she said, trying to catch her breath, "We've got it under control."

Rudy shrugged his shoulders in disappointment and sat back down before his drawings. "Well, okay, but somebody should do something to him."

"You're right. Somebody should do something."

Maybe Heather still could.

* * *

pale shadows

18th Street was a hum of constant activity: cars were creeping bumper-to-bumper down the narrow, two-way lane; herds of human cattle were ambling westward toward The Castro like Islamic pilgrims marching to Mecca; shadow-puppet dancers were animating almost every bay window on the block. In the distance, the dissonant whine of police rollers heralded the follies of the indiscreet.

Such blessed turmoil. Everyone was living out their arcane natures; revealing their secret facets by moonlight.

And what of the moon? It was being split into thirds by the telephone wires above and framed by abandoned sneakers that were swinging like sentenced thieves. Her beauty yet remained; a beauty that was looking as deeply into Laine as he was looking into her. He would spend precious time with this queen, at least.

What was this? A familiar trio was approaching Laine with drunken steps.

"Excuse me, buddy," announced Larry, Marisa's favorite stooge, "but did you just come from The Castro?"

"Yes."

"How's it looking over there?" asked Moe.

"It's thinning out a little, but there're still plenty of gawkers from Marin hanging around, so watch your wallets."

Curly said, "Oh, why soitney!" then followed up with a chicken-cluck laugh as they shuffled away. Impressive costumes indeed.

Laine passed the Woman's Building yet again, then The Dovre Club. He pushed east through the heavy traffic on Valencia and Mission streets until he finally greeted Shotwell again where, by now, Heather should be fast asleep and dreaming sweet dreams. All of the lively lanes of Mission Dolores were now behind him. Only the dead parts of the city remained.

In the deep of the Inner Mission were standing testimonies to moribund industrialism. Defunct factories were displaying the names of companies that had perished over twenty years prior, and diverging from the horizon were disused Pacific Railway tracks gleaming like quicksilver beside abandoned loading docks. Residences were flickering with dying neon and television beams, the occupants already blinded by dream dust, and machines of labors past were donning weary facades under the India ink sky.

This was one of the in-between places; a district within districts that existed everywhere in the natural and unnatural worlds. It may be the size of a house, a forgotten alley, or a residential block. It could be a crossroad in a forest or an oasis between windswept dunes. Where didn't matter. What mattered was in these places, witches found the liminal veils between worlds to be thinnest.

A foraging mutt accompanied Laine for a spell, undaunted by the dark mage's path into a jettisoned automobile. Laine sat in the Karmen Ghia's cremated driver's seat to ground himself while his canine acquaintance stood watch.

Laine was in-between times as well as places. This small region wouldn't stay as it was for much longer. He could sense the specters of future commerce making their stand here and forever changing the psychic flow. Funny how every decade was usually defined by about five of its years. The '60s zeitgeist that The City was currently nostalgic for only really existed from 1964 to 1969, especially in San Francisco and less everywhere else. As far as Laine was concerned, the '80s didn't start until 1983, 1982 at the earliest. This time was all but over, and when it ended, no one would remember what the world was really like before.

This night, however, so deeply kissed by Nuit would live inside of Laine for now and for always.

As he rose from the barbed wire seat, a necropolitan draft curled Laine's long coat, frightening the huge mongrel and chasing it behind the cover of a side street.

A half-mile walk farther and he arrived. The block of man-stone was standing tall and settled on its corner of

Potrero and 17th, and the warehouse's steady 4/4 pulse was folding into itself from off of distant walls. Shapely limbs were swinging gaily from the skeletal fire escape overhead. Laughter, laughter everywhere.

Laine hitched onto the broken line of costumed celebrants snaking into the building's bowels. Another wave of laughter washed over Laine, but something familiar rode the crest: a woman's voice.

Laine squinted ahead and spied a man dressed as Bozo the Clown entertaining three of his friends. He apparently reached the end of an anecdote that tickled half the line. There it was again: Marisa's laugh.

And there was Marisa, looking the way she could look. Laine smiled to himself as he left his place in line and approached her from behind on catlike feet.

"Good evening, milady."

She turned, looked at Laine, and said, "Hi. Do I know you?"

Shit, it wasn't Marisa. Right height, right haircut, right laugh, wrong race. "I'm sorry. I thought you were someone else."

"Oh. No problem," she replied before turning back to Bozo.

Mocking eyes swept Laine's back as he retreated and quietly sang, "'Yeah, you're everywhere that I'm not/I'm not/I'm not.'"

By the time he got back in the queue, it had started to move. He relinquished the requested five-dollar house donation at the door, then ascended the steep, narrow stairs and walked into . . . .

"Eden before The Fall."

Skinheads and scooter wenches; gutter punks and yuppies; models and intellectuals and so many splinters besides filled the cavernous hall. Laine was hammered by sensory overload: drinking and smoking; grimacing and kissing; skanking and laughing. Rows of stout, silver pony kegs were squatting against a wall, surrounded by college types in togas and wallflowers seeking liquid courage.

Plastic spider rings and yawning skulls littered the floor. The only clear space was at the room's center where two rope swings were pitching with human bobs from steel I-beams twenty feet up. The air was overcast with marijuana clouds and sandalwood fogbanks, and while the fluorescent lighting was off, the many burning candles were providing more than enough illumination.

Laine pulled out his shades, gave them a quick polish, then considered what to drink as the DJ cued up something by The Exploited. Budweiser, it looked like. Not much in the way of choice. Laine crouched against the wall long enough to finish two foaming beers and watch the eternal tale of youth unfolding before his hidden eyes. Conversations were rolling over him:

"That's fine and all, but compact discs sound synthetic, man. It doesn't have the soul of vinyl. Just listen to . . . ."

"We gotta drink one for Rickie too. He died last Tuesday. The pneumonia finally . . . ."

"Play I some 'Scratch'!"

"Damn, I never had blue cream soda before. Why does it taste like bubble gum though?"

". . . So she got the editor's position with *On Our Backs* magazine. Lucky, eh? Looks good for a first issue."

"Oh sure, he didn't kill us all during his first term, but just wait! When it's time to kick that fucking cowboy out, BOOM!"

"Play I some Scientist!"

"Hey, I know you!"

Laine's wards thickened reflexively as he rose to face the young man walking up to him. His drunken demeanor and rockabilly pompadour were familiar. "You were at Amy's party, right? With that Chinese betty?"

"Yes," Laine responded, adjusting his black John Lennon shades. "But I'm afraid you have me at a loss."

"I'm Jimmy, Donovan's bud." He offered his hand. Laine just shrugged. "'Dairytown Cream Cheese: The Best!'"

"Oh yeah. Of course." Laine took his hand. He could

prove useful.

"So you wear your sunglasses at night?"

Funny boy. Laine nodded at the booze in Jimmy's hand. "'Have another drink, Deckard.'"

Jimmy just laughed and sniffled. "Ooh, *Blade Runner*: I get it. Best movie ever. Hey, did you see *Aliens*? Man, that was some awesome—"

Sober enough. "So I take it you're tight with Donovan?"

Nodding, Jimmy slipped a Camel Filter between his lips and then started fumbling for a light. "You didn't see this, by the way. If word got out, it could ruin my good-boy rep."

"Mum's the word." Laine pulled out his panther lighter and fired up the cancer stick.

"*Gracé*. Nice lighter."

"Thanks."

Jimmy held up the pack. "Want one?" He was doing a lot of sniffling.

"No, I don't. Thank you." Whatever he was on, Laine wanted none of it. "You were saying about Donovan?"

Jimmy added his tobacco fumes to the dense air. "What, you want to join his fan club or something?"

Laine smirked. "Maybe I want to be the president." He love-tapped Jimmy's shoulder.

"Yeah? Well, you're welcome to that title, pal. We were supposed to hang out tonight. I mean, it's Halloween in San Francisco! You know what that slippery shit did?"

"I haven't the slightest."

"Okay, I told him, 'Look, bud, I can't afford to keep flying up there just to watch you try and do your girlfriend. If I'm coming up for Halloween, fucking A right, we're hitting up parties.'"

What?

"He's all, 'Okay, okay,' and then I get here, and he tells me, 'Hey, it's me and Amy tonight, so if you wanna get bombed so bad, go out by yourself,' and then he fucking bailed! So fuck him! He can bite me!"

No, Amarantha didn't. She wouldn't. But then again,

that *did* explain why Laine couldn't feel her. She had been blocking his skrying eyes. They both had.

"I could've been at a New Order concert tonight," Jimmy griped before his expression went dreadfully blank.

Damn it, he had seen the distress on Laine's face. Now he remembered his connection to Amarantha.

"Oh, wait a minute," he slurred, "That's right, you're Amy's—" The boy's eyes were sweeping the room for an escape route. Laine was sure he was going to lose him, but then Jimmy calmed as quickly as he panicked. He looked straight at Laine and gestured the mage closer.

"Look, you really want to know why I still hang out with Don? It's because he scares me, man. I mean, I don't do all that hoodoo-voodoo shit. It gives me the creeps. Now he's all obsessed with Amy, and he's even scarier when he gets obsessed." Jimmy sniffed again, then pointed at Laine. "And *you*: you should be scared too. He knows all about you, panther-man. He's known about you almost as long as he's known about Amy, and that's been for years. He's been waiting for you."

Villain. Fucking villain.

Jimmy was reviewing his escape options again. Laine only had about one good question left before the guy rabbited. "Jimmy, what happened between Donovan and Lillian?"

Jimmy clicked his teeth. "Lillian was pretty fucked up to begin with, but even she didn't deserve to be treated like a lab rat. She was just a toy for him to practice that magic shit on. Donovan got bored and dumped her, which Lillian takes as a great offense." Jimmy shook his head. "Neither of them like to lose. Sad and simple."

No more bad dreams. No more frail suspicions. Donovan Walsh had to go.

"Look, you didn't hear any of that from me, right?"

"Mum is still the word."

"Thanks, bud. I gotta go salvage this debacle," Jimmy stammered. "The night is young, and so are the ladies. See you around. Tell your fox I said hi." He back-pedaled away from Laine, bumping into a West Indian couple in mid-flight.

Laine knew somehow that Jimmy and he would never cross paths again. Not tonight, not ever. "Thank you, Jimmy," he whispered, knowing the boy couldn't hear his words over Siouxsie's "Spellbound".

"Hey, mon, you dropped yur hearing." The Rasta was pointing at Laine's feet.

"My hearing?"

The tiny bell earring he shared with Amarantha was laying on the floor before him.

"Oh, thank you." Laine knelt to retrieve the token, considering the bauble with urgent eyes. The jewelry's fall was as defining an omen as a comet. Amarantha *had* bedded The Beast, and unless Jimmy was a pawn of misinformation, that Beast knew Laine far too well.

"Did you lose something?" There was that wedding-day white again: Magritte Fornaux.

"No," Laine said, "Not yet, at least." He stashed the earring in his breast pocket.

"What's going on behind those eyes?" That wasn't a flirt. She was displeased with Laine's hidden eyes.

He removed his shades. "Sorry."

"Good. I thought you might like these." Magritte handed Laine a red plastic cup filled with an amber spirit and a wad of Kleenex. She laughed when Laine sniffed the drink. "Don't worry, it's just mead. There are no surprises in it."

Laine unwrapped the two heavy brownies.

"I can't say the same for the pastries though." Ms. Fornaux laughed some more.

Laine took a bite. When in Rome. Besides, he'd never been affected by pot products before. Some kind of innate resistance. "So I've noticed the fire escapes are very popular tonight," he said over the dub music.

"Mm, that's because of the sacrifices."

"Sacrifices?"

"Yes. Everyone who goes out to the escape makes one

sacrifice to the old year so they can start the Pagan year anew. See?"

Laine witnessed two bald lesbians screaming at the top of their lungs toward the cloudless sky, the tempered glass and Kingston prose muting their cries.

"Interesting. But what if you don't have anything left to give?"

"You know the saying: sometimes before you can change your world . . . .'" Magritte's accent suddenly sounded very American.

"'. . . You have to change yourself,'" Laine completed.

The blonde goth eye-locked with Laine, holding him fast. Like a whisper in a forest, she said, "The choice of burnt offerings? That is yours alone."

Laine kissed Ms. Fornaux's supple hand. "I thank you for your courtesy. You have done far more good this eve than you know. Blessed be, Magritte."

"Then I've done my job. Blessed be, Nihthasu." Magritte slipped away with a bow, vanishing behind a tapestry of hale bodies.

Laine drank down his treacle spirit as he waited for a preppie to finish howling at the fading year. Once done, the haggard man knotted his sweater around his neck and stepped down from the sill.

"I guess that's my cue." Laine moved past the swings and kegs with deliberate strides, closing in on the now-vacant fire escape. He placed the hash brownies beneath the window and then stepped out into the warm Samhain night.

There was no traffic to blight the moment; no clamorous construction to defile the ceremony. There were only humid breezes and a bassline by The Specials to season the mood. Perfect.

Laine turned back toward the party inside, watching the celebrants carouse unfettered. Farther back and through squinting eyes Laine saw Magritte Fornaux settled on the loft above the DJ booth. Apparently, she had found her mate for this sabbat: a young goth boy with Peter Murphy features that made Laine envious. Ms. Fornaux jostled her blonde hair a bit, then removed it, uncovering her natural brown bob cut. Cheering, she threw the wig at a bystander. Laine smiled as he shuttered off the brass fanfare of "Ghost Town."

Princess Diana was teetering on the far end of inebriation beneath the grill supporting Laine. The Princess of Wales ambled noisily around the dark street corner, leaving him alone and staring at the sidewalk twenty feet below. He closed his eyes and watched the moon's slow swing over Orion.

Deep, measured breaths were filling and emptying Laine's lungs and mind, setting his daisy chain of chakras afire in succession. His consciousness hovered just above his head as his lips said in silence what his soul said aloud. Laine left the vehicle of his flesh behind, evacuating his mortal body like a hot breath on a cold day, spilling, spilling. At each compass point, he sent the world away with a thought and made all still. Everything became clear as quartz.

"*Maat-a maa pet ab-a nas Tehuti maat-a maa pet ab-a nas Tehuti maat-a maa pet ab-a nas Tehuti.*"

* * *

My hands dug into astral soil and dragged the stella firma into four mounds around me. The mantra assisted me, sending the pillars into a whirl and pulling them upward until they were towering high into the sky. The four monstrous hematite stelai impounded me and my body between them, shutting out any uninvited minds. The slabs were humming like anxious tectonic plates and were graven with the hieroglyphs of four gods of lore: Maat's feather of justice; Neith's sturdy hunting bow; Anubis' golden flail; Thoth's walking crook.

Em Abtet; em Restet; em Amentet; em Mehtet: qet-a sebti em qet-a. *The words were spoken, the wards were raised, and in that timeless time of night, I announced my station. I was Nihthasu, The Darkling King of Nihtheim; I* was Khernifu Pa Kerathi, High Scribe of Amarna, and I had come to kill.

I summoned my champion, and Neteru strolled before me with bejeweled ears and a forehead branded with a silver ankh. This secret knight had been a gift from Neith and Bastet, and his summoned presence meant that the feline goddess was there as well.

Something was caught in Neteru's maw, something velvety to the touch and as small as a pinkie. He dropped the curiosity at my feet, and once I retrieved and smelled it, I knew exactly what it was.

A Janus flower: a piece of home in indigo and buttercup; a symbol of duality in harmony.

There was scraping against the iron-slat floor, and I was overpowered by the smell of funerary soap and unprepared corpses. By reflex, I cupped my face in my hands and drew deep draughts of the Janus flower's perfume. That was when I noticed the simple wood and gold scale before me and the burdens it was weighing.

Upon the scale's right arm was sitting a human heart. It was true what they say: the lump of muscle was the size of my fist. Resting upon the scale's left arm was a dingy ostrich feather. It was the heavier of the two. I knew these signs of Thoth and Maat well.

How then should I tip the scales? It was clear to me that while I held the spear of Moloch, I had been adjusting for its influence just to keep centered. Now with it gone, the evidence of this overcompensation was obvious. The priest in me had prevailed when the warrior in me should have been fighting. I had been reacting with compassion when I should have been acting with intent.

Neteru was the warrior in me, and it was his time now. Unbalanced compassion was as much a weakness as unbalanced strength was cruelty, and I could not afford to be caught lacking again where Donovan was concerned. Twice that compassion had spared him.

No more. It was time to be cruel.

I opened my right hand and considered the flora there,

then I pressed the delicate petals onto my forehead. My crown bloomed again as a silver ankh cold-branded itself there, centering and locking me into Neteru. I was ridden by Neteru; I rode Neteru. Lycanthropy under a full moon.

Ah, to see and smell and hear as a panther does was an unmatched experience. Nothing was hidden, neither deed nor thought. All was laid as bare as a fresh, red kill in low, green grass. The acuity of sight and sound; of sense and presence. Certainty of mind and muscle, of intent and intuition.

The Janus flower fell from my brow like a spider on a web toward the scale. Flickering in gold and purple, it finally set upon the heart and drank of the blood there, becoming a soft bruise. My heart plunged, and Maat's feather was thrown. The gods gasped.

Now would begin the cruel days. Now would begin the book of the waning moon.

SUNDAY, NOVEMBER 2ND

Ⴝ pirouette; a fouette; a gentle adagio. Amarantha Powell was spinning and singing high upon her pointe. From the second through the third and into the fourth position, pink ribbons slithered beneath her toes. She slid from the fifth, and joined Kate Bush in her chorus. "'Let me in-a-your windoOOOW!'"

Terra fled the singing with a rude scuffle. Laughing gently, Amarantha turned to Heather, who was sitting at the vanity and wearing an equally rude grimace.

"Damn, Amy, that sounded more like 'Withering Heights,'" Heather griped, plugging her ears.

"Well, excuse the heck out of me," Amarantha cried, blushing. "Oh, and thanks for the support, Terra!"

Terra yowled repeatedly from the far end of the house. Amy and Heather cracked up laughing.

"So yesterday, Donovan and I had breakfast on The Haight, and then I took him to Curios and Tools of Magick so he could see what our shops are like. We—" Amarantha landed on her feet and sniffed her arms. "I can still smell him on me," she said almost in a whisper. Then she looked at Heather. "Why are you sitting on that chair? It's been ready for the dumpster for ages. Go sit on the bed."

"I'm good." She drank the last of her tea.

Amarantha cocked a brow. "Heather, I *did* change the sheets, you know."

"I should hope so. That'd be pretty—"

"We must've dropped over a hundred dollars of oils and roses in the tub. Needless to say, rose oil got everywhere, especially the sheets."

"Yeah, that's nice," Heather grumbled. "Hey, Amy, what's your Magick name again?"

"Befana Delafey. You remember: it means 'Epiphany of The Fey.' Laine helped me choose it." Amarantha went back to her ballet routine. Despite her lapse in practice, her flexibility remained. Her old instructor would have hated her arabesque though.

"Oh yeah, that's right. Very pretty. Did Donovan tell you his?"

Amarantha shook her head and grinned. "You know I can't tell you that. You wouldn't want me blabbing your Magick name all over the place, would you?"

Heather shrugged in agreement. "Well, if I had one, I guess not."

It then dawned on Amarantha that she'd been doing all the talking ever since Heather arrived, and she was probably boring her friend. "Goddess, I didn't even ask you how *your* ritual went."

Heather gave a small, secret smile. "Good. Very good, actually. I feel like a part of me has been asleep for years, and Laine woke me up."

Wait, Laine woke her up?

"It went very well," Heather added, trying to cover up her ill-considered words. "Man, I can't wait to build my temple."

"Heather, you're not getting a crush on him, are you?" There was a hint of jest in her words, but just a hint.

"Because there are spells for that."

Heather shivered. "Tsk! No. God, Amy, you know me better than that. Plus—duh—he has a girlfriend. All I'm saying is now I have the same rapport with him as you do. And besides, I thought love spells were wrong?"

Amarantha grinned. "They are, mostly. I was just teasing," she said, rolling down a striped leg warmer. "Plus, you can do better."

"Great advice, Amy," Heather said pointedly, "Words to live by."

What did she mean by that? "Remember, his student before me went bad," she added, removing her other legwarmer and tossing it into the closet. "And I'm still not convinced that he didn't attack Donovan first. Just be careful around him."

"Well, what about that girl from Jimmy's party? Wasn't she Donovan's mistake?" Heather's eyes lit up, and she took a deep breath. "And what about *your* old mistakes? Sean cheated on you, Nick swore you cheated on him, Billy the molester at sleepover camp, Klepto Jeff, who probably still has *tus bragas*—" Heather tugged the hips of her jeans.

Amarantha's face was stinging with the blood of her shame. She whimpered, "That's not fair."

Heather continued anyway. "No, no, no, you're right. You're the expert on that love shit, not me. I'll keep my eyes open." Heather smirked past Amarantha toward the bedroom door. "Hi, Laine."

"Heather."

What? How could Laine have snuck up on her so easily? Why didn't she feel him first? Amarantha faced him with barely restrained surprise.

She could only see Laine when she blinked, at the fringe of her sight. He was skinhead-clean in his black long coat and slacks, black t-shirt, and black Lennons. However, her wide-open eyes saw Neteru's monstrous posture; his burning gaze; his light-consuming fur. This wasn't like at her birthday party where a shake of the head could dispel the vision. No, Laine *was* Neteru. He *was* the sable beast, and that was how he'd arrived undetected.

"Hi, Laine. W-where's your hair?" she managed to spit out.

"On the barbershop floor," the panther growled, "Your door was open. Sorry if I startled you." He was absolutely still as if trying to hide a wound.

Amarantha crept toward Neteru with open arms, terrified of his embrace but needing to truly know his intentions. He raised a hand, stopping her just before the hug.

"Can that wait a minute?" he asked.

"Sure. Is . . . is something wrong?"

"Yes. My bladder. It's full." Neteru patted his belly, then said to the cat at his feet, "Hi, Terra." Terra returned the greeting.

"Oh, I'm sorry." Amarantha gestured toward the restroom. "Go right ahead."

Neteru gave a slight bow and then vanished down the hall as quickly and quietly as he had appeared.

Amarantha's guts were churning as she turned back to Heather. "Did . . . did you see that?"

Heather stood and stretched. "What, his haircut? Yeah, I saw it yesterday."

"No, no, he was—never mind."

"He's acting all Darth Vader again. I think he's fighting with Marisa." Heather grabbed her empty coffee mug. "More tea?"

Amarantha forced a casual smile, shook her head, and handed Heather her mug. Heather shrugged before slipping into the hall.

Heather's explanation was limp. There was something more going on. If she shared a rapport with Laine now, how did she miss his were form?

Amarantha snatched off her headband and wiggled a pair of Jordache jeans on over her leotard. If she wanted to discover what Laine was up to and whether or not Heather was in on it, she needed to act now. All Amarantha needed was a few minutes, a few deep breaths, and the sacred words.

* * *

Athené aigis athanaton.
*My eyes shone and searched the cardinals of my home
and scanned the halls and walls. Astral senses extended, I
found my brethren in the dining room; in the ritual space.
Heather's aura was radiant—almost painfully so—as she
stood near the door, watching. Neteru was squatting in the
middle of the room and slowly sweeping his arms around
him like a sundial's shadow, attempting to glean any
residue of the Halloween rite. Their words were muddled to
me except for these: conspicuously clean.*
The door chimes rang.

* * *

"He's here. He's here." Amarantha ran into the hall with
Terra trotting ahead. Upon opening the door, her familiar
stepped aside, allowing smiling Donovan to launch himself
into Amarantha's arms and drown her in kisses.

"Goddess, I missed you," he said, dropping his overnight bag with a thump.

"Silly, you just saw me yesterday." Ah, to swim in those
deep, blue eyes.

"Yesterday was a long day and a long time ago, love.
Look, Terra missed me." He pointed at the cat winding
around her ankles.

She laughed, then said, "And I missed you. It's just that
Laine and Heather are here." As Amarantha nodded toward
the far end of the hall, her heart fell from the heights
Donovan had lifted it to. "He's up to something."

Donovan's eyes followed her gesture as he retrieved his
overnight bag. "Hey, Heather; Laine," he greeted.

Heather was wearing her disgust fairly openly as she
approached them. Laine was once again Laine but
possessed a strange calm.

179

"Donovan," Laine responded in a cold, clinical fashion, removing his shades.

Dread was gripping Amarantha. If Laine harbored ill-intentions, this was when he would act on them. How could he resist striking down his "foe" within the very halls where they met?

Holding Donovan tight, she watched Laine's black lacquered talons reach out and curl around her beloved's grip. Thankfully—surprisingly—they simply shook, but a handshake could be so much more with their kind.

"Be careful of the cat," Laine said of Terra, who was dangerously underfoot.

"Oh, I know. I like the new look." Donovan nodded at Laine's bald pate.

"Got tired of the Grace Jones comparisons," Laine offered as they entered Amarantha's room. It wasn't till she had taken the seat at her vanity that she noticed Heather and Laine had barely entered at all, just lingered near the threshold. As was their will.

Laine asked, "What happened to your shadow, Donovan?"

Donovan cocked his head. "What?"

"Jimmy," Laine interrogated.

Donovan frowned. "You know what Tijuana Boy did?"

"There's no O in 'Tee-hwa-na'," Heather corrected. Amarantha and Donovan cast annoyed glances in her direction.

"Thank you for that, Heather." Donovan went back to addressing everyone. "Anyway, he drank too much on Halloween, gave himself alcohol poisoning, and had to have his stomach pumped."

Both women said, "No!" before Amarantha asked, "Is he okay?"

"He'll live. He flies home today."

"That's too bad. Send him my regards, won't you?" Laine requested in that voice.

"Done." Donovan was matching Laine's surly gaze with one of fearlessness. Good for him. It was good to see he could stand up to her ex-mentor's ire.

Heather had a puzzled look on her face like she was about to ask Laine a question, but he quickly, wordlessly silenced her with a sidelong glance, then reset his sights on Donovan. There was a peculiar squint to his eyes, but then again, he wasn't wearing his prescription glasses and was probably half-blind.

Laine slipped on his sunglasses and announced, "We have to go, Heather. I have to meet with Marisa. Don't want to be late."

"Yeah. Okay, let's book."

Amarantha asked, "Where are you guys heading?"

Laine offered, "A supply run at Curios and Candles."

"Yeah," Heather enthused, "We be getting me a sword." Her friend was grinning and bobbing her head to a secret rhythm. "What about you guys?"

Amarantha looked at Donovan. "I don't know. What are we doing today?"

"I was thinking we could grab something to eat, hit a movie."

While Heather was gathering her jacket, Amarantha got up from her chair and slipped past Donovan, lightly brushing his hand as she walked up to Laine.

"If you need anything, Befana, you need only whisper my name," Laine offered, stilling Amarantha with his eyes.

"Of course," she returned. So Laine was her friend still, if not her mentor. That was almost comforting enough to forgive him his secrets and hostility. It was enough to make her smile again. Amarantha slipped her arms around him and gave him the hug she hadn't been able to earlier. She closed her eyes and dug in deep.

An ultraviolet storm was rolling quietly behind her lids. No throne of hematite sat before her, nor was Lord Nihthasu anywhere to be found here. More alarming was his total lack of wards. He was always shielded by Magick to some degree or other but not now.

Amarantha took a backward step out of the ill weather and into her reflection in Laine's black shades as he stood there impassively. "Good luck with Marisa. Tell her I said hi."

"I'll tell her," he finally said, then turned away and headed for the front door with Heather following obediently behind him. The clicking latch was all there was to fill the silent wake. What Laine was planning remained an enigma.

"That was painless," Donovan offered, his footsteps moving closer behind her as she stared at the shuttered door.

"Yes, it was." Odd that Laine hadn't tried anything, and yet, he had never before hidden himself from her so completely. He was as conspicuously clean as her ritual space. Amarantha warmed the goose pimples on her arms.

"Donovan, when he shook your hand . . . you didn't sense anything, did you? Feel anything?"

He shook his head. "No, nothing at all."

Amarantha faced her love, looking for any signs that Laine had tainted him. "Are you sure? Not even a skry?"

"All I felt was 'goodbye.'"

"A threat maybe?" There had to be something.

Donovan shrugged. "No, just 'goodbye.' Look, worrying about what Laine may or may not do is pointless. Let's go to the movies. *9½ Weeks* is playing at The Strand. Been wanting to check that out."

Look at that smile. Of course he wanted to see it. According to the reviews, it was only the sexiest movie of the year. The flirt returned. "So you 'cool for the kill'?"

Despite all else, Amarantha smiled. "Of course. Except . . . ."

Donovan embraced her waist. "Except what, love?"

"I want to go to church first."

* * *

"The altar, the living room: Amy sure was ready for you, Laine," Heather told him, "Even with your *Manimal* impersonation."

Laine scowled. "*Manimal*? You watched that crap?"

"Some would say *Miami Vice* is 'crap'."

"Yes, but I don't bother with those people."

Heather giggled at his joke as they rounded the corner of Haight and Divisadero. "Too bad though. I mean it was just us there. Perfect time to take Donovan down." She socked her palm.

". . . And come away looking like the villain again? No, as you said, they were ready. I think it is best that I remain unarmed and relatively tame . . . until I am shown to act otherwise."

So he was waiting for another vision? Sounded wise to her. "I noticed you didn't mention to Amy or Donovan that you saw Jimmy on Halloween."

"Donovan knows of what we spoke."

"Did Jimmy look that drunk to you?" Jimmy might have been a horn dog, but she felt sorry for him.

Laine met her gaze. "And then some, though I doubt it was just the booze doing the damage."

Heather remembered what Donovan had said about having already sent Laine's message to Jimmy. There had been something personal between Laine and Donovan in that instant, and she now believed what Laine suspected: Donovan had punished Jimmy for talking to him.

Heather also remembered Amy's earlier prance of love and happiness. Donovan *did* pop Amy's cherry on Samhain, and her friend spilled the details with gusto: how deftly Donovan had put on the condoms; how he liked to talk during sex; how he had definitely improved by the third time; how his skin smelled lightly of over-ripened peaches. It was annoying. It was disgusting. It was kinda sexy. Ew.

Laine and Heather stopped beneath the hand-carved hardwood Curios and Candles sign. Laine peeked through the window and checked out the scene inside before finally pushing open the door and entering with all the reverence of someone attending church.

When it came to one-stop Pagan shopping, Curios and Candles wasn't as pretty as Tools of Magick or Bones of

Our Ancestors, but if you needed to get witching supplies for a reasonable price, this was the place. Everything from electroplated seals of Solomon for ten bucks to silver and gemstone pentacles for forty-five was stocked. They had the weird stuff like jars of bat wings and spider legs— funny, no eye of newt—as well as every shape, color, and size of candle one could imagine: devil-shaped candles, black cat candles, crucifixion candles, even candles of nude men and women that were displayed with their backs to the patrons. Creaky racks were filled with budget books by Anna Riva and New Age greeting cards painted in airbrush, and flood-lit glass cases displayed tiers of tarot decks.

"Hey, Laine!" a blonde girl with a silver nose stud and a Death Angel T-shirt called out from behind a register.

Laine bowed slightly at the shop help as Heather was checking in her book bag. "Hi, Shannon. Where's Julie hiding?"

"Giving a reading."

Laine was looking around the shop. "Still crowded after Halloween?"

"Yeah, it'll probably be like this through Thanksgiving. We hope." Shannon knocked on the wood countertop three times.

"Hmm. Is Jeffrey in back?"

Shannon was ringing up her customer as she shouted, "Yeah. You wanna see him?"

They both frowned, said "Naaah," and laughed.

Heather knew Jeffrey as well, though more by reputation than interaction. She had heard that he could be a crotchety old bastard when riled up, and that was pretty easy to do. Funny thing was he didn't look that old or mean. There was still some red to his male pattern baldness, and every time Heather had bought anything from him directly, he'd been quite nice. But then he did have an all-female staff working for him, so maybe that's why Heather always got the shiny side of his coin. Titties win again!

She and Laine stopped at the bookshelves. Rows and rows of metaphysical topics were spread out before them in a vaguely organized fashion. They started out light enough with typical New Age fluff, astral projection, numerology, divination, and the craft of colors on the left. They gradually reached Wiccan rituals, astrology, fairy Magick, gem lore, herbology, and The Golden Dawn. The end of the library entered darker, more obscure territory: Aleister Crowley and The O.T.O, chaos Magick, LaVey's works, the Goetia, Enochian handbooks, and gematria.

Laine was devoting a lot of his attention to those more intense tomes. He would barely read the spines. He would just wave his hands along the shelves, pause at certain books, read a brief passage, and then slide whatever it was back in its place. Sometimes he grunted or shook his head.

"You have *Spiral Dance*?" he asked, still scanning.

Heather took the wad of watermelon bubblegum from her mouth. "Yeah. Well, my mom does."

"*Earth Magic*?" He tapped his chin.

Heather wrapped the gum up with a Kleenex she found in her jean pocket. "No."

He passed her the book. "*Magical Ritual Methods*? No, of course not." Laine passed it to her and grumbled, "Geez, so many Gardnerian tomes. As if he was the end-all authority on The Art. How about *Creative Visualization*? You have that?"

Great, no wastebasket nearby. Heather'd have to hold on to her gum. "No. What are we doing?"

"Getting your library in order. You don't need books to learn The Art, but they are great for cross-referencing your experiences. I'd visited the Enochian watchtowers many times before I even heard of John Dee or Edward Kelly. Their experiences validated my own, and validation is very important to our work. *Drawing Down the Moon*?"

"No. What can these books tell me that you can't?"

"Nothing. And everything. Sometimes the authors reveal truths beyond their intentions. This book for instance."

Laine squeezed past Heather to pull a rust-colored paperback from a shelf beside her: *How to Meditate* by

pale shadows

Lawrence LeShan.

"In one chapter, the author derides paranormal experiences as distractions to meditation, however if you pay close attention to how his exercises are laid out, you'll find that his four types of meditation correspond nicely with the four elements." Passed it to her. "Besides, you shouldn't restrict your sources of knowledge. There are far wiser people in the world than I. Or Gardner."

Heather turned back to the crowded store and watched Shannon ring up another purchase of Come to Me powder and Money Drawing mojos before almost dropping the stack of books Laine tossed into her arms.

"Look through those, and see which ones you think you'll need."

Heather sorted through the selection while Laine perused.

"Actually, there are exceptions to what I said about books," Laine said, looking for more volumes to burden her with. "I work with a lot of herbs, so books on herbalism would be necessary. Marisa's a crystal witch, so she has a lot of books about gems."

Heather was juggling the remaining books and her gum wad. "So the jewelry she wears—"

"Some are Magickal, others are from the antique store next door to work. You know Hyde and Seek Antiques? Marisa is into their 1920s bakelite and alexandrite mostly. She loves Art Deco—"

The front door slammed open, and a guy who smelled like he just bathed in a sewer strutted in brandishing gold knuckles.

"What's up, y'all? I got some watches here you just gotta check out." Then he spotted Laine. "Yo, yo, cousin, I know a young homeboy like you gotta flash some gold nowadays, and I got a tight Bulova here that—"

Heather saw these guys all the time in The Mission, and she would usually just let it slide, but for some reason, not today. She gave the intruder a long, hard glare, and at that moment, she felt all the other Pagan eyes in the store doing the exact same thing, including Laine's. There were some twenty witchy-types frozen in a witchy store, casting a group banishing at the mundane hustler. The entire shop was graveyard-silent except for the Windham Hill track playing on the stereo.

The ringed hawker stuttered and staggered and then said, "Oh, okay," before creeping back out the door and closing it quietly behind him. Just as suddenly as everything had stopped, the whole store was animated again.

Laine said, "She doesn't wear her Magickal gems too often. She just breaks them out for special occasions."

It was like the watch dealer was never there, except for the lingering funk. That had to be the fourth display of Magickal power Heather had seen today, at least. The witches were on the march for sure.

"I'm sorry, what?"

Laine sighed. "Marisa's jewelry?"

"Oh yeah." Heather shook off the old topic for a new one. "Laine, what do you think Donovan's gonna do now? To Amy?"

His eyes locked onto something behind her, but they weren't really looking outward at all. He was pulling the answer from the ether; from the future. "He'll do what all vampires do: feed." Laine looked back at Heather. "But that won't happen for a while yet. To our advantage, he *is* in love with Amarantha, and that buys us time." He glanced up at the clock that was half-hidden behind busts of King Tut and the god with the jackal head: 3:35. "I'm running late. Go claim your weapon. I have more things to purchase."

"Okay." Now, what books was she left with? Visualization; meditation; *A Witches' Bible Volume One; Earth Magic*. Not too pricey. She could probably afford the rest of her tools.

Heather sat the paperbacks on the case containing the shop's Magickal arsenal. All kinds of dirks, daggers, and Bowie knives were resting on what looked like purple velvet. A dagger like Laine's would be easier to wield in ritual, but—

"Can I help you find something?" Jeffrey had snuck up on her.

"Oh. Hi," she said with pride as she handed him the tissue containing her stale gum. "I need to buy a sword."

Jeffrey discarded her garbage in an unseen trashcan behind the display case. "Okay. Which one?"

Heather squatted and leaned against the counter front with her fingertips. "Heh, that one looks like Excalibur."

"That one? Is that the one you want?"

At 130 bucks? "Naw. Too expensive. Geez, what's that? A fencing foil?"

Jeffrey pointed at the thin blade. "You want that one?"

Heather shook her head. "Too flimsy."

Jeffrey sighed, his fingers tapping out his impatience on the counter.

Laine had mentioned that Cost Plus Imports near Fisherman's Wharf had swords too. If she didn't find one here, she could always—wait. No way.

"That sword there! On the bottom row. No, closer to the front."

Jeffrey's hairy little fingers groped the display floor until he found her sword. The weapon was practically singing as he slid it off the velvet, then it quieted as he set it gently on the glass counter top. "You know you can't sharpen that, right? The blade'll just shred, plus it'll be illegal."

Heather picked it up and began turning it to and fro in her hand, getting used to its weight. That turned out to be easy. The blade was broad, yet light; the hilt was elegant in its simplicity but not fragile; the leather-bound grip felt like it was made for her.

"So is that the one?" Jeffrey asked.

"Oh yeah."

* * *

The Methodist church was literally across the street from Amarantha's house: a good thing since she'd misplaced her keys today, and Heather had forgotten her extra set.

"Remember this?" Hamilton U.M.C Food Program is what the sign read: the sign Amarantha, Heather, and Donovan had helped paint six years ago. She recognized her yellow sunflowers and calligraphy, Donovan's white church with its brown steeples; Hungry Maggie's blue pond; Mondo's red butterflies. All of the kids' touches were still there in strokes of paint.

"Yeah. Yeah, I remember." Donovan was running his fingers through his feathered hair.

"A lifetime away, huh? Shall we go in?"

"I'm sorry. Do you mind if I wait out here?" There was a false joy to his chuckle.

"Why? I don't understand. This is where we met." Why wasn't he looking at her?

"I know, and I'm sorry. It's . . . ." He buried his next thought; his next words. "It's the memories. I can't go in just yet."

"You can't make me go in there alone. I'll end up 'volunteering' for something. At least together—"

Donovan finally looked right at her. "I'm not fucking going in there!"

Amarantha was too shocked by his outburst to be angry at his vulgarity. He could answer for that later. Instead, she slowly nodded. "I'll run in, drop off Joanie's keys, and then we'll go, okay?"

Donovan whispered, "Thank you," while staring sullenly at his shoes.

* * *

"Your cat is showing," Laine's lover sang.

Laine opened his eyes for Marisa. Wrapped in layers of black finery and topped with her wide-brimmed porkpie and Lennon shades, she was standing close enough to Laine

PALE SHADOWS

to be brave, yet far enough to be smart, not that he was currently a threat. Between the absence of the spear's hunger and the presence of Neteru's strength and calmness, Laine was feeling the most centered he had since the vision.

He allowed a smile to emerge as he considered her. "You should've seen him earlier."

"Are you a skinhead now?" She joined him on the worn, evergreen bench and watched the geometries of sails stippling the bay.

"Not even. How was Amron?" Laine asked.

"'Same as it ever was.' Tony says hi."

One of The Metaphysical Church of Amron's resident psychics. During a service a couple of months prior, Tony had called Laine out. He had a vision of Laine dancing—a remote notion indeed—and of someone trying to correct his movements, but apparently Laine went his own way and gained much acclaim. His interpretation: Laine would find lifelong success through his defiance of the rules. At least, that's what Tony had seen, metaphorically.

"Send my regards," Laine offered.

"We need to talk," Marisa announced.

That was how she always went about it: a troubling, formal preamble to a decision made or a question pondered. Can I ask you something? Guess what? We need to talk. The pauses that followed had always been short but deep enough to fill with a thousand lovers' fears. Most of the time the pauses had been followed by something benign: The black or the green? or I got the tickets for the show.

Not so now. She followed up with, "I'm not happy with us; with how things are going. I haven't seen or heard from you in two weeks. I know you had to get Amy's ritual together. I understand that, but still—"

The first volley in their game of Lover's Tennis was served. "After you hung up on me, I didn't think there was anything more to say or that you wanted to talk to me at all." His eyes swept from the north to Marisa. "And I did try to call you."

"Yeah, *on* Halloween and *after* I'd already gone out," she retorted, unblinking. "Why didn't you call me earlier in the day? You could've reached me from the café."

Laine huffed, his calm drawn away by an Alta Plaza Park breeze. "The café was packed with customers and orders all day. You could've called me from your job too."

"Two weeks, Laine. It only takes five minutes to call somebody," she deflected.

"I used about twenty on Wednesday."

"I was stripping liths all day, and I didn't get your calls."

So wearying. "I called your house too. I left messages."

"I didn't see—Mark probably deleted them. Dickhead."

This was exactly what Laine hated: all the arguments about little things that kept shrinking smaller and smaller until they couldn't see what they were feuding over anymore. From money to dates to clocks to time to numbers to fractions to pixie farts until the inevitable what-the-fuck-are-we-fighting-about moment was reached. And then it would begin again, and in the end, Laine always either surrendered or lost.

He thought of the legend of Alexander and The Gordian Knot and decided to end this. "Marisa, what do you want? Tell me what you want."

She sighed. "You. I want you, but I'm not going to waste my time sitting by the phone, worrying if you're going to call or not. Yes, I have my own life, but I want you to be a part of it. Are you a part of it or not?"

He had a choice? "I hope so."

"Me too. Laine, I'm not really mad at you. I mean, I was, but I know what you are, and I know there's a lot of stuff you can't tell me. Probably a lot I don't want to know, but you can't just run out into the night and expect me to always be there when you return. Don't take me for granted because, I'm sorry, but the next argument could be our last."

There was her ultimatum: the new amendment that would bind him, delivered without malice but with much certainty. The Libran had made up her mind.

"I'm sorry," Laine surrendered, "'As is your will, so mote it be.'"

Marisa began stroking his cheeks and whispering a symphony of forevers into his ear, her tears staining his lapel. There was something . . . off about her scent. She smelled like a stranger's home; like stale clove cigarette smoke and missed sleep and the odors that night leaves behind. She smelled chemically sweetened.

After their exchange of kisses, Laine loosened Marisa's hold and slipped his now-free hand inside his long coat and down his sleeve.

"What . . . what are you doing?" Her first sign of worry so far.

Laine handed Marisa the paper sack. "Gonesh incense; jasmine oil; Moon Goddess oil."

"Oooh. Wait," she beamed then reached into her own pockets. She presented an Astropop, those tri-colored cone confections wrapped in thick cellophane and capped on the bottom with wax.

Laine smiled at the childhood favorite. "Thank you." He unwrapped the sucker and relished in the emulsifiers.

"Thank *you*." Marisa punctuated her gratitude with another kiss. "So how did Amy's ritual go?" she asked at last.

Lo, life's imperfections. This should have been the end; the new beginning. "It didn't. Heather's did. Amarantha and Donovan had a ritual of their own while I initiated Heather."

Marisa was watching Laine's jaw flex. "Oh. Ooh, sorry."

A perfectly understated response. "It wasn't too bad. Heather earned it."

Marisa no longer looked like she was paying attention. He couldn't even tell if she really cared that his fight was still on, probably because at that moment, *he* didn't care. For now, he had what he wanted except for . . . .

"Goddess, I need a drink. Want to hit Vesuvios?" Laine

asked. "You can tell me about *your* Halloween."

"Sounds good." Marisa stroked jasmine oil on her wrists. "Oh wait, let's go see *Sid and Nancy*. It's playing near the bar, and I have preview tickets."

"*Sid and Nancy?*"

"You know: Sid Vicious of The Sex Pistols kills his girlfriend Nancy Spungen—"

"Ah yes." Spirits and a tragedy. Sounded like the perfect date. "Sure. Let's go."

* * *

"I'm supposed to sleep with this thing? Really?" Heather thought Laine had been joking when he told her that sleeping with the weapon—along with anointing it with oils—was part of the consecration process, and now she just had to worry about waking up impaled like Lancelot in *Excalibur.*

Heather took a pillow from her bed and dropped it in front of her altar before kneeling on it. Sliding her brass brazier aside, she made room for her new ceremonial pieces.

One by one she laid them out: a silver goblet with a pentagram engraved in its bowl; a wooden disc seven inches in diameter and also engraved with a five-pointed star; four vials of oil for the sword; two vials for her; four out of the seven books Laine picked out earlier plus the latest copy of *Reclaiming.* Even though he had made up the difference, Heather didn't have enough for a wand just yet, so she would just improvise with her quartz crystal for the time being.

There was a creak at the threshold behind her. "Hi, Rudy," she greeted without looking. She had wanted to stash her wares before he knew they even existed. Guess she wasn't fast enough.

"Mama go to the movies already?"

"Yeah. She left with Max for the Roxie a while ago." Heather stood up and turned to her brother, hiding the sword behind her. "They went to some movie called *Parting Glances*. It's supposed to be depressing." Maybe if she could keep Rudy talking—

"What's that?" Damn, he was pointing at the sword.

"Nothing. Hey, you want to order a pizza? Mama—"

"Is that a sword?! Ooh, can I see?!" Rudy's words were just a courtesy. He was already grabbing for it. Heather managed to dodge every lunge, her feet a shoulder span apart. Laine was right again.

"No. No, no, no, no, no. Listen to me." Heather pinned her brother where he stood with her words. "You must promise me that you will never, *never*, touch this sword . . . ."

"Aw, that's bunk," he whined, throwing his lower lip out a mile.

". . . after tonight."

Rudy was finally paying attention to her. There wasn't any fear on his face but rather calm respect. Clearly, her tone and demeanor had tamed him, just as she wanted. "Promise?"

"Okay. I promise," he said with all sincerity.

"Good." Heather tore the rest of the butcher paper from the sword's blade before brandishing it beneath the half-light of her room. Holding it out for Rudy, she said, "Just this once, you can see it."

Heather would find a secure place to store it later. For now, what could it hurt to let Rudy see it just this once, before the consecration? Besides, tonight wasn't the night for workings anyway, not with her brother snooping around. No, she'd work on her temple soon enough.

* * *

"So that movie was something, huh?" Amarantha was nibbling her lips numb. She couldn't wait to get Donovan back home. *Sexiest Movie of The Year*? Absolutely. "Cool for the kill"? Positively.

Donovan just shrugged. "It was okay until the end. The

soundtrack was great though." He started bouncing in place. "Man, it's freezing out here. I knew I should've made our reservations sooner."

"What was wrong with the end?" Amarantha braced against the cold, Market Street winds as well. One would think a fine establishment like Zuni's would have a shelter of some sort for customers waiting outside.

"Okay, I understand that Mickey Rourke did some messed up stuff, but he did warn her at the beginning, and the end—well, I just think Kim Bassinger's character could've shown a little more understanding. He was trying to fix things at the end."

"Don't you think it was too little, too late? Their relationship was pretty harsh. I mean, all those mind games —"

"Not as long as the effort was made to fix it. Elizabeth threw away what could have been the great love of her life. I mean, do you think he was beyond redemption?"

"I think some people are. Some people just can't be fixed."

Donovan just nodded and then turned toward the front of the line, silent. Reflexively, she touched his back and felt him heaving as he wept. "Goddess, Donovan, it was just a movie."

He faced her, his eyes red and tearing. This was how weeping angels looked. Donovan spat out, "I messed up."

"Is this about earlier at the church? I'd already forgotten about that."

Donovan shook his head. "I-I knew I sh-shouldn't have let Ji-Jimmy go out by himself. He-he kept talking about guh-getting wasted, and I just got tired of it!"

"You can't blame yourself for what Jimmy does. He—"

"I cuh-can't? Doesn't that buh-bullshit sound familiar to you?"

It all came back to Amarantha: why Donovan stopped going to the church that brought him to her: his parents' divorce.

"My dad yuh-used to think it was suh-so funny. 'He-

here, Donny, take this pot and guh-go play with your fruh-
friends or something.' 'Hey, guys, yuh-you wanna see Duh-
Donny get drunk?'" Donovan's mucus anointed the
sidewalk. He sniffled. "Whenever they wuh-wanted to get
rid of me so they could fight, they luh-let drugs do the
babysitting. And they said it 'wasn't their fucking fault!'
They should've known better!"

"Donovan . . ." It struck Amarantha as wrong that such
a boyish voice could utter profanities.

"I *do* know better, and I should've stuh-stayed with
Jimmy. I mean, you suh-saw him at his place; at your party.
He wasn't just drunk. But hey, 'the folly of the privileged,'
right?"

"Do you remember my friend Saffron from our
church?" Amarantha moved closer to Donovan. "She and
Jimmy would have loved each other. Saffron turned to acid
and alcohol and boys to cope with her parents' ugly
divorce, at least till the cops caught up with her. I never
wanted my friend to end up that way, but after a while, you
have to realize you can only help so much."

Amarantha wiped Donovan's tears away with her
thumbs. "But you're not like them. You were there for
Jimmy, Donovan. Didn't you see him in the hospital?"

"Yeah," he conceded, still shuddering.

"You did what you could for him. You were a great
friend, but ultimately he's not your responsibility.
Remember what Samhain was about: breaking past chains
and embracing our new life together. I have left my mentor
behind. Forgive me, but maybe 'tis time for you to leave
Jimmy behind, just like Lillian; just like Saffron." And his
influence, for Amarantha would not hazard Donovan's
return to addiction.

She waited for his protest, but instead, Donovan replied
with a kiss so deep that she was lost to him. She shared in
his desperation, his sadness, and finally his relief. So much
color in one kiss.

A woman yelled, "Walsh party, third call!"

How it hurt to have to let him go. Donovan raised a

hand. "That's us," he announced to the hostess as his eyes consumed Amarantha in a way his lips weren't anymore. He mustered, all aglow, "And I'm sorry about earlier at the church."

Amarantha grabbed his cold hands. "It's forgotten," she assured as they entered the restaurant. "You do owe me one though. I ran into Deacon José."

"So how is he?"

"Oh, fine. So fine, in fact, that he talked me into 'volunteering' to cook for the church on Thanksgiving." Amarantha rolled her eyes.

Donovan chuckled, all sadness gone from him. "Wow. I guess I do owe you one."

* * *

"Another Cabernet . . . ," began the barmaid as she passed.

". . . and another whiskey sour," Laine finished.

"Where's your friend?" She nodded at Marisa's coat, purse, and helmet in the chair across from him.

"Restroom. 'One does not buy beer, one merely rents it.' So she says."

She flashed a smile most beguiling, this Constance. It was the content of a smile that was most telling for Laine, and though hers was welcoming, it was ill-timed. Strange these attentions Laine had been enjoying lately. He would never have received a second look before Marisa. That figured.

It was nine in the evening, and from the second story window of Vesuvios, Laine was watching the Adler Street alley, barren except for the occasional bit of foot traffic and Marisa's blue Yamaha Riva. The strip clubs on Broadway, however, and City Lights Books next door were enjoying heavy traffic. That was hardly news. City Lights was one of the last bastions of Beat sensibility and had been thriving for three decades.

Vesuvios was born of that same time and movement,

and it wore its pedigree with pride. Projection screens were flipping through slides of nudes from the '20s, Jazz was in the air, and college students were scaring or enticing European tourists with their candor. Laine couldn't tell if there were any real "beatniks" around, but it didn't matter. The bohemian vibe was still there.

As for the strip clubs, well, there just was no beating the lowest common denominator.

Marisa returned, all smiles. "Did you order?"

Laine nodded. "All better?"

"'I used to be a werewolf, but I'm okay noOOOW!'"

Laughing, Laine wiggled his larynx. "'Werewolf detected. Exterminate! Exterminate!'"

"I remember that!"

"Gotta love *Doctor Who* references. Oh, wait: 'My parents said we'd spend all the money on drugs!' 'Well, we would.'" Laine cracked up.

"Wait! Wait! 'Oh my gawd, I look just like Stevie Nicks!'" Marisa added, laughing at his *Sid and Nancy* paraphrases. "Too bad Fab Mab closed down. I could use a mosh pit right now."

After expending their shared outburst, Laine asked, "Speaking of, may I bum a 'party smoke'?" Neither of them smoked except for at the occasional gig. A pack of incense, a pack of cloves, a live band, and a comfortable corner of the club to haunt were all they needed.

"Sure. I think there are a couple left. Why didn't you just grab one?" she asked, pulling a pack of Djarum from her black "pleatherester" shoulder bag.

"You know I never go through a woman's purse without permission. Sometimes not even when I have it. Mama raised me better."

He twirled the clove cigarette between his lips, moistening the sweet gum on the filter. The steel panther roared, and he took a drag. "So Tori and her new boyfriend were in rare form on Friday, eh?"

"What? Oh yeah." Marisa's emerald eyes rolled. "So you know how Tori is. It was like those damn Siouxsie tickets all over again. Remember, back in June?"

The memory still stung. "Missed the last local show. Missed the *Tinderbox* tour entirely," Laine growled, handing her the cigarette she'd just beckoned.

". . . Because she got all pissy and wouldn't make up her mind, just like Friday. She wanted to go out; she didn't want to go out; her dancing shoes or her stilettos?; did her acid wash jeans make her head look fat?" Marisa's eyes rolled again in remembered frustration. "And Eric kept getting more ape-shit by the second 'cause he doesn't know to just ignore the wild hairs up her butt." Marisa took a drag, careful to keep her green locks clear of the cherry. She must have just put on a fresh coat of Manic Panic. "Good thing I—"

The barmaid had returned. "Cabernet." She set down his order. "And whiskey sour."

Laine's round. He handed the barmaid fifteen and waved away the change. "Thanks, Constance."

"It's a good thing I reminded her Kristen was expecting us," Marisa continued, "Otherwise, we would *still* be debating."

"Mm. Kristen." They toasted silently, then sipped their cocktails. All those unknown names and half-forgotten faces from Marisa's side of their life. He'd been to their parties with her, but Laine still couldn't visualize any of them.

"And guess who was there?"

Laine shrugged, taking another drag.

"Darryl."

A name Laine *did* recognize: Marisa's ex-boyfriend's name. Laine had never met him, but Marisa had told him early on that she'd dumped Darryl for dipping in some other girl's cookie jar. It only took two months and Laine for Marisa to get over him. "Hm. How was that?"

"Okay. We just hung out and talked in the kitchen while Tori and Eric kissed and made-up in the living room." Marisa was pondering the drink she stirred.

"Ah." Laine felt an admission coming.

"We caught up for a while and did a couple of lines."

Laine nodded slowly and swallowed some of his second glass of wine, his head already beginning to spin. "You know how I feel about that coke shit. You said you were done with it before we started going together."

"I'm—" she began.

"Fucking college athletes are dying from that shit." The backs of Laine's eyes began aching.

"I'm sorry, okay? But Darryl was depressed and talking about suicide, and I was pretty much the only person there he knew."

Poor baby. "Was he heartbroken over you?"

"No, his new girlfriend. And if it was Amy, you would be there in a heartbeat."

Laine indulged in a smirk. "True, but I wouldn't be snorting coke."

Marisa's chin met the heels of her palms. "What would you be doing?"

Laine scowled and tamped out the cigarette in the pristine ashtray before him. This nonsense again. The painted hipsters and playing cards under the table's yellowing varnish started dancing together.

"Look, it was just two lines," she pleaded, defusing his anger, "Despite what Nancy Reagan says, you can't get hooked on two lines. And I'm not."

Laine palmed his eyes. "Fine. Fine, just *please* don't do any more." Best to just let it go for now. A warrior knows when to keep his weapon sheathed.

"Are you okay?" Marisa took Laine's hand in hers over the table. She gently drew spirals in his palm with her fingers, their secret signal that promised pleasures to come.

"Yeah. I don't think the cloves like red wine." A spin in his stomach joined the one in his head.

"Do you need a Tylenol?"

"I just need water." Laine was watching Marisa search through her purse for pain relievers. She said more, but he could hear nothing except for a faint, metallic jingle.

In the quiet, Laine saw movement outside the windows

beyond Marisa's left shoulder. Gone were Carol Doda's neon "assets" and Big Al's Tommy gun-toting mobster. Instead, bloated storm clouds were pushing in through the windows, unfurling behind Marisa, and forming a gray tapestry and carpet along the ceilings and floors. They were eating everything and everyone in the bar except for him, and the accompanying downpour was likewise failing to dampen. At the torrent's center, a droning tower backlit by lightning was tethering the rolling charcoal sky to the black earth.

This was a witch storm, and Laine dared not blink. There was a purpose to this vision.

Laine's sight then pulled down, and he found himself in Amarantha's bedroom, watching as his pupil and her lover sat facing each other with their hands entwined. Laine understood and smiled.

"Laine, what are you looking at?" Marisa's head was canted to the right like a curious cockatoo. "Are you okay?"

He blinked the omen away. "Yeah, I just remembered something I have to do soon."

Like the summons that had led him to Amarantha on that crowded Fisherman's Wharf street two years prior, this one required time. Laine would know when the time and the place became now and here, and when that instance came to pass, he would shake the skies.

He would end this crucible during the next summoned storm.

pale shadows

WEDNESDAY, NOVEMBER 12TH

Trees grew in my cave. They were pushing against the grotto walls that enveloped me, yawning and stretching like bored titans. There were waters too, running through hidden veins that swelled in the night and sating the thirsts of wood and flesh.

And if my trees ever lacked light, all I needed to do was breathe.

I was holding a jasper egg: an ovoid, black stone that had entombed the frail skeletons of leaves. Heavy and cool, it listened as I gave it my breath and then pressed it deep into the ground with my palm.

The soil whispered, and columns of fire spit and sparked like charcoal flames around me, leaving behind four driftwood and stone sconces at each cardinal point. Each temple torch was marked with a triangle. Due east and south, the shapes were pointing to the sky. To the north and west, they were pointing earthward. Yellow and red, black and blue, each triangle burned with divine radiance.

pale shadows

The cardinals were set. The elements were in attendance. All that remained was the arrival of Lord Nihthasu.

This was a joyous eve, for on this eve I completed my temple. Half a moon's effort was done, and soon, The Teacher would pass and view our works. It was a struggle at first, erecting the temple around me, but I soon learned how to rouse the corners swiftly.

Something fascinating was occurring: the blue triangle behind me and the yellow one before me were shining the brightest and angriest of the four. Their flames were like an argument to me.

A duel of water and air.

* * *

The business of stirring storms was a simple matter, really. One had to recognize the storm in one's self first, and as Laine faced the eastern dusk, he was turbulent.

The view from his apartment window was magnificent. Heaven's palette was a violent red with wicks of brass awaiting the spark of will. With a gesture, Laine slowed the muggy crimson breeze that was fanning his altar flames and shoved Trump off the window sill and onto the loveseat.

Traffic stopped for signals gone red, the trees of Jefferson Square Park shushed, and the city inhaled. "Nice and still."

No "practical" application of force would be evoked; no clouds would be seeded; nothing would pass that science could gauge, and yet this storm *would* come. Laine was lightning's excitement, thunder's boast, rain's sorrow. The stallions would race tonight, and he held the reins.

He exhaled, igniting the wick. There was a silver flash; there was a guttural boom.

Laine smiled. His witch storm was coming, and soon, he would check in on friends and see what the pupils had brewing.

* * *

Yeah, love spells weren't so bad if you knew they were coming. Not so bad at all.

I am always with you.

The warmth and strength of Deorcloven's finger interlaced with Befana's own. And they shared a breath.

I am always with you.

The tang of his oils; the light of his smile; the weight of his body. All of these remembered sensations were bringing Deorcloven closer to her. And they shared a breath.

I am always—

Befana's eyes were coaxed open by a sudden spark. Deorcloven was sitting skyclad before her on the bed, luminous but dimming like a swift sunset.

"My love, what is it?" she asked his fading presence.

Deorcloven gestured at something behind him in her shadowy candlelit room. They were not alone.

Hanging above and beyond her lover's astral fetch was what looked like two yards of black velvet. A strange flashbulb went off with a buzz outside her window, and the room was bright enough long enough for Befana to make out Neteru's ink-stain body on high near her ceiling. It was moving under its own wind as the ebon night exploded with a dull boom.

Sickening. Maddening. Befana bellowed, "Begone!" A shield burst brilliantly behind her eyes, the sky kicked her room, and both Deorcloven's and that bastard cat's images vanished. Befana could not hold her lover's presence while banishing her former mentor's, not in that moment of rage.

"Damn you!" Amarantha stomped both feet onto her bedroom floor and grabbed her coral night robe from the vanity, concealing her nudity before hazarding a glance outside.

The downpour was like lead against her windowpane. The hail Amarantha was expecting to see was absent, but the rain was bouncing off the street all the same. There was another lightning strike somewhere near the bay, it seemed to her, closely followed by its noisy sibling.

This was Nihthasu's witch storm, to be sure. It felt like him; sounded like him. This was his message, and she read it loud and clear.

Amarantha should have put up stronger wards. She should have been more disciplined about her daily affirmations, and more regular with her meditations. Above all, she should have been honest with herself about the one true thing she wouldn't admit, even after the attack and the broken oath.

"This is *not* letting go. This is *not* 'goodbye.' This is desecration." Her first proper ceremony with Donovan in over a week, and Laine had to defile it! He was biding his time all along, just as she had suspected.

The stormy skies above Amarantha appeared to be posing a question, a challenge: Why not send a message of her own? Why not return the favor in full?

*   *   *

We had fallen as one, Neteru and I. We were staring up into the rains of Nihtheim, flat upon our back as if we had plummeted from a great height. Our hands assured us we lay not on skulls, but how had we arrived there when we should have been in my pupil's temple? It seemed we'd been utterly banished.

We heard the summons of tortured metal and rolled onto our belly. Standing far ahead against the burnt-sugar horizon was a windmill, grinding and calling. Even on four padded paws, it would be a long trek, so we dissolved into the tempest and resolved ourselves at the base of the keep.

It was not a place of refuge, as the clamor belched louder still from the besotted structure. It was muting the troubled sky and deafening us to all else. We had to make it cease. We pounded the soot-coated walls with our fists thrice.

The din stopped, but the storm was still unheard to us.

Eyes ever locked, we stepped back cautiously as an electric charge stood our fur on its end. The torrent was extinguishing us.

All went white, and we were grateful for our lack of hearing. A lance of sky-fire hit its mark squarely, and its mark was the windmill. The vaned tower split like fruit sections before imploding into itself. Dust and fog danced, and all that remained were fractured buttresses and crushed Janus flowers.

Then we heard the tune: a duet of discord sung by unfound strangers. This chant was not for us, but for what was piercing the soil before us: the spear of Moloch had returned to claim the rubble as its own.

We were not fool enough to touch the angry thing; to venture near it, but we had been the kinds of fools who'd let remain that which should have been completely banished. We narrowed our gaze and began uttering words of sending.

Alas, we saw the spear come for us far too late. We heard our queen thrashing. I heard my cat hissing. I heard myself screaming as the shaft ran our right eye through.

I, too, was claimed.

* * *

The city had been drowning for two days, and now Hyde Street was a river of gray too perilous for speed. Wiper blades were squeaking, umbrellas were dashing past, and steam accompanied every breath. The deluge was soaking Amarantha to her bones, and it felt good.

Russian Hill O' Beans looked barren through the window, especially when compared to Halloween. If it weren't for the lights, Amarantha wouldn't have guessed it was open at all. She wrung the excess rain from her shirttail and hiked up her blue skirt a tad before entering.

Laine was there, sitting at the table closest to the espresso machine and writing in a green subject book.

"Ah, you're here," he greeted, stabbing a page from his

notebook with a nasty-looking silver device. "I'll cash out, then you can—" The fool finally looked up and smiled weakly. "Oh, Amarantha. Hi. I'm waiting for Diana to show. I thought you were her."

"No. Sorry." Now that Amarantha was sitting across from him, she could see that he was drawing circles with one of those pencil compasses. He seemed to be inventing new Magick symbols, and Amarantha tilted her head to decipher the markings.

Laine closed the notebook and started to rise. "Do you want me to get Heather?"

"No."

"Can I get you a latté?"

Amarantha gestured him down. "No, thank you. I'm wired enough." She gave him a secret smile, toying with the bell dangling from her ear. "Quite a storm we've been having, hm?"

"I try." The mage adjusted his glasses. "It won't fix the drought, but a little rain is better than none. You look like you're enjoying it." Laine's eyes were lingering on the white Lauren dress shirt Donovan had loaned her during a generous visit. The half-buttoned, drenched garment left just enough of her breasts visible to tempt the imagination, and Amarantha did nothing to hide them, letting Laine enjoy the snare. It was the exact kind of distraction she— *they*—wanted. The earring chimed thinly.

I am always with you.

She grabbed a cord of her golden hair and squeezed a small lake onto the hardwood floor. "Oops. I'm sorry," she apologized sweetly and smugly.

"No problem. Of course, you should have an umbrella." Laine's gaze slid from her breasts to her eyes. Suspicion was finally claiming him, and if she didn't keep talking, he'd figure out that she wasn't alone.

"I have my smock in my bag. I just didn't feel like wearing it." Amarantha looked around. "Slow day?"

He nodded. "The problem with my handiwork is that no one leaves home for their coffee now," he announced to the empty café, "So I await the arrivals of Diana and Marisa so I can bail."

"A barista's life." Amarantha glanced at the wall clock above the grinder. "Wait, it's only 4:00."

"Yeah. One of my managerial duties is to open shop at seven in the morning a couple of days a week. Diana is running behind, so I stayed a little longer" Laine stifled a yawn and asked, "Why aren't you in class?"

"I went to my earlier classes, but then I ran late after lunch, and my instructor Cashman is a jerk, and the rain was so nice, so I just said fuck it."

Laine's jaw dropped an inch at Amarantha's profanity as if she'd never used such language before. He was disarmed just enough for Amarantha to slip in past his mind's notice.

Touch him.

"I just wanted to come by and see what's been going on lately." Amarantha took his hand in search of a cat and found his old shadows instead. She was sitting before Nihthasu. "We haven't spoken in over a week."

There was this strange inner response to her statement like he'd heard it before. "I've been busy," he said simply to a cinnamon shaker.

Ask him.

Amarantha nodded. "How's Marisa?"

"She's fine, I guess."

"That doesn't sound good."

"Sometimes I can't tell. We'll be fine for a month or a week and then blow up over the most insignificant—" Nihthasu sighed.

"On Wednesday, we started out having a perfectly civil discussion that turned into a verbal firefight. She read that Magickal rituals must be followed by practical efforts, and I told her that theurgic rituals meant to cause subtler changes don't always operate that way. You would think the virtue of my experience would have sufficed but no. She disagreed, we started yelling, and I hung up the phone." Nihthasu chuckled more to himself than to any witness. "That's when I summoned the storm. How's that for 'practical'? Anyway, she apologized an hour ago, so . . . ."

The poor dear. "You two fight a lot. If things are that bad, why don't you just break up with her?"

There was no change in his black wards, but anger was stirring behind Nihthasu's glance. "Now, why do you think, '*famulus*'?"

"I know you love her, 'milord', but is it really worth it? Is it worth her suspicions, insults, and disrespect?" Even mentors had their pride, after all.

He growled, "Maybe. Maybe not. Anyway, I could not do so lightly."

Show him.

"How hard could it be for you? She's on her way here, right?"

"Yes, from work." He was calming now.

An electric motor's hum.

"It's pretty wet out there." She drew little spirals in Nihthasu's open palm with her nails.

He nodded, a drowsy scowl carved into his face. "Especially on California."

The metallic blue chassis leaned into a right turn.

"Lots of cable car tracks . . . ," she purred.

"Lots of places to fall."

Steel and water stole the rear tire's traction. The world tipped on its side, and there was a thump.

"No!" Amarantha's old mentor flinched and snatched his hand away from hers. "No! Not like this."

The tire found the asphalt again, and the strangest updraft set the world aright.

The vision broken, Amarantha now faced the murder behind Nihthasu's eyes. He was towering over his end of the table, slowly sinking the stabbing end of his compass deep into the varnished wood.

"What . . . what are you doing?" he asked with a serpent's lisp.

He wouldn't dare touch her. "Just a suggestion." Amarantha smiled sweetly just long enough to show her old mentor that someone else was behind her eyes.

I am always with you.

Laine's wards abated and his shoulders sloped and his fury diminished. He slowly grabbed his notebook, pulled the compass point out of the table with a *twang*, and then stammered, "I . . . I'm gonna get my jacket. I'll send Heather out to say hi."

Amarantha shrugged as she squeezed another puddle from her hair. Just as Laine started turning toward the office, she added, "Oh wait, we did just see you. On Wednesday night." She let her smile darken as she fidgeted with her bell earring, then joked, "How did I forget that?"

Laine nodded as he backed into the hall where the closets were and closed the door.

Amarantha whispered, "'Class dismissed,'" with satisfaction.

* * *

Just a suggestion. That's all it was, right? A touch and a vision meant to shake him? Well, it worked. Laine was deeply shaken, right down to his soul's core. It took a couple of paces in the hall before he noticed Heather sitting on the short steps in front of the office, looking equally terrified.

Heather stammered, "What the hell was that?"

Laine whispered, "That . . . was revenge."

"I looked at Amy's face, but I saw Donovan."

"Then it wasn't just me." Small assurance.

"What is he doing to her?" Heather's voice was hushed but urgent. "Is she possessed?"

Laine's own whisper was hoarse. "A consensual possession, to be sure. Donovan used Amarantha to get to me, and Amarantha used me to get to Marisa."

What time was it? Was Marisa running late? Laine's fists tightened as he tread another ring into the floorboards, then tore off his green apron and threw it into a closet.

"Are you okay?"

"You have no idea, Heather. I was so close to—ending

this right then." Laine almost admitted he could've killed Amarantha where she sat. She had Donovan's astral stink all over her, and Laine's impulses almost won out again. "But we're too late. Amarantha and Donovan *are* bound to each other, and we *are* fighting both of them."

Heather suddenly stood up and grabbed Laine's left shoulder. She had her decision face on. "What do you need? I'll do anything you want."

He cocked a brow. "Anything?"

Heather smiled. "Anything."

"That's a very dangerous promise, Heather." Laine retrieved his long coat from the closet as the comforting electric hum of Marisa's scooter rode into his ears. "You should never make that promise."

She shrugged. "Too late. What do you want me to do?"

Laine slipped into his trench coat, then cracked open the hall door and watched as Marisa locked up her bike. There was nothing in her movements that belied an injury. The suggestion had been just that; only that. Marisa was fine for now.

"This has gone on long enough." His eyes pinned Heather where she stood. "Do . . . whatever you have to do to divide them." Laine glanced over his shoulder toward Amarantha. "Before I do dire harm to her."

Without levity, Heather drew an invoking star in the air between them. "As is your will, so mote it be."

Heather followed Laine onto the café floor, but detoured into the kitchen, probably for Mohammed's oolong fix. Laine couldn't look at Amarantha yet, not without assaulting her. Instead, he kept his attention on the register. Cash it out now, and he could depart swiftly when Diana arrived.

"There you are." Amarantha's greeting still had a tinge of menace. "How's it going, Heather?"

There was a crash, and what was left of the poor door bell fell to the floor, defeated by Marisa's entrance. Heather couldn't have done it better herself. "Hi. Hey, Heather; Amy."

"Hey. What's up?" Keep the greeting casual.

"Oh, nothing, except I almost scrubbed on my scooter."

Laine just stared at Marisa, shocked stupid. He stole a glance at Amarantha, who was mimicking his eyebrow cock. For some reason, "Hm," finally came out of Laine. Too casual. That was *not* the right response.

"That's all you have to say?" Marisa went slack with outrage. "I could've been killed, and all you say is 'hm'?"

"You *are* okay, right?" That wasn't much better.

"Yeah, thanks to this." Marisa dropped her helmet next to the register. "Look. Now I have to shell out a hundred bucks for a new one. I'm surprised the motor didn't stall."

Laine had seen what gravel could do to skin as a boy. As he examined the claw-cut grooves in her helmet, he visualized the fiberglass as Marisa's flesh. "Goddess."

"Thanks for the concern." Marisa cut Laine with her eyes.

"So what happened, Marisa?" Amarantha chimed in. Everyone looked at her.

Marisa said, "I was taking the turn onto Hyde from California when my rear tire lost it on some tracks. I tried to get the scooter to straighten out, but it wouldn't, and I started thinking about the cable car I saw two cars behind me and how I was going to be the new Rice-a-Roni billboard."

You wanna see how we make Rice-a-Roni out here?

Laine caught the glance Heather shot him from the kitchen. Their memory of Samhain.

Amarantha smiled at Marisa's gag. "Eew. What then?"

"It was weird: I heard my helmet hit the ground, and I gave the handlebars a jerk, and there was, like, this wind or —I don't know what it was, but the scooter went right back up."

Amarantha was gazing at Laine conspiratorially. "Wow. It sounds to me like someone was watching over you."

Laine winced from the chill that shot up his spine and down his right forearm.

Just then, Diana strolled in, her Walkman chattering

like a punk rock mouse. Laine could tell she was taking stock of the situation: front door wide open, even with the rain; four witches suddenly silent, two of them lovers. No, it didn't take more than a heartbeat before she asked, "Okay, what did I miss?"

They all answered, "Nothing." The same word, but utterly different voices.

* * *

Two hours had passed, and Amy still seemed normal, sitting across from Heather at Double Rainbow and plowing through her cup of Coffee Almond Fudge ice cream like nothing weird had ever happened. She looked like a tired cherub bathing in the parlor's prismatic lighting.

But something weird *did* happen, and Heather had to get answers without giving herself away. It was like what Laine once said about The Laws of Secrets: the first law was never reveal the secret; the second law was never admit that there was a secret; the third was if asked about the secret, deny it.

"What are you thinking about, Heather?" The rainbow projector had turned Amy's face pink. "You haven't touched your ice cream."

Heather spooned down some of her pumpkin ice cream. "I was just thinking about Laine. He was royally stressed out at the shop. I mean, even before Marisa told us she crashed on her scooter."

Amy scoffed. "Well, he is a witch, after all. Maybe he saw it coming." It was like Amy didn't remember or care that Marisa could've died.

"Maybe." And maybe not. "Did you feel anything? Because I sure didn't, and I know your link to him is stronger than mine."

"I don't want to talk about Laine." Amy snatched off the earring their mentor had given her and tossed it on the table before shoving another heap of ice cream into her mouth. "It's because of him I haven't been doing too well in the Art department lately," she added. It wasn't just hunger that was making Amy risk brain freeze, it was frustration.

"What do you mean?"

Amy sighed and turned into a plum. "As a witch, one comes to accept that the occasional spell will fail. The tides ebb and the trade winds falter, after all." She tossed her plastic spoon into her empty ice cream cup. "But for almost two weeks, I've failed at every working. I can't ground anymore. My candles won't light, my incense won't burn, and I can't mirror walk anymore." Amy had sad, ultraviolet eyes. "I miss home."

Heather shared Amy's Smurf skin. "When's the last time one of your spells worked?"

"I don't know. Donovan and I had a little success last Friday changing the color of candle flames, and then Laine messed up our ritual on Wednesday, but—"

"So the only time your Magick works is when you're with Donovan? That's interesting." But not surprising. That was why Heather saw Donovan in Amy earlier. Just like Laine said, they were fighting both of them now, and it looked like Vampire Boy was keeping Amy on a tight, astral leash. "How do you know it's Laine?"

"Oh, come on, Heather, why do you keep defending him?! Who else could—" Amy froze, staring into Heather's eyes from her Frankenstein face.

Shit. Heather was trying to keep her face blank, but she could feel the panic begin to twitch her muscles. She had to say something before Amy skryed her. "What, Amy?"

"Goddess," she finally said, "Lillian! It must be Lillian!"

"Holy shit. Why didn't I think of that?" Heather took a deep breath of relief, and then shoved a spoonful of ice cream into her mouth.

"Right? There're only two people that have the power to foul up my spells *and* the gall to mess with Donovan and me: Lillian and Laine. Now I see it. My solo workings failed because Donovan wasn't around to strengthen them. That doesn't mean Laine's not a suspect, but still . . . ."

215

Heather nodded in agreement, and it was no act. If Amy was right, Heather had help in splitting Amy and Vampire Boy apart. Ooh, all Heather had to do was let Lillian do her thing and then let Laine know when everything was ready. Neither Amy nor Donovan would suspect her. The thing was she still didn't know how the fuck she was going to make it work.

Then it hit her. "So what shall we do about it?"

"'We?'" Amy gave her a buttercup smile.

"Yeah, 'we'. I'm a witch now too, and two witches are better than one. If the trouble is with Lillian, I can help. If it's not, well, we haven't done a ritual together in years." Knowing which key to strike, Heather added, "Not since Saffy. It'll be fun."

Amy was smiling for the first time today without Donovan's face in the way. "Like old times?"

Heather drew a measured breath and exhaled all thoughts of Laine and their plans before Amy took her hand. Better safe than sorry. "Like old times."

"Can we do it tonight?"

"How about tomorrow? Mama's new girlfriend is coming over tonight for dinner and—oh shit, what time is it?" Heather checked her Swatch: 6:30. "I gotta bail! I'm gonna be late for dinner with Max."

Amy was ruby red again. "That's okay. Go. Tell them I say hi."

"I will. You need my set of keys?" Heather asked, slapping her jean pockets. "I remembered them this time."

"No," Amy chuckled, "I found mine in a fanny pack in the closet." She picked up the jewelry but didn't wear it.

"Cool. Tomorrow night?" Heather's bomber jacket had dried out enough to slide on easily.

"Tomorrow night is perfect. I'll even make dinner."

This was perfect. Heather could feel for Lillian's presence during the ritual, and if she showed up, maybe boost the signal and start the divide and conquer. Yeah, she was on it.

* * *

Laine couldn't shake the memory of seeing Donovan in Amarantha's eyes, nor the cyan vision of Marisa's subsequent fall, but what kept him from his comfort most was how natural and strangely arousing his attempt on his lover's life had felt. True, what happened earlier was Donovan and dear Amarantha's doing, but Laine certainly shouldn't have found it pleasurable. The confusion of whys constricted Laine's brain and snuffed the coals in his heart's furnace.

Laine sat up on the mattress when Marisa entered her room bearing two white dinner plates laden with Parisian-brand sourdough bread and enough cold cuts and cheese to empty out a small deli. She closed the door quietly with her foot. "Look what I got," she announced, wiggling the Miller bottles tucked under her armpits.

"So I see. Bread and beer: the Egyptian staples." Laine set his Sade cassette cases on the nightstand littered with molded plastic rocket ships from Star Magic. "How's your head?"

"It's fine. I was just shaken up from the crash. Sorry I was so pissed before."

He opened his beer and touched bottles with Marisa. "Understandable. If you start to feel dizzy or anything, say something."

"I'm fine, but I will."

For a moment, there was just the shared consumption of prosciutto; a verse of "Sweetest Taboo"; the chatter between Beeker and Misha; the soft sound of warm rain on glass. Good company in bad times.

Marisa washed down some turkey and bread. "Laine, why are you staring at me? I said I'm fine."

He smiled thinly. "'Forever?'"

She returned the smile and the line from *The Hunger.* "'Forever and ever.'" They lingered sweetly, and there was an instance where Laine felt warmth again.

"You know, if you were to ask me, I'd give up The Art

for you," he blurted. "I don't just mean taking on pupils but completely."

Marisa chuckled, "No, you wouldn't."

"Yes, I would. In a heartbeat."

She matched his serious demeanor. "I wouldn't ask you to do that. It's a big part of who you are."

Perhaps, perhaps not. What remained in Laine now was largely wrath and worry, and he could do without them both. No, right now he envied the conventional. He was wishing his worldview was a little smaller; his understanding, more mainstream; his responsibilities, fewer. He was wishing he could just be Laine the Man and not Lord Nihthasu the Magickian.

Marisa added, "You'd be miserable."

Ignoring her possible skry, Laine insisted, "But if it made you happy—"

"I *am* happy." Her smile was true. "Besides, where would that leave me? I practice too, you know, thanks to you."

"I know. Have you been practicing lately? Any gem work or tarot readings?"

"I can't do my own tarot readings," Marisa griped, folding a slice of Monterey Jack into quarters. "They never make any sense."

"That's not unusual. Which deck are you using?"

Marisa looked at the altar nestled beneath her window. "Uh, *Tarot of The Cat People*. Why?"

"I've heard that deck can be finicky." Laine clapped sourdough powder from his hands. "Hand me your Egyptian deck."

"You're giving me a reading tonight?"

"Sure." Knowledge was power, after all.

Rising, Marisa said, "By the way, I finished that horror novel we got at Safeway."

Ah, checkout stand libraries. "I finished mine last night too. How was yours?"

"Worst subterranean-werewolf-in-a-New-England-town plot I ever killed a brain cell with. The characters were alright, but the rest of the story read like it was written by someone drowning. How about yours?" Marisa whistled at her lovebird as she got the wooden tarot box from her altar.

Once Laine stopped laughing, he reviewed, "Worst virgin-sent-to-an-exclusive-Luciferian-school-as-an-unwilling-sacrifice story I've ever read. The writer didn't even bother to make any real characters, and the ceremonies read like something out of *Ghostbusters*. And the 'twist' ending: ooh, I didn't see *that* coming on page one. 'We give it two thumbs down.'"

"If it's that bad, I have to read it. That wasn't a King novel, was it?"

"Of course not. Stephen's a much better writer, even though I can't read his stuff anymore. Too self-referential." A dull thump came from the next room: the sound of a closet door being slammed. "Your esteemed housemates?"

Marisa shook her head in shame as she returned to their rainy day picnic. "Apparently, Mark's band did a show last night, and Kelli got a bug up her ass because he didn't look at her when he sang some love song. They've been at it ever since."

Laine's normal pitch went up an octave. "Are you shitting me?"

"I shit you not," Marisa assured, sliding the stained-wood tarot box across the comforter. "What did she expect from a guy who named his band after himself? Hard to believe Kelli and I come from the same gene pool."

"Oh, well that's just bloody—"

There were three strident knocks on Marisa's door.

Laine hissed, "Obnoxious."

Marisa sighed sharply as she went to her bedroom door and brought the lights up a little. Five more knocks. "You ready?"

"No, but go ahead." Laine removed the *Egipcios Kier* tarot from its box and started shuffling while Marisa opened her door.

"Hi. Can we come in?" Kelli's saccharine greeting stoked Laine's anxieties. Marisa stepped aside, allowing her elder sibling entrance with Mark close behind, donning a stern expression better suited for a Greek statue. His first move was to turn down Marisa's Pioneer stereo, silencing Ms. Adu's ballad. Laine's card riffling suddenly sounded like splitting timber.

Kelli plopped down next to Laine on the bed. *So the game begins.* What would it be tonight? A melodramatic round of "Good Cop/Bad Cop"? They'd been favoring that approach lately.

He could just kill them in their sleep, you know.

The first shot was Mark's. He wouldn't have it any other way. "We need to discuss our living arrangement again."

"We want you to understand it's nothing personal against you, Laine," added Kelli, placing a friendly hand on Laine's unfriendly shoulder. Her smile begged for hostility.

"It's just that you're here every weekend, man. It's only fair you pay your part."

"Wrong," Marisa declared, "Last week was his first time here in a while."

Mark's brow went all Neanderthal. "And he's here again."

"If you want to move in, you're more than welcome to," Kelli assured as she tried to burp Laine. At least, that's what her back-patting suggested.

These two should not breed.

Laine laughed through his nose and shuffled again. This didn't go unnoticed.

"By the way, Laine, congratulations on your manager's position at the café," Mark bellowed, cocksure. "And Marisa: you're working at your dad's print shop during the week and Pier 1 Imports on the weekend. You two should be able to handle half the rent."

Laine looked into Mark's eyes for the second time since his intrusion and said, "Actually, you know what? You're right. We should be able to swing the rent. We've talked about it, and well, Marisa has something to say."

Marisa was leaning on her stereo cabinet, toying with her yellow and green budgie. "Yes. We've decided that we're going to move into our own apartment as soon as we find one we like."

Laine shuffled the cards loudly. Kelli started backing off.

"That way," Marisa continued, "we can't eat up all your food or hog up the living room anymore. Oh wait, we don't do that now." Marisa was cranking Sade back up and waving her flatmates bye-bye.

Kelli left the room with a dead man's grin on her face. What was that condition called? *Risus sardonicus*? Mark followed her, mumbling to himself in what Laine guessed was colorful language.

Once confident that they were gone for good, Marisa turned the music down a little, returned to her previous spot on the bed, and grabbed her beer. "You know we probably won't get to move until January."

"Yeah."

"And you know you'll have to pay them some kind of tribute."

Laine frowned. "I'll bake the fools a Bundt cake."

Fuck that. He should just kill them in their sleep.

Marisa stopped in mid-sip. "Laine . . . ."

"All right, all right. I'll give them some meager recompense," he surrendered, giving the deck another shuffle. "A cleaning deposit or something."

"Thank you."

"Next time, though, we'll just sneak you into my place. I don't think security will care. They know you."

"Goddess, I hate your elevator."

"You hate elevators, period. Here." Laine offered Marisa her deck. "*You're* supposed to be shuffling these."

* * *

Heather really liked Max. It was easy to see how the bookish brunette had captured Mama's heart. She certainly had the smarts, and even though she wasn't as intense as Mama could be, she spoke her mind.

As she stirred her linguine, Heather was listening to Mama and Max lament the loss of the club where they had met, occasionally pinching Rudy's thigh whenever he kicked her chair. She was already feeling the buzz from the sangria her mom let her have.

"Marga's taking Culture Clash on the road; Tom's talking about really getting into politics; Ron closed Valencia Rose to open a new comedy venue." Max wiped eggplant sauce from her chin, but totally missed the spray on the corner of her black, cat-eye glasses. Now Heather would be fixating on that stain for the rest of the meal. "I'm telling you," she continued, "the cultural landscape of the city is changing."

The alcohol in Heather asked, "Wasn't The Rose where you had that fight with Gina?"

Mama looked like someone stuck her with a pin. "It wasn't exactly a fight." She turned to Max. "My ex showed up at the club one night wearing a dress she stole from my closet."

Heather giggled. "Tell her what you did."

Mama said plainly, "I took it back. Right then, right there, everyone watching."

Everybody laughed except for Rudy, who didn't quite get it.

Mama smiled despite herself. "It's not something I'm proud of."

"Yeah, right, what you said," Heather jabbed.

"I really liked that dress." Mama reached across the table and took Max's glasses off. "Anyway, everyone's moving on, true, but it's better than the alternative." Wiping the specs off with her napkin, she said, "That's what made the Halloween party so sad: so many of our friends died because of that damn virus, and no one cares because 'only the fags are dying.'" Mama handed the glasses back to Max, but she was looking straight at Heather. "That's why you have to make sure he wears a condom."

Sparkling cider shot out of Rudy's nose and snuffed out one of the dinner candles as he almost fell out of his chair laughing. Mama was royally pissed, but both Heather and Max were laughing too. She yelled at Rudy in Spanish so fast even Heather missed most of what she said, but Rudy got up looking all sullen and left the room. He was finished eating anyway.

Once she stopped laughing, Heather told Mama, "I have condoms. I doubt I'll ever need them, but I have them." Damn it.

"What about that boy Laine?"

"Mama, I told you already he's—"

Mama started mimicking Heather's whine. "'. . . He's just my friend. There's nothing going on.' Yeah, yeah, yeah." Mama touched Max's hand. "Cute boy, though. He looks like Grace Jones. Well, he did before he cut his hair. You know, one night I thought they were smoking the marijuana in her room?"

Then Max joined in. "Margarita, stop it, you're embarrassing her. Look, she's all red now."

Oh, *that* really helped. "It's the sangria! And I told you, we were meditating."

"*Sure* you were. Whatever's going on, don't let anybody distract you from your goals. Which reminds me . . ." Mama produced a glossy brochure from the shoulder bag hanging from her chair and handed it to Heather.

Max squinted. "What are those?"

"Applications for NEC!"

"That's right," Mama said proudly. "I know it'll be a while before you make enough to go. When you can, you'll go to school for a while, work with some doctors, and maybe find a cure for this fucking plague that's killing all our friends."

Heather's tears tickled her tingling cheeks. "I will, Mama."

* * *

"I think I know why I've been having trouble with my workings lately," Amarantha said into the receiver. "I even think I know who's behind it, but I need you there to be sure. Don't ask any questions yet, but answer this one: can you come over tomorrow night?"

There was some brief, slightly-congested breathing at first, then Donovan answered, "Yes, I can come over tomorrow night. The City's better for my allergies anyway."

* * *

There was a crash when time flew. Forty-five minutes passed on its side, gauging in ruby-red LEDs the length of Laine's Tantric agitations with Marisa. Her aviary thrashed, lunar modules toppled, and a white Gund teddy bear sporting a *Rocky Horror* pin cowered on the carpet.

The tiger stripes Marisa had clawed into his back stung, so his pelvis battered hers in pain. Their pentacles were clashing like pixie swords, and laminated card stock creased beneath Laine's left knee.

"How are you still conscious?" he demanded, singeing her ear with his whisper. "Let go."

A long, dry sigh escaped Marisa's lips when Laine's hands threatened the contours of her neck. She couldn't respond vocally, not with his weight on her throat, but did so with an aimless gaze that stared into eternity.

The last candle died as the twelve-inch of Kraftwerk's "Tour De France" started again, and the sky strobed and drummed.

Third eye blooming, Laine sat upon his heels and pulled Marisa's hips onto his bare thighs. Her arms were swimming slowly on the navy-blue bed sheets, spreading the red and white toy astronauts around her. If Marisa were lying in snow, she would have sculpted herself a pair of wide angel wings.

"Are you crazy enough yet? Huh? You really think you can keep up?"

Marisa moaned and gasped, her body glistening with sweat.

She looks ready to me.

"Hello?" Laine almost knocked on Marisa's skull.

"Nuh-now. Cuh-cum now," she pleaded, splayed in crucifixion grace.

"Are you sure?" Laine balled his fists. "You want it now?"

He's stalling.

"I can't . . . I can't . . . ." Her breastplate beckoned.

Laine's hands were heavy with a long, metal shaft. "As is your will."

He shifted his weight, filling Marisa with exquisite friction. She was too weak to help him churn but strong enough to cry out, "Do it! Do it!"

"Good night, baby," he growled. Laine raised the spear over his head, the ebon shaft branding his palms with its barbs, its tip poised to puncture.

Get this over with. Kill her already!

"Goddesssss," pushed past Laine's teeth as what felt like a frozen drill bit bored into his forehead accompanied by a metallic click and the agonizing sensation of his optic nerves twisting.

Is this where you've led your life? Is this where your life has led you?

Laine gasped, "Maat?" He knew those words. They were her first words to him.

Marisa's trembling centered him, her dead eyes reflecting the darkness.

The accident! Laine's fear overpowered his pain. "Marisa. Are you okay?"

She replied with shudders and was panting like she was suffocating.

"Marisa?" What should he do? Should he call a hospital? Laine still remembered his mouth-to-mouth lessons from the Cub Scouts. Maybe— "Marisa?"

Laine shook the spear loose from his charred hands, dropped it next to the bed, and waited for the laceration to ease before skrying Marisa's head with his fingertips. Their two halves joined, and he shared in her vertigo, but no trauma was found, nor was bone fractured.

Laine broke the link, pulled out of her, and crawled off the foot of the bed. Nude on the coarse carpet, he was finally given the sign of life he sought when Marisa inhaled deeply, moaned, "Wow," with a final orgasmic shudder, then rolled onto her side and immediately slept.

Laine took his time rising from the floor. Once up, he turned off the stereo and waited out his horror before retrieving one of the *kimonos* at his feet. Its length told him he chose the right one. He slipped into it and cinched the *obi* as he went to the bathroom, quiet as ghosts.

The fluorescents turned Laine's pupils into pinpoints. He checked his palms for any blisters the spear may have caused, but that fire had stayed in its own plane, for his hands were unscathed. His forehead was likewise unmarked by the strange, icy spike he'd felt. If only he could think clearly.

An irritation to his thigh that had almost gone unnoticed eased itself by falling to the bathroom floor. Laine recognized the back of Marisa's Egyptian tarot well enough. He picked it up and slowly turned it over.

A lance of sky-fire hit its mark squarely, and its mark was the windmill.

The card revealed a teal tower shattering under the force of a salmon lightning bolt. Two figures were falling from its top and plunging headfirst into a cobra-filled lake. In this deck, the card was named The Obelisk, and it was an ill portent far worse than Death, worse than The Moon, even worse than The Devil. The Tower of Destruction—as it was called in traditional decks—spelled sudden and utter cataclysm, and it had followed Laine.

SATURDAY, NOVEMBER 15TH

heather cracked up when Max yelled, "Don't let the rain slow you down, asshole!" at the black XR4Ti that sped through the intersection of Waller and Clayton streets. "Ugly car. Sorry about the language," Max apologized as she rolled up her window and accelerated. "Witch of a storm, wasn't it?"

Heather's laughter stammered. "What?"

"Serious storm, huh? Is that it on the corner?" she asked, nodding toward Belvedere.

That was weird. "Yeah, that's it."

The white Volvo's tires crunched up wet gravel as it made the left kiddy-corner turn to the front of Amy's place. As they stopped, Heather took in the Victorian facade. The windows in the front of the house were dim, so maybe Amy had already lit the candles.

Heather shook Max's hand. "Are you eating with us on Thanksgiving?"

"I don't know. I don't see why not." There was something in Max's eyes that told Heather her mother's girlfriend wasn't welcomed in her own family's home.

Grabbing her duffel bag, Heather said, "Well, you are most welcome to dine with us. Thanks again for the ride, Max." She kissed Max on the cheek, smiled, then left the sedan. Heather jogged up Amy's stoop and waved at Max's departing car.

"Okay. Let's see what we can see." Turning toward Amy's door, she took a couple of grounding breaths before pressing the doorbell. She measured out a few more breaths in the time it took for the footsteps at the far end of the hall to reach her. The door opened, and she froze.

Donovan filled the threshold with his Adonic glory: blue 501s; white T-shirt; gray, single-breasted blazer unbuttoned with his fancy pentagram a-swinging. The most intriguing part of his attire was his expression, though, as it was the same damned expression Heather had on her own face. Their thoughts had to be the same too: What the hell are *you* doing here?

Donovan sputtered, "I—Amy didn't say—"

"I know. She didn't tell me either."

"Huh," he said, nodding, "Our little witch must be up to something big."

"Yeah." So what the fuck was Heather supposed to do with this?

Donovan smiled and shrugged. "Well, anyway, hi. We're all in the dining room." He stepped aside for her and then closed the door behind them.

"'We're'? Who-who else is here?" The sound of Donovan's trailing steps made Heather's skin crawl.

"Oh, Amarantha, me, Joanie, and now you."

"Joanie's here?" That was a relief and a surprise.

"Yeah. Amarantha couldn't get her out the house." Donovan couldn't hide his disappointment. "But *no problemo*. She made plenty of food."

They entered the candlelit dining room, and man, Donovan didn't lie about the size of the dinner. There was more than enough for four people. "Wow, someone's been busy," Heather said to Amarantha, setting her duffel bag and jacket aside.

"Yup, and I just made your plate. I figured I'd show off what they've been teaching me in class. Dig in."

Heather greeted Joanie and kissed her on the cheek, then took the empty seat. The dinner scene was absolutely picture-perfect. Seriously, it looked just like a painting. Donovan sat directly across from Heather and silently filled her wine glass; Joanie was at one end of the dining table, silently shoveling small mounds of brown rice into her mouth; Amy was sitting at the other end silently twirling her French-cut green beans and glancing at Donovan. The whole family was there, plus Vampire Boy.

Yep, quiet as a painting too.

As the meal went on and the Pinot Noir flowed, Heather and Joanie played catch up. Joanie asked about Mama and Rudy, and Heather asked about Joanie's volunteer work until, after a while, Heather was over Donovan's surprise appearance. In fact, his presence could make her job easier. If she could find a way to prove Donovan was up to no good tonight, he'd have to face Amy with nowhere to run. Now, how to out him?

Heather looked over at Donovan when he cleared his throat at Amy and pointed at the floor beneath the dining table. Amy smiled. Heather didn't know what was going on at first, but then she looked down, and she totally got it: the two lovebirds were remembering that this was the room where they first "did it." Heather rolled her eyes with revulsion.

"Is there more of this chicken?" Joanie asked, breaking the tension.

The three witches cackled. Leave it up to Joanie to think with her stomach.

"What?" Amy's mom cried with a shrug.

"Nothing. Yes, there's plenty more," Amy assured.

"Is that fennel I taste?" Donovan inquired through his candlelit grin. Heather gave a small snort.

"Yes. I found a patch of it growing in the garden." Amy

was so close to cracking up again. "It's not in the recipe, but I figured I might as well use some before it takes over the backyard."

Smiling at her plate, Heather said, "The bacon's a nice touch. What is this called?"

"*Coq au vin*," Amy said through her smile.

Heather frowned. "What does that mean?"

Amy whimpered, "'Cuh-cock with wine.'" The three witches cackled louder.

Joanie stood up and said in her small voice, "Okay, I'm going to my room now. It's getting silly in here." She grabbed the bottle of red from the oak dining table.

Amy managed, "I'm sorry, Joanie."

Joanie was smiling so hard her cheeks hid her bespectacled eyes. "That's okay. *Mike Hammer* will be on in a little bit anyway."

As Joanie headed down the hall for her room, Amy whispered, "Now see what you did? She took the wine."

Heather whispered, "Me? How is that my fault?" After Mama's world-famous sangria last night, one glass of wine was enough for her anyway. Besides, she was already buzzed.

Donovan whispered back, "I brought more."

Heather mumbled, "Of course you did," into her glass of water.

Donovan dropped his fork on his plate. "And of course you're busting my balls for it. Nice to see some things never change."

Amy took their hands in hers and declared, "Okay, okay, truce. I spent a long time on dinner, and I'd appreciate it if you two didn't fight over it. Please?"

"You're right, Amy." Heather gave Donovan a pacifying smile. "I'm sorry, Donovan."

Donovan returned the smile with a shrug. "Truce. Aren't you hungry? You've only cleared half of your plate."

Heather speared some dark meat with her fork. "Oh no, I'm fine, and the dinner's great. I'm just trying to drop a few pounds for the holidays, that's all." Heather looked at Amy, setting her utensil down. "Besides, I discovered that my Magick works better if I'm not hungry or full."

Amy finished the last of her wine, pinky upright. "So I guess you're both pretty confused about what we're all doing here tonight," she started. "As I've told you both, I've been having problems with my workings lately, and I think there's an outside force that's responsible."

She directed her gaze toward Heather. "Last night you said, 'Two witches are better than one.' I figured three had to be even better, so I asked Donovan to come and help us."

Heather just said, "Hmm." Funny how Amy neglected to mention she suspected Lillian. She probably wanted to keep Donovan in the dark on that part.

Amy said to Donovan, "I need you both here to help me bolster my seals. Between the three of us, we should be able to hold off whatever's behind my problem, if there is in fact someone or something behind it."

Donovan was frowning. "So you don't think we'll have any more 'intrusions' tonight?" He meant Laine.

Amy shrugged. "I just think we should keep open minds and open eyes. For all I know, it could be astrological. Or astronomical."

"Wise," Donovan said simply.

Heather asked, "So we're going to raise a cone of power tonight?"

"That's right, Heather. We'll use the energy to strengthen the wards. Textbook stuff, just like the old days."

Perfect. Heather now knew how to get into Donovan's head.

* * *

The black moon hid, as was its nature: hidden by the position of the sun; hidden above the high, deep clouds; hidden beyond the mage's clenched lids.

Laine wiped off the chrome pencil compasses in his fists. There were about twenty unbanished phantom cadavers at his feet now. Not good to leave the dead like this, not even the astral dead, but he had to accustom himself to being knee-deep in gore. He could let neither his mind nor constitution be shaken when it was time for his true enemy's fall.

Although Laine desired a prolonged sparring session, he had to cut the brawl short. He sensed a mortal audience and figured it was time to open his eyes.

The girl before him couldn't have been more than twelve. The leash in her hand and hooded jogging suit on her back said she was out walking her dog. She whispered, "*Brujo*."

The mage's high school Spanish covered that. She knew what he was and perhaps even sensed the carnage surrounding them just beyond the nether-veil. Maybe she saw the inhuman limbs her feet were straddling. What a tale this would make for her grandchildren.

"You should be getting home where it's safe," Laine advised with a smile. "It's getting darker faster these days, these nights."

The Latina curtseyed—of all gestures—before catching up with her pet. The animal expelling its dinner looked like a close relative of another black mongrel: the one he had met on Samhain half a moon ago. Synchronicity and his sister Déjà Vu made for interesting company.

So the rain had stopped. Fortunately, San Francisco was also good for wind, and the wind was perfect for sweeping away a field of dead souls. A brief inner submission later, Laine and the air did just that. Skin became bone, bone became dust, and then nothing.

A carpet of wind-pitted skulls stretched farther than the glare would allow me to see.

His upper lip twitching at the memory, the wizard checked his watch: it was almost 9:00. Laine guessed he had energy and time enough for a few more corpses after all, despite his evasive slumber. He paced a widdershins course, trampling the rain-burdened grass beneath his soles.

This unrest was uncharacteristic of him. The new moon

was a cloistral phase, so why did it drive him from his apartment? He was only ever this anxious during the full moon when her rays kept him happily wired.

There was no such exuberance this eve, just the intent to move and hunt and injure.

* * *

They were sitting hand in hand in hand on Amarantha's bed. Buttocks on calves, their names were racing around them like frightened foals. The glass candles bearing the likeness of a guardian angel were dim in comparison to the trio's auras as they breathed electricity.

Tethered to the Earth's core while summoning to the heavens, Amarantha was elastic light. She sent a wick's worth of that light into the center of their ring with one word: "Heather."

The deed was now passed on to her best friend.

"Donovan." The flame at the center breathed, casting light into the cowl of Heather's shift. Her eyes were half-shuttered, looking somewhere slightly beyond the northern wall, as they should be.

"Amarantha." They did not use their Magick names tonight, for Heather still had none. Amarantha knew what he meant, and Donovan's call rang as Befana in her mind.

"Heather." The astral flame was brighter still.

"Donovan." Heather quickened the beat half a pulse. Goddess, she was radiant, and Amarantha couldn't help but be impressed with Heather's great progress. She was playing her part perfectly.

"Amarantha." It was her best friend's new powers that were the worry, though. Amarantha had caught a glimmer of Laine's plan last night at Double Rainbow and knew Heather was a key part of it.

"Heather." Before this ritual was done, Amarantha would know the whole truth of it, no matter what it took.

"Donovan." Yes, Lillian was a possibility—and the reason why tonight was perfect—but she wasn't a convincing one, despite Amarantha's suggestion. After all, Donovan handled her.

"Amarantha." No, it had to be Laine. It had to be—

"Heather."

Each round fed the fire as each witch contributed their light, and with growing haste, their names were chasing each other's heels. Soon, Amarantha would quarter draw the astral flame and send the parts to her wards. Soon, the truth would be revealed.

* * *

"Donovan."

Heather knew this ritual very well. After all, they used to do it with Saffy all the time.

"Donovan."

In a couple more rounds, Amy would begin her chant, which would be Heather and Vampire Boy's cue to sing her name.

"Donovan."

He'd be focusing on Amy, and Heather would be quick. He'd eaten a lot, so he should be sluggish and drowsy. When the flame finally rose to turn their ring of light into a cone, she'd sneak a peek.

"Donovan."

Heather almost felt sympathy for the devil. Donovan *had* been nice all evening, and there was no doubt that he loved Amy as deeply as anyone could, but that was the problem.

"Donovan." A love that deep could easily become an obsession. Hell, it was *possession* just yesterday. No, Heather had to find a way to split them up.

"Donovan." Questionable acts for the greater good: yeah. Oh shit, she'd forgotten to call Laine. He didn't know Heather was there doing what had to be done.

"Donovan." Then again, he couldn't help now anyway since Amy's wards were almost at full power. No, this was her time. Heather refocused.

"Donovan." Weird. Every time Heather said Donovan's name, she felt a little weaker. That had never happened with Amy or Saffy.

Amy said something in Greek, and Heather and Donovan called out her name in unison. It took a couple of rounds before they got a rhythm down; made the chant almost musical.

The lavender room wobbled strangely as the walls started breathing, and static electricity snapped at Heather's skin before settling to a hum. They were in-between worlds now.

Heather lowered her head, shading her eyes from the rising light before them. Now for the skry.

Her sidelong glance caught Donovan's skyclad thighs, and she almost gasped. Instead, she took a deep breath and said, "Amarantha."

Still watching his naked thighs, Heather realized they weren't really naked at all. She hazarded a glimpse at Amy and found she too was wearing translucent clothes. Heather was seeing their astral shells burning bright beneath their attire. They were like living x-rays.

"Amarantha."

Heather slowly turned her gaze back to Donovan and continued her sweep of him. She took in his hips; torso; shoulders; the grasp they shared.

Goddess, he was looking right at her: a grinning, wing-less angel all afire!

"Amarantha."

He was staring with white-gold eyes, his head slightly tilted.

She felt it then: the liquor-sodden body crushing her lungs.

No. What was he doing?

"Amarantha."

The angel was so close that Heather could feel his cold flames.

Her wrists struggling against the sofa cushions; the hot, putrid gasps against her young breasts.

Donovan was deep in her head, stirring through her memories like a stick in her mind's mud. He was skrying her.

"Amarantha."

He parted her thighs with his as she slowly reclined.

Goddess, her pelvis.

Heather did not resist. She didn't want to, and she knew she should have.

"Amarantha."

Not a word passed between them as his unblinking glare consumed her.

Heather gritted her teeth against the sting of her rug burned back.

She wanted him. She hated him.

"Amarantha."

The angel stopped, and his face was etched with fear when he looked away.

He pushed himself off of her, smiling with satisfaction.

Heather followed his terrified gaze then screamed, "Amarantha!"

Whose eyes were—?

* * *

Vertigo pushed Amarantha sideways when Heather snatched her hand away and scurried off the bed.

"Heather, what's wrong?"

Heather said nothing. She just grabbed her half-open bag of clothes from the floor and raced for the bedroom door, her shift flowing behind her.

"I'll be right back," she told Donovan before chasing Heather into the hall, begging for a response. "Heather, tell me what happened. We still have to close the ceremony."

Heather was wordlessly leading Amarantha down the outside steps. Maybe she sensed what Amarantha was up to and was making her silent escape, or maybe she couldn't speak, just like at the café; just like all the times before. Amarantha couldn't tell.

The rain had passed, but everything moving on Waller Street gave off a wet, gritty crunch. At the speed that Heather was walking, Amarantha feared her friend would slip and fall.

She stumbled. It was enough for Amarantha to catch up to Heather as she lurked beneath a streetlamp. She grabbed her friend's shoulders and turned her, but Heather shrugged the hands off, her face still hidden beneath her shift's hood.

"Heather, please, just say it!" Amarantha growled with frustration, "Just tell me the truth! What is Laine making —"

Exposed to the salmon-colored light, Heather's painted lips took on the strangest hue as eyeliner tears streaked down beside them. She reached out for Amarantha's cheek, but Amarantha dodged her hand like—

The world stopped, all sound silenced, and visions of volleyed balloons and teenage partiers were flashing behind Amarantha's eyes.

Heather rasped, "If you would not drown, little one, then you shall relent."

Those words, that gesture: they were Lillian's. Amarantha had not shared those details with anyone.

The chilling proclamation halted any protest Amarantha could raise or any attempt to stop Heather, who had fled across the street and past the church. Shaken, Amarantha turned on her heels and went inside as drizzle fell again.

Donovan was standing next to her altar, holding a now-desiccated red rose from Samhain. "Where's Heather?" he asked, using the flower like a wand to draw a widdershins star in the air.

"I couldn't . . . I couldn't stop her."

"Did she say anything?" He turned toward her door and banished again.

Amarantha shook her head.

Donovan asked plainly, "And why didn't you tell me that you were summoning Lillian the whole time?"

"What? I wasn't trying to—"

"I felt her, you know. I saw her in your mirror, and I

think Heather did too. I mean, by The Goddess, Amarantha, Lillian's a Hecatean! She is strongest by the new moon." Donovan jabbed a finger at the sky. "Guess what tonight is? That was dangerous and foolish. Why would you do that?" He banished the summoned energy over her bed.

Amarantha hadn't overlooked that fact: she was counting on it, despite her doubts. She knew what Lillian was the instant she saw her. "Because you said you'd handle her. Clearly, you didn't," she reminded. "She's been blocking my spells for almost a month, and I just wanted to banish her permanently if she did show up."

Donovan drew the final star near her northern windows, then threw the rose back onto Amarantha's altar. "And how do you know she's blocking your spells? Magick fails sometimes, you know. We don't create it, we channel it."

"I know what we do, sir, and I also know when someone's keeping me from doing it!"

Donovan surrendered, his white palms standing in for a white flag. "Okay, fair enough. I still think it's Laine, but if you want me to take care of this, I'll take care of it. My dad wants me back in SD next Saturday anyway. I'll deal with Lillian then."

"Thank you."

"Consider yourself damned lucky Heather broke up the ritual, and I was able to send Lillian away. She is psychotic, Amarantha, and you would be wise to stay away from her in any manner." There was a pointed emphasis on the last part of Donovan's sentence. "Besides, now that she knows that we know, your Magick is probably back anyway."

"Probably." After all, it always was when Donovan was around.

* * *

"Stop it," Heather whispered, "No more crying." She had cried enough on the way home, she was hysterical during her phone call to Laine, and she'd wept deeply during her long, intense shower. Now standing in the dark outside of Mama's bedroom, Heather haunted the hallway silently, rocking back and forth near the front door. Laine would be there soon, and she didn't want to wake Mama. Heather couldn't share tonight with her, not yet.

Steps creaked, and Heather opened her front door partway before Laine could knock, and before he could speak or even get a good look at her, she shushed him.

Heather led the way to her room, trailed by her angry shadow of a teacher. Laine had been pretty pissed over the phone until Heather's crying convinced him that something went FUBAR. After that, he'd obviously wasted no time getting to her house.

"You should have waited," he finally spit out in her room. "You should have told me you were doing it tonight. We could have reinforced your wards again beforehand—"

He stopped seething when Heather finally turned and faced him. The white, worn-down bathrobe she was wearing gave away the shower she'd just taken, and even in her room's half-light, Laine was noticing her neck and limbs were cherry-red from her rigorous attempt to scrub the memory of Donovan off of them. Her tears flowed again, her breath shuddered, and the silence around them thickened.

Laine's expression went from aggro to concern as he placed a comforting hand on her shoulder. "Goddess, Heather, what happened?"

Her Pandora's box of misery blew wide open. "I-I was 'sposed to spend the night, and fuh-fuckin' Donovan was there, and Amy wanted to do a rit-ritual. I didn't know he was guh-going to be there 'cause Amy didn't tell me, and I wanted to see, that's all. I just wanted to take a peek. I thought maybe I could skry him and see what he wuh-what he's really up to." She wiped her nose on a terry cloth sleeve. "But he skryed me first!"

Laine's lips were pursed, but he loosened his jaw enough to say, "Go on."

Heather wiped up some spilled snot with her slippered foot. "We were on Amy's buh-bed," she whispered to keep from screaming, "and we were ruh-raising the cone." She showed Laine the torture behind her eyes. "Donovan was on me! He was in me! I wanted him to stop, but I couldn't make him—"

"That's enough."

"And Amy didn't know 'cause she wuh-was tranced out. Sh-she probably put him up to it. He fucking went through all my worst memories. He shuh-showed me my every pain, and he made me like it." Her whispering failed. "He made me like it!"

"That's enough. That's enough. It's okay, I've got you." Laine had both of her shoulders now, massaging away the tension and anguish.

"What a fuh-fucking freak show." Heather usually would've been embarrassed after just emotionally hurling all over Laine, but she wasn't really. Instead, she sank into the comfort of his embrace, still sobbing, but growing calmer and feeling safer. "I-I want him dead," Heather admitted.

"Me too."

Laine smelled lightly of patchouli and sweat, and soon that old electric tingle Heather felt when she was around him came back. He gave her a peck on the forehead that made her tremble, and she looked up at him, catching his eyes with hers. Goddess, she wanted to kiss him back so badly.

"Oh, God. I'm . . . so attracted to you." She glanced away timidly. "I'm sorry. I shouldn't have said that."

"I know that must have been very hard for you to admit, especially after tonight."

Heather caught his gaze again. "Can you stay with me? Help me forget, just for tonight? I just—I know you have Marisa, and I'm not trying to mess that up, but I need—" Heather wiped the fresh tears from her face.

"You . . . kept a dangerous promise, Heather, and you paid for it. I can't leave you to hurt alone." Laine's face was mostly blank, but there seemed to be a little sadness and maybe fear in his eyes. "So what are you proposing?"

Heather walked past him toward her bed, slowly faced Laine, and shrugged the terry cloth from her body, suddenly worrying about the weight she hadn't lost yet. Her tits always attracted attention, but face it, she wasn't built like Amy or Marisa. What if her extra curves grossed him out?

"You're The Earth Mother," he commented. "You're Ruben's muse. You are a Goddess. There's no reason to be ashamed of that."

Heather smiled. "Thanks."

He closed the distance between them, moving into the light of her lamp. Heather opened her nightstand drawer, revealing the two dozen or so doubloon-like condom coins inside.

Laine couldn't help himself. "For a rainy day?"

"Or night. I've never needed them before."

Laine said, "Oh," and then the meaning behind her words caught him. "Oh. In that case, I am truly honored, Heather, but are you sure I'm the one to do this?"

"Yes, absolutely. I trust *you*, Laine. But no kissing, okay?"

"Very well. No telling either." Laine removed his black long coat and muffler and then searched her room for someplace to put them.

"Can I?" Heather offered. She took both items from him and dropped them on the floor. Laine gave a small smile as Heather grabbed his turtleneck by the waist and untucked it. His arms were so long that he had to help her get it over his head. The sweater then joined the pile.

Laine was as rail-thin as she'd expected, but he wasn't skin and bones, he was sinews and bones. Heather didn't think he had an ounce of fat on him—the lucky asshole—but his shoulders were surprisingly broad, and he was cut. Heather traced his pecs and abdomen with her fingertips, happy that he wasn't hairy and that his skin was as smooth as polished *manzanita* wood.

She kneeled to remove his shoes and socks. That old stereotype about the size of a man's feet came to her, and suddenly Heather got *really* worried. If there was any truth to the myth, Laine would prove to be a big boy.

Heather stood back up and worked on his belt next. When she unbuckled it and slipped it from his slacks in one pull, Laine said, "Well, that was easy," laughing like it was a private joke. Heather let it slide, chuckling nervously.

Now came the hard part. With a tug of his waistband, she slid his pants and briefs down, dropping them around his ankles. Laine stepped out of them, leaving himself naked before her. Heather didn't dare look down.

His eyes asked again if she was sure. Her eyes answered yes.

* * *

This was how suspicious lovers slept: back to back and inches apart with just enough room in between for a napping cat. Donovan was suspicious of Amarantha, and Amarantha was suspicious of everything. Terra kept her suspicions to herself. Even with the down comforter and her familiar's company, the bed was cold now that Donovan was apparently loathing Amarantha's touch.

True, Lillian was Donovan's problem, and he probably would handle her better than Amarantha, but that loose skin at the roof of her mind was still bothering her. The pieces weren't fitting at all. Why would Lillian suppress Amarantha's powers if she wanted to make contact, even if Lillian was—as Donovan said—psychotic?

And then there was Heather. Whether she was conspiring with Laine or not, what happened to her best friend tonight was all Amarantha's fault, and she owed Heather an apology. The problem was that Heather probably hated her now. Still, it was odd that Lillian possessed Heather to deliver her message rather than send it directly. Why? To make sure Amarantha listened? To get around Donovan? To prove that she could? Amarantha hoped Heather got home okay.

Amarantha rolled onto her back and began uneasily

stroking the frayed edge of her childhood blanket. She had originally intended to utterly banish Lillian, but the warning she sent through Heather changed all that. Now she wanted to connect with the Hecatean more than anything.

* * *

"So after the enlightenment of Rooftop, I was thrust headlong into the smothering cocoon of adolescence. I was dogged by high school thugs, frustrated by girls, dis-illusioned by religion, unanswered by science, and angry with mankind. I decided that life on this side of the veil was more chaos than I could stand. I wanted out."

Laine's silhouette spoke, backlit by Heather's lamplight, the bed sheets pulled up to his neck, and his arms tucked in at his sides. He looked ready for burial as he told Heather about his Calling.

"My room was cramped and in teenage disarray with special effects manuals, 'kit-bashed' models, and Dungeons and Dragons maps strewn all over the place. The only knowing eyes belonged to the family of mice living in the old wall-mounted radio."

"What about your mom and your sister?" Heather asked.

"Asleep at the other end of the house. I can't remember how many pills were in that black jewelry box, or what kind of pills they were, but I knew I had enough of them to do the job. I'd leave this world one way or another."

A wind rattled Heather's window. She slithered closer to Laine and toyed with the moonstone pentacle that lay loose around his neck, wondering when she'd get hers.

Laine pointed his chin at Heather. "You know, like in that Prince song, I wanted to die so I could be free: free from the tether of the flesh; free of the troubles of the mind and soul. This alone would have been good enough for me. I spoke the only prayer I knew, trying to will my heart to a standstill as my body grew heavy from the drugs.

"Then I heard a familiar, unseen voice say 'Is this where you've led your life? Is this where your life has led you?'

"'Yes,' I replied with a whisper of my mind.

"'Are you willing to do anything to change your life; your world?'

"'Yes.'

"'Even die?'

"'Yes,' I said."

"The Goddess?" Heather asked.

Laine's profile nodded. "She was Nieth; Bastet; Venus; Isis; Diana; Hecate; Maat; all of the other ancient and divine names for femininity. She was The Great Mother, and I could ask for no better teacher."

"And what did she teach you?"

Laine was silently reading the cracks in Heather's ceiling before answering. "I learned enough technique to at last fill the canyons of my curiosity. I learned when to wound, when to heal. I learned how to bend forces, light and dark, to my will. I learned that remembering the future is just as easy as remembering the past, and that now is eternal. All of that and so much more."

For some reason, one phrase sang to Heather: remembering the future. Was it really as simple as that?

"Do you know you have Australia on your ceiling?" Laine had noticed the familiar paint chips over them.

"Yeah. The Hawaiian Islands and Iceland are over there." Heather pointed at a shadowy area of her ceiling close to the door.

"Aha," Laine said with a smile. "Well, anyway, I learned that reality is created by consensus, and I found my place not only in this world but in others. More than that, I found the silence and succor I was looking for. The Goddess taught me Magick." Laine shook his head. "Seven years ago: it seems like a lifetime away."

Heather remembered an old biology class. "You know, technically it was."

"What do you mean?"

"Did you know that every seven years, we regenerate all new cells? Not all at once, but it's like we get a new body every seven years. Wait, you're twenty-one, right?"

Laine nodded. "Yeah."

"So not only is this your third body, but it's also your first adult body. I've got three years to go before I get mine."

"A lifetime away . . . ."

Before he even moved to do so, Heather knew Laine would leave soon. Their night of passion and compassion was over. He was scheduled to be at work later, and she desperately needed sleep too, even though she wanted him to stay. Laine and the evening had worn her out.

"Laine, what sign are you?"

"Pisces, with a whole lot of Scorpio." After throwing away the used condom, Laine began searching through his clothes by lamplight. "You?" he asked, pulling on his black slacks.

Heather propped herself up on one elbow. "Capricorn. Hey, what did you mean by 'remembering the future'?"

"Well," he started, "when you try to remember something, you usually start with one detail and then link it to the rest of the memory, right?" He was tying his laces. "Just do the same thing with a future detail."

"Wait, how do you know which detail if it hasn't happened yet?"

Laine had just finished pulling his turtleneck over his head when he leaned close to Heather. She wondered who made up the word "swoon".

"If the future hasn't happened yet, why not choose any detail you like?" He slowly stood straight again as he tucked himself in. "A gesture in a certain room; a personal item glimpsed; a comment made during a commercial break. Anything can serve as the key. Think of it as . . . déjà vu under will."

Heather sat up. "So you know how this is going to end then?"

"No," he whispered. "No, I don't. I can't see that." His

frown showed Heather that it was bothering him. Laine put on his coat and muffler and became a living shadow again. He reached inside his turtleneck and freed his pentacle. "Heather, do you think I'm . . . evil?"

Heather laughed to herself, falling back onto her bed. How could she think him evil after tonight? "They say 'evil is as evil does,' so no, I don't think you're evil. I think you're dark . . . and a little naughty, and I think you've spent a lot of time with—I don't know—things I'll never understand, but you're not evil. *¿Por qué?*"

Laine was gripping the doorjamb so hard it squeaked. "I've come to believe that angels are the broken parts of gods, and that demons are the broken parts of men," Laine said, his eyes pinning her in the dark. "I've never felt closer to pure evil before in my life. I've never felt more broken."

Heather shook her head and swayed her legs. "If that was true, you wouldn't be here. I trust *you*, Laine, and you know me, I don't do that too easily." She couldn't resist putting a little flirt in her voice. "You seem all right to me."

"I hope you're right, Heather," Laine finally said. "Goodnight." He slipped into the darkness of her hallway as quiet as ghosts.

"That was a pretty cryptic end to the evening." Why was Laine—Heather sat up suddenly. "Oh shit. Is he going to kill Donovan?"

Her blankets settled, blowing a breath of Laine's ritual oil past her face. Heather calmed and smiled while lying back down.

"No, he won't. He can't. Laine's no murderer."

* * *

Evil is as evil does. What was said about the yet undone? What witty platitudes covered murderous intent? What axiom addressed Laine's singular goal of slaying Donovan in his sleep tonight? Revenge is a dish best served cold. That was it.

For Amarantha's possession, for his part in the attempt

on Marisa's life, for the assault on Heather's sanity, Donovan would die tonight. His bell had tolled, and Laine had the evilest of intentions.

About time. Kill them all, and let The Goddess sort them out.

"It's about time indeed."

Even without Neteru, Laine strolled Mission Street at a panther's pace. His long-legged strides made short work of the journey between 22nd and 20th. It wouldn't be long before he was standing over Donovan and Amarantha as they slept, and once he was, he would render Donovan as gray and bloated as the rat that had just cut across Laine's path. There was something about that—

Slow-time kicked in as Laine stopped to watch the beer bottle performing a trapeze act a foot from his face. "Budweiser. How disappointing," he lamented as the bottle exploded near the fleeing rat's ass.

"FUCKING NIGGER!" A red Dodge pickup accelerated as the passengers threw Laine a double gesture of profanity.

Ooh, practice time.

Laine resumed his pace; sped up his breathing; let them think they were losing him. By the corner of 19th, he started gaining. By halfway down the block, Laine was looking the passengers in the eyes, smiling. He was still just walking.

The long-haired payload in the back banged on the cab window. The truck stopped, and the passenger-side door choked out a two hundred pound redhead in a yellow Izod shirt. He joined his shaggy friend as they approached Laine.

Go for the big one first!

The mage planted his feet a shoulder span apart.

"You got something to say, faggot?" the longhair asked, a fresh beer in his hand.

Damned Twin Cities kids. They never pronounced "nigger" properly, and they always assumed that all San Franciscan men were "faggots" whether they wore makeup or not. They probably called Laine's city "Frisco" too.

"Nope. Nothing at all," Laine responded.

The redheaded sasquatch shifted his weight to throw a punch, but his right eye popped like a grape when the spike went in. Laine's fist snapped back to his side and wiped the gel off of his pencil compass. The giant started screaming.

The longhair inhaled with shock. His brain was telling him to swing the beer bottle, but his reflexes were slow. Laine's second blow buried the compass spike into the Bud fan's red neck so deeply that his knuckles made contact. A follow-up side kick threw the longhair a safe distance away. The redhead was now rolling around on the sidewalk, crying blood.

Now the truck driver wanted in on the fun, jumping out of the cab. Laine readied the pencil compasses and moaned, "Ooh, a bonus kill." He so rarely got live sparring partners.

"Puh-please, man, I'm sorry," the driver begged. "Let me just help my friends."

Laine took a step forward. The driver flinched an inch back into the middle of the street.

"They're drunk. I'm sorry. Please let me get them to a hospital."

"Not my problem," Laine declared, "As far as I'm concerned, you're all dead."

Just then mental tumblers clicked, and Laine's forehead felt like it was exploding into small icebergs.

"Please—"

"Take them. Juh-Just go." Laine turned and stumbled away, squeezing the pieces of his frozen skull together. What was wrong with his head?

Now that was fun. What a night.

Laine's stomach did an unwelcome jig. "Shut up."

Get to kill the villain and get the girl.

"Sh-shut up!"

Hell, he's got two *girls.*

"That's enough!" Laine protested aloud, "I couldn't leave Heather the way she was."

Except one can't know about the other.

"Stop! I couldn't—" Laine's feet turned to lead.

A virgin. He bagged himself a virgin.

He couldn't move anymore. He found purchase against a chain-link fence as guilt and shame spread through his weakening limbs. "What . . . what did I—"

Love the way she laughed when she came.

Laine collapsed and emptied his stomach through the corroded fence. Shaking and hurling, he stammered around his last meal, "Guh-Go the fuck away!"

Well, this is no good.

We've lost him again.

"Fuck! Fuck!" Laine was kneeling among black discs of forgotten chewing gum on the sidewalk, his face melting into misery. "You've had your blood. Why can't you just leave? Why can't I banish you?"

What's he bitching about? He's bulletproof now.

I think he's missing the point: we are here for Donovan.

And anyone else who opposes us, like that bird-bitch.

That was why Laine had been so eager to spill Amarantha's red contents the week before. *That* was the source of Laine's night terrors about Marisa: they both opposed the spear. Marisa had kept him from striking Donovan in the beginning, and Amarantha had stood against him ever since. The two people Laine had embarked on this crucible for were no longer safe from him.

Well, he ain't killing anybody in this state. C'mon, let's get the king home.

Yes. We have him for a while. We'll try again later.

pale shadows

TUESDAY, NOVEMBER 18TH

*T*he *king was his land, and the land was its king.*

Wherever I roamed, I found black earth bent against an ashen sky and Janus flowers following the arteries of mana beneath Nihtheim's skin from tower to tower. Forever, the flowers followed the veins, and thereupon, they thrived.

However, the sacred flora were no longer marigold and violet rivers now, but instead plum scabs stitching the landscape. Nearly all the Rede Towers were gone, and wherever a sanctuary lay toppled, the ruins were interred beneath blood-filled petals and fallen char. All were downed save one: The Tower of Union, and it wouldn't be long before that too was claimed by fell gardens.

I would not let it be so. I could not let the encroaching bruise befoul the emerald spire, the symbol of my love for my Queen. I would stop it there.

But to do it, I needed Queen Seawing's strength.

* * *

"Laine?"

"What?"

"Did you hear me?"

"Oh. I'm sorry, Diana. I was remembering a vacation I never took."

The day had been too generous with happier hues now that the rain had ended. It lulled Laine into a peacefulness he felt he had no right to enjoy, and his mind kept wandering.

Laine watered the last ivy plant and then climbed down from the ladder near the front door. "What did you say?"

Diana was sitting at one of the café tables near the wall. She'd been steadily picking, picking, picking at her stale, over-toasted apple Danish for almost forty-five minutes. "I asked if you know Seth."

"I don't think so."

"Tall, White guy? Wears lots of black velvet and makeup? Sky-high black Mohawk—"

Laine's memory jogged as he headed for the kitchen. ". . . Wears an inverted pentagram, hangs out on Haight? Yeah, I *have* seen him handing out club flyers."

"Seth said they didn't know when the club's anniversary really was." Diana laughed, "So they set it on the date of their first bathroom overdose."

"Ah. Quaint." Laine ran a palm across the stubble on his skull. Time for a touch-up. "Which club is this again?"

"Sub Club. No, it's called The Underground now. It's over on Ninth and Howard. You should check it out with Marisa." Scorched Danish dandruff cracked beneath her fork. "Your kind of music."

"Hm." Laine had serious doubts that would ever happen. Not now. He stifled a yawn as he slid the empty watering can beneath the sink.

Diana heard him anyway. "So you okay? You look like you haven't slept in days." She dripped the rest of the Guatemalan Antigua from the French press into her cup. "You should have some of this. It'll keep you 'moving and shaking.'"

"Glad to see you're enjoying the 'perks' of the job, but I've had enough coffee today." And it still wasn't helping. Bad visions still came when the sun was high, and the company still chattered by the moon.

Thoroughly caffeinated, Diana shrugged and asked, "So how did 'San Francisco's coolest couple' meet in the first place?"

Laine smiled at the title. The regulars had dubbed them that a year ago, and it had stuck. He didn't know if it was because of Marisa's green locks and vintage jewelry or his black and purple apparel; their heathen beliefs or eclectic music tastes. Perhaps it was because they were an interracial couple or that their knowledge greatly exceeded their ages. Whatever had captured their favor, the locals held Laine and Marisa in high regard.

And now, at the end, when their love was proving dangerous, Laine would tell of their beginning. He started tossing out the rest of the stale pastries from the display case before Diana decided she needed another victim.

"We met at 'Stinkin'' Lincoln High. No, we weren't sweethearts, we just orbited within the same system of friends: The Little Theater Group. Man, Marisa was cool even then. She was the token punk in our circle of nerds and artists." Laine scattered a swarm of houseflies with a semi-successful swat. They, too, were after the ancient pastries.

"Psychotic Pineapple, Killing Joke and Two-Tone buttons on her trench; Docs dragging her feet down; hair all spiked up. She was tight with local bands the rest of us had never heard of and had the most polite 'fuck you' attitude towards life I'd ever seen.

"But as will happen, a lot of us lost touch after graduation, and I wouldn't see her again for another two years."

Diana was spreading the gelatinous apple filling into a disc, flattening any fruit chunks that got in the way. "Let me guess: you were slammin' to some Oi band, you spotted her from across the crowded dance floor, your skulls met, and at that moment, you knew that she was meant to be yours. Am I right?"

Laine shook his head while he wiped sweaty sugar glaze from his fingers. "Not even close. More like a mutual high school friend of ours ran into Marisa at Safeway, and they swapped our numbers."

Diana gave a disappointed, "Oh."

"But I had dreamt about Marisa a week prior to her phone call, so I guess it was a case of synchronicity, if not destiny. Our first date certainly felt destined."

"What happened then?"

"We went out for Mandarin food, I gave her a back rub. The rest is none of your business." Stale pastries thudded into the garbage pail.

"No doy. That sex stuff is obvious."

"I guess it is." Laine was remembering their first night and his first time in fine detail: the meal at Yet Wah, and the massage with the clumsy stripping; the look in her eyes that told him she was ready; the afterglow that made an idiot of him. He remembered how she kissed him awake the next morning, and the pleasant realization that he now had a "side of the bed". Laine remembered, and he knew he always would even when he'd rather not.

"I take it that's dead?" He pointed at Diana's eviscerated pastry.

She nodded and handed him the paper towel bearing the cake's remains.

Laine shook his head and quipped, "That's just wrong, Diana." The pastry splattered when it hit the bottom of the can. He sighed and turned toward the rumble of a passing cable car.

"Did Heather get the day off?"

"Yes," he said to the Russian Hill afternoon.

"Lucky. It's boring in here. Hey, you gonna' check out The Dead Milkmen tomorrow night?"

Laine knew the band well. One of Marisa's obscure favorites. "I doubt it."

KKHI was airing the title track from *Webber's Requiem* as Laine walked slowly to the front door. The composition was marvelously appropriate. It sounded like today. It sounded like the end.

Laine remembered the oath he had sworn at the start of his bond with Marisa: he had promised her that in the unlikely event that he should lie with another, his beliefs would require an admission. In light of her previous lover Darryl, Marisa responded that if that were to happen, she wouldn't want to know.

So which oath to honor? The Goddess made him the mage he was, but Marisa made him a man. Was there a way to honor both?

Hyde Street was left a liquid gold in the wake of the weeping sky, and Laine had to break the heart he had loved for fifteen months to the day in order to save its life.

"To the day," he whispered to the door, fogging the glass with his breath. "Today is wrongfully beautiful."

"What?"

"Nothing, Diana. I'm leaving now."

* * *

Amarantha was walking between row after row of heavily shellacked pews, her fingertips bouncing off each armrest as she passed. The red carpeting she was treading upon was too threadbare to worry about static shock. What remained of the afternoon sun was painting the sanctuary with stained glass light, while the shadows concealed the flaws of the wall paneling and the dried spills under her feet.

Back at Hamilton Methodist where so much of her life had begun.

Amarantha stood toe to toe with Christ's graven image. The wooden effigy returned her solemn gaze, his fingers encircling the sacred heart beveled into his chest. It seemed so strange to her to be able to look Jesus in the eyes. When Amarantha first came to the Methodist church over six years ago, the statue's height and demeanor seemed to demand her piety, but now she was in danger of dwarfing him.

Amarantha supplicated and crossed herself. Even she was subject to bouts of Christian guilt.

Many—like Laine—found it odd that Amarantha still had Christian ties, but all the young witch had to do was remember which belief came first, and she had no conflict. Christmas was once Yule; Easter was once Ostara. As far as Amarantha was concerned, Jesus was born on one Pagan holiday and died on another, and that didn't diminish his role in the world. While her brethren could not forgive Christianity's aggression towards them, Amarantha had learned to strike a balance. If one's faith brought solace to the soul, then it was good, period. After all, Amarantha was a "Methodist" in every sense of the word, and while God may have breathed the first breath, The Goddess always had the last word.

After a moment of stillness, she opened her backpack and pulled out a bundled linen napkin. Amarantha untied the corners before Christ's sandaled feet, unveiling three *brioches à tête* she'd made in class that day. She crossed herself again. "The Father, The Son, The Holy Ghost."

Amarantha reclaimed her center and ran the events since Saturday's through her mind. The encounter with Lillian had been terrifying and telling, and every day since Heather either couldn't or wouldn't return Amarantha's phone calls. Going to Russian Hill 'O Beans was out of the question because Laine was always there, and the shame of what she did to Marisa and the fear of what Laine would do to her kept Amarantha away. She wept gently.

Exposed to the salmon-colored light, Heather's painted lips took on the strangest hue as eyeliner tears streaked down beside them. She reached out for Amarantha's cheek, but Amarantha dodged her hand like—

"Wait a minute—"

The witch reached out to touch Amarantha's cheek, but Amarantha dodged her hand as if it were full of angry vipers. "If you would not drown, little one, then you shall relent."

"Lillian was . . . ."

Near the sunset shore, likewise hovering, was a black-cloaked figure accompanied by two pitch hounds. It too offered a hand, but this one filled me with dread as albino serpents bound its wrists and fingers like reptilian manacles and rings.

". . . The Crone. That means . . . ." Amarantha's mind turned.

Near the sunrise shore, just above the water's surface, was an angel dripping with white brilliance. I felt its reassuring smile as it extended a flaming hand toward me.

". . . Donovan was The Angel. *He* has been standing between me and Lillian. *He* has been blocking my spells."

Amarantha dried her tears and stole another glance inside her backpack, spying the other bread bundle she had made for her home altar. The offerings would mark the start of her new grounding regimen. If Donovan had been clouding her thoughts, she needed isolation and clarity. Amarantha's wards were charged now, and her room was cleansed. She would enter her world and discover what The Crone held and The Angel hid. That gave Amarantha till Donovan's return home to meditate and re-consecrate her mirror.

Amarantha crossed herself in gratitude, shrugged her backpack onto one shoulder, and headed for the church door. Four days. That wasn't a lot of time.

* * *

Seawing was soaring above the blood-sopped petals, broad of wing and keen of eye. She circled our Tower of Union, surveyed what remained of Nihtheim, and shrieked woefully.

Talons to feet and feather to flesh, she joined me atop the spire. Melancholy blossomed on her face as the cresting smell of rotting vegetation announced that our monument was next to fall. The tendrils were encroaching, their heavy, slick vines sparing nothing but grief.

I showed my Queen one of the last unsullied Janus flowers. The five slender petals were displaying their night colors now: violet on each tongue with gold underneath. By day, the hues reversed but were powdered with an iridescent hint of their opposites. Seawing inhaled its honeysuckle and jasmine bouquet. I apologized. We embraced.

I held her head to my chest. She need not see the rest.

I gathered a gem engraved with the glyph of Nieth from my robes and let it fall. It burned quickly in amber and orange, and there was the briefest of clatters as the dropped stone struck the side of our emerald tower before vanishing in the crimson dark below us. There was a thick, wet hiss followed by the iron stench of scorched blood. The flowers followed the veins, and thereupon, they would die.

Flame light was dancing through the curtains of my eyelids as we wept.

Our tower would never see light again.

* * *

Laine's skin felt like a stiff suit that was two sizes too large, and his feelings were the emotional equivalent of looking down the wrong end of a telescope. The spear's return was to blame for his swelling dissociation, and by increments, it robbed him of the exhaustion that let him sleep; the hunger that made him eat; the balance that made him sane. Three hours of slumber and one meal a day were all Laine was permitted, and with the remaining hours, he witnessed his life rather than lived it. He was utterly fractured and profoundly delirious; an illusion passing through a dream.

Freshly shorn and darkly adorned, he was sitting stoically with Trump and a single red rose on his lap and U2's *The Unforgettable Fire* in the air. By now, Marisa had signed in and braved the elevator's ascent. All Laine could do was sit and watch what followed unfold, a voyeur to his heart's calamity.

The apartment door clicked open just as "Bad" began playing with cinematic timing.

He's gonna love this.

Yeah, break-up sex is the best!

"Shut up." Laine managed to keep his voice lower than The Edge's intro.

Oh, here she is, dressed in black again.

Laine swallowed a rising profanity as his room was breached. Altar flames bowed at Marisa as she closed the door behind her. "Have I told you how much I hate your elevator?" she asked facetiously.

"Yes."

"Just making sure. Are we doing witchy stuff tonight?" That smile—

"No."

"Why are you sitting in the dark?"

"It wasn't dark when I sat down."

"Oh." Marisa lay her long coat and new helmet on Laine's bed, never breaking eye contact with him. "I ran into Jack Slater at Green Apple Books."

A mutual Stinkin' Lincoln alumni. "How is Jack?"

"Pretty good. He looks like David Gahan now." By the time she'd finished her sentence, suspicion had slowed Marisa's body language. "So are you gonna tell me what's going on? You were cryptic on the phone."

It took effort for Laine's emotions to animate his mouth. "I'm remembering your ultimatum. I remember how you said that you'd no longer await my many late returns."

Marisa nodded. "I remember, too."

"Marisa, I'm not coming in from the night." A brittle wind blew in.

She was close now, standing just slightly taller than Laine was sitting. "Laine, just tell me the truth: are you sleeping with Amarantha?" The scent of Marisa's white jasmine oil touched him at the same time as her biting words.

The truth came easily. "For the thousandth time, no!"
What a convenient truth.
He learns quickly.
"I'm sorry. I had to ask."

"That's exactly my point, Marisa. I'm tired of tiptoeing through every conversation with you. I never know when I'll say something that'll set you off." Laine's sigh rattled toward the ceiling. "Right now, I don't need the drama, and you don't need the trouble."

"What do you mean by 'trouble'?"

"Things are not faring well." Recalling their argument at Amarantha's long-ago party, Laine added, "I haven't been careful enough."

Marisa nodded her understanding. "When we were making love on Friday, I noticed something different in you." She cupped Laine's face, her thumbs gently stroking his temples, his jaw. "Something dark and scary as fuck. You were lying over me with a sword or some spear in your hands, and you were going to stab me with it, but you didn't." The city's indigo horizon was captured in her eyes. "Until now, I thought that was just part of the Tantra."

Laine cast a sideways glance at his TV stand. "I wish that's all it was." Marisa had seen the spear of Moloch, but she hadn't guessed its threat. Marisa could never know. "Chivalry is . . . much harder than I expected. That must be what murdered it."

That a boy!

Marisa took the rose from Laine and straddled his lanky lap, her tears already in place. She was sobbing and slowly tapping his shoulder with the rosebud, then she began kissing him as if she were mapping every contour of his face. It was the prelude to their last great kiss. "Is there anything I can—"

Laine shook his head, wishing he could feel something, anything. He wanted to cry for Marisa; to blame her; to lie and say it wasn't that bad; to hold her until their bodies fused. In the end, Laine knew that the only words that would save her from his pact with the spear were the last words in the world he wanted to utter. The eventide was deepening, and a serpent of Gonesh smoke slithered out the window.

"Say it, then," Marisa finally gasped, her face violet from the night sky.

"Must I?"

"Say it!" Marisa's eyes dared him.

"Marisa, we have to break up."

* * *

Three strokes of oil for the edges of my sword. Three strokes over seven nights made twenty-one strokes total.

Two plus one made three.

This was how I would consecrate my sword and ultimately give her a name: firmly anchored to La Luna Trinidad.

I applied the oil of Diana first while facing the eastern torch. Once both edges and the tip were saturated, I wrapped my forefinger and thumb around the base of it and rubbed the lubricant down the length of the blade. My cleansing gloves kept me from injury.

Citrus and blossoms dazzled my nose, and I was reliving every spring day I'd ever enjoyed.

I touched the tip of the sword to the torch flame. Yellow fire wound itself around the blade.

Next to the south was the oil of Selene the Moon Goddess. This blend was as confident as it was mysterious. I didn't know what it was made of, but it smelled wonderful.

I touched the tip of the sword to the torch flame. Red fire wound itself around the blade, setting it ablaze with orange.

To the west, I used the oil of Hecate. It was a surprisingly light scent that one would have to be close to notice. Once discovered though, its aroma hinted at dragon's blood resin and myrrh and was impossible to forget.

pale shadows

I touched the tip of the sword to the torch flame. Blue fire wound itself around the blade, setting it ablaze with white.

At last to the north, I used the oil of Cernunnos. Patchouli and musk identified this lusty god and consort to the Goddesses. The scent reminded me of a night not too long ago.

I smiled as I touched the tip of the sword to the torch flame. Black fire wound itself around the blade, extinguishing all the others.

Three strokes in four directions over a span of seven nights would make eighty-four strokes.

Eight plus four equals twelve. One plus two equals three. The trinity again.

I set the sword upon my lap, breathing my light into it. As I drew The Blessing Star over my chest, my fingers got snagged. I was wearing a familiar pendant, but I couldn't understand why it was so.

A door opened in my temple, and the driftwood and stone torches died. I didn't flinch.

A male silhouette filled the rectangular threshold. He lurked there momentarily as if deciding what to do next, then eventually stepped into the temple, reeking of alcohol.

I tried to ready my sword against the intruder, but it was gone.

* * *

Laine's emotions were dawning with the sun. It looked like it was going to be another gorgeous fucking day, and his inevitable sense of loss and guilt were awakening as Marisa climbed onto her scooter. He kept his gaze remote, turning away from the pain of the eastern light as Marisa walked her bike onto the tarmac. It must have been too early to ticket her.

Facing westward on Turk, Marisa was ready for her journey to work. "So . . . ," she said.

"So . . . ." Laine adjusted his shades, but the sun was

still agonizing.

"Are we—can we still be friends?"

"Of course. I don't want to lose that too." Friends in jeopardy.

"Me neither." Marisa smiled weakly. "Do you still want to come over for Thanksgiving? We don't have to tell my folks anything. It's just we already made the plans—"

"I'd love to have Thanksgiving with you." Laine felt her heart breaking. Another cliché only she made real; a bitter trite that they were both suffering. He moved close enough to touch her but didn't.

Eyes sparkling with tears, Marisa looked at Laine with a love and gratitude he was unworthy of. This was her final gift. This was the last great kiss.

* * *

We were embracing high above the smoldering landscape. The brief day had begun, and warm sea breezes gave my queen and I respite. I was sampling her scent while I still could and praying the memory would last me through the trials ahead.

Her hair became feathers beneath my touch; her lips calcified. Now avian, Seawing turned toward the western dawn of Nihtheim and leapt into the morning sun.

My queen was gone, but she had passed me a gift. I opened my hand to find one of her feathers. It was vibrant and green in a way the tower on which I stood would never be again. I hid it within my cloak's folds, then turned to face my burning sovereignty.

The king was his land, and the land was the king. It was nearly time to kill. It was nearly time to die.

pale shadows

SATURDAY, NOVEMBER 22ND

Sipping her Orangina, Amarantha didn't need to turn around to know Heather had arrived at Cybelle Pizzeria, nor that she brought uninvited company. She felt their entrance.

"Hi, Amy." Heather turned a sauce-stained chair around and straddled it, all smiles and bubble gum. Laine was far more formal and almost as buoyant as he sat primly in the other seat across the table from Amarantha. His face revealed little of what truth lay beneath.

"Hey, Heather; Laine." A familiar electronic whine signaled the death of another Pac-Man.

"Good thing we picked here, Amy. Escape From New York is packed. Our pizza would have taken forever. What are you having?" Heather asked Amarantha.

"Just this." Amarantha displayed her drink. "I'm not very hungry."

Heather popped back out of her chair. "Well, I'm starving. I'm getting a slice."

Laine droned, "Better make it to go."

Heather slouched a little. "Oh. Okay."

As Heather joined the line, Laine wasted no time in touching the shell of Amarantha's mind. She winced psychically and stared off to the side as her shame returned anew, widening the vast, silent gulf between them.

The row of customers was inching toward the counter, laughing and contemplating their next meals, while the father/son team at the electric table beside Amarantha and Laine digested sausage slices and pursued computerized ghosts.

"So how are you doing?" she finally asked as stoically as she could.

Laine shrugged. "Been better, been worse. How's Donovan?" His question bore a murderous ring.

"I—he's fine." Amarantha nibbled her lower lip. "And Marisa? Is she okay?"

Laine's tardy storm clouds arrived. "We've broken up."

That explained the mood his nonchalant smirk was trying to dismiss. "I'm sorry to hear that. I know what she meant to you. Are you okay?"

"Been better, been worse."

He seemed strangely divided, like he was at war with himself; like he was torn between glee and morosity. She doubted any apology would matter to him, but she had to try. She owed him and Heather.

"I know we haven't been talking lately, but I'm sorry about that day at the café. If you ever—"

Heather returned to the table, pizza box in hand.

"Did they burn your slice?" Laine asked.

Heather did a take, then checked the contents of her box. "Looks okay to me."

"Smells like something's burning." Laine was sniffing the air.

They all joined in, but eventually surrendered when the source was unfound. Amarantha returned her attention to her company. "Anyway, what's this surprise of yours, Heather? The one you mentioned on the phone?"

Heather's smile was wide and thin with suspense as she looked at Laine. He nodded.

"It looks like you were sorta right about me," she said.

"About what?"

Heather blushed. "Laine and I . . . slept together."

Amarantha's lips tightened. "I . . . I kinda thought something was going on."

"Nothing was at first, but last Saturday—"

"I meant to ask about that. Are you okay?"

"I don't want to talk about it," Heather said, head shaking.

"I just want to apolo—"

"I said I *don't* want to talk about it!" Heather leaned against Laine's shoulder, her narrow glare reinforcing the topic ban. "Besides, I'm better now."

"Much better," Laine practically sang. "You're looking a little stressed yourself, Befana. Mayhaps I should bed you too and complete the set?"

With this simple statement, all sympathy, all respect, for Laine became a revulsion that made Amarantha's blood boil and breath shudder.

Then, Heather's smile suddenly grew daring as she leaned deeper into the arms of the witch Amarantha no longer trusted. "Yeah, what are you up to tonight, Amy?" she purred. Her tongue flashed between her painted lips.

The implied proposition paralyzed Amarantha where she sat. In all their years together, Heather had never made such an incestuous offer outside of jest.

Wait a minute, Heather was skrying her too. She had been ever since she walked through the pizza parlor door with Laine. It was all so clear to Amarantha now: they were angry; they were lost.

Amarantha nodded slowly and rose, shaking with fear. "You know what? I . . . have to go." That was it. Neither of them would help her. Amarantha was on her own.

* * *

267

"Did you really mean what you said to Amy about sleeping with her to complete your set?" Heather swore she knew his answer. She just needed to hear Laine say it.

"Of course not. Our tryst didn't shock her enough for you to skry her, so I dropped a bigger bomb. Now *that's* how one plays The Skrying Game." Laine laughed. It wasn't a jolly laugh, to be sure. "You didn't tell her I was showing up, right?" he asked, still smirking.

"No. I thought it would work better that way. You know, 'the element of surprise' and shit. Besides, I owed Amy one for last week. That's the only reason why I bothered calling her. And because you asked me to." Up until then, Heather was doing a masterful job of dodging Amy's phone calls at work and home. Damn, it was probably a personal best. "So what happened to you this morning?" Heather asked, "I thought we were going to watch *Pee Wee's Playhouse* together, but you were already gone."

"I . . . couldn't sleep, so I walked to work. I had to since I took yesterday off in addition to my 'weekend.'"

Heather recalled Laine was off Wednesdays and Thursdays now. "Oh, right."

Laine slowed his long strides and grabbed Heather's right shoulder, saying, "Thank you for the company last night, Heather. I needed it." He sped up again and asked, "So what did you see? In Amarantha, I mean?"

Back to business again. That must be as intimate as Laine was going to get now that their act was finished. "I didn't see Donovan," Heather said of her skry of Amy. "She *was* pretty disgusted, though."

"But it was *Amarantha's* disgust, not his. That's good. Your efforts have met with some success." Laine spared her a satisfied glance over his glasses. "She may even ask for our help in the end."

The thing was, Heather got the feeling that her old friend wanted that help tonight, but Amy changed her mind when Laine made his fucked-up offer. "I hope we didn't miss our chance. Could you slow down a little?" she asked, juggling her pizza box.

They slowed to a mosey, and Laine began frowning into the air.

"You still smell something burning?"

"Yeah, I do. Then again, maybe I just smell Christmas." Laine nodded at the wreaths going up in Great Expectations' storefront window across the street.

Heather spied the volumes of large red, white, and green book covers lassoed with gold ribbons. "No doy! Nobody even waits for Thanksgiving anymore. Even The Space Lady is singing Christmas carols now."

Laine wiggled a finger at the bookstore. "You know, if we live through all this, I must write a book about it."

"The way you use words, that could be cool. What's the title?"

Laine shrugged. "*The Devil and the Vampire*, maybe?"

Heather pretended to yawn. "Boring."

"How about *Black Celebration*? I can use an album title, right? Or maybe *Waning Moons*."

"*Waning Moons*, huh?"

What the hell was that? Laine's distorted reflection wasn't alone in Aardvark's plate glass window. Its company looked like smoke rising from a burning tire, but the smoke had his eyes.

Someone angry and unseen shoved past Heather, nearly knocking her on her ass.

Heather went cold. "Laine, your reflection—"

He didn't look, just kept dodging pedestrians. "What about it?"

"It doesn't look like you."

"I am not my flesh," was his answer.

A 7-Haight bus whined to a stop in front of them. Laine gestured like the bus was a carriage when the doors slapped open. "Here we are."

Heather was stepping up into the stairwell. "Where are we going?"

"*We're* not going anywhere. *I* have a dinner date with Marisa, and *you* need to go home and prepare for what's to come." The orange and white doors shut off any reply or complaint Heather could have made. Laine yelled, "Just days now, child, I can feel it!"

Days? That wasn't enough time, not if Marisa was still inviting Laine to dinner.

* * *

Amarantha gave the mugwort a couple more stirs before mashing the wormwood against the bottom of the pot and setting the wooden spoon to rest. Three-quarter ounces of the fluffy, yellow buds and one pint of water were brewing into a stiff tea. Far too bitter to drink, this wash was legendary for dream and astral workings.

Everything was just about prepared. The mugwort was nearly done, the pomegranate was blessed, and the altar cleared of the beige incense ash; Donovan's dry roses; the pink candle stubs; the three *brioches à tête*. Amarantha threw away or set aside it all in preparation for her return beyond the veil. She may not have been ready for Laine and Heather, but she was ready for Lillian.

The white wall phone rang. "Hello."

"Hey, love, it's Donovan." His voice was backed up by The Human League's latest hit. "Are you okay? I just got this weird vibe a minute ago."

Donovan was already keying in on her. "I'm fine. Just a little busy with school stuff." Though not the school she was leading him to believe. "It's also been a . . . very weird day. Where are you?"

"At my old man's. We just watched the Tyson/Berbick fight. Two rounds and it was over. That Tyson—"

"How's your dad?"

Donovan snorted. "Same as always. While I've got you, have you had any more ritual problems?"

Amarantha was mashing pulp again. "To be honest, I haven't checked. Did you—"

Donovan whispered in a dash, "I've lost track of Lillian, and I'm getting nothing from her family." His words slowed. "Don't worry, though. She won't stay hidden for long."

He hadn't located her yet, which meant Amarantha had a chance of getting to Lillian first. "I'm sure she won't, but there's no hurry. Will you be back by Thanksgiving?"

"Yeah, I'll be back in time to help you out at the church. I still owe you one. I'll let you know how everything went with Lillian by then."

"Sounds good," Amarantha said, wiping condensation from her brow. "I have to go now. I have something on the stove."

"Mmm, save me some. I'll see you on Thursday. I love you."

"I love you too." Amarantha hung the phone up, turned her attention back to the saucepan, and slowly drained the golden decoction through a sieve into the silver bowl.

* * *

"Smooth move, Ex-Lax, now you're sprung," Heather mumbled to herself. She couldn't even walk down 22nd from the bus stop without remembering how much Laine loved this nasty-ass neighborhood. Man, she hated being whupped. "It's not like it's going to do me any good. He's just gonna run right back to Marisa."

Of course, that was assuming everything went according to whatever scary shit Laine had planned, because if that shit hit the fan, Laine could easily end up in jail or 'under observation' at Langley Porter.

Heather rounded the corner onto Shotwell and got hit by an early-evening gust as cold as the facts. "If we beat Donovan, I lose Laine; if we lose to him, I lose Laine." She sidestepped a dog turd and admitted, "I have to tell Laine how I feel. I have to tell him I love him." Goddess, this was stupid. Heather was starting to sound like Amy.

"Hey, *chiquita*!" A homeboy in a green and blue flannel shirt buttoned at the neck and blue jeans had swung in front of Heather like a drunken barn door. He was one of the fluorescent lamp ninjas from a few weeks ago, but he was unarmed right now.

She zipped up her bomber jacket partly because of the cold, but also because of the way his crusty, older partner was practically drooling. "*Mmm, que guapa,*" the pervert growled.

"Come on, baby, don't be shy," the younger one said, squinting like he was using x-ray vision on Heather's tits.

These two were small problems. Heather did all she had to do: close her eyes, take a deep breath until she was large, and exhale her outrage. She didn't speak a word, just locked the fools in place with an ancient gaze.

The homeboys' lusts ran away, leaving the wannabe molesters standing there with their mouths hanging open. There was calm respect in their eyes as they stepped aside to let Heather pass. It was just like with that watch guy at Curios.

"*Lo siento,*" the old fart apologized. "*Soy ignorante.*"

"Hey, have a nice night, ma'am," his young partner added as he pulled his knit cap low over his shy eyes.

Heather still never said a word to them, but she did sing, "Keep feeling fascination . . . ," to herself as she climbed the stairs to her home.

Heather called out, "Mama, I'm home!" as she closed her front door, but the only greeting she got back was the ticking of central heating. Mama must have taken Rudy out shopping with her.

"That's cool. I can eat my pizza in peace." Heather tossed the box containing the half-eaten slice on her bed, then unzipped her bomber jacket, catching her reflection in the mirror.

"Wait a minute." Heather's jacket joined dinner on her bed as she took a closer look at her altar. No doubt about it: Rudy was clever about the sword this time. It was facing the right way; leaning properly against the wall.

"An almost perfect crime, Rudy," Heather admired. In Heather's cookie-stealing youth, that's how she would've done it too: moved the altar effects aside like a curtain so they'd be easy to put back in their proper place; stood on the altar in her socks so as not to leave behind footprints; braced herself against her window frame with one hand while tipping the sword off its screws with the other, probably with gloves or another pair of socks on her hands. When it was time to stash the evidence, simply reverse the order.

Rudy had gone for speed and traction instead of guile though. His un-socked footprints gave away the "curtain" breach, and even though the sword was unmarked, greasy little fingerprints along the mirror revealed the offense. Standing on her toes, Heather grabbed ahold of her mirror to retrieve *La Trinidad* and ready it for another cleansing.

A male silhouette filled the rectangular threshold. He lurked there momentarily as if deciding what to do next.

The vision planted Heather's feet right back on the floor. "I know you," she whispered.

* * *

Laine recognized the smell now: the one that had been clinging to his nostrils for the past two nights. At first, he suspected an elderly Asian neighbor was conducting Buddhist services in the apartment building, but the scent haunted Laine beyond those concrete walls. The "incense" was Janus flowers and charred flesh, and wherever the company followed, so did their funereal perfume.

"You guys stink," Laine griped while dabbing Moon Goddess oil on his upper lip.

It's your doing.

"So it is." The flames of Nihtheim had captured Nihthasu's company unprepared. When the Janus flowers burned, so did the spear, and now the spirits that had once inhabited it smoldered and stank just out of sight, veiled by venous smoke and ocular blind spots.

Putting the oil vial back in his pocket, he asked, "Did you kill Neteru?"

What do you think?

He didn't want to think about it. "We'll discuss my champion later."

Yes, boss.

Marisa's invitation had been equally cryptic when she called Laine that afternoon: We have to talk. Can you come over for dinner? Her gate buzzed open, and Laine and company ascended the stucco and brick stairway into Marisa's home.

There was no music playing, no fireplace razing, and no lights except for in the kitchen and dining room. "Marisa?" The door boomed when he closed it.

"I'm in the dining room," she called out without emotion.

Laine followed her voice toward the front of the house and found her sitting at the far end of the long table, hands tucked out of sight. No roses, no candles, no smiles. The dinnerware and napkins were there, but the food was absent except by scent. "Sit down," Marisa summoned.

Laine obeyed like a good Pagan consort.

"I figured I'd wait until after we talked to serve dinner," she explained, resplendent in her mourning colors. "You might not be hungry then."

Oh shit.

You should have let us—

Laine raised his hands and looked Marisa dead in the eyes. "Just say it, Marisa."

She sighed, breaking his gaze. "I think I'm pregnant."

There was a gasp that chilled the room, but neither witch made it, and Marisa seemed not to notice the sound.

"What do you mean?"

"I mean I'm almost a week late."

Laine closed his eyes, counted several breaths, then looked at Marisa more deeply. If nothing else, the spear did augment his skrying abilities immensely. What would have taken Laine thirty seconds to determine regularly he now did in ten. Laine announced, "You're not pregnant."

Marisa blinked, surprised at his certainty. "Are you sure?"

"Positive. It's stress." Laine's reassuring smile was too weighty to sustain. "You need to relax. Everything will be fine."

Marisa let go of the air she was holding. "Okay. Are you hungry?"

No, Laine wasn't, but he would try to eat as a courtesy. "Yeah, dinner sounds good. I need to go wash up first. I've got French Roast under my nails."

"Sure." Her smile was relaxed but fragile. "I'll make your plate."

Laine bowed and rose from the table, then ventured into her restroom. The door shut, and he rinsed the day's labors from his hands; the day's wear from his face. He was pondering the final destination of the ink he'd washed down the drain nearly two moons ago as he dried off.

Next to Laine's foot was an off-white scale. He centered his stance on it and watched the wheel turn: one hundred and fifteen pounds at six-foot-three inches tall. About twenty-five pounds were lost in a month. People were dying to be able to do that. Amazing, the power of stress: it could make a childless woman think she's pregnant and turn a healthy man into the walking dead.

Damn, he looks like one of us now.

Laine groaned darkly. "Appearances can be deceiving."

So true. Your bird, for instance.

"The same old threats? Marisa no longer opposes you. She's no longer a part of this." She hadn't even smelled them.

Oh, but we so love children.

"Marisa is *not* pregnant," Laine affirmed, his heavy scowl still affixed. "And I know what you are; what you both truly are."

Enlighten us.

Laine caught the fire in his reflected eyes. "You are no more and no less than my imbalances. You are my fury and my despair, and tradition also dictates that you are my doom. But you know what?"

What?

"You are the coinage of my mind, and I can cash you in verily. You are no more real than fog; no greater substance than a whisper. I deny my demise. I deny The King's Tradition."

Fair enough.

If we measure so little, then look at us.

Yes, look upon your handiwork, King.

A simple enough request, but Laine's eyes wouldn't move. In the way that old truths surfaced in the seeking mind, so did Laine realize that to trade gazes with the company was to assure his damnation and demise.

Look at us!

Laine's ears were ringing as he squeezed his eyes shut. "You know what? Maybe later."

It's a date, boss.

They were of The Qliphoth, these twins of the spear; these joyless seraphim of Moloch. Their passion was for death, and Laine knew that they would not leave unsatisfied.

* * *

The glow of flickering white tapers revealed Terra eyeing Amarantha from the bed. Between those altar candles, the statue of Athena was keeping watch over a silver bowl scored with a pentagram, a spud of sea sponge, and an overripe pomegranate.

The mugwort infusion sang as it circled clockwise within the shallow bowl Amarantha was tilting. *"Athené aigis athanaton."*

Amarantha drew decoction into the sponge, then stood before her armoire mirror and wiped it down with long sweeps. Her reflection broke as she coated the glass, then gradually settled into the image of Amarantha's higher self, Befana Delafey. Her likeness was donning a white tunic cinched with ivy vines.

Satisfied with the vision, Befana returned to the altar. Three firm strokes split the red seed and spilled the red juice. She took a bleeding half of pomegranate to the looking glass and painted it with the autumn fruit. "*Athené aigis athanaton.*"

The Crone—or Lillian as the case may be—had used serpents to draw out Befana, and as sacred as serpents were to Athenians, so were pomegranates to those who followed the darker goddesses Hecate and Persephone. The fruit was her key to gaining an audience with Lillian.

* * *

Terra would not follow me beyond the veil, but instead, she safeguarded my passive body. Perhaps it was for the best. I had no idea what or whom I would find upon returning to my realm.

I, Befana, knew who I sought and who I wished to avoid. Neither The Crone nor The Angel could be found, though. In fact, I found no indication of life in my draining lowlands. My feet plodded on compacted mud and dead cedar, and a clear, mute dusk was rolling over my head. The only drowning possible here was under the silence.

I sought to leave, but my withdrawal was halted by the loss of traction. I stared at the slippery patch of soil beneath my feet and found it wasn't earth at all but hide. Deep musk was stinging my nostrils as I dug up the dead animal, and barely halfway through my task, I recognized the corpse I was releasing.

What remained of my horned charger—my unicorn— lay before me, puffy and green-gray with its tongue bulging between blood-stained teeth and its coat embossed with boils.

My heart tumbled; my body followed. I laid my hands upon my friend's remains and cried a quiet requiem. That The Crone could destroy and desecrate so fine and powerful a beast was all the warning I needed. My love had been right: the Hecatean was quite mad, and that madness would keep me true to my promise.

I would seek Lillian no more.

pale shadows

WEDNESDAY, NOVEMBER 26TH

"So how'd the deliveries go?" Laine was standing in the same old place: under the clock and in front of the scale with his back to the door. "Did Mr. Hitachi fry our coffee machines again?"

Mohammed had pushed the café door open wide so Heather could follow him in and give her report. "No, he kept them clean. Your visit straightened him out. Imagine that."

"'Imagine that.'"

Mr. Hitachi at Fujitsu Corporation downtown had the bad habit of warming his lunches on the heating pads of their rental machines. Sometimes there was scorched ramen with bits of blackened coffee filter bonded to the plates. The last time it happened, Heather called him out on it, and he cussed her out. He turned out to be a Japanese chauvinist pig with a real shogun mentality, so Mohammed sicced Laine on him. Mr. Hitachi's attitude had since entered the 20th century.

Mohammed asked, "What you work on, Len?" as he and his jangling key ring went to the register.

"Bryer Electric called for their pound of flesh: two bags of Colombian. I'm just about done."

Just then, the new bug zapper sizzled a gnat. Heather cringed at the pop.

"Okeh, okeh. I mek phone calls." Mohammed dropped a wad of receipts on the counter. "Tech sees eenvoices and cash out when Diana come. Sorry I mech you to work todeh."

Laine was waving their boss off with one hand and shoveling with the other.

"Eat slow, so you go home too, Hehser. I see you bose on Fuhriday."

That was cool. Heather didn't think she'd get out of there before five with all the orders that had come in. Out by three. "Thanks."

Mohammed did one of those movie takes, pointed at them, and said, "Oh yeah. 'You guys be cool . . . .'"

Laine finally looked up as he and Heather grumbled, "'. . . or be cruel.'"

Mohammed grinned and winked into his office.

Now that they were alone, Heather asked, "Okay, so what the hell is that supposed to mean?"

Laine admitted, "I don't know, he made it up. It probably sounds cooler in Arabic or something."

"I guess. You know, the whole trip he kept performing 'Stand By Me' in spoken word."

"Well, at least he didn't sing it."

"No doy." Another fly fried loudly. "That thing is gross."

"But brutally effective. Those are all the invoices?" He'd just weighed the last bag of the order.

Heather nodded as she stepped aside for Laine, but remained close. "So my 'visitor from down under' arrived."

"You have an Australian friend?"

Heather cracked up. "No, my 'monthly visitor.'"

He got it now, but she could tell he didn't think it was

anywhere near funny. He just said, "Oh. Well, that's good news." Another fly died, and Laine said, "What?"

"What?"

"Sorry, it's nothing."

"Are you okay?"

"Of course not." He was tallying the paperwork and cash in front of him.

"You want to come by later? We could talk or—"

Laine kept counting. "I think I should sleep in my own bed for a while."

Bullshit. Laine looked like he hadn't slept in a month. "I'm not talking about sex. Like I said, I'm on the rag. There's something else I need to talk to you about."

Laine closed himself off from Heather, and for the second time since she'd known him, he looked terrified. He stopped counting the register's take. "What do you think is going on here, Heather? Between us?"

Every possible answer he could give was flying through her head except for the one that would hurt.

Café regular Claire was pulling up outside, and it wouldn't take her long to lock up her pink ten-speed bike. And dammit, Diana was coming in right behind her.

A horsefly exploded. "Well?"

Heather locked eyes with her mentor; her friend; her heart. She sent to him, *I love you.*

Laine went tragically limp. *You can't. I can't.*

Heather just nodded but kept smiling. That was that: the right answer; the one that hurt.

Diana and Claire entered just as Heather turned and went mutely into the office and plopped into her chair.

Mohammed was pacing the room, laughing into the phone receiver smashed against his cube-shaped head, so he hardly noticed her, which was fine. If Heather started bawling, she might be able to hide it from her boss. With surprising coolness, Heather grabbed some sheets of red construction paper, Scotch tape, and a Magic Marker from the yellow desk organizer, her eyes totally dry.

She still had one more confession to spill.

pale shadows

"Hey, Laine, you want a baby?"

"A baby?" Laine managed. Blue lightning killed a fly.

Tell that baby yeah!

"Uh-huh. Here." Claire dropped four plastic gum-machine babies about an inch long each on the counter, all as carnation-pink as the purse they came from, the Schwinn she rode on, and the Karmann Ghia she drove.

Laine's sigh was part relief and part disappointment. "Thanks. You had me going there for a second."

Claire's slight smile and wink were most inviting, as was her alabaster, dancer's body when she slinked away. Why were women always drawn to Laine when he was at his worst?

He lined the plastic talismans atop the register and announced, "I'm almost finished cashing out, Diana."

Diana was already in the green company apron and at the espresso machine, squeezing Graffeo's Italian nectar from steel udders. "All right."

What about our deal?

As Claire took the table closest to the register, she said to Diana, "So yeah, you were giving me your opinion on the whole witchcraft thing:" She gave Laine a sly side-glance as she finished her cone of strawberry ice cream from Swensen's. "What do you think? Is it real?"

He *had* to hear this. Diana set Claire's latte before her, sighed, and said, "I can tell you this much: one day, during the worst part of the storms a couple of weeks ago, I had an appointment to go to, and I didn't have my umbrella."

Ready for that peek, milord?

By sun and moon, the grim critics spoke, longing for the actor to die. Their stench and smoke were never far from the mage's nose and eyes.

"Laine told me he would it clear up long enough for me to get where I was going, and it did. It stopped as soon as I left the store and started again as soon as I got to my appointment." Diana shrugged. "You can call that whatever you want."

"So what do *you* call it?" Claire badgered, running a hand through her cinnamon pixie haircut.

A woman scorned.

Heather's pace was swift and direct as she dropped a red letter on the counter and continued out the café door. She said nothing but still went noticed.

Is she going to be problematic?

"She'll be fine," Laine defended quietly.

"What was that about?" Diana asked.

Laine pocketed the letter and half-whispered, "Her moon."

Diana tamped used espresso grounds into the garbage. "What's that mean?"

"That's a nice way of saying 'female troubles.'"

Diana's eyes rolled along the ceiling. "Just say 'period.'"

"Yeah, right, what you said."

The topic was ended with the entrance of two women with a baby carriage. A fly went off like a cap gun.

"I'll get this. Cash in."

Claire pushed her palms against her lower spine and bowed back slowly. As vertebrae popped, her braless breasts hissed against the ribbed cotton of her pink tank top. "Don't change the subject: what do you call what happened?"

Mmm, pretty in pink.

Isn't she?

"Hey, Thalia," Laine greeted the new arrivals. "What can I get you today?"

A piece of Claire.

Fuck Claire, look at the little baby.

"Let's not," Laine said small.

"I call it over my head," Diana admitted.

A stiletto heel impaling bubble wrap.

"But I don't know. Anything's possible." Diana strolled up to the register.

"Hi, Laine. I've been telling my friend Abby here about your cappuccinos, and she came down from Santa Rosa to put you to the test."

What's the baby's name?

"I'll try not to disappoint. Two capps?" Laine pulled his drifting gaze away from Abby's child.

A car tire rolling over a ketchup packet.

Marisa could be packing one right now.

Again with the threats of fatherhood.

"Fair enough." Claire conceded to Diana's assessment, then nodded at the electrified tower between the shelves. "That thing's loud."

"It can be." The milk was firmly foamed. "What are you reading today?"

Ignoring us?! Fine!

Laine flinched.

"*Sexus* by Miller. Ever read any Henry Miller?" Claire waved the wide-bound tome.

A teenager snapping gum.

"No." A nervous, pulsing motion caught Laine's peripheral attention. Something along the walls—

"You know what? The register's fine, Laine." Diana violated Mohammed's radio station policies and settled on "Papa Don't Preach."

One of the company laughed intimately.

Laine growled, "You've got to be fucking kidding me."

He's not listening. No honor at all.

Diana said, "What, you don't like Madonna?"

He hadn't realized he said that so loudly.

There was a peculiar pop in Laine's ears, and the café sounded like it was three rooms over. The twitching at the corner of his eyes increased, and Laine faced the frenzied writhing of the creepers along the shop wall. Their colors shifted from ivy-green to bruise-violet as they multiplied, concealing the ceiling over Laine's head strand by gruesome strand.

The tendrils were encroaching, their heavy, slick vines sparing nothing but grief.

Laine shook the vision off and leaned on the open refrigerator door. "I have to break this mad motif. I have to break this mad motif . . . ," he whispered again and again.

Forget it, milord. No chants or charts will save you.

One child's the same as any other to Moloch.

"Enough. Marisa is not pregnant."

He loves a mother's lament.

"Not today." The refrigerator door closed heartily, and Laine's hearing cleared.

A fresh fuse snapping on.

"That was a big one," Claire commented with a wince.

Diana laughed, "Yeah."

"So Miller: a sexist pig, but a *clever* sexist pig," Claire said, completing her review, "You should read *Tropic of Cancer*. For some reason, all the guys I know call it 'liberating.'"

"Maybe you're hanging out with the wrong guys." Laine spanked cocoa powder on the awaiting beverages, then carried them onto the floor, hiding his breath's shuddering. Eyes on the cups, he crept to Thalia and Abby's table. "Here you are, ladies."

Today.

Mohammed's footfalls were approaching from the office stairs. No doubt, he had come to investigate the pop music.

Now!

"Hey, Nihthasu, look!" A barbecued limb jutted from behind Laine and pointed at the infant. He looked.

Blackened flesh fell from the smoldering figure crouching behind the stroller. It was twirling a scorched Janus flower over the infant's head like a crib toy while cooing. The spear's agent glared at Laine, its jaw cracking open with the sound of rupturing pottery. A hundred agonized screams spilled from the apparition's mouth, its glossy, gray eyes daring Laine not to faint.

Laine's flaccid grip let the cappuccinos slip. The tumbling cups and saucers missed the child; the molten liquid didn't. Someone asked about a burning smell, and

Laine went deaf again, but not before hearing Thalia's lament; not before hearing Abby and the baby's screams.

The rest was a strange, slow dash of white washcloths drenched with cold water; Mohammed's polyester backside following the matrons to their car; assurances from Claire that went unheard; Diana's unfelt pacing behind the register. When sound returned, Laine found he had sunk to the café floor, washcloths draping cold and wet in his clutching hands.

Made you look.

Laine pounded scuffed wood with his fists, then toppled the pastry case while pulling himself to his feet. As he closed in on the counter, Diana backed into the coffee jars with a clatter.

"Give me the warehouse keys." He relinquished the soaked towels.

"What?"

"Did I stutter?!"

"No."

"Then give me the fucking keys!" His words rang off the walls. Claire jumped. Diana obeyed.

Where are we going?

Mohammed's summons chased Laine from Hyde to the Russell Street alley, surrendering when their quarry made the turn. The lock on the newly-forged security gate fared better in slowing the witch's will. Normally, his anxiety would have happily broken off the key in the lock, but instead, Laine was a storm's calm, dark eye.

We can't hear the screams from here.

"You'll get your screams."

What is this, guilt?

"It's time to feel." The stiff switch snapped on, and pale fluorescent light flooded the palettes burdened with ware. Lipton's dehydrated soup cases towered along the un-paneled walls beside Bigelow herb tea and Carnation hot chocolate powder boxes.

Farther back in the still-unlit portion of the dank warehouse stood the awaiting target: the sugar stack five boxes high and weighing more than Laine. C&H packed in cardboard and wrapped in more cardboard. He growled and swung.

What is he doing?

Blow after blow exploded into the side of the boxes. Laine's screams were shriller than he would have preferred, and the annoyance of it fueled his aggression. Blood darkened his vision, and the sting of his raw knuckles was spurring him on.

What is he doing?!

By degrees, he left his skin and anguish on the corrugated paper, and when the boxes split and spilled their saccharine contents, Laine moved on to the cocoa powder.

Damn him! He's still not ready!

Each strike was evicting the spear from Laine. With every punch, the company's voices grew fainter until their numb fleece of apathy was drawn from him. Eventually, his arms stopped working, the crimson veil fell from his eyes, and Laine was spent for the first time in almost a month.

"You feel better now?" Mohammed's footsteps registered late in Laine's head.

"Slightly," Laine replied, turning to his boss.

The Egyptian stared at the beach of white and brown sand beneath them. "What habben?"

Laine's arms kept trying to float away. "Another spill."

"Okeh, okeh. Len, go home."

"What, am I fired now?"

Mohammed's glasses slid to the end of his nose. "Are you on duhrugs?"

Was that a joke? "Definitely not."

"You suhbeel ze duhrinks on bur'bus?"

"Of course not!"

"Sen you not fired . . . yet. But you need some suhleeb. You working too hard, yes?" Mohammed patted Laine's left shoulder. "Go home. I call you letter about Cellia."

That simple generosity was humbling. "Thank you, Mohammed," he choked out. "Really, thanks."

His boss' words had never been truer. Laine was overdue for a very long sleep.

* * *

Did Laine even care about Heather, or was he just using her all this time? She never should've gotten close to him, no matter what she thought she felt. The only things he loved were Marisa and revenge. That was it. Everyone and everything else was obviously moot.

The hall to Heather's room was thick with the Thanksgiving aromas of cloves, turkey, and stuffing, and it almost chilled her out.

"I see Mama started cooking," she said to Rudy, who was loitering outside Heather's door.

Rudy munched down the last of a sandwich and said, "Yup. Hey, you wanna see the new *Star Trek* movie Friday? It all happens in San Francisco, and these whales—"

"Can we talk about it later, Rudy?" Heather gave the boy a slight shove as she went into her room. "I just got home from work, and I've had a bad day."

"Oh. Okay." Rudy looked inside Heather's room nervously for a second, then ran toward the kitchen and Mama's cooking.

"That was suspicious." Heather immediately cased her room, stopping only when she looked up at Trinity. The sword was facing the wrong way.

Heather growled, "Rudy," as she charged up to *Trinidad* and snatched it from above the altar. Remnants of her brother's peanut butter meal squished between Heather's fingers and the grip when she stepped back onto her floor. Heather switched hands and absently wiped peanut butter on her blouse.

"Goddammit!" Rudy hadn't even tried to be sneaky; he hadn't even tried to clean off the evidence even after her warning. He didn't care any more than Laine did.

Something inside of Heather broke loose.

"Why?!" Heather screamed at Rudy. "Why?!" she screamed at Amy. "Why?!" she screamed at Laine and

Donovan and Marisa. Facing her crying, peanut-butter-wearing, worthless, useless reflection, Heather screamed at herself screaming at herself. "Whyyyy?! Fuuuuck!"

Trinidad would have maimed or killed someone if it had hit a person instead of Heather's reflection. The explosion of glass and steel sounded like rusty wind chimes when the thrown sword and ruined mirror crashed to Heather's floor.

Her panting slowed. She regarded the shards through tear-drenched eyes; moved a couple of the large fragments around with her toes. "Why?" she whined again.

Heather fell to her knees with a thump that she felt up to her hips, then sobbed among the sharp remains.

Mama screamed, "*¡Dios mio!*" from her doorway.

* * *

I love you, Marisa: a fitting end to Laine's final journal entry. If lucky, she would read the sentiment, provided someone unearthed his spiral-bound revelations. Pity that there was so much written within that would damn him in her eyes and others'. He closed the notebook one last time.

Laine's mania stained every page, and it was likely those lurid passages would garner the greater scrutiny. They would be his ruling and his legacy, and the living would judge the dead harshly. Infernal Magick would be blamed instead of human frailty, and insanity would be declared instead of desperate compassion. Had he consorted with demons disguised as gods or gods in demon's garb? Did it really matter?

Perhaps it was no less than Laine deserved. No innocents were to be harmed, yet harm had befallen by his hand.

"I cannot remain. I betrayed and damned near killed Marisa, I intended to kill Donovan, I resisted killing Amarantha, and I harmed an innocent child. And Heather —" He held up her letter and viewed it by candlelight. Laine understood her better now that he'd read her note.

Goddess, what she'd been through and what he had put her through.

Laine opened the TV stand drawer and deposited his chronicles and the red letter inside, displacing the replica . 45 and occult tomes. He closed the drawer, then strapped on his ceremonial mask as he rose.

Silver satin caught the silver candles' glow, and all other fetishes and talismans had been removed from the altar save Trump, an open bottle of Gallo wine and half-full goblet, and the black jewelry box.

The suicide box. The right word to the right Mission Street grocer could garner as much Mexican Valium as one could safely carry. Laine guessed that a large jewelry box's worth should suffice, and if not, he had more in the bottle he bought before going home. He'd know his killer this time.

He took the box and goblet to his window and faced the beautiful moon outside. Luna's perfume was soaking through Laine's black suit, leaving an astral film on his skin. His bell earring chimed. He almost smiled.

Stirring the baby-blue pills with his fingers, Laine played the discomforts of death through his mind. One's body always fought its demise. It had to be prepared and settled down first, made compliant. The wine would help with that.

Moonbeams broke against the tears trapped in his eyelashes as he took another deep swallow. Pouring the drugs into his hand, he proclaimed, "I'll threaten my kin no longer." The last crucible was over. Laine had failed. He had become the greater menace.

"*Em Abtet; em Restet; em Amentet; em Mehtet: qet-a sebti em qet-a.*" The chant was giving the king no comfort: none was deserved.

'Twas no way for a servant of the Goddess to present himself.

Laine's forehead began burning painfully cold, right where the cat mask bore its silver *ankh*.

* * *

"I'm not suicidal, Mama, I'm pissed off."

"You could have fooled me. Don't ever do anything like that again." Mama was looking down at Heather from Australia and gently stroking her hair as she sat on the bed.

"Don't worry, I won't," Heather griped. "Now I know why you hate men. They can eat shit and die."

Mama wagged a finger and said, "*Yo no odio hombres, Heather, me encantan mujeres. Hay una gran diferencia. Tu sabe que.*"

"Not even—"

Mama knew Heather meant her ex. "*Ni siquiera él.*"

"*¿Por qué no? Era tu novio, confiabas en él, y me violó.*"

Mama sighed. "*. . . Y yo lo lastime tambien, y la policía separó a nuestra familia, y pasamos por años de terapia mientras* Joanie *actuó como tu mamá. ¿Valió la pena mi enojo?*"

"*Talvéz valió la pena. Nos resultó bien.* Anyway, it's still not fair. I was there for Laine when his girlfriend wasn't, and I believed in him." Heather swiped a tear from her cheek. "I love him, Mama."

"I know."

"And you didn't stop me."

Mama groomed Heather's curls with her fingers. "*Tu es casi una mujer ahora, dulce, y tu sabías lo que ibas recibir. Tu sabías que* Laine *tenia una novia, y sabías que si tu tratas de amarlo podría haber problemas.* You have to trust your own decisions, not mine. All I can do is point out what you can't see. You still have to walk in the dark alone."

"Fine, then here's a decision: maybe I'll narc on him and tell Marisa about us."

Mama was nodding, but her frown said she disapproved. "*Quizá tu debe, y quizá tu no debería, pero si lo haces, tendrás dos enemigos con los que luchar. Eso es el doble de problemas. Ambos* Laine *y . . . ,*"

". . . Marisa . . ."

pale shadows

"... *Te odiarian. Eso casi nunca vale la pena romper una relación de pareja.*" Mama smirked down from the off-white continents. "And anyway, Laine'll probably do that himself."

"Shit, Mama, what should I do then?"

"As I say, that's up to you. Do what you think you have to. Just don't tempt another seven years of bad luck while you do it." Mama pointed her chin at *Trinidad* and the bits of broken mirror. "They say sometimes the best way to win a battle is not to fight, you know? Sometimes, you find a better way." Mama slid her lap from under Heather's head and stepped around the broken glass as she left the bedroom.

Mama was right as usual. There was nothing Heather could do about Laine. He belonged to Marisa. It sucked, but it was true, and there was no point in being mad at the truth.

Amy, though. Forget everything else, Amy was still Heather's best friend, and she couldn't leave her to Donovan. That asshole messed with Heather's head and mentally raped her. She couldn't forgive that.

The mirror pieces on her floor resembled islands of ice drifting on a hardwood sea. She reached over the edge of her bed and picked up a triangular shard, staring hard at her flushed reflection. How to get Donovan back?

Heather gasped. "Holy shit! The mirror."

* * *

And I opened my hand and found it filled not with the Valium, but with an emerald feather and the last Janus flower.

Maat emerged from surrounding shadows, appearing as a winged child who couldn't have circled the sun more than seven times. A plain, linen, Egyptian tunic was hanging from her shoulders; a tall staff was filling her tiny fist.

I threw a furious gaze at the minor fetch and demanded

she explain why she had come as a child when a goddess was needed, and why at so late an hour.

Maat cast a gaze of her own, unimpeded by my disguise and rage. She touched my brow, and my crown fell, ringing as it hit the metal floor. My mind split, and I recognized the glacial pain that had stayed my hand against Marisa and Donovan. In that instance, I was shown how everything had gone so wrong and how Maat had tried to keep it right.

I could have simply walked away and retired after Samhain, playing out The King's Tradition honorably. Instead, the entire pantheon bore witness to my failings. My ignorance had helped the spear and its company claim dominance over me, and my obsession prevented me from heeding the gods' intentions. Because of my animosity and hubris, I tipped the scales when I had only been meant to watch them. So concerned was I with Amarantha's ascension that I'd forgotten about my own and the rewards it promised. I had even sued to violate the first rede: Do what thou will, save that it harm none.

My folly lost me my knight, my queen, and my fief. Originally, I was not meant to be the deodand that I had become, but now I must die by The Qliphoth's hands, by decree, no illusions to the contrary.

All of my shame visited upon me at once and wrested me of my tears. I wept my apologies. The goddess silenced me by pressing a holy finger upon my lips, then she retrieved my diadem and slung it from her waist.

Child Maat extended her feathered hand to unworthy me. I took it, and we walked seven steps away from my window and onto the corner of Jefferson and Jones. I smiled at the memories of my truant youth and the times I had spent dropping quarters into pinball machines and critiquing the latest video games at Museé Méchanique; the hours whiled away at The Galactic Starport, admiring their latest sci-fi memorabilia. Just to my left across the street was the seafood stand where I used to spend almost as many quarters on rolls of Parisian sourdough bread to gnaw on; to my right stood the gift shop that promised that all of their oysters bore pearls. While a welcomed sight, I didn't understand why Maat had brought me to The Anchorage.

A familiar figure skulked past me at a determined pace. About my height, I let my vanity judge his unkempt hair and weather-beaten wardrobe before I realized I was looking at myself two years earlier.

I knew where he was heading. I knew where we were heading. We were trailing Laine eastward down the crowded street, yet were unaffected by the crowd. We dogged his heels past caricature artists, novelty photo booths, and T-shirt merchants for almost two blocks before he slowed up behind a trio of teenagers. Once the two boys had split off, Laine tapped the girl's shoulder, and of course, Amarantha turned around.

I watched as we briefly caught up and expressed how we missed each other; how she had returned home that day and wanted to resume her training; how she had met up with an old friend.

Amarantha's companions were rocking on their heels in the threshold of a camera store. Jimmy was complaining about the cold San Francisco air, and Donovan was trying to get a good look at Laine and a good listen to our conversation.

And so it was. Proof that even then Donovan had me in mind, before I knew he even existed. Jimmy had been true on Samhain, but there was another truth to this vision.

Before long, Amarantha rejoined her chaperones while Laine skulked away into the night. She was hugging the bastard's arm as they continued toward Mason Street and she explained the nature of our friendship. Maat and I followed my pupil and her love past a haunted goldmine, designer jellybean shops, and more video arcades. It was within the tungsten glow of a salt-water taffy house that our quintet halted. Amarantha called toward the handful of people watching the pulling machine stretch pink and green confections. One of their number responded, and Heather walked toward us, all broad smiles.

Amarantha introduced Heather to Jimmy and reintroduced her to Donovan. Heather considered Donovan, and her face had that look on it like she'd just made an important decision about something. Her grimace said that despite his new smile and beauty, she still didn't like him.

The vision froze, silenced. Child Maat left my side to join Heather's and smiled up at her like she was her beloved mother. I joined them and knelt. Maat looked upon me and spoke wordlessly. I knew what I was meant to do.

Grabbing the crown from the goddess' hip, I found my footing and slowly placed the radiant symbol of my station upon Heather's head. I had performed the task that fate had willed: I had trained a new goddess. The rest, now that she was ready, was up to Heather. So where did that leave me?

Maat walked past me, and there came again to my ears the groan of distressed wood. I turned and found her standing with her staff extended along her shoulders. Each end bore a plate: one was still without its quill while its contestant was weighing heavy, red meat.

I opened the hand where drugs once laid and looked upon the tokens. The last Janus flower was all that was left of my Magickal self. The emerald feather was all that remained of my queen. One of these two fetishes would have to be sacrificed if I had any hope of restoring balance to the scales.

I joined the woman/child who was the fulcrum and stared down into the suspended brass plate.

The choice of offerings wasn't hard at all. The last pure Janus flower to ever grow in Nihtheim proved equal to my bleeding heart.

* * *

I buried the black egg and started the fires, east, south, west, and north. The trees bowed and parted in a gesture of farewell as I settled into my shift and crossed the threshold of my sanctum.

There I was in Amy's kitchen, though it looked like it was underwater. The light seemed lazy, and everything had a halo. Amy was with me, but she didn't know it as she slid a tray into the oven. She was no doubt preparing for Thanksgiving as well. Amy's features became clearer as she set her kitchen timer, picked up a nearby paperback, and started down the hall towards the front of the house. I shadowed her, step for step.

About halfway to Joanie's room, Amy stopped, slowly turned around, and looked right at me. Sort of. I kept my breathing easy as she looked through me, shook her head, then continued on her journey with me swimming behind her until I reached her bedroom.

The armoire was my target. I remembered what Amy had said about being unable to mirror walk, and I also remembered what Donovan had been staring at during the dark moon ritual. If I wanted to seriously bind Amy's powers, her mirror would be my first stop. If I seriously wanted to restore her powers, that would be my same stop.

Her mirror was conspicuously clean and shimmering like lights in a swimming pool. My guess was she had mugwort cooking the other night. Too late again, unless it wasn't really the mirror itself that was tampered with.

There it was! A mark on the trim! One would have to be tall and deft to place it. I breathed and I rose until my vision was level with the furnishing's top. I didn't know what the smudge was made of, but I doubted I would have seen it with my earthly eyes. In the astral though, the blemish looked like a glowing Pac-Man or a Corn Nut.

No, it was shaped like a hoof print. Definitely a hoof print.

I drew a circle with a cross in the center in white flame. It traveled three inches from my fingertip to the hoof symbol. The mark didn't make a sound when it vaporized.

The job was only half-completed though. This sort of spell usually had a physical anchor, and I now knew where to find that anchor. I'd have to return to Amy's room in the *flesh.*

As I descended to the floor, a strange ringing from Amy's altar distracted me. I moved through the astral fluid until I was standing at her ceremonial space. There it was: the source of the jingling. The earring that Amy shared with Laine was buzzing unnaturally as it hung from one of Athena's stone hands. I breathed deeply and slowly and drew a banishing star in the air, then I muted the jewelry with a pinch.

On my way out, I caught my reflection in the looking glass. There was a new radiance around my head like a tiara of pure light. I gasped, and both confusion and elation filled me when I ran my fingers along the band.

* * *

In about fifteen minutes, the stuffing-filled mushrooms for the church supper tomorrow night would be done. The first batch had come out overcooked, but if this sheet worked out, Amarantha would prep more and refrigerate them for the church's oven. She would top them with a dollop of cranberry sauce on-site.

Joanie had no problem acting as court taster as she had soundly demonstrated her mettle by snacking on the scorched fungi experiment while watching *Magnum, P.I.* "You actually finished them, huh?" Amarantha's landing on her mother's bed jostled Terra, who was dozing nearby.

"Yeah. They weren't too bad, just a little burnt."

"I set the timer for fifteen minutes this time. These should be perfect." Amarantha reclined and reopened her copy of Richard Adams' *Maia* to the bookmark.

Two pages of dense reading later, the character Occula had entered The Streels of Urtah at the bidding of spirits, but as her revenge drew near, Amarantha was suddenly distracted from the narrative by the rising bay of hounds. They were close, easily within the next house or two, and they sounded angry, like they'd cornered a cat. "You hear that?"

"Yeah, Cary Grant died today," Joanie said of a news teaser. "What a shame. He didn't make it to Thanksgiving."

"No, I think our neighbors got a new dog." Terra's ears were now pricking up, and her eyes were now bugging. She had heard it too.

"Oh really? What's it look like?"

"No, I hear bark—never mind. Wait, wasn't Cary Grant British? I'm pretty sure they don't celebrate Thanksgiving."

Gurgling howls sounded from somewhere inside the house now. Amarantha closed her novel and sat erect.

"You didn't hear that?"

"No, nothing. Just the TV." Tom Selleck had Joanie's undivided attention.

Words from another tome came to Amarantha: a poem from long ago. "'The hounds of Hecate,'" Amarantha whispered. "Lillian."

Amarantha dropped her book and gestured for Terra to follow. She promised Joanie, "We'll be back."

The floral reliefs of the hallway walls seemed damp as if the plaster petals were sweating. It was an illusion of the gloss paint, but it was an unsettling one nonetheless. The howls grew louder as Amarantha approached her bedroom door. She looked to Terra for her bravery; the white cat appeared to be doing the same to her.

"Fine." Amarantha stole the first slow peek. Her room was as silent as it was dark. Not a candle lit nor a mastiff heard. "See, Terra, just nerves."

The white long-haired cat sniffed the threshold suspiciously, then crept inside.

The kitchen timer chimed. Amarantha trotted into the kitchen, opened the oven door, and shut off the flame. Fifteen minutes was definitely the time. "Perfect."

Then three barks sounded followed by a pain-wracked *yipe*. Amarantha glanced down the hall just in time to see Terra scattering for Joanie's room.

"That *wasn't* just nerves." Amarantha set the sheets of stuffed mushrooms on the stovetop, then passed from the kitchen's tungsten cast into the corridor's dusk. No more sounds were heard save the shuffling of her socked feet.

Amarantha's shadow stretched long on her bedroom floor as she went to a window, keeping her light off. There was no one on Waller that brisk holiday eve. Certainly no battered canines. There was just the muted sound of Joanie's show in the front room and the bangs of the cooling oven.

An animal whimpered, its cry distant and yet strangely intimate.

"Where are you, girl?" Amarantha turned and dropped slowly to her hands and knees. Nothing lurked beneath her canopy bed except dust bunnies and her old blue slippers. "I won't hurt you."

Another cry came from near. Amarantha's vision snapped to her armoire, and she noticed something sharing her reflection. A black mongrel sat on its broken haunches at the other side of the looking glass. Unclear and unresolved, the specter staggered into the depths of Amarantha's furnishing and faded away.

"Here, girl." She was meant to follow the lame fetch.

* * *

Propping his head up on a pillow, Laine inhaled the full moon's glow and the wind that chilled it. He exhaled the night sky when he said, "I have been spared from Ammut's maw, and yet I remain damned."

What did Laine have left? His life certainly, but also a dire debt. He'd made a pact when he summoned the spear of Moloch, yet that contract must remain unfulfilled. Laine could not kill Donovan, nor would he sacrifice his pupils, and yet the company must somehow be satisfied.

And then there was Marisa. He couldn't vie for her love again until the spear was quelled; until he was made honorable again. "At least no one will get to Marisa again." That thought alone guaranteed Laine would get a good night's sleep.

That was really all that mattered to him. That was what

pale shadows

Laine had left: this night, this moment, these breaths. That was all anyone ever had. He could afford to be damned tomorrow.

*   *   *

The shore where the unicorn had fled and serpents had writhed was now circling a pool of gore. The reek of decomposing pomegranates assaulted my senses as I traveled above the acrid stew. Then I heard the abuse sound again from deep within the pomegranate woodland.

I tripped over tree knuckles breaking through crimson soil and called out from beneath grisly canopies but was given no aural compass. The hound I was pursuing was quiet now, and I was finally afraid.

The yawning, cherry sky made the thickets seem endless, even for me. My eyes were screwed red and black, and I was half-blind when I broke into the clearing where a tree stump was belching. The corpses of two black hounds laid gutted at the foot of the wooden basin. I was too late. I slumped and wept at the altar.

That's when I heard Lillian ask if her pupil was gone. I declared I didn't know who she meant, but that we were alone. Her nearby voice asked again about her consort, the hunter. Deorcloven. She asked if it was safe.

Now standing, I searched for the source of Lillian's voice. So closely did it ring that the only possible place it could have come from was the gurgling stump. I plunged my arms elbow-deep into the thin, fallow membrane and bruised peelings, and stirred the stump until I found Lillian's hands, then I pulled her to the surface of the thick, spoiling vegetation.

Lillian's blue eyes were staring up at me; her raven hair was strewn with canine and fruit remains. Both alien and familiar, I recognized something as she was buoying within the eldritch broth: with the slightest of cosmetic changes, Lillian and I could have passed for sisters.

I pinned Lillian against the inside of the stump and

threatened to call Deorcloven back to finish her as revenge for slaughtering my unicorn.

Lillian called me a fool and said that Deorcloven and I had killed it on Samhain when I lay with him. Unicorns died when virginity did, and this lesson in obvious lore was wasting Lillian's fleeting time.

I leaned closer as Lillian told of when she first fostered Deorcloven's calling and initiated him. They were both using Magick to end their addictions and traumas and had made a pact on it out of love for The Art and each other. What she hadn't foreseen were Deorcloven's spiritual dependencies. The hunter suffered from psychic anemia, and Lillian soon became his new drug. Lillian was not as strong as his addictions, and when Deorcloven went bad, Lillian tried to break the pact, damming his source of psychic flux.

The breaking of any Magickal contract carried karmic consequences: it was doubly so with Deorcloven and—as with a tick—the remedy proved more injurious than the ailment. Lillian had paid for the breach with her sanity and his cruelty. She blamed herself for Deorcloven: he was her failure, and she should have seen it coming.

Now Deorcloven had a new source; a more powerful yet compliant source. Lillian pointed at me, her body shaking like she was standing on her tiptoes.

Her buoyancy began giving way, and her ice-blue eyes were filling with pulp. She was afflicted, but by what I did not know. Her palms turned as she began to thrash, displaying the long white and red snake tattoos writhing up her forearms. The red ones were bleeding.

I asked what I could do to help. Lillian said it was too late for her, and that if I wished to be spared, I must keep no more company with Deorcloven. I must make no pact and no longer share his bed.

I screamed to her that I was Handfasted to him already. Lillian gargled and clutched as she stated that it was too late for me then, and commanded me to flee before I was found. Lillian's desperate grasping threatened to drag me

pale shadows

into the trunk with her, but death finally stole her strength, and she went under with a final, violent yank.

I wept again.

Lillian Crane, my sister. It is too late.

THURSDAY, NOVEMBER 27TH

THANKSGIVING

λ silver Porsche whipped down Beach Street pumping "Bizarre Love Triangle" into the sky. Whatever happened to Jimmy? Heather remembered he loved New Order.

Heather didn't let Laine know that she was in the near-empty gallery. She just watched him stare at an Erté print on the wall with his back to her. When Heather finally crept deeper into the gallery, Laine appeared to be playing with his glasses as he critiqued the piece, flipping his specs up and down with his right hand.

Heather's red envelope was in his left one.

"It's funny: as much as I love Erté's Alphabet series," he commented without looking at her, "I've never really noticed the details in this one before now." Laine flipped his glasses back down. "Makes me wonder how many other details I've missed; how many patterns I've misread."

Heather lifted each sneakered foot off the carpet,

breaking the static charge she'd built up. "Maybe you just need to wear contacts."

Laine chuckled. "That's what Marisa says." A delayed grimace crushed his profile when he mentioned her name. There was no doubt where Laine's mind and heart were lingering.

Heather took in the posh surroundings. "I'm surprised they're open today."

Laine finally looked at her, his bright eyes showing that he finally got that sleep he was missing. He nodded toward the Italian stud up front. "Half a day. Andre's closing up in an hour. Sorry I had you come all the way across the city. I had to check in with Mohammed."

Heather said, "No problem. I'm used to it. Why am I here?"

Laine displayed her letter: the full misery and horror of her adolescent rape scrawled on construction paper. "I think we should discuss this outside."

Heather nodded. "Yeah, we should."

While he turned toward the front door, Heather got a good look at the picture he had been obsessing over: the letter M burning with orange and yellow flames. Two identical black figures kneeled face-to-face underneath the blazing consonant, imprisoned in what looked like olive butterfly wings. She remembered Laine's reflection on Haight Street and gave in to the heebie-jeebies.

Heather caught up to Laine and followed him into the quiet holiday haze. The intersection the gallery shared with Ghirardelli Square had plenty of foot traffic—as that area always did—but little of it was tourists. Dancing on the curb, a street artist with some serious rhyming skills was trying to charm the cash out of a couple of locals and failing.

"Please don't go/Give me some dough!" he shot at Laine.

Laine frisked himself. "Sorry, I don't have any cash on me."

Then to Heather. "Don't be shy/Slide me a five!"

Heather dug around in her jean pocket and pulled out a buck. "Happy Thanksgiving."

"Thank you, sister/I'm a happy mister." They both laughed.

Heather added, "Hey, check out Glide or Hamilton Methodist off of Haight Street. They're both serving free dinners," as she and Laine cut across Bay Street.

The homeless man waved. "I'm already there with time to spare!" he yelled before laughing again.

The creak of the old clipper ship that had been turned into a historical museum called them to the city's northern edge. Heather was walking on the black bricks hugging the small beach. Laine took the sand, yet she was still shorter than him as they strolled.

Waving her red letter in the ocean air, he announced, "I had my suspicions that you were the one abused, but I figured you'd tell me when you were ready. It would have been rude of me to pick that lock."

Always the gentleman, more so than Donovan, at least. Laine was making it really hard to stay mad at him. "Thank you for that. Wanted to tell you, but it's really hard to talk about, even with you."

"What I don't understand is you said you were still, you know, a virgin."

"As far as I'm concerned, I was. My rape doesn't count."

Laine nodded a little and put his hands together like he was praying. "May I apologize on behalf of the male animal for what happened to you?"

Heather snorted. "No, you may not. Not for that, anyway. The asshole that did that to me wasn't like you. I've let it go: you can too." She knew too well how Laine was. Next thing you know, he'd be trying to find Mama's ex to get revenge. "Mama already dealt with him. Just let it go."

Laine smiled and nodded again as he took off his glasses. "Still, I assume that everyone should know better: that we all have an internal ethics compass that we follow, and it really pisses me off when humanity demonstrates otherwise." Then his smile went away, and he stared north toward the fog of Marin. "Shit, I should have known better too. You're only seventeen, aren't you?"

"I . . . I'll be eighteen next month. I swear I won't tell nobody. It's our business." She added, "Anyways, Mama knows already."

Laine groaned and exhaled. "You know what? I can't do this anymore, Heather."

"I know you can't. You still love Marisa, and like I said, I'm not going to fuck that up."

"It's not just that, it's everything," he growled, his arms spread. "I was planning to retire from Magick after Amarantha's Wiccaning, you know. Now between dealing with Donovan, losing Marisa, and fighting my—well, that purpose is gone."

"Get Marisa back if that's what you want. Start painting again if that's what you want. You are a High Magickian, so stop bitching and manifest. I'll take care of Amy and—" Heather made her bloodsucking noise. They both laughed, but Laine's laughter was tense.

"I know you will. You were meant to."

Heather wanted to hug him just one more time and comfort him, but she knew that wouldn't happen. Their time was done. Instead, she took Laine's hand.

And that's when she saw it: a glimpse of black ash and of twins on a burning horizon. Was she just projecting Erté's art, or was this the fight from his broken sentence?

Wait, where was Laine's crown? "What's going on behind your eyes, milord? I see darkness before you."

"I'm just going to Marisa's folks' for dinner. I guess that's pretty scary." He had one of his fake smiles on.

"You know that's not what I mean."

Laine's gaze was like a pointing finger. "And you know that's all you're going to get out of me."

It was true: there would be no more breaking through his walls today. His silver wards were thicker now.

"I will say this though: I'm not going into the darkness

unprepared. That should be comforting enough."

"Okay." Heather returned Laine's sly smile and asked, "Milord, be honest: did you know this is how it would all end?"

"Goddess, no." Laine's head shaking convinced her. "Besides, it's not finished yet."

"You're right. I still have something to take care of at Amy's." Heather still had to banish the physical anchor to Donovan's spell. Otherwise, last night's deed wouldn't matter. Vampire Boy could just charge it back up the next time he went to Amy's.

"What I meant was I believe I still owe you a name." Laine let go of Heather's hand, leaving his cold fingerprints behind, then played with the silk cord of his pentacle.

"At different stages of my Magickal life, I have worn different pentacles. When it's time for me to move on to the next stage, I give my retired pentacles to whomever is worthy. That's how Amarantha and Marisa got theirs."

Laine finally slipped the talisman free and turned it in his hand as he stepped closer.

"This one belongs to you now, Nefertamut." Laine looped the cord over Heather's head and let the silver amulet fall gently on her breasts. "Blessed be."

I was wearing a familiar pendant, but I couldn't understand why it was so.

Now she did, and her remembered future never felt nearer. "Won't you need it?"

Laine dismissed the notion with a head shake. "I assure you, it's been replaced." He slipped his thumbs underneath another cord around his neck and yanked a polished silver *ankh* from his dress shirt collar. "Besides, I always wear a spare." He then flashed the pentacle ring on his right index finger.

"As is your will, so mote it be. And thank you. Wait, what's my name again?"

"Nef-er-tah-moot," he repeated slowly, "It's Egyptian for 'Beautiful Earth Mother'. Well, according to Budge, anyway. I thought it an appropriate name for a Capricorn healer, but if you don't like it—"

"Actually, I love it." Heather had everything she needed.

"I laid the pentacle on some sea salt overnight, but you should still cleanse it properly when you get the chance."

"I will. So . . . ." Heather wiped away a tear of pride.

Laine folded his lanky arms. "So what will you do now, Lady Nefertamut?"

"Make sure we finish what we started. What about you, Lord Nihthasu?"

The tall wizard smiled and shrugged. "The same thing." This time, his grin was real.

* * *

The church basement was empty now except for Amarantha, Joanie, and the other six volunteer food servers. The subterranean space was usually filled with the cots, sleeping bags, and partitions of the homeless family shelter. They were standing against the unpaneled walls now, displaced by beige, laminated dining tables and those metal folding chairs with the cushions that farted when sat upon.

"Did you see the line outside?" Joanie asked as she pulled the aluminum shield off a tub of turkey gravy. "It's twice what it was last year."

Stuffing steam was already dampening Amarantha's brow. She tried wiping it away with the back of her hand, but the plastic gloves made the gesture pointless. "Tell me you're exaggerating."

Footsteps began pounding like bass drums overhead. Apparently, José's service was over, and soon a flood of hunger would roar through the doors. This wasn't Amarantha's first Thanksgiving feast to be sure, but ever since Hamilton U.M.C. opened the Homeless Family Center, it had promised to be her busiest. Oh well, it was good practice, serving a crowd.

Amarantha's eyes shot towards the murmurs and

laughter cresting beyond the main door. She took in her fellow servers, and they all had the same anxious expression.

She pleaded, "Joanie, please tell me you're exaggerating."

Her mom just shook her head and hid her eyes with her smiling cheeks. "Sorry, sweetie, I can't. The sad thing is most of them are street kids. Isn't Donovan going to help out today?"

"Yeah, he is." It would be a surprise if he made it on time after what Lillian had shown her last night. If he showed up before the banquet finished, his innocence defied doubt, but if he arrived late, Amarantha hoped his reasons would prove more convincing than Lillian's claims.

A woman giggled. All the volunteers turned toward Sister Anna Beth, who was wearing a delirious grin as she stood over her mountain of sweet potatoes. "I'm sorry. I'm just a little nervous," she explained.

Amarantha said, "That's okay. We all are."

The main door opened as Amarantha cinched her apron.

* * *

Laine exited his apartment lobby, following the concrete awning overhead to the purring, blue Riva scooter. Back to Marisa again. He stopped about a yard from where they broke up an eternal week ago.

"Hey. You're right on time." Laine slid the black nylon duffel he was carrying into a steep angle, prepping it for the ride. Its contents rang.

"Hey." Marisa stood on her tiptoes and gave him an unexpected kiss on the cheek. "I'm not pregnant," she whispered quickly before gravity pushed her off her toes. "My period started Tuesday night. Yippie!" she chirped.

The world got much lighter. "That's . . . good news. *Great* news." Now the spear truly had no leverage.

"I tried to call you at work yesterday: Mohammed told me what happened." Marisa frowned. "Is the baby okay?"

Laine took the spare helmet and nodded, remembering his relief. "Yeah, everything's fine. Not a scar or a welt. Hell, even Mohammed joked about it today." He imitated his boss' thick Arabic accent. "'See, your cappuccinos not hot enough.'"

Laughing, she said, "I'm a little nervous about tonight." Marisa smiled at Laine's burden but didn't question it. She knew him well enough to know he never traveled without some pack or other.

Laine sighed deeply as he locked the chinstrap. "Me too."

He mounted the bike and coiled his arms tightly around Marisa's waist, soaking in her warmth. He could have taken Marisa right then; ravished her back into his apartment and tried to make it all okay again. Problem was, he couldn't even if they hadn't split up; even if they hadn't rolled away from the curb. Though the spear's company was silent, he knew they were near, waiting for the moon's pale shadow. God was bigger, but The Devil was always closer.

Midas's plight came to Laine's mind, but at least he could share this necessary embrace. As they rode toward the Sunset District, his satchel chimed and clattered from the brass sconces and steel dagger within. Black and silver candles, a fresh twenty-dollar bottle of '83 Cabernet—the Gallo wasn't cutting it, dragon's blood incense sticks, and a scarab-graven incense holder were all contained. No suicide boxes. Tonight's ritual would have a wholly different function. When the voices came again, he'd be ready.

And Trump. For some reason, he knew he had to bring Trump. Beyond that, Laine kept the load simple; kept it light. His duffel bag would probably attract questions from Marisa's folks. Best to have a ready answer.

* * *

"Rudy, I thought you were drawing something for Thanksgiving?"

Heather's little brother grinned as he flapped his art in the air. "It *is* for Thanksgiving: I call him The Gobbler."

Heather laughed, "The Gobbler?"

"Yeah, he's a mutant. He was a farmer that got caught in a turkey plucking machine, and all the turkeys on the farm turned on the machine, and the farmer got crunched."

Her stomach hurt so hard from laughing, that Heather had to roll onto her back.

"Now he's a deformed turkey, and he wants revenge against Thanksgiving."

"You know who should fight him? Wolverine," Heather suggested, sitting up again on her bedroom floor. "'Light or dark meat, bub?'"

"Yeah. The Gobbler was supposed to be a drawing of Sasquatch, but I messed it up."

Turning her head sideways, Heather could see the resemblance to the Alpha Flight member. "It's not too bad. He looks like Sasquatch dressed like a turkey."

"Yo mama."

"My mama and your mama are the same." They could cap like that for hours.

"'So, so suck my toe/All the way to Mexico.'"

Just then Mama poked in her head. "*La cena estará lista en unos cinco minutos. Límpiate.*"

Heather and Rudy said, "Okay."

Heather was rolling their sketches into butcher-paper tubes when Rudy asked, "Is that Laine's?"

"What?"

Rudy was pointing at Heather's chest. "That. That's Laine's, right?"

The pentacle. Heather rubbed her thumb on the smooth moonstone.

"It was Laine's, but it's mine now."

"I saw one of those in a movie once, but it was the other way around."

"Upside-down?"

"Yeah, I guess." Rudy wrapped a rubber band around a bunch of markers.

"Those were Satanists. We don't do that."

"I didn't think so." No doubt, the kid was smart.

"Come here, I'll show you what it means."

Rudy scooched closer, leaving art supplies in his wake.

"See, there are five points. The four points on the bottom are the elements: Air, Fire, Water, and Earth. The point on top—" She tapped the symbol. "—is The Spirit. That is, it represents the spiritual ideal over the earthly. When it's upside-down—" Heather rotated the pentacle "—it represents the earthly over the spiritual. That's how Satanists wear theirs. And by the way, we witches were here waaaay before Satanists."

"Ohhh. Okay."

Heather's stomach told her the lesson was over. "Man, I'm really hungry."

Rudy said, "Me too. Beat you to the table!" then tore down the hall toward the kitchen.

Heather wouldn't eat too much though. Just enough to shut her stomach up. Her Magick always worked better that way. She stood and stretched, then turned toward her altar; her sword.

"You ready to eat, *dulce*?" Mama asked from the bedroom door.

"*Si, Mama, pero* Amy *es en la iglesia. Necesito ver luego.*"

Mama just smiled. "*De nada.* Better eat now then before it gets late. Max can give you a ride."

Before Mama could leave the room, Heather added, "Actually, I think I'll bus it."

Mama's smile turned suspicious. "You hate walking through The Mission."

"Usually." But not today. Heather could take anything the mean streets dished out.

* * *

"Don't be rude/Pile on the food!"

"What?" The disheveled, Black poet had surprised

Amarantha.

"It's alright, Amy," Deacon José assured as he passed behind her, "We're pretty much finished for the year anyway. Give him the rest."

"Whatever you say. Here you go, sir." She scooped two perfect spheres of savory Stove Top stuffing onto his Chinet plate. "Happy Thanksgiving."

The poet returned the holiday cheer, tipping his herringbone fedora before finding himself a vacant seat. Even from her serving station, Amarantha heard the hiss when his butt compressed the seat cushion half a row away. When José came back around, she asked him, "What time is it?"

Deacon José always wore his watch with the face on his inner wrist. Amarantha never understood why guys did that. They probably thought it made them look cool. "Almost 6:30."

"It's that late already?" She uttered the question more for herself than José. The evidence was in front of her: three empty aluminum troughs that were once bursting with prepackaged dressing. Her duties had been exhaustively mechanistic: greet, scoop, thank. Between all of that was the watching of the door, waiting for her lover to breach it. "Have you seen Donovan?"

The young minister leaned collapsed chairs against the beige wall behind them and slapped his forehead. "That's right: Joanie said Donny was lending us a hand today. I haven't seen him though. Hang on." José scanned the still-crowded basement that was gradually converting back into a shelter. "Margaret!"

Amarantha was about to tell José to just forget it, but about three families over a girl with auburn braids looked their way. Summoned by José, she walked up to them. Amarantha knew the girl from somewhere.

"Margaret, have you seen Donovan around?"

"No, but I *have* been seeing a lot of the kitchen."

José sighed and smiled. "Okay, I'll be right in. Can you call the church members and volunteers into—"

"Already did it."

"What would I do without you?"

"Go prematurely bald is my guess."

Amarantha knew friendly banter when she saw it, and obviously, they'd known each other for a long time. It was funny: when José wasn't acting like *Deacon* José, it was easy for Amarantha to remember he was only seven years older than she was.

Margaret turned to her. "Hey, Amy. Your stuffing mushrooms were incredible."

Who the heck was she? "Thanks."

"Why don't you two go up?" José said, "I'm sure Donny will be here in time for a meal. He'd be a fool to miss out on Amy's dish. Plus you two can catch up."

Wait a minute. "Maggie?" Amarantha almost called her "Hungry Maggie".

"Yup." The shorter woman's smile widened. She had changed a lot in five years.

* * *

All residents of the Sunset District had one thing in common: their homes. With one east-west flip and the rotation of a couple of rooms, the Spanish-style flat Marisa's parents called home could have easily been the Spanish-style flat Nihthasu's queen called home.

His queen. Right.

It had been an evening of deep hugs and deeper guts, little of which Laine shared. He ate his share when badgered and coaxed out as much conversation as was warranted, but the bottom line was he was utterly distracted by Marisa and what he'd have to do that night to try to get her back.

He stumbled back into his dialogue with her dad Jerry. "So I don't get it. What exactly did Reagan's boys do again?"

"Haven't you seen the news?"

Laine glanced at Marisa, then down at his lap. "I've

been a little out of it lately."

"They sold arms to Iran—which is illegal . . ."

"Okay . . . ." Despite the fact the weekend sportsman expressed the first misgivings about Marisa's mating choice, he and Laine had established a rapport of sorts over the past year. The witch's frequent print shop visits had paid off.

His wife, Kim, admonished, "Calm down, Jer, it's Thanksgiving," as she gathered dishes.

"And gave the money they made to the Contras, which is also illegal."

Marisa was pinned close to Laine on the loveseat, dressed in black and smelling of white jasmine oil. He called her effect on him "skintoxication", and it made pretending to still be a couple both easy and difficult. Every brush of her jewel-spangled hand and every fragile smile made him keenly aware of what he had lost and what he stood to lose.

"Suh-so what's the big deal? I figured the government did dirty stuff like that all the time." Laine leaned forward casually, breaking some of his physical contact with Marisa.

"Would you like more potato salad, Laine?" Marisa's mom offered. "You're so skinny."

"Thank you, Mrs. Chang, but I think I've reached my limit." Laine's white tuxedo shirttail and un-slung suspenders signaled his surrender. It was easy to see where her daughters got their good looks.

"Good point, Laine," Jerry jumped in. "Think of it—"

Kim interrupted, "I tell you what: I'll pack some up for you to take home later."

"Thanks." Laine's grandfather would appreciate the meal, no doubt, though he had no idea when he'd get home.

Jerry's stature shrunk conspiratorially. "Think of it: they just got caught *this* time. I mean they caught that soldier and the secretary that shredded all the files." The graying patron of the Chang clan packed a Marlboro Light on the back of his tan hand. "What about the stuff they're doing that we *haven't* caught yet? Think about it." Jerry scratched his chest through his sky-blue Izod shirt while wiggling the index of his free hand. He probably excelled at patting his head and rubbing his stomach.

"Okay."

Kim was in the kitchen with Marisa's brothers, flapping open a brown paper bag. "Calm down, Jer, it's Thanksgiving."

Jerry gave the tip of his unlit cigarette a thumbs-up. Sympathetic, Laine produced his panther lighter from a pants pocket and silently offered it to Jerry when he leaned forward, but Kim stepped between them and sniped the cigarette out of her husband's mouth. "Only one per day, Jer. You know what the doctor said."

"Sorry." Laine chuckled quietly.

"You shouldn't even be smoking *one*, dad," quipped Kelli Chang, who was sitting in the love seat directly across from Laine and Marisa. Mark was ensconced on the floor between her calves, receiving an omnipresent shoulder rub from his paramour. Her efforts were doing nothing to remove his caveman glares which were as deep as hugs and guts. They probably knew about the split, but were sworn to secrecy by Marisa. From where he was sitting, Laine could have skryed both of them with ease, but he'd walked through their minds before when they first met and had no interest in a return visit.

Jerry turned to his oldest daughter. "See this is what happens when the kids move out of the house: the parents treat each other as kids." All the Chang siblings laughed.

"Are we doing this again with your family this weekend?" Marisa whispered sweetly into Laine's ear.

"Yes, if you still want to." He was acutely aware of the missing kiss as her warm thigh pressed against his. Laine and Marisa lingered. The electricity was unbearable; the temptation could kill. "I—"

"Are you okay?" Marisa's emerald gaze narrowed into his. "Your cat is showing."

"Really?" That was such good news. It meant that some

part of Laine's champion still remained, and he could use the backup. He whispered, "I better bail."

Standing with him, she said, "I'll walk you out."

Mark mumbled, "Leaving so soon?"

Marisa flipped him off openly, but Kim was back in the kitchen gathering the doggy bags, Jerry was still trying to plea bargain an extra smoke, and the rest of the family were locked in nostalgia, so they missed it. Laine smirked as he retrieved his black duffel bag laying ever close to his feet.

"Wait." Kim hurried from the kitchen with two doubled-up brown paper bags laying sideways in her grasp. From her gait, it seemed her stirrup pants were giving her issues. "Don't forget your food."

"Actually, I don't think I've got enough room for them." Laine gave his bag a shake, letting them hear the contents ring.

Marisa slipped an arm around Laine's waist. A heavy gasp caught in his throat. "Yeah, Ma," she agreed, "I'll take it to him at work tomorrow."

"Oh. Okay." Marisa's mom set the bags on the dining room table.

"What's in there anyway?" A new cigarette was fluttering between Jerry's lips.

"Art supplies from earlier today." The half-lie came easily. Laine shook the dad's hand and waved to everyone else. "Thank you very much for inviting me. It was great meeting the whole family."

Jerry's slap on Laine's shoulder was firm even though he had to reach up. "Thank you for coming."

His cancer stick vanished, and Kim now had two. She looked up at the mage and smiled. "It was really good sitting down and getting to know you, Laine."

"You too, Mrs. Chang."

"Aw, come on, they're *light* cigarettes!" Jerry protested.

"Call me Kim." She ignored Nihthasu's offered hand and hugged him instead. Marisa looked as shocked as Laine felt. Things had changed indeed.

Departing down stucco caverns and outside steel gates,

Laine and Marisa were finally alone beneath Nuit's navy canopy.

"I told you they'd like you in the end," Marisa reminded.

"'In the end.'" He shrugged against the bite of his bag strap.

"Off into the night again?"

That wasn't Marisa's real question, simply an easy one. "For the last time, I think."

She frowned at his shoes. "Be careful. Don't do anything stupid."

"Stupid might be all I have left."

"No, it isn't."

Laine could have laughed or cried right then, but did neither. If Marisa knew what he had planned that evening and why, she would have called his intentions stupid to be sure, but then there was so much she didn't know; so many other elements that were driving him to this night's destiny. He made no promises and no confessions. This would be his last secret. "I'll see you tomorrow at the shop?"

Marisa nodded, paving over her emotions with a blank visage. He allowed his hands to cup her face; his thumbs to stroke her cheeks. So did she.

"I've got to go."

* * *

Heather hugged the walls of Haight and Waller like a shadow. She saw to it that the lantern light of Belvedere Street did not touch her, her hooded shift deflecting any radiance that did. There were no pedestrians to witness her passage, just as she wanted.

Amy's house looked empty enough, but Heather waited it out in case Joanie had to return home for some forgotten thing. Five minutes passed before Heather drifted across the lane like a feather on the wind. Once at the front door, Heather found her set of keys with ease and entered.

All within was quiet and still as Heather closed the

door. Terra's paws drummed the wooden floor as the cat approached from Amy's room.

"Hi, Terra." Heather kneeled and gently scratched the white feline along her neck. Terra tumbled onto her side and purred. "Any strangers tonight?"

Terra mewed.

"No, huh? Don't worry, he'll show." Heather stood to her full height, staring into the darkness of the hall. "He'll show." Especially if he wanted to keep Amy snug around his finger. She even left the front door unlocked for him.

Heather brought up the light in Amy's room just enough to make out the features of the armoire. No astral glow, but it, like the rest of the room, was recently cleaned. Heather's reflected silhouette dropped a backpack on the bed, pushed the cowl from its head, and searched her pockets for her Bic lighter. Found, she took it to Amy's altar.

The white candles caught fast. Heather found an anonymous stick of incense among the stalks of sage, the natural sea sponge, and Athena's gentle stance. She lit it, then drew a star of smoke in the air before her. Heather faced Amy's door and drew another; turned to the bed and drew another above it; finally facing the windows, she drew the last.

"Nag Champa." It always smelled like Halloween to her. She placed the incense in the rosewood holder on the altar top and grabbed some tissue from a floral box of Kleenex.

"I need water." There was a shallow bowl with what smelled like tea in it. She dipped the wad of tissue in the tea, then dabbed the frame of Amy's armoire right where Donovan's mark was the night before.

Heather let out an "Eew," at the rusty stain left behind on the tissue. She knew blood when she saw it, and this sample was shaped like a hoof, just like from her vision. Keeping her fingers away from the blood, she folded the wad tightly and stuck it into a backpack pocket. "Okay Amy, now I have proof." There was no way Amy could deny Donovan was no good.

pale shadows

Satisfied, Heather turned to Amy's bed and sat on it cross-legged, facing her likeness in the armoire mirror. "Nef-er-ta-mut, Nef-er-ta-mut, Nef-er-ta-mut." She sang her Magickal name, eyes slowly closing into narrow slits. The mantra vibrated the witch's limbs and chained her spine to the Earth's core. She felt the moon rolling over her head like an immense pool ball; the ceiling of stars spinning like a vast carousel. Nefertamut smiled down at the pentacle around her neck and caressed its moonstone with two fingers.

Then the front door opened. "Amarantha?" the stranger summoned.

Nefertamut gave no reply. A shadow filled the threshold of Amy's bedroom: She knew Donovan's shadow even though her cowl cropped off his head. He loitered there for a second like he was deciding what to do next, then when he finally stepped into the room, Nefertamut stole a full glimpse.

By candlelight, Donovan looked like he'd seen a ghost. "Luh-Lillian?"

Lillian? That was interesting. "Hello, Donovan," she greeted evenly.

Donovan crouched low enough to peek under Nefertamut's hood and sighed with relief. "Heather, it's you."

She'd seen Donovan hammered before, so the current signs were comically obvious. From his ruddy cheeks to his toxic breath, Vampire Boy was all stagger and slur.

"Yes." She spied his creased gray suit. "Rough flight?"

"I've . . . had a rough night. What are you doing here?"

She smiled and nodded toward the mirrored wardrobe. "Cleaning up. Care to join me?"

He went serious again. "No. No. I just saw the light from outside. Where's Amarantha?"

"Still at church, waiting for you."

A tell-tale fidget. "Right, right," he mumbled to the armoire. He *had* come to check his mark again, just as Nefertamut suspected, but something besides drink was

320

tangling his mind. "I should get to the church."

"As is your will, so mote it be. I'll be along shortly."

Defeated, Donovan muttered, "Okay," then turned toward the exit. He added somberly, "I'm sorry I disturbed you," before leaving the room.

Nefertamut nodded her head, and when the front door closed, replied, "Truce. For now."

* * *

"Hey, there he is!" José heralded Donovan's entrance into the gym, wiping his mouth with a napkin. "We thought you got lost."

Donovan approached between the aisles of feeding church members, nodding and smiling with false ease at the ones that greeted him.

"*He's* your boyfriend now? I didn't recognize him without the headgear," Maggie appraised, apparently remembering Donovan from his tragic years. She love-tapped Amarantha on the shoulder with admiration. "Way to go."

"Thanks." Had Donovan shown up sooner, Amarantha would have had enough doubt in Lillian and faith in him to forgive any crime; to accept any fable. That time had passed, and all that remained were her suspicions.

"I'm sorry I'm late," he apologized before kissing her lips. She winced at the intensity of his alcohol vapors. "We need to talk."

Amarantha rose. "Yes, we do. Excuse us a minute," she said to the table before leading Donovan out of the basement as casually as possible without touching him again.

Amarantha held her tongue for as long as she could stand as they passed through the hallway leading into the dim sanctuary. Donovan's silence assured the first words would be hers. "You're drunk," she finally uttered.

Donovan nodded as he leaned against the ticking radiator below the stained glass image of trumpeting angels. He rubbed his red eyes as if he were trying to spoon them from their sockets. "Lillian's dead."

"Huh-how did it happen?"

A tell-tale fidget. "S.D.P.D found her body in a hotel bathtub."

The question, "Slit wrists?" got past Amarantha's common sense.

Donovan gasped both psychically and physically. He considered her in the filtered half-light. "How did you know?"

Damn, Amarantha had said too much. "Seems like the death rock way to go, is all," she covered, "And I saw her scars when we met. This wasn't the first time, was it?"

Donovan's snort steamed up an angel's illuminated wing. "Why all the questions? Lillian's gone. I thought you'd be pleased. You wanted me to deal with her."

"Did you?"

His boastfulness retreated clumsily. "What? I told you she killed herself."

She stared him down. "And I know the power that our kind wields. Driving a madwoman to suicide is as simple as breathing for us."

Drunkenness fed the outrage he coaxed. "That doesn't mean I killed her," he hissed, eyes sweeping for witnesses that weren't there.

"Then . . . why are you so late?"

"Why do you think? I've been mourning, and I came here for your comfort."

"Mourning or celebrating?"

"Amarantha, we decided—no, we made a pact on Samhain that no mage would come between us." Donovan cradled Amarantha's chin in his right palm. "Don't let Lillian's suicide undo all that."

Amarantha surrendered into Donovan's arms and squeezed him. Goddess, the smell of him; the warmth of him. She could only go so deep into his embrace, she knew, before she'd forgive him everything again. Amarantha wiggled herself free.

"Donovan?"

"Yes?"

"I want you to go home. To your mom's." She stroked a gray flannel lapel. "You shouldn't be here in your condition, and you're not sleeping with me like this."

Donovan's face was puckering and creasing with anger again. "You're gonna do it, aren't you?" He barely got the words past his clenched jaw. "You're going to let that dead bitch foul up everything—"

"Donovan! We're in a church!" He used to utter such sweet poison. Now there was only acid. "Just go! You're too drunk!"

"That's it, isn't it? You *did* contact her. You did it anyway, even after I told you how unstable she was." Donovan softened just enough where he could move close to Amarantha again and brush her cheek with a thumb. "Whatever she said or you think she said, Lillian was a psychotic, maybe even delusional. Don't let those delusions mess up what we—"

Pushing Donovan's hands from her cheek, Amarantha recalled Jimmy's party when Lillian too rejected his advances.

Amarantha was drawn into Lillian's diamond-blue eyes like light into a prism of sorrow. Lillian's woes became Amarantha's, and she felt her soul wrung for tears without knowing why.

The untold story had been there, hadn't it? Of Lillian's previous suicide attempt to keep Donovan close and from hurting others of their kin? It had all been revealed in that one, eternal glance. An ounce of doubt led to a pound of truth, and the sudden revelation brought Amarantha's tears.

"No, I didn't go to her, Donovan. Please, just leave. Go!" Amarantha pushed him back a step by his chest.

"You know what? I don't need this. You're just like—" A dry heave stopped Donovan's sentence. He collected himself, but his face was still twisting. "Fine!" His finger stopped an inch from impaling Amarantha's chest.

As Donovan turned on an inebriated heel and headed

for the sanctuary door, Amarantha tried gagging her sobs
with her palms, but just made a noisy, wet mess of herself.
Grief pulled her down the brown wall to the threadbare
carpeting. "No, no, no."

She was deaf to everything but her despair and did not
notice the closing footsteps until— "Heather?" she asked
when her best friend's sneakered feet entered her line of
sight. Amarantha wiped her tear-tacky cheeks dry.

"Donovan just blew right past me." Heather's pause told
Amarantha she was digesting the scene. Her friend's voice
turned furious. "What did that—what did Donovan do to
you?"

The expectation on Heather's face told Amarantha that
if she gave the word, Heather would have gladly gone after
Donovan and given him more than a piece of her mind.
Amarantha couldn't allow that. Besides, Heather didn't need
to know how badly Amarantha had messed up. Again.

"Donovan didn't do anything to me. I . . . I think we've
broken up."

"Really? Why? What happened?"

"Lillian . . . is dead."

Heather's jaw slackened, and her eyes bugged. She
seemed to be looking for an explanation from the air
around her. "Oh shit." An uneasy veil fell upon Heather's
face as she joined Amarantha beneath the dim radiance of
the amber seraph. "Wait a minute. Did Donovan have
something to do with it?"

Amarantha shrugged despite her suspicions, and she
hated the gesture as soon as she made it. It was practically
an invitation for Heather to start railing against Donovan.
Amarantha sighed sharp and shallow, bracing for the tirade.

"Love sucks," was all Heather said.

Nodding, Amarantha noticed Heather's new pentacle.
"What *is* going on with you and Laine?"

Heather puffed out a breath and rolled her eyes.
"Nothing. He's probably making up with Marisa right
now."

"You know there's an old folklore about witches and

love," Amarantha said, recalling her long-ago conversation with her mentor and rubbing her sodden eyes.

Heather's snort said she'd heard it already. "No doy."

Amarantha sunk into Heather's embrace and wept.

* * *

From atop the woven steel of the fire escape, the drop didn't seem so bad. Granted, even with a good sprint and spring, Laine wouldn't have reached its ladder, especially with Trump and a bottle of wine in tow, but with the help of a nearby dumpster, he had made up the distance easily, and his effort was rewarded with solitude.

He opened the blessedly-unlocked six-paned window and stepped into the cold, dark concrete of the second-story space. Laine was back in the warehouse on 17th and Potrero he had enjoyed on Samhain. "Now to end this."

Laine found a patch of moonlit floor to settle upon, laid his long coat down, and pondered the catacomb stillness surrounding him. Whereas a moon ago those walls could scarcely contain the life within them, now there was isolation and echoed breathing. The duffel bag zipper tore through the quiet, and Laine laid out his Magickal panoply.

"Four candles for the devil." Laine stroked a thick layer of Binding oil on the four black tapers before ensconcing them in the cardinal candle holders and lighting them with the tip of a stick of dragon's blood. When it came to Hermetic evocations, the rule was to create a pen for the summoned entities to inhabit, just in case the solicited harbored dire intentions. It was quartz-clear that the agents of Moloch intended nothing but the dire.

Laine kissed the tip of his black-handled falcon athamé and carved the air, connecting the tapers with a shimmering astral ring. *"Em Abtet; em Restet; em Amentet; em Mehtet: qet-a sebti em qet-a."*

The remaining four silver candles were for Laine. Now seven feet west of the summoning circle, he set fire to the torches at the cardinal points around him. If the company breached their circle, they wouldn't breach his, not until he was ready. He drew the second ring around himself with the dagger and droned, *"Em Abtet; em Restet; em Amentet; em Mehtet: qet-a sebti em qet-a."*

Laine decanted the Cabernet, then blew lint out of his goblet before filling it with wine. "While I'm waiting . . . ." He drank until his lips numbed, then freed Trump from the bag.

The porcelain pirouette was the bait. Identical to one Prince had in his storm cellar bedroom in *Purple Rain*, it was one of Marisa's earliest gifts and was thus embedded with the history of their love. The company would hate it.

Laine closed his eyes and gave Trump a tight squeeze. It was time to open the infernal dialogue.

New Year's Eve, 1985: I attended my first viewing of The Rocky Horror Picture Show at The Strand with Marisa. Afterward, we had managed to squeeze into Broadway Street's dense revelries before the bell tolled twelve. The kiss. The kiss.

"I am Nihthasu, The Darkling King of Nihtheim!"

Silence still, except for the last ring of his proclamation against the walls. He hugged Trump again.

February: I'm watching my grandmother's worldly remains interred in a mausoleum wall. My family loudly mourned, but I was beyond expressing grief. Marisa's fingers interlaced with mine, and I pulled her close. I managed to weep a little more.

"I am Khernifu Pa Kerathi, High Scribe of Amarna!"

Silence. Strange, The Qliphoth were usually so willing to speak. Perhaps Nihthasu had been found out. He embraced the fool again.

December, 1985: Headlines on Polk was packed with Christmas shoppers. Marisa and I spied a stack of Zoids, those robotic dinosaurs that came unassembled from Japan. Marisa had charmed the manager into letting us assemble a menagerie for display, and in exchange, we promised to buy a few for our collection. We must've assembled robot toys for three hours that day, smiling the whole time.

June: Marisa and I were enjoying a bottle of White Zinfandel on Ocean Beach. Moonlight and libations raised more than just our spirits. Wine was spilled and a glass goblet was broken when Marisa pounced on me, pinning my head to the sand with kisses. Too cowardly to rut in public, I nervously laughed.

"I have come to die!"

Nihthasu's voice bled away, leaving behind the sound of scraping metal and the stench of burnt Janus flowers. Eyes still closed, he tried to place the din's origin. The windmill? The scales? It could have been both or neither, but the one certain thing was the wisdom in keeping his eyes shut: the noise was coming from the summoning circle seven feet east of him.

"Is that you, brothers?"

Yes. It is we.

Look at us.

"In due time, brothers, in due time."

Your time is overdue, King Nihthasu.

We will be satisfied.

"Yes, you will, but a little indulgence on my part ere then. I would know my executioners."

We'll indulge you fairly. Open your eyes!

"No," Nihthasu denied sternly. "I assume you two have names. Of The Qliphoth, you may be, but you are not legion."

M.

H.

We're not of The Qliphoth, though they sustain us.

We were once angels.

Before our descent and tainting.

Nihthasu grunted, "Fallen angels. I have undone your lot before."

Aye, with our help.

"You lie. Every demon felled has been by my hand."

And with our weapons.

The spear of Moloch hadn't been the only armament

he'd borne against their kind, it was true. Every victory had fed Nihthasu's pride and arrogance; fed the personal demons he had wished vanquished and strengthened their hold over him. All they had to do was wait. Nihthasu happily, blindly, did the rest.

We are the spear.

We are you.

And every other dread weapon you've ever turned against us and ours.

Now you are undone.

Now that weapon is turned against you.

We will be satisfied. We shall feed.

As per the compact, King.

An almost audible smile pulled across Nihthasu's face. "About that: contracts can be a tricky thing. The simplest change in condition can render most pacts obsolete."

Windmill blades moaned. Scale arms creaked.

"Come now, surely you've noticed the difference."

Your crown. It's gone.

"Yes, it is, for I was deposed by the goddess Maat. Your pact was with *King* Nihthasu, and since I no longer have a crown, queen, or kingdom, that pact is void."

Now you lie!

"Why would I lie to you, brothers, when you've been so honest?" Demons never lied when the truth was more damning. Neither would Nihthasu.

We will be satisfied!

"Yes, you will. With me. I am all that's left: a lowly mage who once was Magickal royalty. You see, when I became the liege of Nihtheim and ere my oath to you, I swore another pact, and that pact now dictates that I, Nihthasu, must die per The King's Tradition. So yes, you will be satisfied." Nihthasu opened his eyes but kept his gaze earthward and angry. "Reclaim your arsenal, but Donovan, Amarantha, Heather, Marisa: they are barred to you. Any harm that you intended for them will befall me."

Ah, Marisa.

The heart makes for a poor shield, sir.

She is why you defy us. She is why you will die.

"As Nihthasu, yes. You can have my arcane power, my Magickal identity, my divine destiny. I just want her." Nihthasu nodded at the black-and-white clad porcelain clown at his knees.

Laughter jangled unseen chains.

Even if we agree, you can not hope to keep her.

Neither deception nor revelation will curtail her departure.

Nihthasu found himself responding with, "That remains to be seen."

Very well then.

See.

Nihthasu swept his arms around him, extinguishing his ring of candles, then stood to his full height as if suspended and pulled open his tuxedo shirt to free the *ankh*. "Let's get nuts."

Seven-feet distant and cornered by tapers there stood neither tower nor windmill nor scales, though what Nihthasu's eyes were beholding had accents of all those things. A small cairn of skulls acted as the foundation for a four-armed crucifix made of mottled bone and rusted metal. Two of the gnarled arms bore the inverted, scorched bodies of "M" and "H" by their ankles above the warehouse floor. They were shedding black scabs, and as they rotated, Nihthasu saw the scars and nubs welting their scapulae that were once seraphic wings.

Nihthasu unbound them with a gesture. The black candles expired, the cairn dissolved, and the company vanished, their screams like nails scraping a blackboard.

So still now. So quiet. "Is that all?" Nihthasu asked the empty room. "Where have you gone, brothers?"

There grew a chill that came from no draft. Tremors started in Nihthasu's head, then seized his shoulders; his hips; his calves until he toppled onto his side, stricken. His legs began peddling, his eyes rolled back in their sockets, and mucus was pouring from Nihthasu's gurgling mouth.

The company was where they had always been. They

pale shadows

were inside him.

* * *

They began by shredding my organs; they were rending my mind. They were clawing and laughing with cruel zeal, and by degrees, I felt my soul tearing.

"No! Wait!" Exquisite pain demanded my submission and ignored my suffering as chunks of my self fell away. Their barbed bodies twisted and rolled inside me until my rib cage yawned, and The Qliphoth finally pushed their way out.

Two emaciated shadows loomed through the veil of my watery vision. Each infernal angel grabbed an outstretched arm and wrenched it, hoisting me up onto my knees. I wailed pitifully.

A twin incised my right forearm with a brittle thumbnail, peeled the tendons apart, and withdrew the impossibly long spear of Moloch from my limb at a tortuously slow pace. The serrated shaft clattered when it hit the concrete. I fell again.

"Stop! Stop!" They attacked once more, and my pleading served only to encourage their savagery.

"No life . . . ," H growled.

"No destiny," M gloated.

My bones felt as though they were curdling. My body was bleeding vigor. I was dying.

Then suddenly the assault stopped and another sound caught my notice, this one low and rumbling. I hazarded a glimpse and was met by one emerald eye. "Neh-Neteru?"

That one-eyed bastard of a cat fought the company hard. It was all teeth and talons and tendons until the panther successfully wounded and routed the un-anticipating demons. Their panicked curses retreated at last, and a final whimper pierced my delirium as Neteru collapsed beside me in agony. The scent of the panther's bodily contents flooded my nose.

I stroked one of the panther's heavy paws. There were

no more screams; there was no more laughter. All that remained was Neteru's rapid labored breaths that eventually slowed and joined mine in stillness.

I whispered, "Good night, brother," then surrendered to the blackness.

There came a frail sound from some great distance in my mind. It tugged at my notice and, despite my lethargy and pain, roused me. Music couched the noise, and as both rose, I was lured by the familiar nimbus of a backlit parasol.

It took only six steps to bring me to Marisa's bedside. She was lying there with her back to me, weeping and shuddering, her bare body and emerald "tail" visible through the veil of mosquito netting. Bono was crooning our breakup song, muting all avian incantations and blanketing my descent beside my queen.

Yes, my queen. Only she would cry so for me. Queen Seawing: my last perfect thing.

I reclined and coiled my arms around my love, squeezing her misery away. Cries became sobs; sobs became sniffles, and our shared comfort remained unspoken. Our two halves were a whole again, and for me, that was enough. I shut my eyes against the night.

*   *   *

Sunlight was painting Laine's eyelids red; the heat pried them open. His head was still heavy from wine as he peeled it from the concrete floor. His stomach was feeling the libation's effects as well, but at least he knew a good meal would settle it. He pushed himself up into a crouch with trembling arms, the change in altitude causing his mind to cloud and stomach to churn. Laine couldn't remember the last time he felt so weak, so helpless, so useless.

No, that wasn't true. The last time Laine felt this insignificant was the last time he was a mere mundane. Seven long years ago: a lifetime away.

By dawn's light, the warehouse more closely resembled

what Laine had found on Samhain. Behind him was the DJ booth and loft where Ms. Fornaux had reveled. The rope swings were gone as were the pony kegs and Halloween decor, but the rest was the same, save Laine's ritual trappings. Black and silver wax drippings had welded his brass candlesticks to the floor, and Trump was now laying amongst fine incense ash. Laine picked the token up.

"We did it, Trump." Laine cleared phlegm from his throat. "They're gone. The spear is gone." It also hit Laine keenly that his Magick was gone as well. "It's all gone. The gates of Nihtheim are locked. The king is dead."

Laine found his full footing and stared down at the spent wares around him. "What have I done?" Short breaths came, and his shoulders sloped with emotional gravity. "Oh my god, what have I—"

Someone else was in the warehouse. Laine didn't actually hear any footfalls or slamming doors, but his passive psychic faculties told him he was no longer alone. Somewhere beneath him, a stranger was treading.

Adrenaline took hold of Laine as he crammed his ritual trappings into the black duffel bag, his tearing eyes aimed at the fire escape he had used to trespass the building.

* * *

"It was my fault," Donovan conceded, "I was way too drunk last night. And in our church."

Sitting at the vanity, Amarantha felt Heather's eyes practically burning through the back of her quilted bathrobe. She hadn't meant to awaken her visiting friend, but once she started crying, it was hard for Amarantha to control her volume. Amarantha's whispers into the Princess phone had been too harsh, too conspicuous to go unnoticed, even by slumbering ears. All she could do now was stare at her vanity's worn, oak top as she forgave Donovan.

"It's okay, love. You had every reason to be upset. After all, Lillian died."

"She killed herself. It's so stupid."

"It is."

The sound of Heather's jean zipper ripped behind Amarantha, and she knew she wouldn't be able to ignore her best friend's presence for much longer. Eventually, Amarantha would have to face her. She and Heather had been growing apart for a while now, like two branches of the same willow, and a branch was due to fall.

"I'm sorry about taking it out on you," Donovan sang, his sweet poison returning. "You're the most important thing in my life right now, and I just don't want to lose that."

"You won't. I'm not Lillian." Donovan's vow sprang from Amarantha's lips. "I am always with you. I will always be with you. We can fix this, together."

Heather was standing close behind her, her gaze singeing Amarantha with anger. Now she had to turn around.

Heather was towering over Amarantha, now fully dressed in her brown bomber jacket, blue jeans, and an aquamarine T-shirt that read Stop Staring At My Tits in bold, black letters. Her cornflower eyes were as furious and ashamed as Lillian's had been sad and desperate. She had a fist shoved in an outer pocket of her backpack, slowly stirring some unseen content therein. Heather looked like she was about to slap Amarantha, and she honestly couldn't blame her. She closed her eyes and braced herself.

"I love you, Amarantha," he sobbed.

"I . . . I love you too." That was the shameful part. It was true. True enough to think she could fix it all, that she could fix Donovan.

Heather's slap never came. Instead, footsteps left Amarantha's room, then her front door opened and shut. When Amarantha opened her eyes again, she was alone.

* * *

Heather stopped at the dumpster on the windy corner of Haight and Clayton, sifted through her backpack, and pulled out the blood-stained Kleenex. It would have been easy to show Amy the evidence of Donovan's meddling spell and break up their little weep-fest on the phone, but she recalled what Mama had said. If breaking up Laine and Marisa would just mean more trouble for Heather, then that was also true of Amy and Donovan. Shit, it already had been.

Heather chucked the soiled tissue into the garbage bin, watching it land among the Big Mac wrappers and empty Marlboro packs. If Amy wanted Donovan so bad, she could have him. She drew a banishing star across her chest and grumbled, "You're on your own, Amy."

*   *   *

Marisa shoved her way in through the café door with two sideways brown paper bags filling her arms and redness ringing her eyes. As she stopped near the register, Laine became acutely aware of Diana's curiosity beaming from behind the counter.

"Hey," he greeted.

"Hey." Marisa set the leftovers down on a nearby serving table.

"Looks like your mom really packed on the food."

Diana's chin settled quietly into her palms.

Marisa's smile was as fragile as Laine's heart and nerves. "There's some lasagna in there you missed out on." She handed him the red rose that had been concealed beneath the offerings. "Are you okay?"

"I'm better now." Laine nodded at the flower. "What's this for?"

The first tear fell. "I felt you last night. I felt you come to me, then you faded away, and all the flowers were gone." She glanced at the rose.

"It's okay. That's all over now. We can always grow new flowers." Ignoring Diana's stares from the counter, he leaned closer. "Marisa, listen to me: I can live without a lot of things in my life, but I can't live without you. I . . .

deeply, eternally, love you, Marisa."

The words she was waiting for. "I love you too."

They kissed and kissed and kissed again. Diana clapped and whistled with exaggerated volume, then asked, "Wait, did you guys break up?" Marisa and Laine broke their reunion long enough to laugh.

A wind-blown figure outside the café entrance caught Laine's attention. He squeezed Marisa tightly as he and Heather shared a knowing glance through the open glass door, his former pentacle utterly visible. Laine dry-swallowed.

Heather smiled weakly, then continued up the grade toward the company warehouse.

pale shadows

EPILOGUE

WEDNESDAY, NOVEMBER 25TH, 1987

"This is the right storm: the one that will end it all."

Grey currents almost suitable for rafting were flooding Nob Hill's grades. The rains and winds were whipping Pine Street with the dusty smell of startled mold and pungent ozone. Laine had no hand in this deluge. If he had, it would have stopped before his walk home.

The hunter-green awning sheltered Laine as he sifted through the day's mail. He could make a deck out the fliers for imported jewelry shops, hair salon discounts, and night-clubs Marisa received. Almost nothing ever arrived in his name.

The warm aroma of the old hallway followed Laine to the second floor, breaking only when Vince from down the hall passed him. "How's it going, Laine?"

"*Vivre la vie*. You?"

"Ready for the holidays." Vince waved farewell with

his derringer-like umbrella. That was the usual extent of Laine's exchanges with his neighbors, which was fine with him.

The door to the apartment—like the one to its left—was painted in black gloss paint, and since the one hallway light fixture didn't quite illuminate the door, Laine had to get his keys ready while he could still see. As he approached, Marisa's aviary was chirping above the musical strains of Translator and the banging of woks. The aroma of stir-fry teased him, and Laine's stomach growled as he turned the key in the lock and pushed open the black door.

Laine's entrance echoed in the empty studio apartment; the door's closure echoed even louder. No birds, but there was dried bird shit that would never come off the hardwood floors, not that Laine cared; no woks, though there were a couple of pots and pans left behind, not that he ate much at home.

No Marisa.

The music had been real enough, though. His answering machine was playing "Everywhere That I'm Not", a sentiment that he chimed in on. "'It was just someone who/Sounded a lot like I remember you do.'"

The machine clicked, and a robotic voice announced, "This is Pacific Bell's Quality Service Division. This automated message is to confirm that customer Laine Douglas phone line is restored and operational." The squall's damage to the phone lines had proven to be fleeting after all.

The phone service was one more thing Marisa had taken with her last week, but a call from the café reestablished the number under Laine's name. No harm, no foul. A glance at his answering machine told him that there were no new messages aside from PacBell's.

Laine shook off the rain and the ghosts as he went to his room and dropped his long coat onto Marisa's side of the bed. Blinds down, he paced the dimmed floor lightly while scratching his goatee.

Three stiff bangs popped the soles of Laine's feet: his

downstairs neighbor, the wife-beater. It was okay if the whole building heard him abuse his mate, but heaven forbid Laine should pace in the privacy of his own bedroom.

"Fuck that." Laine leapt up and stomped three times, high and hard. The storm was quiet by comparison. He waited for a retort that never came.

Laine pushed through the pair of frosted glass doors separating the bedroom from the living room. Juniper trees were casting harried shadows on the living room walls as he went to the steam radiator. He gave the black wheel a crank, and soon the heater was spitting and knocking, restoring the warmth the storm had stolen. Now sitting cross-legged on the floor, Laine grabbed the thurible from the shrine at the radiator's feet. A charcoal disc was already present. "Let's get this over with."

The lighter he removed from his pocket had seen better days. It was once the proud profile of a panther, but had since lost most of its black-coated luster, revealing the steel body beneath. It looked back at Laine with its remaining blue costume-jewelry eye as he flicked the skullcap for a flame. The disc sputtered quickly.

The love letters he and Marisa had written each other over the years began fuming in the thurible. That and Marisa's mail would make for great kindling.

Laine flipped through the pages of his nearby green journal. The lunar calendar Marisa had found buried inside the damning entries fell out with a shake. The only missing passages were some of his sigils and the notes from his Samhain ritual with Heather the previous year. His sins remained.

He had picked at the scab of his guilt so often that it was inevitable Marisa would notice the wound and wonder. She always had the option of not reading Laine's journal, of course, and he half-expected her not to. She said she almost didn't. In truth though, he had *wanted* Marisa to find the notebook; even left it out so that temptation would drive her to open the pages herself. The Goddess had made him the mage he was, but Marisa had made him a man.

Laine threw the journal on the fire while fists of air punched the living room windows.

The electric stutter of Laine's phone sounded. He drew a measured breath like it was a prayer, then picked up the black receiver. "Hello?"

"Hey, Laine."

"Hi, Heather." Of course, it *wasn't* Marisa. Laine didn't get that lucky. No good deed went unpunished, and there were no rewards for honesty.

"How are the contact lenses going?"

Laine rubbed black smoke from them. "Fine. Hardly noticed they're in. How's Fruitvale?"

"It's okay." Laine could imagine Heather sitting on a mattress and staring around the room. "Everything is still in boxes."

Marisa had hand-doctored the Maxell cassette Laine picked up next. There was a gold label on one side and an indigo one on the other, just like a Janus flower. After she'd read the journal, Marisa had filled the blue side of the two-hour tape with all of the venom her anger could secrete, while she devoted the gold side to melancholy and disappointment. Both sides were infused with her love and her fury; neither side had been easy for Laine to listen to. Duality in disharmony.

He tossed the last Janus flower into the flames.

"And it gets kinda boring sometimes," Heather continued, "but it's cheaper than The City. I never thought I'd actually miss The Mission. So are we still on for tonight?"

"Definitely. We're a year overdue."

"I just wanted to check because of the storm and all."

"I rather like the violent monochrome." The sky flashed blue.

"I'm surprised we're still doing Amy's Wiccaning at all. I mean, she never apologized to us, she never thanked us —"

Laine looked at Trump's indelible smile. "You know what? None of that really matters to me anymore." Thunder rolled. "Besides, if we did our job right, she probably doesn't even know. That's why it's called the occult."

"Yeah, I guess you're right. And she *did* break up with Donovan."

"Yes, she did." On All Saint's Day, the same day Marisa Chang read Laine's journal. "You know, Claire at work said something interesting today. She said it takes twice as long to get over a relationship as the relationship's length."

"Wuh-what does that mean?"

Laine waved smoke aside. "It means Amy has a long two years ahead of her. And I have a long four-and-a-half."

"I'm sorry. You know, if you need anything—"

"Show up tonight." Laine knew she meant well. The problem was it was a similar offer that had lost him everything in the first place and put Heather in harm's way. "That's all I need. I have to finish getting ready. I'll see you at eight." Laine didn't wait for Heather's confirmation before hanging up.

He was topping off the fire with more mail when he came across a club flyer. Black ink on white card stock announced that DJ Steve Masters was spinning at Lipps Underground, now serving breakfast as well as cheap beer and a cheaper cover. Diana had recommended the place to Laine a few times, and it seemed to him an under-lit, subterranean goth club was the perfect place for a former High Magickian to haunt incognito; to heal; to start over. Perhaps in time, he would redeem himself in The Goddess' eyes even if he had failed to do so in Marisa's. Or his own.

"Hell, I've been a closet goth for years anyway." He pocketed the flier.

Laine closed his eyes tight and kissed Trump on his porcelain lips, then raised the doll over his head. "Goodbye, friend." He struck the pirouette hard against the wood floor.

It sounded like a rupturing skull when it shattered.

* * *

"*¡Cuelga, Rudy, estoy al teléfono!*" Heather announced.

pale shadows

"*I'm* on the phone!"

Why didn't Laine just call Amy himself? They lived in the same damn city. "*I'm* on the phone!"

"*I'm* on the phone!" he yelled again from down the hall.

"Rudy, hang up!" Instead Heather got to run up her phone bill. Whatever.

There was a loud click in Heather's ear when Rudy finally obeyed followed by, "Hello?"

"Hey, Amy, it's Heather."

"Oh hey. I just got out of the shower. I thought you might be Bill. We went out for sushi last night."

Fine, Amy's boyfriend drama first. "How was that?"

"Dating an older guy is different. He was definitely mellower, although . . . ."

Rudy's head slowly peeked around the edge of Heather's doorway, then ducked out of sight again. Heather grabbed a nice firm pillow from a nearby cardboard box. "What, Amy?"

"I don't know, you think twenty-seven is too old?"

Heather cracked up laughing.

"What?" That Peter Gabriel/Kate Bush duet was playing behind Amy's voice.

"Twenty-seven ain't old, Amy, not nowadays."

"I guess you'd know, Doctor Dominguez."

Heather smiled. "Please, I ain't even *Nurse* Dominguez yet. Max found me the intern job, but I still have to go to school next year."

Rudy's head made a return appearance from behind a bookcase in the hall, tongue-a-flipping. Man, he was growing up so fast. He must have gained three inches since last Thanksgiving. Rudy would break some girl's heart, for sure.

Heather shot her pillow hard at the target, nailing Rudy straight in the face. They cracked up at her surprising accuracy before he sped away again.

"Oh, it won't be long now. So what else is going on?"

Okay, back to business. "Laine says we're still on for tonight."

"What time?"

"8:00. We're sleeping at his place, so bring pajamas. Are you working the church banquet tomorrow?"

There was a brief pause before Amy answered, "No. I made some puff pastries, but somebody else can serve the masses this Thanksgiving. Besides, I worked the booth at the Haight Street Fair, so I'm off the hook." Heather heard Amarantha's front door ring through the phone. Amy said, "Oh great, that's probably José. Guess I spoke too soon. I'll see you later tonight, Heather."

"See you tonight." Heather hung up the phone. Rudy was back again, sticking his tongue out at Heather and wiggling his hips. Before Heather could grab more ammo, Mama appeared and bum-rushed her son down the hall.

"That's enough, Rudy. Finish unpacking," Mama commanded, then turned her attention to Heather. "Going out tonight?

"*Sí*, Mama. I'm staying over at Laine's with Amy. I'll be back way before Thanksgiving dinner."

"Laine, huh?"

Heather sighed. "*No significa nada*, Mama. *Le estamos haciendo un favor a* Amy." That was the only reason why Heather agreed to tonight: because Amy had asked; because Laine had asked. A harmless favor for the coven.

Mama nodded slowly. "*Muy bien*. Tell Amy—and I guess Laine—that I said hello. And don't be late tomorrow. You wouldn't want to miss our first holiday in our new house." Mama blew Heather a kiss and vanished down the hall.

Heather caught her reflection in the new wall mirror and smiled. "I won't." That was a promise she would have no problem fulfilling.

* * *

Amarantha Powell cinched her robe and scurried down the hall, only to find Terra had beat her to the front door. The cat turned her gaze from the door to Amarantha and mewed.

"Donovan?" They'd only been split up three weeks. Of course, that's who was at her doorstep. Terra stepped aside when the wind blew in.

Donovan Walsh was drenched with tears and rain. "Hi."

"What do you want?"

"What do you mean, 'What do you want?' I want to come in." His teeth were grinding.

"You're not coming in. I gave you your year-and-a-day. I was *not* satisfied."

"I just want to talk." The way Donovan was eyeing Amarantha in her bathrobe said he wanted much more.

"So talk."

He was hugging his chest and rocking slowly back and forth. His swaying was almost giving Amarantha motion sickness. "I had to see you. Everywhere I go, I hear your voice; smell your perfume. I can't get you out of my head, Amarantha."

"Maybe you're taking the wrong drugs."

"I'm clean! I have been for—"

"Don't come darkening my threshold reeking of speed and who knows what else and then claim that you're clean. I know what you smell of, Donovan, or have you forgotten about my mother?"

"Well, wuh-what do you expect? Yuh-you left me, Lillian killed herself, Jimmy—"

"You should be ashamed of yourself. Do you know that? You should be ashamed of using your mentor's death as an excuse for your drug problems."

Donovan shivered, and it wasn't just from the storm. He didn't deny his true relationship with Lillian, and his stymied expression confirmed it.

"And I won't be your scapegoat either. The addictions were one of the things that broke us up." Amarantha began closing the door, but Donovan's sneakered foot and Terra's cry stopped her.

"You're right, Amarantha, and I'm sorry." He used those words so often that his apologies became an insult. "See, that's why I need you. You can help me get off of the shit once and for all. Please, Amy, help me."

"I wasted a year trying to help you."

"And you were, I just need—"

"Your lies are the other reason we split, Donovan. If I could prove half of what I suspect you did to Lillian Crane, your life would be equally forfeit. You know that, don't you?"

"Amarantha, I told you I didn't kill—"

"You should be thankful I can't and just go away." Amarantha's index finger gave him directions.

As Donovan turned to leave, Terra rubbed against Amarantha's calf, still crying for attention, and a sudden knowledge sprung into Amarantha's head: he held a secret.

"Donovan, wait."

The foolish boy almost skipped back up the steps. When he got to her door, Amarantha held out her hand. Donovan tried to hold it, but she snatched it away, then held it out again. "I believe you have something of mine."

"I didn't even come in," Donovan whined, "How could I take anything?"

"Your right hand."

Donovan was caught. He sighed and closed his eyes before offering her the small dram of oil in his palm. Amarantha grabbed it.

It wasn't oil. The small vial was two-thirds filled with Amarantha's blood; the same blood she gave Donovan during their Samhain ritual so long ago. Two-thirds full: she didn't want to know what he did with the first third.

"Goodbye, Donovan." Amarantha's door boomed a final farewell.

* * *

Nihthasu moved aside the white votive and the bowls bearing seeds and water at his bare feet, clearing space for his former pupils to stand. Nefertamut entered the ring of four silver taper candles and awaited his instructions, keeping her hooded shift clear of the open flames.

"Shall I bring Befana in?" Thunder shook the living room. "Wow. It's pretty intense out there."

"Yes, it is." Equally so inside. "Make sure you blind-fold Befana securely, then escort her in."

Nefertamut bowed. "As is your will, Lord Nihthasu." Her words were softened by a reverence he didn't feel he deserved.

"Angel." The broken part of a god.

"Wuh-what?"

"Lord Nihthasu is dead. It's *Angel* Nihthasu now." His tiny brass bell earring rang.

"Oh. Okay, *Angel* Nihthasu." Confusion danced in the *famulus'* eyes as she turned toward the double glass doors leading to his bedroom.

Nihthasu strapped on his panther mask, tied a black patch over his right eye in tribute to Neteru, then closed the sacred circle with a sweep of his arms, feeling no difference in the room's energy. Freeing his *ankh* from within his black tuxedo shirt, he began chanting. *"Em Abtet; em Restet; em Amentet; em Mehtet: qet-a sebti em qet-a . . ."*

The effort of raising the power for the ritual was unmistakable despite the mantra and the glyphs he was scribing in the air with his athamé. Once—long ago, it seemed—Nihthasu could have summoned the necessary forces with ease, but with his lapse in practice and loss of will came a lack in facility. He was breathing measured breaths but failing to anchor. His mind's eye was blind; his gaze could no longer penetrate the astral spheres.

Nihthasu shook his head and hoped that the mystery of the rite would suffice in exalting Befana Delafey when his own efforts could not.

The doors opened again, and Nefertamut was standing just behind Befana, who was now blindfolded with white silk and adorned in a Grecian tunic and her matching bell earring. Nihthasu nodded that he was ready for her.

Nefertamut took Befana's hand and led her into the living room, smiling with subdued pride. There was the crackle of static electricity in the air, and the stomping night outside sounded like it was at the far end of a short hallway.

Nihthasu announced, "Five are the rules; five are the tools for this Great Art of Making/From ash to pool, from breath to jewel, in this there's no mistaking."

Nefertamut turned Befana Delafey toward the eastern quarter by her bare shoulders and handed Nihthasu the brazier and a Chinese folding fan. Befana smiled while he flapped myrrh smoke around her head, but she had no radiance.

"The breath of intelligence has embraced you," he said, face to face with Befana, "sweeping away mental penury; filling the sky of thought with the gale of clarity; refreshing the stagnant mind. You are the design and the designer. You are the wind."

Nefertamut picked up the white votive next and handed it to Nihthasu. Passing it seven inches to either side of Befana's head, he uttered into her right ear, "The fire of will has embraced you, igniting the spark grown dim; innerving the flame gone cold; inspiring the despairing heart. You are the idea and the ideal. You are the flame."

Nefertamut held up two silver bowls, one containing water and the other carrying anise seeds. Nihthasu dipped his forefinger into the water bowl and touched five separate drops onto Befana's forehead, breasts and shoulders, then circled her clockwise.

"The tides of purpose have embraced you, eroding the steadfast barriers; linking shore to distant shore; filling the drought-drained heart." Lightning flashed just outside the room. Nefertamut and even blind Befana jumped. "You are the purpose and the practice. You are the storm."

Nihthasu showered Befana with blond anise seeds. Her sidewalk penny-brown hair caught a few grains in its streaks. Her tresses also lacked radiance, their former golden glory gone dim like the setting sun. Was that what a year with Donovan had done to her? Nihthasu hoped the discoloration was a fashion choice.

"The potency of stone has embraced you, providing resources where there seems to be none; creating context to the mysteries of life; granting signposts to the misplaced wanderer. You are the carpenter and the tool. You are the earth."

Nefertamut put the bowls down and mirrored Nihthasu's clockwise circle around Befana. They were close. Now the question of spirit and how much Befana had left.

"Desire and design, construction and completion: these are the provinces of The Elements. Each vies for dominance over the others. Each claims perfection in its own right. 'Tis not these things alone that make up existence, but the relationships between them. One note is not a song; one word is not a sonnet."

The wind was kicking up outside, and for a second, Nihthasu thought one of the living room windows might shatter. He glanced out at the black and gray night to the south. The rain was so heavy, it looked like a team of firefighters were trying to knock down the building with their hoses.

Returning his attention, Nihthasu asked, "To whom does the fire answer? To whom does the wind cower? What gives rise to the oceans and makes the mountains tower? Who is your mother's mother, and how does she touch her kin? How do we hear our mother's voice when trapped in this worldly din?"

Befana nibbled her lower lip. She must not have rehearsed her part. "Um," was how she answered.

Nihthasu gave Befana a few seconds to think before he rephrased his question. "What is the fifth element, and what is its tool/Without which we are unable to rule?" Simple enough: Spirit was the element, and silence was its tool.

"Um." Nihthasu almost didn't hear her. It was the wrong kind of silence: the kind born of indecision. His patience fled, and he glanced at Nefertamut, who was sharing his sad tension in her eyes.

He asked Befana again, "What is the last element?

What is its tool?"

Nihthasu could have fallen into the quiet that followed and never touched the chasm walls. He stared at Befana's feet and shook his head before removing his eye patch and mask.

Heather quietly, sadly, sat on the living room floor, watching the storm roll outside the southern windows. Her thoughts were her own, but Laine could easily guess at them: after all of their sacrifices, it had come down to this.

Amarantha slowly removed her blindfold, admitting, "I'm sorry. I-I don't know."

Laine turned and took in the brew outside as well. No new goddess would be born tonight.

Bells chimed. The sky cried. The brief ceremony ended.

Angyl Nihthasu is the *nom de arte* of the author and
former High Magickian. In addition to writing,
Angyl is a photographer and musician.
He lives in San Francisco with his wife,
two children, four cats, and one dog.

Additional copies at http://stores.lulu.com/paleshadows

Also by Angyl Nihthasu

EDGINGS

Erotica for The Broken

WHETHER IT'S UNSPEAKABLE RENDEZVOUS,
BROKEN TRUST, OR TRAGIC LONGINGS, AGONY
LURKS BEYOND THE EDGES OF LOVE, AND
LUST BREEDS MONSTERS AND VICTIMS.

"If Edgar Allen Poe, H.P. Lovecraft, and William S. Burroughs got together
and decided to collaborate on a book of short erotica stories,

EDGINGS would be that triumphant and bizarre result."

ISBN: 978-1-6781-8197-0